Daniel Defoe

The life and most surprising adventures of Robinson Crusoe

Of York, mariner, who lived eight-and-twenty years in an uninhabited island on the coast of America, near the mouth of the great river Oroonoque. With an account of his deliverance thence, a

Daniel Defoe

The life and most surprising adventures of Robinson Crusoe
Of York, mariner, who lived eight-and-twenty years in an uninhabited island on the coast of America, near the mouth of the great river Oroonoque. With an account of his deliverance thence, a

ISBN/EAN: 9783742808769

Manufactured in Europe, USA, Canada, Australia, Japa

Cover: Foto ©Andreas Hilbeck / pixelio.de

Manufactured and distributed by brebook publishing software (www.brebook.com)

Daniel Defoe

The life and most surprising adventures of Robinson Crusoe

iv   P R E F A C E.

The Editor believes the thing to be
a juſt hiſtory of fact ; neither is there
any appearance of fiction in it: and
though he is well aware there are many,
who, on account of the very ſingular
preſervations the author met with, will
give it the name of a romance ; yet, in
which ever of theſe lights it ſhall be
viewed, he imagines, that the improvement of it, as well to the diverſion, as
to the inſtruction of the reader, will be
the ſame ; and, as ſuch, he thinks,
without farther compliment to the
world, he does them a great ſervice in
the publication.

THE

LIFE and ADVENTURES

OF

ROBINSON CRUSOE.

I Was born at York, in the year 1632, of a reputable family. My father was a native of Bremen, who, by merchandising at Hull for some time, gained a very plentiful fortune. He married my mother at York, who received her first breath in that country: and as her maiden name was Robinson, I was called *Robinson Kreutznaer*, which not being easily pronounced in the English tongue, we are commonly known by the name of Crusoe.

I was the youngest of three brothers. The eldest was a lieutenant-colonel in Lockhart's regiment, but slain by the Spaniards: what became of the other, I could never learn.

No charge nor pains were wanting in my education. My father designed me for the law; yet nothing would serve me but I must go to sea, both against the will of my father, the tears of my mother, and the intreaties of friends. One morning my father expostulated very warmly with me: What reason, says he, have you to leave your native country, where there must be a more certain prospect of content and happiness, to enter into a wandering con-

A

dition

dition of uneasiness and uncertainty? He recommended to me Agur's wish, *Neither to desire poverty nor riches;* that a middle state of life was the most happy; and that the high towering thoughts of raising our condition by wandering abroad, were surrounded with misery and danger, and often ended with confusion and disappointment. I intreat you, nay, I command you, (says he,) to desist from these intentions. Consider your eldest brother, who laid down his life for his honour, or rather lost it for his disobedience to my will. If you will go, (added he,) my prayers shall however be offered for your preservation; but a time may come, when, desolate, oppressed, or forsaken, you may wish you had taken your poor despised father's counsel.———He pronounced these words with such a moving and paternal eloquence, while floods of tears ran down his aged cheeks, that it seemed to stem the torrent of my resolutions. But this soon wore off, and a little after I informed my mother, that I could not settle to any business, my resolutions were so strong to see the world; and begged she would gain my father's consent only to go one voyage; which, if it did not prove prosperous, I would never attempt a second. But my desire was as vain as my folly in asking. My mother passionately expressed her dislike of this proposal, telling me, *That as she saw I was bent upon my own destruction, contrary to their will and my duty, she would say no more, but leave me to myself to do whatsoever I pleased.*

I was then, I think, nineteen years old, when one time being at Hull, I met a school-fellow of mine going along with his father, who was master of a ship, to London; and acquainting him with my wandering desires, he assured me of a free passage, and a plentiful share of what was necessary. Thus, without imploring a blessing, or taking farewell of my parents, I took shipping on the first of September 1651. We
set

set sail soon after; and our ship had scarce left the Humber astern, when there arose so violent a storm, that, being extremely sea-sick, I concluded the judgments of God deservedly followed me for my disobedience to my dear parents. It was then I called to mind the good advice of my father; how easy and comfortable was a middle state of life; and I firmly resolved, if it pleased God to set me on dry land once more, I would return to my parents, implore their forgiveness, and bid a final adieu to my wandering inclinations.

Such were my thoughts while the storm continued; but these good resolutions decreased with the danger; more especially when my companion came to me, clapping me on the shoulder: *What, Bob!* said he, *sure you was not frightened last night with scarce a capful of wind?—And do you,* cried I, *call such a violent storm a capfull of wind? A storm, you fool you,* said he, *this is nothing: a good ship and sea-room always baffles such a foolish squall of wind as that: But you're a fresh water-sailor: Come, boy, turn out, see what fine weather we have now, and a good bowl of punch will drown all your past sorrows.* In short, the punch was made, I was drunk, and in one night's time drowned both my repentance and my good resolutions, forgetting entirely the vows and promises I made in my distress: and whenever any reflections would return on me, what by company, and what by drinking, I soon mastered those fits, as I deridingly called them. But this only made way for another trial, whereby I could not but see how much I was beholden to kind providence.

Upon the sixth day we came to an anchor in Harwich road, where we lay wind-bound with some Newcastle ships; and there being good anchorage, and our cables sound, the seamen forgot their late toil and danger, and spent the time as merry as if they had been on shore. But on the eighth day there

A 2

arose

arofe a brifk gale of wind, which prevented our ti-
ding it up the river; and ftill increafing, our fhip
rode forecaftle in, and fhipped feveral large feas.

It was not long before horror feized the feamen
themfelves, and I heard the Mafter exprefs this melancholy ejaculation, *Lord have mercy upon us, we fhall
be all loft and undone!* For my part, fick unto death,
I kept my cabin, till the univerfal and terribly dreadful apprehenfions of our fpeedy fate made me get
upon deck: and there I was affrighted indeed. The
fea went mountains high: I could fee nothing but
diftrefs around us; two fhips had cut their mafts on
board, and another was foundered; two more that
had loft their anchors, were forced out to the mercy
of the ocean; and, to fave our lives, we were forced to cut onr foremaft and main-maft quite away.

Who is there fo ignorant as not to judge of my
dreadful condition! I was but a frefh-water failor,
and therefore it feemed more terrible. Our fhip
was very good, but over-loaded; which made the failors often cry out, *She would founder:* Words I then
was ignorant of. All this while the ftorm continuing, and rather increafing, the mafter and the more
fober part of his men went to prayers, expecting death
every moment. In the middle of the night one cried
out, *We had fprung a leak:* another *That there was
four foot water in the hold.* I was juft ready to expire with fear, when immediately all hands were called to the pump; and the men forced me alfo in that
extremity to fhare with them in their labour. While
thus employed, the mafter efpying fome light colliers
fired a gun as a fignal of diftrefs; and I not underftanding what it meant, and thinking that either the
fhip broke, or fome dreadful thing happened, fell
into a fwoon. Even in that common condition of
woe, nobody minded me, excepting to thruft me a-
fide with their feet, thinking me dead, and it was
a great while before I recovered.

Happy

Happy it was for us, when, upon the signal given, they ventured out their boat to save our lives. All our pumping had been in vain, and vain had all our attempts been, had they not come to our ship's side, and our men cast them a rope over the stern with a buoy to it, which after great labour they got hold of, and we haling them to us, got into their boat, and left our ship, which we perceived sink within less than a quarter of an hour; and thus I learned what was meant by *Foundering at sea.* And now the men incessantly laboured to recover their own ship; but the sea ran so high, and the wind blew so hard, that they thought it convenient to hale within shore; which, with great difficulty and danger, at last we happily effected, landing at a place called *Cromer*, not far from Winterton light-house; from whence we all walked to Yarmouth, where, as objects of pity, many good people furnished us with necessaries to carry us either to Hull or London.

Strange, that after all this, like the prodigal son, I did not return to my father; who, hearing of the ship's calamity, for a long time thought me intombed in the deep. No doubt but I should have *shared in his fatted calf,* as the scripture expresseth it; but my ill fate still pushed me on, in spite of the powerful convictions of reason and conscience.

When we had been at Yarmouth three days, I met my old companion, who had given me the invitation to go on board along with his father. His behaviour and speech was altered, and in a melancholy manner asked me how I did, telling his father who I was, and how I had made this voyage for a trial only to proceed farther abroad. Upon which the old gentleman turning to me gravely, said, *Young man, you ought never to go to sea any more, but to take this for a certain sign, that you will ne'er prosper in a seafaring condition.* Sir, *answered I,* will you take the same resolution? *It is a different case,* said he, *it is my calling, and conse-*

quently

quently my duty; but as you have made this voyage for a trial, you see what ill success heaven has set before your eyes; and perhaps our miseries have been on your account, like Jonah *in the ship of* Tarshish. *But pray what are you, and on what account did you go to sea?* Upon which I very freely declared my whole story; at the end of which he made this exclamation. Ye sacred powers! what had I committed, that such a wretch should enter into my ship, to heap upon me such a deluge of miseries! But soon recollecting his passions, *Young man,* said he, *if you do not go back, depend upon it, where-ever you go, you will meet with disasters and disappointments till your father's words are fulfilled upon you.* And so we parted.

I thought at first to return home; but shame opposed that good motion, as thinking I should be laughed at by my neighbours and acquaintance. So strange is the nature of youth, who are not ashamed to sin, but yet ashamed to repent; and so far from being ashamed of those actions for which they may be accounted fools, they think it folly to return to their duty, which is the principal mark of wisdom.   In short, I travelled up to London, resolving upon a voyage; and a voyage I soon heard of, by my acquaintance with a captain who took a fancy to me, to go to the coast of Guinea. Having some money, and appearing like a gentleman, I went on board, not as a common sailor or foremast-man; nay, the commander agreed I should go that voyage with him without any expence; that I should be his mess-mate and companion, and I was very welcome to carry any thing with me, and make the best merchandise I could.

I blessed my happy fortune, and humbly thanked my captain for this offer; and acquainting my friends in Yorkshire, forty pounds were sent me, the greatest part of which my dear father and mother contributed to, with which I bought toys and trifles, as the captain directed me. My captain also taught me navigation,

gation, how to keep an account of the ship's course, take an observation, and led me into the knowledge of several useful branches of the mathematics. And indeed this voyage made me both a sailor and a merchant; for I brought home five pounds nine ounces of gold dust for my adventure, which produced, at my return to *London*, almost three hundred pounds. But in this voyage I was extremely sick, being thrown into a violent calenture through excessive heat, trading upon the coast from the latitude of fifteen degrees north even to the line itself.

But alas! my dear friend the captain soon departed this life after his arrival. This was a sensible grief to me; yet I resolved to go another voyage with his mate, who had now got command of the ship. This proved a very unsuccessful one; for though I did not carry quite a hundred pounds of my late acquired wealth, (so that I had two hundred pounds left, which I reposed with the captain's widow who was an honest gentlewoman,) yet my misfortunes in this unhappy voyage were very great. For our ship sailing towards the *Canary* islands, we were chased by a *Salee* rover; and in spite of all the haste we could make, by crouding as much canvas as our yards could spread, or our masts carry, the pirate gained upon us, so that we prepared ourselves to fight. They had eighteen guns, and we had but twelve. About three in the afternoon there was a desperate engagement, wherein many were killed and wounded on both sides: but finding ourselves overpowered with numbers, our ship disabled, and ourselves too impotent to have the least hopes of success, we were forced to surrender; and accordingly were all carried prisoners into the port of Sallee. Our men were sent to the Emperor's court to be sold there; but the pirate captain taking notice of me, kept me to be his own slave.

In this condition, I thought myself the most miserable creature on earth, and the prophecy of my father

came

came afresh into my thoughts. However, my condition was better than I thought it to be, as will soon appear. Some hopes indeed I had that my new patron would go to sea again, where he might be taken by a Spanish or Portugnese man of war, and then I should be set at liberty. But in this I was mistaken; for he never took me with him, but left me to look after his little garden, and do the drudgery of his house, and when he returned from sea, would make me lye in the cabin, and look after the ship. I had no one that I could communicate my thoughts to, which were continually meditating my escape; no Englishman, Irishman, or Scotsman here but myself; and for two years I could see nothing practicable, but only pleased myself with the imagination.

After some length of time, my patron, as I found, grew so poor, that he could not fit out his ship as usual: and then he used constantly, once or twice a-week, if the weather was fair, to go out a-fishing, taking me and a young Moresco boy to row the boat; and so much pleased was he with me for my dexterity in catching the fish, that he would often send me with a Moor, who was one of his kinsmen, and the Moresco youth, to catch a dish of fish for him.

One morning as we were at the sport, there arose such a thick fog, that we lost sight of the shore: and rowing we knew not which way, we laboured all the night, and in the morning found ourselves in the ocean, two leagues from land. However, we attained there at length, and made the greater haste, because our stomachs were exceeding sharp and hungry. In order to prevent such disasters for the future, my patron ordered a carpenter to build a little state-room or cabbin in the middle of the long-boat, with a place behind it to steer and hale home the main sheet, with other conveniences to keep him from the weather, as also lockers to put in all manner of provisions, with a handsome shoulder-of-mutton sail, gibing over the cabin.

In this he frequently took us out a-fishing; and
one time inviting two or three persons of distinction
to go with him, made provisions extraordinary, providing also three fusees with powder and shot, that they
might have some sport at fowling along the sea-coast.
The next morning the boat was made clean, her ancient and pendants out, and every thing ready; but
their minds altering, my patron ordered us to go
a-fishing for that his guests would certainly sup with
him that night.

And now I began to think of my deliverance indeed. In order to this I persuaded the moor to get
some provisions on board, as not daring to meddle
with our patron's; and he taking my advice, we sto-
red ourselves with rusk biscuit, and three jars of water. Besides, I privately conveyed into the boat a
bottle of brandy, some twine, thread, a hammer, hatchet, and a saw; and in particular some bees-wax,
which was a great comfort to me, and served to make
candles. I then persuaded Muley (for so was the moor
called) to procure some powder and shot, pretending
to kill sea-curlieus, which he innocently and readily
agreed to. In short, being provided with all things
necessary, we failed out, resolving for my own part
to make my escape tho' it should cost me my life.

When we had passed the castle, we fell to fishing;
but tho' I knew there was a bite, I dissembled the
matter, in order to put further out to sea. Accordingly we ran a league further; when giving the boy
the hem, and pretending to stoop for something, I
seized Muley by surprise, and threw him overboard.
As he was an excellent swimmer, he soon arose, and
made towards the boat; upon which I took out a
fusee, and presented it at him: *Muley*, said I, *I never
yet designed to do you any harm, and seek nothing now
but my redemption. I know you are able enough to swim
to shore, and save your life; but if you are resolved to
follow me to the endangering of mine, the very mo-*

ment

ment you proceed I will shoot you through the head. The harmless creature, at these words, turned himself from me, and I make no doubt got safe to land. Then turning to the boy Xury, I perceived he trembled at the action; but I put him out of all fear, telling him, that if he would be true and faithful to me, I would do well by him. *And therefore,* said I, *you must stroke your face to be faithful, and, as the* Turks *have learned you, swear by* Mahomet, *and the beard of your father, or else I will throw you into the sea also.* So innocent did the child then look, and with such an obliging smile consented, that I readily believed him, and from that day forward began to love him entirely.

We then pursued our voyage; and left they should think me gone to the Streight's mouth, I kept to the Southward to the truly Barbarian coast: but in the dusk of the evening I changed my course, and steered directly S. and by E. that I might keep near the shore; and having a fresh gale of wind, with a pleasant smooth sea, by three o'clock next day I was 150 miles beyond the Emperor of Morocco's dominions. Yet still having the dreadful apprehension of being retaken, I continued sailing for five days succeffively, till such time as the wind shifting to the southward, made me conclude, that if any veffel was in chace of me, they would proceed no further. After so much fatigue and thought, I anchored at the mouth of a little river, I knew not what, or where: neither did I then see any people. What I principally wanted was fresh water; and I was resolved about the dusk to swim ashore. But no sooner did the gloomy clouds of night begin to succeed the declining day, when we heard such barking, roaring, and howling of wild creatures, that one might have thought the very strangest monsters of nature, or infernal spirits, had their residence there. Poor Xury, almost

moſt dead with fear, intreated me not to go on
ſhore that night. *Suppoſing I don't, Xury, ſaid I,
and in the morning we ſhould ſee men who are worſe
than thoſe we fear, what then? O den we may give
dem de ſhoot gun,* replied *Xury* laughing, *and de
gun make dem all run away.* The wit, and broken
Engliſh which the boy had learned among the captives of our nation, pleaſed me entirely ; and to
add to his chearfulneſs, I gave him a dram of the
bottle: we could get but little ſleep all the night
for thoſe terrible howlings they made; and indeed
we were both very much affrighted, when, by the
rollings of the water, and other tokens, we juſtly
concluded one of thoſe monſters made towards our
boat. I could not ſee it till it came within two
oars length, when taking my fuſee, I let fly at
him. Whether I hit him or no, I cannot tell ; but
he made towards the ſhore, and the noiſe of my
gun increaſed the ſtupendous noiſe of the monſ-
ſters.

The next morning I was reſolved to go on ſhore
to get freſh water, and venture my life among the
beaſts or ſavages, ſhould either attack me. Xury
ſaid, he would take one of the jars, and bring me
ſome. I aſked him why he would go, and not I?
The poor boy anſwered, *If wild mans come, they
eat me, you go way.* A mind ſcarcely now to be
imitated, ſo contrary to ſelf-preſervation, the
moſt powerful law of nature! This indeed increaſed my affection to the child. *Well, dear Xury, ſaid
I, we will both go aſhore, both kill wild mans, and
they ſhall eat neither of us.* So giving Xury a piece
of ruſk bread to eat, and a dram, we waded a-
ſhore, carrying nothing with us but our arms, and
two jars for water. I did not go out of ſight of
the boat, as dreading the ſavages coming down the
river in their canoes : but the boy ſeeing a low
deſcent or vale about a mile in the country, he
wandered

wandered to it; and then running back to me with great precipitation, I thought he was purfued by fome favage or wild beaft; upon which I approach-ed, refolving to perifh or protect him from danger. As he came nearer to me, I faw fomething hang-ing over his fhoulders, which was a creature he had fhot like a hare, but different in colour, and longer legs; however, we were glad of it, for it proved wholefome and nourifhing meat; but what added to our joy was, my boy affured me there was plenty of water, and that he *fee no wild mans.* And greater ftill was our comfort, when we found frefh water in the creek where we were when the tide was out, without going fo far up into the country.

In this place I began to confider that the Canary and Cape de Verde iflands lay not far off; but having no inftrument, I knew not what latitude, or when to ftand off to fea for them; yet my hopes were, I fhould meet fome of the Englifh trading veffels, who would relieve and take us in.

The place I was in was no doubt that wild coun-try, inhabited only by a few, that lyes between the Emperor of Morocco's dominions and the Ne-groes. It is filled with wild beafts, and the Moors ufe it for hunting chiefly. From this place I thought I faw the top of the mountain Teneriffe in the Canaries; which made me try twice to at-tain it; but as often was I drove back, and fo for-ced to purfue my fortune along fhore.

Early one morning we came to an anchor un-der a little point of land, but pretty high; and the tide beginning to flow, we lay ready to go further in, but Xury, whofe youthful and pene-trating eyes were fharper than mine, in a foft tone, defired me to keep far from land, left we fhould be devoured: *For look yonder, mayter,* faid he, *and fee de dreadful monfter faft a fleep on de fide of de hill.*

hill. Accordingly looking where he pointed, I espied a fearful monster indeed. It was a terrible great lion that lay on shore, covered as it were by a shade of a piece of the hill. Xury, said I, *you shall go on shore and kill him.* But the boy looked amazed: *Me kill him,* says he, *he eat me at one mouth;* meaning one mouthful. Upon which I bid him lye still, and charging my biggest gun with two slugs, and a good charge of powder, I took the best aim I could to shoot him through the head; but his leg lying over his nose, the slug broke his knee bone. The lion awaking with the pain, got up, but soon fell down, giving the most hideous groan I ever heard; but taking my second piece, I shot him through the head, and then he lay struggling for life. Upon this Xury took heart, and defired my leave to go on shore. Go then, said I. Upon which taking a little gun in one hand, he swam to shore with the other, and coming close to the lion, put a period to his life, by shooting him again through the head.

But this was spending our ammunition in vain, the flesh not being good to eat. Xury was like a champion, and comes on board for a hatchet, to cut off the head of his enemy; but not having strength to perform it, he cut off and brought me a foot. I bethought me however that his skin would be of use. This work cost Xury and me a whole day; when spreading it on the top of our cabin, the hot beams of the sun effectually dried it in two days time, and it afterwards served me for a bed to lye on.

And now we sailed southerly, living sparingly on our provisions, and went no oftener on shore than we were obliged for fresh water. My defign was to make the river Gambia or Senegal, or any where about the Cape de Verde, in hopes to meet some European ship. If Providence did not so favour me, my next course was to seek for the islands, or lose my life among the negroes. And in a word, I put my whole stress upon this; " Ei- " that I must meet with some ship, or certainly " perish."

One day as we were sailing along, we saw people stand on the shore looking at us; we could also perceive they were black, and stark naked. I was inclined to go on shore: but Xury cried, No, no; however I approached nearer, and I found they run along the shore by me a good way. They had no weapons in their hands, except one, who held a long stick, which Xury told me was a lance with which they could kill at a great distance. I talked to them by signs, and made them sensible I wanted something to eat; they beckoned to me to stop my boat, while two of them ran up into the country, and in less than half an hour came back, and brought with them two pieces of dry flesh, and some corn, which we kindly accepted: and to prevent any fears on either side, they brought the food to the shore, laid it down, then went and stood a great way off till we fetched it on board, and then came close to us again.

But while we were returning thanks to them, being all we could afford, two mighty creatures came from the mountains, one as it were pursuing the other with great fury, which we were the rather inclined to believe, as they seldom appear but in the night; and both these swiftly passing by the negroes jumped into the sea, wantonly swimming about, as though the diversion of the waters had put a stop to their fierceness. At last one of them coming nearer to my boat than I expected or desired, I shot him directly through the head; upon which he sunk immediately, yet rising again, would have willingly made to the shore; but between the wound and the strangling of the water, he died before he could reach it.

It is impoſſible to expreſs the conſternation the poor negroes were in at the firing of my gun; much leſs can I mention their ſurpriſe, when they perceived the creature to be ſlain by it. I made ſigns to them to draw near it with a rope, and then gave it to them to hale on ſhore. It was a beautiful leopard which made me deſire its ſkin: and the negroes ſeeming to covet the carcaſe, I freely gave it to them. As for the other leopard, it made to ſhore, and ran with a prodigious ſwift-neſs out of ſight. The negroes having kindly fur-niſhed me with water, and with what roots and grains their country afforded, I took my leave, and, after eleven days ſail, came in ſight of the Cape de Verde, and thoſe iſlands called by its name. But, the great diſtance I was from it, and fearing contrary winds would prevent my reaching them, I began to grow melancholy and dejected, when upon a ſudden Xury cried out, *Maſter, maſter, a ſhip with a ſail!* and looked as affrighted as if it was his maſter's ſhip ſent in ſearch of us. But I ſoon diſcovered ſhe was a Portugueze ſhip, as I thought bound to the coaſt of Guinea for negroes. Upon which I ſtrove for life to come up to them. But vain had it been, if through their perſpective glaſſes they had not perceived me, and ſhortened their ſail to let me come up. Encouraged at this, I ſet up my patron's ancient, and fired a gun, both as ſignals of diſtreſs; upon which they very kindly lay to, ſo that in three hours time I came up with them. They ſpoke to me in Portugueze, Spaniſh, and French, but neither of theſe did I underſtand; till at length a Scots ſailor called, and then I told him I was an Engliſhman, who had eſcaped from the Moors at Sallee; upon which they took me kind-ly on board with all my effects.

Surely none can expreſs the inconceivable joy I felt at this happy deliverance! who, from being

a late miferable and forlorn creature, was not only relieved, but in favour with the mafter of the
fhip, to whom, in return for my deliverance, I offered all I had. *God forbid*, faid he, *that I fhould take
any thing from you. Every thing fhall be delivered to you when you come to* Brazil. *If I have faved your life, it is no more than I fhould expect to
receive myfelf from any other, when, in the fame
circumftances, I fhould happen to meet the like deliverance. And fhould I take from you what you
have, and leave you at* Brazil, *why? this would be
only taking away a life I have given. My charity teaches me better. Thofe effects you have will
fupport you there, and provide you a paffage home
again.* And indeed he acted with the ftricteft juftice in what he did, taking my things into his poffeffion, and giving me an exact inventory even to
my earthen jars. He bought my boat of me for
the fhip's ufe, giving me a note of eighty pieces of
eight, payable at Brazil; and if any body offered
more, he would make it up. He alfo gave me fixty
pieces for my boy Xury. It was with great reluc-
tance I was prevailed upon to fell the child's liberty, who had ferved me fo faithfully; but the boy
was willing himfelf; and it was agreed, that after
ten years he fhould be made free, upon his renoun-
cing Mahometifm, and embracing Chriftianity.

Having a pleafing voyage to the Brazils, we arrived in the Bay de Todos los Santos, or All-Saints
Bay, in twenty-two days after. And here I cannot forget the generous treatment of the captain.
He would take nothing for my paffage, gave me
twenty ducats for the leopard's fkin, and thirty for
the lion's. Every thing he caufed to be delivered, and what I would fell he bought. In fhort,
I made about 220 pieces of my cargo; and with
this ftock I entered once more, as I may fay, into
the fcene of life.

Being

Being recommended to an honeft planter, I lived with him till fuch time as I was informed of the manner of their planting and making fugar; and feeing how well they lived, and how fuddenly they grew rich, I was filled with a defire to fettle among them, and refolved to get my money remitted to me, and to purchafe a plantation.

To be brief, I bought a fettlement next door to an honeft and kind neighbour, born at Lifbon, of Englifh parents, whofe plantation joining to mine, we improved very amicably together. Both our ftocks were low, and for two years we planted only for food: but the third year we planted fome tobacco, and each of us dreffed a large piece of ground the enfuing year for planting canes. But now I found how much I wanted affiftance, and repented the lofs of my dear boy Xury.

Having none to affift me, my father's words came into my mind; and I ufed to afk myfelf, If what I fought was only a middle ftation of life, why could it not as well be obtained in England as here? When I pondered on this with regret, the thoughts of my late deliverance forfook me. I had none to converfe with but my neighbour; no work to be done but by my own hands; it often made me fay, my condition was like to that of a man caft upon a defolate ifland. So unhappy are we in our reflections, fo forgetful of what good things we receive ourfelves, and fo unthankful for our deliverance from thofe calamities that others endure.

I was in fome meafure fettled, before the captain, who took me up, departed from the Brafils. One day I went to him, and told him what ftock I had in London, defiring his affiftance in getting it remitted; to which the good gentleman readily confented, but would only have me fend for half my money, left it fhould mifcarry; which if it did, I might ftill have the remainder to fupport me:

and

and so taking letters of procuration from me, bid me trouble myself no farther about it.

And indeed wonderful was his kindness towards me; for he not only procured the money I had drawn for upon my Captain's widow, but sent me over a servant with a cargo, proportionable to my condition. He also sent me over tools of all sorts, iron work, and utensils necessary for my plantation, and which proved of the greatest use to me in my business.

Wealth now accumulating on me, and uncommon success crowning my prosperous labours, I might have rested happy in that middle state of life my father had so often recommended; yet nothing would content me, such was my evil genius, but I must leave this happy station, for a foolish ambition in rising: and thus, once more, I cast myself into the deepest gulf of misery that ever a poor creature fell into. Having lived four years in Brasil, I had not only learned the language, but contracted acquaintance with the most eminent planters, and even the merchants of St. Salvadore; to whom, once, by way of discourse, having given an account of my two voyages to the coast of Guinea, and the manner of trading there for mere trifles, by which we furnish our plantations with negroes, they gave such attention to what I said, that three of them came one morning to me, and told me they had a secret proposal to make. After injoining me to secrecy, (it being an infringement on the powers of the kings of Portugal and Spain,) they told me they had a mind to fit out a ship to go to Guinea, in order to stock the plantation with negroes, which, as they could not be publicly sold, they would divide among them; and if I would go their supercargo in the ship, to manage the trading part, I should have an equal share of the negroes, without providing any stock. The

thing

thing indeed was fair enough, had I been in another condition. But I, born to be my own deſtroyer, could not reſiſt the propoſal, but accepted the offer, upon condition of their looking after my plantation. So making a formal will, I bequeathed my effects to my good friend the captain, as my univerſal heir; but obliged him to diſpoſe of my effects as directed, one half of the produce to himſelf, and the other to be ſhipped to England.

The ſhip being fitted out, and all things ready, we ſet ſail on the firſt of September 1659, being the ſame day eighth year I left my father and mother in Yorkſhire. We ſailed northward upon the coaſt, in order to gain Africa, till we made Cape Auguſtine; from whence, going farther in the ocean, out of ſight of land, we ſteered as though we were bound for the iſle Fernand de Norenba, leaving the iſlands on the eaſt; and then it was we met with a terrible tempeſt, which continued for twelve days ſucceſſively, ſo that the winds carried us whereſoever they pleaſed. In this perplexity, one of our men died, and one man and a boy were waſhed over board. When the weather cleared up a little, we found ourſelves eleven degrees north latitude, upon the coaſt of Guinea. Upon this the captain gave reaſons for returning; which I oppoſed, counſelling him to ſtand away for Barbadoes, which, as I ſuppoſed, might be attained in fifteen days. So altering our courſe, we ſailed north-weſt and by weſt, in order to reach the leeward iſlands; but a ſecond ſtorm ſucceeding, drove us to the weſtward; ſo that we were juſtly afraid of falling into the hands of cruel ſavages, or the paws of devouring beaſts of prey.

In this great diſtreſs, one of our men, early in the morning, cried out, *Land, land*; which he had no ſooner cried out, but our ſhip ſtruck upon a

ſand,

fand, and in a moment the fea broke over her in fuch a manner, that we expected we fhould all have perifhed immediately. We knew nothing where we were, or upon what land we were driven; whether an ifland or the main, inhabited or not inhabited; and we could not fo much as hope that the fhip would hold out many minutes, without breaking in pieces, except the wind by a miracle fhould turn about immediately. While we ftood looking at one another, expecting death every moment, the mate lays hold of the boat, and with the help of the reft got her flung over the fhip's fide, and getting all into her, being eleven of us, committed ourfelves to God's mercy, and the wild fea. And now we faw that this laft effort would not be a fufficient protection from death; fo high did the fea rife, that it was impoffible the boat fhould live. As to making fail, we had none; neither if we had, could we make ufe of any. So that when we had rowed, or rather were driven about a league and a half, a raging wave, like a lofty mountain, came rolling aftern of us, and took us with fuch fury, that at once it overfet the boat. Thus being fwallowed up in a moment, we had hardly time to call upon the tremendous name of God: much lefs to implore, in dying ejaculations, his infinite mercy to receive our departing fouls.

Men are generally counted infenfible, when ftruggling in the pangs of death; but while I was overwhelmed with water, I had the moft dreadful apprehenfions imaginable; for the joys of heaven and the torments of hell, feemed to prefent themfelves before me in thefe dying agonies, and even the fmall fpace of time, as it were, between life and death. I was going, I thought, I knew not whether, in a difmal gulf unknown, and as yet unperceived, never to behold my friends, nor the light of this world any more! Could I even have
thought

thought of annihilation, or a total diffolution of foul as well as body, the gloomy thoughts of having no further being, no knowledge of what we hoped for, but an eternal *quietus*, without life or fenfe; even that, I fay, would have been enough to ftrike me with horror and confufion! I ftrove however to the laft extremity, while all my companions were overpowered and intombed in the deep: and it was with great difficulty I kept my breath till the wave fpent itfelf, and retiring back, left me on the fhore half dead with the water I had taken in. As foon as I got on my feet, I ran as faft as I could, left another wave fhould purfue me, and carry me back again. But, for all the hafte I made, I could not avoid it; for the fea came after me like a high mountain, or furious enemy; fo that my bufinefs was to hold my breath, and by raifing myfelf on the water, preferve it by fwimming. The next dreadful wave buried me at once twenty or thirty foot deep, but at the fame time carried me with a mighty force and fwiftnefs toward the fhore; when raifing myfelf, I held out as well as poffible, till at length the water having fpent itfelf, began to return, at which I ftruck forward, and feeling ground with my feet, I took to my heels again. Thus being ferved twice more, I was at laft dafhed againft a piece of a rock, in fuch a manner as left me fenfelefs; but recovering a little before the return of the wave, which, no doubt, would then have overwhelmed me, I held faft by the rock till thofe fucceeding waves abated; and then fetching another run, was overtaken by a fmall wave, which was foon conquered. But before any more could overtake me, I reached the main land, where, clambering up the clifts of the fhore, tired and almoft fpent, I fat down on the grafs, free from the dangers of the foaming ocean.

No tongue can exprefs the ecftafies and tranfports

sports that my soul felt at this happy deliverance. It was like a reprieve to a dying malefactor, with the halter about his neck, and ready to be turned off. I was wrapt up in contemplation, and often lifted up my hands, with the profoundest humility, to the divine powers, for saving my life, when the rest of my companions were all drowned. And now I began to cast my eyes around, to behold what place I was in, and what I had next to do. I could see no house nor people: I was wet, yet had no cloaths to shift me; hungry and thirsty, yet nothing to eat or drink; no weapon to destroy any creature for my sustenance, nor defend myself against devouring beasts. In short I had nothing but a knife, a tobacco-pipe, and a box half filled with tobacco. The darksome night coming upon me, increased my fears of being devoured by wild creatures; my mind was plunged in despair, and having no prospect, as I thought, of life before me, I prepared for another kind of death than what I had lately escaped. I walked about a furlong to see if I could find any fresh water, which I did, to my great joy; and taking a quid of tobacco to prevent hunger, I got up into a thick bushy tree, and seating myself so that I could not fall, a deep sleep overtook me, and for that night buried my sorrows in a quiet repose.

It was broad day the next morning before I awakened; when I not only perceived the tempest was ceased, but saw the ship driven almost as far as the rock before mentioned, which the waves had dashed me against, and which was about a mile from the place where I was. When I came down from my apartment in the tree, I perceived the ship's boat two miles distant on my right hand, lying on shore, as the waves had cast her. I thought to have got to her; but there being an inlet of water of about half a mile's breadth between

R. Crusoe Saving his Goods out of ye Wreck of ye Ship P. 22.

tween it and me, I returned again towards the
ship, as hoping to find something for my more immediate subsistence. About noon when the sea
was calm, that I could come within a quarter of
a mile of her, it was to my grief I perceived, that
if we had kept on board, all our lives had been
saved. These thoughts, and my solitude, drew
tears from my eyes, though all in vain. So resolving to get to the ship, I stripped and leaped into the water; when swimming round her I was
afraid I should not get any thing to lay hold of;
but it was my good fortune to espy a small piece
of rope hang down by the forechains so low, that,
by the help of it, though with great difficulty, I
got into the forecastle of the ship. Here I found
that the ship was bulged, and had a great deal of
water in her hold; her stern was lifted up against
a bank, and her head almost to the water. All
her quarter, and what was there, were free and
dry. The provisions I found in good order; with
which I crammed my pockets; and, losing no time,
ate while I was doing other things; I also found
some rum, of which I took a hearty dram; and
now I wanted for nothing except a boat, which
indeed was all, to carry away what was needful
for me.

Necessity occasions quickness of thought. We
had several spare yards, a spare topmast or two,
and two or three large spars of wood. With
these I fell to work, and flung as many of them
over board as I could manage, tying every one of
them with a rope that they might not drive away.
This done, I went down the ship's side, and tied
four of them fast together at both ends, in form
of a raft, and laying two or three short pieces of
plank upon them crofs-wise, I found it would bear
me, but not any considerable weight. Upon which
I went to work again, cutting a spare topmast in-

to

to three lengths, adding them to my raft with a
great deal of labour and pains. I then confidered
what I fhould load it with, it being not able to
bear a ponderous burden. And this I foon thought
of, firft laying upon it all the planks and boards I
could get; next I lowered down three of the feamen's chefts, after I had filled them with bread,
rice, three Dutch cheefes, five pieces of dried
goats flefh, and fome European corn, what little
the rats had fpared; and for liquors, I found feveral cafes of bottles belonging to our fkipper, in
which were fome cordial waters, and four or five
gallons of rack, which I ftowed by themfelves.
By this time the tide beginning to flow, I perceived my coat, waiftcoat, and fhirt fwim away,
which I had left on the fhore; as for my linen
breeches and ftockings, I fwam with them on to
the fhip: but I foon found cloaths enough, though
I took no more than I wanted for the prefent.
My eyes were chiefly on tools to work with; and
after long fearch, I found out the carpenter's cheft,
which I got fafe down on my raft. I then looked
for arms and ammunition, and in the great cabin
found two good fowling-pieces, two piftols, feveral powder-horns filled, a fmall bag of fhot, and
two old rufty fwords. I likewife found three barrels of powder, two of which were good, but the
third had taken water, alfo two or three broken
oars, two faws, an axe, and a hammer. I then
put to fea, and in getting to fhore had three en-
couragements. 1. A fmooth calm fea. 2. The
tide rifing and fetting into the fhore. 3. The little wind there was blew towards land. After I
had failed about a mile, I found the raft to drive
a little diftance from the place where I firft landed, and then I perceived an opening of the land,
with a ftrong current of the tide runing into it;
upon which I kept in the middle of the ftream. But
.great

great was my concern, when on a sudden the fore part of my raft ran aground; so that had I not, with great difficulty; for near half an hour, kept my back straining against the chests to keep my effects in their places, all I had would have gone into the sea. But after some time, the rising of the water caused the raft to float again, and coming up a little river, with land on both sides, I landed in a little cave, as near the mouth as possible, the better to discover a sail, if any such providentially passed that way.

Not far off, I espied a hill of a stupendous height, surrounded with lesser hills about it, and thither I was resoved to go and view the country, that I might see what part was best to fix my habitation in. Accordingly, arming myself with a pistol, a fowling piece, powder and ball, I ascended the mountain. There I perceived, I was in an island, encompassed by the sea; no distant lands to be seen, but scattering rocks that lay to the west: that it seemed to be a barren place, and, as I thought, inhabited only by wild beasts. I pereeived abundance of fowls, but ignorant of what kind, or whether good for nourishment. I shot one of them at my return, which occasioned a confused screaming among the other birds; and I found it, by its colours and beak, to be a kind of a hawk, but its flesh was perfect carrion.

When I came to my raft, I brought my effects on shore, which work spent that day entirely; and fearing that some cruel beasts might devour me in the night time while I slept, I made a kind of hut or barricade with the chests and boards I had brought on shore. That night I slept very comfortable; and the next morning my thoughts were employed to make a further attempt on the ship, and bring away what necessaries I could find, before another storm should break her to pieces. Accordingly I got on board as before, and prepared a fecond raft, far more nice than the firft; upon which I brought away the carpenter's ftores, two or three bags full of nails, a great jack-fcrew, a dozen or two of hatchets, and a grindftone. I alfo took away feveral things that belonged to the gunner, particularly two or three iron crows, two barrels of mufket bullets, another fowling-piece, a fmall quantity of powder, and a large bagful of fmall fhot. Befides thefe, I took all the men's cloaths I could find, a fpare foretop-fail, a hammock, and fome bedding; and thus, compleating my fecond cargo, I made all the hafte to fhore I could, fearing fome wild beaft might deftroy what I had there already. But I only found a little wild cat fitting on one of the chefts, who not feeming to fear me, or the gun that I prefented at her, I threw her a piece of bifcuit, which fhe inftantly ate and departed.

. When I had gotten thefe effects on fhore, I went to work, in order to make me a little tent with the fail and fome poles, which I had cut for that purpofe; and having finifhed it, what things might be damaged by the weather, I brought in, piling all the empty chefts and cafks in a circle, the better to fortify it againft any fudden attempt of man or beaft. After this, I blocked up the doors with fome boards, and an empty cheft, turned the long way out. I then charged my gun and piftol, and laying my bed on the ground, flept as comfortably, till next morning, as though I had been in a Chriftian country.

Now, tho' I had enough to fubfift me a long time, yet defpairing of a fudden deliverance, or that both ammunition and provifion might be fpent before fuch a thing happened, I coveted as much as I could; and fo long as the fhip remained in that condition, I daily brought away one neceffary or other; particularly the rigging, fails, and cordage, and fome twine, a barrel of wet powder, fome fugar, a barrel of meal, three casks of rum, and, what indeed was most welcome to me, a whole hogshead of bread.

The next time I went, I cut the cables in pieces, carried off a haulser whole, with a great deal of iron work, and made another raft with the mizen and sprit-sail-yards; but this being so unwieldy, by the too heavy burden I had upon it, and not being able so dexterously to guide it as the former, both my cargo and I were overturned. For my part, all the damage I sustained was a wet skin: and at low water, after much labour in diving, I got most of the cables, and some pieces of iron.

Thirteen days had I now been in the island, and eleven times on board, bringing away all that was possible; and, I believe, had the weather been calm, I should have brought away the whole ship piece by piece. As I was going the twelfth time, the wind began to rise; however, I ventured at low water, and rummaging the cabin, in a locker I found several razors, sciffars, and some dozens of knives and forks; and in another thirty-six pounds in pieces of eight, silver and gold. *Ah! simple vanity,* said I, *whom this world so much dotes on, where is now thy virtue, thy excellency to me? you cannot procure me one thing needful, nor remove me from this desolate island to a place of plenty. One of these knives, so meanly esteemed, is to me more preferable than all this heap. E'en therefore remain where thou art, to sink in the deep as unregarded, even as a creature whose life is not worth preserving.* Yet, after all this exclamation, I wrapt it up in a piece of canvas, and began to think of making another raft; but I soon perceived the wind begin to arise, a fresh gale blowing from the shore, and the sky overcast with clouds and darkness. So thinking a raft to be in vain, I let myself into the water with what things I had

C 2

about

about me; and it was with much difficulty I got a-
fhore, when foon after it blew a fearful ftorm.

That night I flept very contentedly in my little
tent, furrounded with all my effects; but when I
looked out in the morning, no more fhip was to
be feen. This much furprifed me for the prefent:
yet, when I had confidered I had loft no time, a-
bated no pains, and had got every thing ufeful
out of her, I comforted myfelf in the beft manner,
and entirely fubmitted to the will of Providence.

My next thoughts were, how I fhould defend
and fecure myfelf from favages and wild beafts,
if any fuch were in the ifland. At one time I thought
of digging a cave, at another I was for erecting a
a tent, and, at length, I refolved to do both:
The manner or form of which will not, I hope,
be unpleafing to defcribe.

When I confidered the ground where I was, that
it was moorifh, and had no frefh water near it,
my refolutions were to fearch for a foil healthy
and well watered, where I might not only be fheltered from the fun's fcorching heat, but be more
conveniently fituated, as well to be fecured from
wild men, and beafts of prey, as more eafily to
difcover any diftant fail fhould it ever fo happen.

And indeed it was not long before I had my defire. I found a little plain near a rifing hill, the
front towards which being as fteep as a houfe-
fide, nothing could defcend on me from the top.
On the fide of this rock was a little hollow place,
refembling the entrance or door of a cave. Juft
before this place, on the circle of the green, I refolved my tent fhould ftand. This plan did not
much exceed a hundred yards broad, and about
twice as long, like a delightful green before my
door, with a pleafing, tho' irregular defcent every
way to the low grounds by the fea-fide, lying on
the N. N. W. fide of the hill, fo that it was fheltered

tered from the exceſſive heat of the ſun. After
this I drew a ſemicircle, containing ten yards in
its ſemidiameter, and twenty yards in the whole,
driving down two rows of ſtrong ſtakes not ſix
inches from each other. Then with the pieces of
cable which I had cut on board, I regularly laid
them in the circle between the piles up to their
tops, which were more than five feet out of the
earth, and after drove another row of piles looking within ſide againſt them, between two or
three feet high, which made me conclude it a little impregnable caſtle for men and beaſts. And
for my better ſecurity I would have no door, but
entered in and came out by the help of a ladder,
which I alſo made.

Here was my fence and fortreſs, into which I
carried all my riches, ammunition, and ſtores.
After which, working on the rock, what with the
dirt and ſtones I dig out, I not only raiſed my
ground two feet, but made a little cellar to my
manſion houſe; and this coſt me many days labour
and pains: One day in particular a ſhower of rain
falling, thunder and lightening enſued, which put
me in terror leſt my powder ſhould take fire, and
not only hinder my neceſſary ſubſiſtence, by killing me food, but even blow up me and my habitation. To prevent which, I fell to making boxes and bags, in order to ſeparate it; having by
me near 150 weight. And thus being eſtabliſhed
as king of the iſland, every day I went out with
my gun to ſee what I could kill that was fit to
eat. I ſoon perceived numbers of goats, but very ſhy; yet having watched them narrowly, and
ſeeing I could better ſhoot off the rocks than when
in the low grounds, I happened to ſhoot a ſhe-
goat ſuckling a young kid; which not thinking its
dam ſlain, ſtood by her unconcerned; and when I
took the dead creature up, the young one follow-

C 3   ed

ed me even to the inclofure. I lifted the kid over the pales, and would willingly have kept it alive; but finding it could not be brought to eat, I was forced to flay it alfo for my own fubfiftence.

Thus, entered into as ftrange a fcene of life as ever any man was in, I had moft melancholy ap-prehenfions concerning my deplorable condition; and many times the tears would plentifully run down my face, when I confidered how I was debarred from all communication with human kind. Yet while thefe defponding cogitations would feem to make me accufe Providence, other good thoughts would interpofe and reprove me after this manner: Well, fuppofing you are fo de-folate, is it not better to be fo than totally pe-rifh? Why were you fingled out to be faved, and the reft deftroyed? Why fhould you complain, when not only your life is preferved, but the fhip driven even into your reach, in order to take what was neceflary out of her for your fubfiftence? But to proceed: It was by the account I kept, the 30th of September, when I firft landed on this ifland. About twelve days after, fearing left I fhould lofe my reckoning of time, nay, even forget the Sab-bath-days, for want of pen, ink, and paper, I car-ved with a knife upon a large poft, in great letters, and fet it up, in the fimilitude of a crofs, on the fea-fhore where I landed, *I came on fhore* Sept. 30. 1659. Every day I cut a notch with my knife on the fides of this fquare poft, and that on Sabbath was as long again as the reft; and every firft day of the month as long again as that long one. In this manner I kept my calendar, weekly, monthly, or yearly reckoning of time. But had I made a more ftrict fearch, (as I did afterwards,) I need not have fet up this mark. For among the par-cels belonging to the gunner, carpenter and cap-tain's mate, I found thofe very things I wanted: parti-

particularly pens, ink and paper; alfo I found two or three compaffes, fome mathematical inftruments, dials, perfpective glaffes, books of navigation, three Englifh Bibles, and feveral other good books, which I carefully put up. Here I cannot but call to mind our having a dog and two cats on board, whom I made inhabitants with me in my caftle. Though one might think I had all the néceffaries that were defirable, yet ftill I found feveral things wanting. My ink was daily wafting: I wanted needles, pins, and thread to mend or keep my cloaths together; and particularly a fpade, pickaxe, or fhovel, to remove the earth. It was a year before I finifhed my little bulwark; and having fome intervals of relaxation, after my daily wandering abroad for provifion, I drew up this plan, alternately, as creditor and debtor, to remind me of the miferies and bleffings of my life, under fo many various circumftances.

EVIL.	GOOD.
I am caft upon a defolate ifland, having no hopes, no profpect of a welcome deliverance.	*But yet I am preferved, while my companions are perifhed in the raging ocean.*
How miferably am I fingled out from the enjoyment or company of all mankind.	*Yet fet apart to be fpared from death. And he, who has fo preferved me, can deliver me from this condition.*
Like an hermit (rather fhould I fay a lonely anchorite) am I forced from human converfation.	*However, I have food to eat, and even a happy profpect of fubfiftence whilft life endures.*
My cloaths after fome time will be worn out; and then I fhall have none to cover me.	*At prefent I enjoy what is abfolutely needful; and the climate is fo hot, that had I never fo many, I fhould hardly wear them.*

E v i l.	G o o d.
When my ammunition is wasted, then shall I remain without any defence against wild men and beasts.	*Yet if it does, I see no danger of any to hurt me, as in Africa: and what if I had been cast away upon that coast.*
I have no creature, no soul to speak to ; none to beg assistance from: Some comfort would it be to resound my woes where I am understood, and beg assistance where I might hope for relief.	*Is there not God to converse to, and is not he able to relieve thee ? Already has he afforded thee sustenance, and put it in thy power to provide for thyself till he sends thee a deliverance.*

And now easing my mind a little by these reflections, I began to render my life as easy as possible.

I must here add, to the description I have given of my habitation, that having raised a turf-wall against the outside of it, I thatched it so close, as might keep it from the inclemency of the weather ; I also improved it within; enlarged my cave, and made a passage and a door in the rock, which came out beyond the pale of my fortification. I next proceeded to make a chair and table, and so began to study such mechanical arts as seemed to me practicable. When I wanted a plank or board, I hewed down a tree with my hatchet, making it as thin with my axe as possible, and then smooth enough with an adze to answer my designs : yet though I could make no more this way than one board out of a tree, in length of time I got boards enough to shelter all my stores, every thing being regularly placed, and my guns securely hanging against the side of the rock. This made it a very pleasant sight to me, and being the result of vast labour and diligence ; which leaving for a while,

and

and me to the enjoyment of, I ſhall give the reader an account of my Journal from the day of my
landing, till the fixing and ſettling of my habitation, as heretofore ſhewn.

◄◄◄◄◄◄◄◄ ◄◄◄◄◄◄◄◄◄◄◄◄◄◄◄◄◆►►►►►►►►►►►►►►►►►►►►►►►

J O U R N A L.

SEptember 30th, 1659, I unhappy Robinſon
Cruſoe, having ſuffered ſhipwreck, was driven
on this deſolate iſland, which I named the Deſolate
iſland of Deſpair, the reſt being ſwallowed up in
the tempeſtuous ocean. The next day I ſpent in
conſideration of my unhappy circumſtances, having
no proſpect but of death, either to be ſtarved with
hunger, or devoured by beaſts or mercileſs ſavages.

Octob. 1. That morning with great comfort I
beheld the ſhip drove aſhore. Some hopes I had,
that when the ſtorm was abated, I might be able
to get ſome food and neceſſaries out of her; which
I conceived were not damaged, becauſe the ſhip
did ſtand upright. At this time I lamented the
loſs of my companions, and our misfortune in
leaving the veſſel. When I perceived the ſhip as
it were lye dry, I waded through the ſands, then
ſwam aboard, the weather being very rainy, and
with ſcarcely any wind.

To the 14th of this month, my time was employed in making voyages, every tide getting what
I could out of the ſhip. The weather very wet
and uncertain.

Octob. 20. My raft and all the goods thereon
were overſet; yet I recovered moſt again at low
water.

Octob. 25. It blew hard, and rained night and
day, when the ſhip went in pieces, ſo that nothing
was

was feen of her but the wreck at low water. This day I fecured my goods from the inclemency of the weather.

Octob. 26. I wandered to fee where I could find a place convenient for my abode. I fixed upon a rock in the evening, marked out a half-moon, intending to erect a wall, fortified with piles, lined within with pieces of cables, and covered with turf.

Nov. 1. I erected my tent under a rock, and took up my lodgings very contentedly in a hammock that night.

Nov. 2. This day I fenced myfelf in with timber, chefts, and boards.

Nov. 3. I fhot two wild fowl, refembling ducks, which were good to eat, and in the afternoon made me a table.

Nov. 4. I began to live regularly. In the morning I allowed myfelf two or three hours to walk out with my gun; I then worked till near eleven o'clock; and afterwards refrefhed myfelf with what I had to eat. From twelve to two I would lye down to fleep. Extreme fultry weather. In the evening go to work again.

Nov. 5. Went out with my gun and dog, fhot a wild cat with a foft fkin, but her flefh was good for nothing. The fkins of thofe I killed I preferved. In my return I perceived many wild birds, and was terrified by fome feals which made off to fea.

Nov. 6. Compleated my table.

Nov. 7. Fair weather. I worked till the 12th, but ommitted the 11th, which according to my calculation, I fuppofed to be Sunday.

Nov. 13. Rain in abundance, which, however, much cooled the earth; with thunder and lightening, caufed in me a terrible furprife. The weather clearing, I fecured my powder in feparate parcels.

Nov.

Nov. 14.—16. I made little boxes for my powder, lodging them in several places. I also shot a large fowl, which proved excellent meat.

Nov. 17. I began to dig in the rock, yet was obliged to defist for want of a pick-axe, shovel, and wheel-barrow. Iron crows I caused to supply the place of the first; but with all my art I could not make a wheel-barrow.

Nov. 18. It was my fortune to find a tree, resembling what the Brasilians call an iron-tree. I had like to have spoiled my axe with cutting it, being very hard and exceeding heavy: yet with much labour and industry, I made a fort of a spade out of it.

Nov. 23. These tools being made, I daily carried on my business; eighteen days I allowed for enlarging my cave, that it might serve me, not only for a ware-house, but kitchen, parlour, and cellar. I commonly lay in the tent, unless the weather was rainy that I could not lye dry. So wet would it be at certain seasons, that I was obliged to cover all within the pale with long poles, in the form of rafters, leaning against the rock, and load them with flags and large leaves of trees, resembling a thatch.

Dec. 10. No sooner did I think my habitation finished, but suddenly a great deal of the top broke in, so that it was a mercy I was not buried in the ruins. This occasioned a great deal of pains and trouble to me, before I could make it firm and durable.

Dec. 17. I nailed up some shelves, and drove nails and staples in the wall, and posts to hang things out of the way.

Dec. 20. Every thing I got into its place, then made a fort of dresser, and another table.

Dec. 24. 25. Rain in abundance.

Dec. 26. Very fair weather.

Dec.

Dec. 27. I chanced to light on fome goats, fhot one, wounded another; I led it home in a ftring, bound up his leg, and cured it in a little time; at length it became fo tame and familiar as to feed before the door, and follow me where I pleafed. This put me in mind to bring up tame creatures, in order to fupply me with food after my ammunition was fpent.

Dec. 28, 29, 30. The weather being exceffive hot with little air, obliged me for the moft part to keep within doors.

Jan. 1. Still fultry. However, obliged by neceffity, I went out with my gun, and found a great ftore of goats in the valleys; they were exceedingly fhy, nor could any dog hunt them down.

Jan. 3, to 14. My employment this time was to finifh the wall before defcribed, and fearch the ifland. I difcovered a kind of pigeons like our houfe-pigeons in a neft among the rocks. I brought them home, nurfed them till they could fly, and then they left me. After this I fhot fome, which proved excellent food. Some time I fpent vainly in contriving to make a cafk; I may well fay it was vain, becaufe I could neither join the ftaves, or fix the heads, fo as to make it tight; fo leaving that, I took fome goats' tallow I had by me, and a little oakum for the wick, and provided myfelf with a lamp, which ferved me inftead of candles.

But now a very ftrange event happened. For being in the height of my fearch, what fhould come into my hand, but a bag which was ufed to hold corn (as I fuppofed for the fowls,) fo immediately refolving to put gunpowder in it, I fhook all the hufks and dirt upon one fide of the rock, little expecting what the confequence would be. The rain had fallen plentifully a few days before; and about a month after, to my great amazement, fomething began to look out very green and flourifhing:

ing: and when I came to view it more nicely, every day as it grew, I found about ten or twelve ears of green barley appeared in the very ſame ſhape and make as that in England.

I can ſcarce expreſs the agitations of my mind at this ſight. Hitherto I had looked upon the actions of this life, no otherwiſe than only as the events of blind chance and fortune. But now, the appearance of this barley, flouriſhing in a barren ſoil, and my ignorance in not conceiving how it ſhould come there, made me conclude, *that miracles were not yet ceaſed:* nay, I even thought that God had appointed it to grow there without any ſeed, purely for my ſuſtenance in this miſerable and deſolate iſland. And indeed ſuch great affect this had upon me, that it often made me melt into tears, through a grateful ſenſe of God's mercies; and the greater ſtill was my thankfulneſs, when I perceived about this little field of barley, ſome rice ſtalks, alſo wonderfully flouriſhing.

While thus pleaſed in mind, I concluded there muſt be more corn in the iſland; and therefore made a diligent ſearch narrowly among the rocks; but not being able to find any, on a ſudden it came into my mind, how I had ſhaken the huſks of corn out of the bag, and then my admiration ceaſed, with my gratitude to the divine Being, *as thinking it was but natural,* and not to be conceived a miracle; tho' even the manner of its preſervation might have made me own it as a wonderful event of God's kind providence.

It was about the latter end of June when the ears of this corn ripened, which I laid up very carefully, together with 20 or 30 ſtalks of rice, expecting one day I ſhould reap the fruit of my labour; yet four years were expired before I could allow myſelf to eat any barley bread, and much longer time before I had any rice. After this,

D

with

with indefatigable pains and induſtry for three or
four months, at laſt I finiſhed my wall on the 14th.
of April, having no way to go into it, but by a
ladder againſt the wall.

April 16th I finiſhed my ladder, and aſcended it;
afterwards pulled it up, then let it down on the
other ſide, and deſcended into my new habitation,
where I had ſpace enough, and ſo fortified, that
nothing could attack me, without ſcaling the walls.

But what does all human pains and induſtry a-
vail, if the bleſſing of God does not crown our
labours?--Or, who can ſtand before the Almighty,
when he ſtretcheth forth his arm? For one time,
as I was at the entrance of my cave, there happened
ſuch a dreadful earthquake, that not only the roof
of the cave came tumbling about my ears, but the
the poſts ſeemed to crack terribly at the ſame time,
This put me in great amazement; and running to
the ladder, and getting over the wall, I then plainly knew it was an earthquake, the place I ſtood
on ſuſtaining three terrible ſhokes in leſs than three
minutes. But judge of my terror when I ſaw the
top of a great rock roll into the ſea; I then expected the iſland would be ſwallowed up every moment: And what made the ſcene ſtill more dreadful, was to ſee the ſea thrown into the moſt violent
agitations and diſorders by this tremendous accident.

For my part, I ſtood like a criminal at the place
of execution, ready to expire. At the moving of
the earth, I was, as it were, ſea-ſick; and very
much afraid leſt the rock, under which was my
fence and habitation, ſhould overwhelm me and it
in a laſting tomb.

When the third dreadful ſhock had ſpent itſelf,
my ſpirits began to revive; yet ſtill I would not
venture to aſcend the ladder, but continued ſitting
not knowing what I ſhould do. So little grace had
I then, as only to ſay, *Lord, have mercy upon me !*
and

and no sooner was the earthquake over, but that pathetic prayer left me.

It was not long after, when a horrible tempest arose, at the same time attended with a hurricane of wind. The sea seemed mountains high, and the waves rolled so impetuously, that nothing could be perceived but froth and foam. Three hours did this storm continue, and in so violent a manner, as to tear the very trees up by the roots, which was succeeded by abundance of rain. When the tempest was over, I went to my tent; but the rain coming on in a furious manner, I was obliged to take shelter in the cave, where I was forced to cut a channel through my fortification to let the water out. It continued raining all that night, and some time the next day. These accidents made me resolve, as soon as the weather cleared up, to build me a little hut in some open place, walled round to defend me from wild creatures and savages; not doubting, but, at the next earthquake, the mountain would fall upon my habitation and me, and swallow up all in its bowels.

April 16, — 20. These days I spent in contriving how and in what manner I should fix my place of abode. All this while I was under the most dreadful apprehensions. When I looked round my habitation, every thing I found in its proper place. I had several resolutions whether I should move or not: but at length I resolved to stay where I was, till I found out a convenient place where I might pitch my tent.

April 22. When I began to put my resolutions in practice, I was stopt for want of tools and instruments to work with. Most of my axes and hatchets were useless, occasioned by cutting the hard timber that grew on the island. It took me up a full week to make my grindstone of use to me; and at last I found out a way to turn it a-

bout

bout with my foot, by help of a wheel and a ſtring.

April 28, 29. Theſe days were ſpent in grinding my tools,

April 30. My bread falling ſhort, I allowed myſelf but one biſcuit a day.

May 1. As I walked along the ſea-ſhore, I found a barrel of gunpowder, and ſeveral pieces of the wreck, which the ſea had flung up. Having ſecured thoſe 1 made to the ſhip, whoſe ſtern was torn off, and waſhed a great diſtance aſhore; but the reſt lay in the ſands. Theſe 1 ſuppoſed was occaſioned by the earthquake. I now reſolved to keep my old place of abode: and alſo to go to the ſhip that day, but then found it impoſſible.

May 3. This day I went on board, and with my ſaw ſawed off one of the beams, which kept her quarter deck. 1 then cleared the ſand till flood.

May 4. 1 caught ſome fiſh, but they were not wholeſome. The ſame day I alſo catched a young dolphin.

May 5. This day I alſo repaired to the wreck, and ſawed another piece of timber; and when the flood came, I made a float of three great planks, which was driven aſhore by the tide.

May 6, 7, 8, 9. Theſe days I brought off the iron bolts, opened the deck with the iron crow, and carried two planks to land, having made a way into the very middle of the wreck.

May 10, 11, 12, 13, 14. All this time I ſpent in bringing off great quantities of iron and timber.

May 15. Took with me two hatchets, on purpoſe to cut off ſome lead off the roll, but all in vain, for it lay too low under water.

May 16 I omitted going to the wreck this day; for employing myſelf in looking out pigeons, I outſtaid my time.

May 17. I perceived ſeveral pieces of the wreck blown aſhore, which I found belonged to the head of the ſhip.

May

May 24. To this day I worked on the wreck, and with great difficulty loofened fome things fo much with the crow, that at the firft flowing tide feveral cafks floated out, and many of the feamen's chefts; yet that day nothing came to land but pieces of timber, and a hogfhead which had fome Brafil pork in it. I continued working to the 15th of June, (except neceffary times for food and reft;) and had I known how to have built a boat, I had timber and plank enough: I had alfo near a 100 weight of fheet-lead.

June 16. As I was wandering towards the fea-fide, I found a large tortoife or turtle, being the firft I had feen on the ifland, tho' of it as I after-wards found, there were many on the other fide.

June 17. This day I fpent in cooking it, found in her threefcore eggs, and her flefh the moft fa-voury and pleafant I ever tafted in my life.

June 18. I ftaid within this day, there being a continual rain; and it was fomething more chilly and cold than ufual.

June 19. Exceeding bad, taken with a trem-bling and fhivering.

June 20. Awake all night, my head racked with pain, and feverifh.

June 21. Sick unto death, and terrified with the difmal apprehenfions of my condition. Prayed to God more frequently, but very confufedly.

June 22. Something better, but ftill uneafy in my mind.

June 23. Again relapfed much as before.

June 24. Mended a fecond time.

June 25. A violent ague for feven hours, cold and hot fits, fucceeded with faint fweats.

June 26. Better, but very weak; yet I fcrambled out, fhot a fhe-goat, brought it home, and broiled fome of it: I would willingly have ftewed it, and made fome broth, but had no pot.

June 27. All this day I was afflicted with an ague; thirsty, yet could not help myself to water: Prayed to God in these words; *Lord, in pity, look upon me; Lord have mercy upon me; have mercy upon me!* After this I fell asleep, which I found had much refreshed me when I awaked. I fell asleep a second time, and fell into this strange and terrible sort of dream:

Methought I was sitting on the same spot of ground, at the outside of the wall where I sat when the storm blew after the earthquake; and that I saw a man descending from a great black cloud, and light upon the ground. He was all over as bright as a flash of fire that a little before surrounded him; his countenance inconceivably terrible; the earth as it were trembled when he stept upon the ground, and flashes of fire seemed to fill all the air. No sooner I thought him landed upon the earth, but with a long spear or other weapon he made towards me; but first ascending a rising ground, his voice added to my amazement, when I thought I heard him pronounce these dreadful words, *Unhappy wretch! seeing all these things have not brought thee to repentance, thou shalt immediately die.* In pronouncing this dreadful sentence, I thought he went to kill me with the spear that was in his hand.

Any body may think it impossible for me to express the horrors of my mind at this vision; and even when I awaked, this very dream made a deep impression upon my mind. The little divine knowledge I had, I received from my father's instructions, and that was worn out by an uninterrupted series of seafaring impiety for eight years space. Except what sickness forced from me, I do not remember I had one thought of lifting up my heart towards God; but rather had a certain stupidity of soul, not having the least sense of fear of the

omnipotent

omnipotent Being when in diftrefs, nor of gratitude to him for his deliverances. Nay, when I was on the defperate expedition on the defart African fhore, I cannot remember I had one thought of what would become of me, or to beg his confolation and affiftance in my fufferings and diftrefs. When the Portugal captain took me up, and honourably ufed me; nay, farther, when I was even delivered from drowning by efcaping to this ifland, I never looked upon it as a judgment, but only faid I was an unfortunate dog, and that's all.- Indeed fome fecret tranfports of foul I had, which was not through grace, but only a common flight of joy, that I was yet alive, when my companions were all drowned, and no other joy could I conceive but what is common with the failors over a bowl of punch, after they have efcaped the greateft dangers.

The likelihood of wanting for neither food nor conveniencies, might have called upon me for a thankful acknowledgment to Providence. Indeed the growth of my corn touched me with fome fenfe; but that foon wore off again. The terrible earthquake pointed to me as it were the finger of God, but my dreadful amazement continued no longer than its duration. But now, when my fpirits began to fink under the burthen of a ftrong diftemper, and I could leifurely view the miferies of death prefent themfelves before my eyes; then my awakened confcience began to reproach me with my paft life, in which I had fo wickedly provoked the juftice of God, to pour down his vengeance upon me.

Such reflections as thefe opprefled me even in the violence of my diftemper. Some prayers I uttered which only proceeded from my fear of death. But when I confidered my father's advice and prophecy, I could not forbear weeping; for

he

he told me, *That if I did persist in my folly, I should not only be deprived of God's blessing, but have time enough to reflect upon my despising his instructions; and this in a wretched time, when none could help me.* And now concluding it to be fulfilled, having no soul in the island to administer any comfort to me, I prayed earnestly to the Lord, that he would help me in this my great calamity. And this, I think, was the first time I prayed in sincerity for many years. But now I must return to my journal.

June 28. Something refreshed with sleep, and the fit quite off, I got up. My dream still occasioned in me a great consternation; and fearing that the ague might return the succeeding day, I concluded it time to get something to comfort me. I filled a case-bottle with water, and set it within the reach of my bed; and to make it more nourishing, and less chilly, I put some rum into it. The next thing I did was to boil me a piece of goat-flesh, of which I ate but little, I was very weak; however, walked about, dreading the return of my distemper; and at night I supped on three of the turtle's eggs, which I roasted and ate, begging God's blessing therewith.

After I had eaten, I attempted to walk again out of doors with my gun; but was so weak, that I sat down, and looked at the sea, which was smooth and calm. While I continued here, these thoughts came into my mind:

In what manner is the production of the earth and sea, which I have seen so much of? From whence came myself, and all other creatures living, and of what are we made?

Our beings were assuredly created by some almighty invisible power, who framed the earth, the sea, and air, and all therein. But what is that power?

Certainly

Certa'nly it muft follow, that God has created
it all. Yet, faid I, if God has made all this, he
muft be the ruler of them all, and what is relating thereto; for certainly the power that makes,
muft indifputably have a power to guide and direct them. And if this be fo (as certainly it muft,)
nothing can happen without his knowledge or appointment. Then furely if nothing happens without God's appointment, certainly God has appointed thefe my fufferings to befal me. And here I
fixed my firm belief, that it was his will that it
fhould be fo; and then proceeded to inquire, why
fhould God deal with me in this manner? Or
What have I done thus to deferve his indignation?

Here confcience flew in my face, reprehending
me as a blafphemer; crying with a loud and piercing voice, *Unworthy wretch! dare you afk what
you have done? Look upon your paft life, and fee
what you have left undone?* Afk thyfelf, why thou
wert not long ago in the mercilefs hands of Death?
Why not drowned in Yarmouth roads, or killed
in the fight when the fhip was taken by the Sallee
man of war? Why not intombed in the bowels of
wild beafts on the African coaft, or drowned here
when all thy companions fuffered fhipwreck in the
ocean?

Struck dumb with thefe reflections, I rofe up in
a penfive manner, being fo thoughtful that I could
not go to fleep; and fearing the dreadful return
of my diftemper, it caufed me to remember that
the Brafilians ufed tobacco for almoft all difeafes.
I then went to my cheft, in order to find fome,
where Heaven no doubt directed me to find a cure
for both foul and body; for there I found one of
the Bibles, which till this time I had neither lei-
fure nor inclination to look into; I took both the
tobacco and that out of the cheft, and laid them
on the table. Several experiments did I try with
the

the tobacco: First I took a piece of leaf, and chewed it; but it being very green and strong, almost stupified me. Next I steeped it in some rum an hour or two, resolving when I went to bed to take a dose of it; and in the third place, I burnt some over a pan of fire, holding my nose over it so long as I could endure it without suffocation.

In the intervals of this operation, though my head was giddy and disturbed at the tobacco, I took up the Bible to read. No sooner did I open it, but there appeared to me these words, *Call on me in the day of trouble, and I will deliver thee, and thou shalt glorify me.*

At first this sentence made a very deep impression on my heart; but it soon wore off again, when I considered the word *deliver* was foreign to me. And as the children of Israel said, when they were promised flesh to eat, *Can God spread a table in the wilderness?* in like manner I began to say, Can God himself deliver me from this desolate island? However, the words would still return to my mind, and afterwards made a greater impression upon me. As it now was very late, and the tobacco had dozed my head, I was inclined to sleep; but before I would lye down, I fell on my knees, and implored the promise that God had made to me in the holy scriptures, that *if I called upon him in the day of trouble, he would deliver me.* With much difficulty I after drank the rum, wherein I had steeped the tobacco; which flying in my head, threw me into such a profound sleep, that it was three o'clock the next day before I awaked; or rather, I believe, I slept two days, having certainly lost a day in my account, and I could never tell any other way. When I got up, my spirits were lively and cheerful; my stomach much better, being very hungry; and in short, no fit returned the next day; which was the 29th, but I found myself much altered for the better.

The 30th, I went abroad with my gun, but not far, and killed a sea-fowl or two, resembling a brand-goose, which, however I cared not to eat when I brought them home, but dined on two more of the turtle's eggs. In the evening I renewed my medicine, excepting that I did not take so large a quantity, neither did I chew the leaf, or hold my head over the smoke: but next day, which was the 1st of July, having a little spice of the cold fit, I again took my medicine as I did the first time.

July 3. The fit quite left me, but very weak. In this condition, I often thought of these words, *I will deliver thee;* and while at some times I would think of the impossibility of it, other thoughts would reprehend me, for disregarding the deliverances I had received, even from the most forlorn and distressed condition. I asked myself, what regard have I had to God for his abundant mercies? have I done my part? *He has delivered me, but I have not glorified him;*—as if I had said, I had not owned and been thankful for these as deliverances, and how could I expect greater? So much did this sensibly touch my heart, that I gave God thanks for my recovery from sickness in the most humble prostration.

July 4. This morning I began seriously to ponder on what is written in the New Testament, resolving to read a chapter every morning and night as long as my thoughts would engage me. As soon as I set about this work seriously, I found my heart deeply affected with the impiety of my past life; these words that I thought were spoken to me in my dream revived, *All these things have not brought thee to repentance.* After this, I begged of God to assist me with his Holy Spirit in returning to my duty. One day, in perusing the scriptures, I came to these words, *He*

is

*is exalted a Prince and a Saviour, to give re-
pentance, and to give remiffion:* Immediately
I laid down the book, and, with uplifted hands
to heaven, loudly cried, *O bleffed Jefus, thou fon
of David, Jefus, thou exalted Prince and Saviour,
give me repentance!* And now indeed I prayed
with a true fenfe of my condition, and a more certain hope founded on the word of God. Now I
had a different fenfe of thefe words, *Call on me,
and I will deliver thee,* that is, from the dreadful
load of guilt, which oppreffed my finful foul, and
not from a folitary life, which might rather be
called a bleffing, (feeing I wanted neither food nor
raiment,) when compared with living among the
human race, furrounded with fo much oppreffion,
mifery, and affliction: In a word, I came to this
conclufion, that a deliverance from fin was a much
greater bleffing than a deliverance from affliction.
But again I proceed to my journal.

To the 14th of July, I walked about with my
gun little and little at a time, having been reduced to the greateft extremity of weaknefs. The
applications and experiments I ufed were perfectly new; neither could I recommend them to any
one's practice. For though it carried off the fit,
it very much weakened me; and I had frequently
convulfions in my nerves and limbs for fome time.
From hence I learned, that going abroad in rainy
weather, efpecially when it was attended with
ftorms and hurricanes of wind, was moft pernicious to health. I had now been above ten months
in the ifland; and as I never had feen any of the
human kind, I therefore accounted myfelf as fole
monarch; and as I grew better, having fecured
my habitation to my mind, I refolved to make a
tour round my kingdom, in order to make new
difcoveries.

The 15th of July I began my journey. I firft

went to the creek, where I had brought my rafts
on shore; and travelling farther, found the tide
went no higher than two miles up, where there
was a little brook of running waters, on the bank
of which were many pleasant Savannas or mea-
dows, plain, smooth, and covered with grass. On
the rising parts, where I supposed the water did
not reach, I perceived a great deal of tobacco growing to a very strong stalk. Several other plants
I likewise found, the virtues of which I did not
understand. I searched a long time for the Cassa-
va root, which I knew the Indians in that climate
made their bread of; but all in vain. There were
several plants of aloes, though at that time I
knew not what they were; likewise I saw several
sugar-cane, but imperfect for want of cultivation.
With these few discoveries I came back that night,
and slept contentedly in my little castle.

The next day, being the 16th, going the same
way, but farther than the day before, I found the
country more adorned with woods and trees. Here
I perceived different fruits in great abundance.
Melons in plenty lay on the ground, and clusters
of grapes, ripe and very rich, spread over the trees.
You may imagine I was glad of this discovery, yet
ate very sparingly, lest I should throw myself into a flux or fever. The grapes I found of excellent use, for when I had dried them in the sun,
which preserved them as dried raisins are kept,
they proved very wholesome and nourishing, and
served me in those seasons when no grapes were
to be had.

The night drawing on apace, I ascended up a
tree, and slept very comfortably, though it was
the first time I had lien out of my habitation. And
when the morning came, I proceeded with great
pleasure on my way, travelling about four miles,
as I imagined by the length of the valley, direct-

E

ing

ing my courfe northward, there being a ridge of
hills on the fouth and north fide of me.   At the
end of this valley, I came to an opening, where the
country feemed to defcend to the weft; there I found
a little fpring of frefh water, proceeding out. of
the fide of a hill, with its chryftal ftreams running
directly eaft.   And indeed here my fenfes were
charmed with the moft beautiful landfcape nature
could afford: for the country appeared fo flourifhing, green, and delightful, that to me it feemed
like a planted garden.   I then defcended on the
fide of that delicious vale, when I found abundance
of cocoa, orange, lemon, and citron trees, but very wild and barren at that time. As for the limes,
they were delightful and wholefome, the juice of
which I after ufed to mix in water, which made it
very cool and refrefhing. And now I was refolved to
carry home and lay up a ftore of grapes, limes
and lemons againft the approaching wet feafon.
So laying them up in feparated parcels, and then
taking a few of each with me, I returned to my
little caftle, after having fpent three days in this
journey.   Before I got home, the grapes were fo
bruifed that they utterly fpoiled; the limes indeed
were good, but of thefe I could bring only a few.

July 19. Having prepared two bags, I returned
thither again; but to my great furprife found all
the grapes fpread about, trod to pieces, and abundance eaten, which made me conclude there were
wild beafts thereabouts. To prevent this happening again, I gathered a large quantity of the grapes,
and hung them upon the out-branches of the trees,
both to keep them unhurt, and that they might
cure and dry in the fun: and having well loaded
myfelf with limes and lemons, I returned once
more to my old place of refidence.

And now contemplating on the fruitfulnefs of
this valley, the pleafantnefs of its fituation, its
                                                        fecurity

security from storms, and the delightfulness of the adjacent woods, I concluded I was settled in the worst part of the country, and therefore was thinking to remove my habitation. But when I confidered again, that though it was pleasant, it was off from the sea-side where there was a possibility, some time or other, a ship might either be driven or sail by; and that to inclose myself among hills and woods must certainly put an end to my hopes of deliverance; I resolved to let my castle remain where Providence had first assigned it. Yet so ravished was I with this place, that I made me a little kind of bower, surrounding it with a double hedge, as high as I could reach, well staked, and filled with bulrushes; and having spent a great part of the month of July, I think it was the first of August before I began to enjoy my labour.

Aug. 3. Perceiving my grapes to be dry, I took them from the trees, and they proved excellent good raisins of the sun? the most of which I carried to my cave; and happy for me I did so, by which I saved the best part of my winter food.

Aug. 14. This day it began to rain; and tho' I had made me a tent like the other, yet having no shelter of a hill to keep me from storms, nor a cave behind me to retreat to, I was obliged to return to my old castle. The rain continued more or less every day, till the middle of October; and sometimes so violently that I could not stir out of my cave for several days.

This season I found my family to increase? for one of my cats that ran away from me, and who I thought had been dead, returned about August, with three kittens at her heels, like herself, which I thought strange, because both my cats were females, and the wild cats of the island seemed to be of a different kind from our European cats; but from these cats proceeded such numbers, that

I was

I was forced to kill and deſtroy them as I would do wild beaſts or vermin.

To the 26th of this month I could not ſtir out, it raining inceſſantly; when beginning to want food, I was compelled to venture twice, the firſt of which I ſhot a goat, and afterwards found a very large tortoiſe. The manner of my regulating my food was thus: A bunch of raiſins ſerved me for breakfaſt; a piece of goat's fleſh or turtle broiled for my dinner, and two or three turtle eggs for my ſupper. While the rain laſted, I daily worked two or three hours at enlarging my cave, and by degrees worked it on towards one ſide, till I came to the outſide of the hill, and made a door or way out, which came beyond my fence or wall, and ſo I came in and out this way. But after I had done this, I was troubled to ſee myſelf thus expoſed; though I could not perceive any thing to fear, a goat being the biggeſt creature I had ſeen upon this iſland.

Sept. 30. Caſting up my notches on my poſt, which amounted to 365, I concluded this to be the anniverſary of my landing; and therefore humbly proſtrating myſelf on the ground, confeſſing my ſins, acknowledging God's righteous judgments upon me, and praying to Jeſus Chriſt to have mercy on me, I faſted for twelve hours till the going down of the ſun; and then eating a biſcuit and a bunch of grapes, laid me on the bed, and with great comfort took my night's repoſe. Till this time I never had diſtinguiſhed the Sabbath day; but now I made a longer notch than ordinary for the days of reſt, and divided the weeks as well as I could, though I found I had loſt a day or two in my account. My ink failing ſoon after, I omitted in my daily memorandum things of an indifferent nature, and contented myſelf to write down only the moſt remarkable events of my life. The rainy

and

and dry seasons appeared now regular to me, and experience taught me how to provide for them; yet, in one thing I am going to relate, my experience very much failed me. You may call to mind what I have mentioned of some barley and rice which I had saved; about thirty stalks of the former, and twenty of the latter; and at that time the sun being in its southern position, going from me, together with the rains, made me conclude it a very proper season to sow it. Accordingly I dug up a piece of ground, with my wooden spade, and dividing it in two parts, sowed about two-thirds of my seed, preserving by me about a handful of each. And happy it was I did so; for no rains falling, it was choked up, and never appeared above the earth till the wet season came again, and then part of it grew, as if it had been newly sown.

I was resolved still to make another trial; and seeking for a moister piece of ground near my bower, I there sowed the rest of my seed in February, a little before the vernal equinox; which having the rainy months of March and April to water it, yielded a noble crop, and sprung up very pleasantly. I had still saved part of the seed, not daring to venture all; and by the time I found out the proper seasons to sow in, and that I might expect every year two seed-times and two harvests, my stock amounted to above half a peck of each sort of grain.

No sooner were the rains over, but the stakes which I had cut from the trees, shot out like willows the first year after lopping their heads. I was ignorant of the tree I cut them from: but they grew so regularly beautiful, that they made a most lively appearance, and so flourished in three years time, that I resolved to cut more of them;

and thefe foon growing, made a glorious fence, as afterwards I fhall obferve.

And now I perceived that the feafons of the year might generally be divided, not into fummer and winter, as in Europe, but into wet and dry feafons as in this manner.

Half	February, March, April,	Rainy, fun coming near the Equinox.
Half	April, May, June, July, Auguft,	Dry, fun getting north of the line.
Half	Auguft, September October,	Wet, the fun being then come back.
Half	October, November December, January, February,	Dry, fun running fouth of the line.

The wet feafons would continue longer or fhorter as the winds happened to blow. But having found the ill confequences of being abroad in the rain, I took care before hand to furnifh myfelf with provifions; and, during the wet months, fat within doors as much as poffible. At this time I contrived to make many things that I wanted, tho', it coft me much labour and pains, before I could accomplifh them. The firft I tried was to make a bafket; but all the twigs I could get proved fo brittle, that I could not then perform it. It now proved of great advantage to me, that, when a boy, I took great delight in ftanding at a bafket-maker's in the fame town where my father lived, to view them at work : and, like other boys, curious to fee the manner of their working thefe things, and very officious to affift, I perfectly learned the method of it, and wanted nothing but the tools. And it coming into my mind, that the twigs of that tree of which I made my ftakes, might be as tough as fallow, willow, or ofiers, growing in England, I refolved to make an experiment, and went the next day to my country-feat, and found fome fit for my turn ; and after cutting down a quantity with my hatchet, I dried them in my pale, and, when fit to work with, carried them to my cave, where I employed myfelf in making feveral forts of bafkets, infomuch that I could put in whatfoever I pleafed. It is true, they were not cleverly made, yet they ferved my turn upon all-occafions.

But ftill I wanted two neceffary things. I had no cafk to hold my liquor, except two rundlets almoft full of rum, a few bottles of an ordinary fize, and fome fquare cafe-bottles ; neither had I a pot to boil any thing in, only a large kettle, unfit to make broth, or ftew a bit of meat : I wanted likewife at the beginning of this dry feafon a tobacco pipe; but for this I afterwards found an expedient.

I kept myfelf employed in planting my fecond row of ftakes. But remembring that when I travelled up to the brook, I had a mind to fee the whole ifland, I now refumed my intention, and taking my dog, gun, hatchet, two bifcuit-cakes, a great bunch of raifins, with a larger quantity of powder and fhot than ufual, I began my journey. Having paffed the vale where my bower ftood, I came within view of the fea lying to the weft ; when, it being a clear day, I fairly defcried land, extending from the W. to the S. W. about 10 or 15 leagues, as I concluded ; but could not fay
whe-

whether it was an island or a continent. Neither could I tell what this place might be; only thought it was part of America, and where I might have been in a miserable condition, had I landed. Again, I confidered, that if this was the Spanilh coaft, certainly, one time or other, I fhould fee fome fhip pafs by ; and if it was not, then it muft be the Savage coaft, between the Spanifh country and Brafil, which abounds with cannibals or man-eaters.

As I proceeded forward, I found this fide of the island much more pleafant than mine; the fields fragrant, adorned with fweet flowers and verdant grafs together with feveral very fine woods. There were parrots in plenty, which made me long for one to be my companion ; but it was with great difficulty I could knock one down with my ftick ; and I kept him at home fome years, before I could get him to call me by my name.

In the low grounds I found various forts of hares and foxes as I took them to be, but much different from thofe in England. Several of thefe I killed, but never ate them; neither indeed had I any occafion ; for abounding with goats, pigeons, turtle, and grapes, I could defy Leadenhall market to furnifh me a better table. In this journey I did not travel above two miles a-day, becaufe I took feveral turns and windings to fee what difcoveries I could make, returning weary enough to the place where I defigned to reft all night, which was either in a tree, or to a place which I furrounded with ftakes, that no wild creature might fuddenly furprife me. When I came to the fea fhore, I was amazed to fee the fplendor of it. Its ftrand was covered with fhells of the moft beautiful fifh, and conftantly abounding with innumerable turtles, and fowls of many kinds, which I was ignorant of, except thofe called Penguins. I might have fhot as many as I pleafed, but was fparing of my ammunition, rather chufing to kill a fhe-goat, which I did with much difficulty, on account of the flatnefs of the country.

Now, though this journey produced the moft pleafing fatisfaction, yet my habitation was fo much to my liking, that I did not repine at my being feated on the worft part of the ifland. I continued my journey, travelling about twelve miles further towards the eaft, where I fet a great pile on the fhore for a mark, concluding that my next journey fhould bring me to the other fide of the ifland, eaft from my caftle, and fo round till I came to my poft again. As I had a conftant view of the country, I thought I could not mifs my way; but fcarce had I travelled three miles, when I defcended into a very large valley, fo furrounded with hills covered with wood, that I having no guide but by the fun, nor even then, uhlefs I knew well the pofition of the fun at that time of the day; and to add to my misfortune, the weather proving very hazy, I was obliged to return to my poft by the fea fide, and fo backwards the fame way I came. In this journey my dog furprifed a kid, and would have killed it, had I not prevented him. As I had often been thinking of getting a kid or two, and fo raifing a breed of tame goats to fupply me after my ammunition was fpent, I took this opportunity of beginning: and having made a collar for this little creature with a ftring made of rope-yarn, I brought it to my bower, and there inclofed and left him; and having fpent a month in this journey, at length I returned to my old habitation.

No body can doubt of my fatisfaction, when I returned to my little caftle, and repofed myfelf in my hammock. After my journey I refted myfelf a week, which time I employed in making a cage for

for my pretty poll. I now began to confider of the poor kid I had left at the bower, and I immediately went to fetch it home. When I came there, I found the young creature almoft ftarved; I gave it fome food, and tied it as before: but there was no occafion, for it followed me like a dog; and as I conftantly fed it, it became fo loving, gentle, and fond, that it commenced one of my domeftics, and would never leave me.

The rainy feafon of the autumnal equinox being now come, I kept the 30th of September in the moft folemn manner, as ufual, it being the third year of my abode in the ifland. I fpent the whole day in acknowledging God's mercies; in giving him thanks for making this folitary life as agreeable, and lefs finful, than that of human fociety; and for the communications of his grace to my foul, in fupporting, comforting, and encouraging me to depend upon his providence, and hope for his eternal prefence in the world to come.

Indeed I often did confider how much more happy I was in this ftate of life than in that accurfed manner of living I formerly ufed: and fometimes when hunting, or viewing the country, the anguifh of my foul would break out upon me, and my very heart would fink within me, to think of the woods, the mountains, the defarts I was in: and how I was a prifoner locked up within the eternal bars and bolts of the ocean, in an uninhabited wildernefs without hopes, and without redemption. In this condition, I would often wring my hands, and weep like a child: And even fometimes in the middle of my work this fit would take me; and then I would fit down and figh, looking on the ground for an hour or two together, till fuch time as my grief got vent in a flood of tears.

One morning as I was fadly employed in this man-

manner, I opened my Bible, when immediately I fixed my eyes upon these words; *I will never leave thee, nor forsake thee!* Surely, thought I, these words are directed to me; or else why should they appear just at a moment when I am bemoaning my forlorn condition! and if God does not forsake me, what matters it, since he can make me more happy in this state of life, than if I enjoyed the greatest splendor in the world? But while I was going to return God thanks for my present state, something seemed to shock my mind, as if it had thus said: Unworthy wretch! can you pretend to be thankful for a condition, from which you would pray to be delivered! Here I stopt;—and though I could not say, I thanked the Divine Majesty for being there, yet I gave God thanks for placing to my view my former wicked course of life, and granting me a true knowledge of repentance. And whenever I opened or shut the Bible, I blessed kind Providence, that directed my good friend in England, to send it among my goods without my order, and for assisting me to save it from the power of the raging ocean.

And now beginning my third year, my several daily employments were these, *First,* My duty to Heaven, and diligently reading the holy scriptures, which I did twice or thrice every day. *Secondly,* Seeking provision with my gun, which commonly took me up, when it did not rain, three hours every morning. *Thirdly,* The ordering, curing, preserving, and cooking what I had killed, or catched for my supply, which took me up a great part of the day: for in the middle of the day the sun being in its height, it was so hot, that I could not stir out; so that I had only but four hours in the evening to work in: and then the want of tools, of assistance, and skill wasted a great deal of time to little purpose. I was no less than two

and

and forty days making a board fit for a long shelf,
which two sawyers, with their tools and saw-pit,
would have cut out of the same tree in half a day.
It was of a large tree, as my board was to be
broad. I was three days in cutting it down, and
two more in lopping off the bows, and reducing
it to a piece of timber. Thus I hacked and hewed off each side, till it became light to move; then
I turned it, made one side of it smooth and flat as
a board from end to end, then turned it downward,
cutting the other side, till I brought the plank to
be about three inches thick, and smooth on both
sides. Any body might judge my great labour and
fatigue in such a piece of work; but this I went
through with patience, as also many other things
that my circumstances made necessary for me to do.

The harvest months, November, and December,
were now at hand, in which I had the pleasing
prospect of a very good crop. But here I met
with a new misfortune; for the goats and hares,
having tasted of the sweetness of the blade, kept
it so short, that it had no strength to shoot up into a stalk. To prevent this, I inclosed it with a
hedge, and by day shot some of its devourers; and
my dog, which I had tied to the field-gate, keeping barking all night, so frightened these creatures,
that I got entirely rid of them.

But no sooner did I get rid of these, than other
enemies appeared, to wit, whole flocks of several
sorts of birds, who only waited till my back was
turned to ruin me. So much did this provoke me,
that I let fly, and killed three of the malefactors;
and afterwards served them as they do notorious
thieves in England, hung them up in chains as a
terror to others. And indeed so good an effect had
this, that they not only forsook the corn, but all
that part of the island, so long as these criminals
hung there.

My

My corn having ripened apace, the latter end
of December, which was my second harvest, I
reaped it with a scythe, made of one of my broad
swords. I had no fatigue in cutting down my first
crop, it was so slender. The ears I carried home
in a basket, rubbing it out with my hands instead
of threshing it; and when my harvest was over,
found my half peck of seed produced near two
bushels of rice, and two bushels and a half of
barley. And now I plainly foresaw, that, by
God's goodness, I should be furnished with bread:
but yet I was concerned, because I knew not how
to grind or make meal of my corn, nor bread,
neither knew how to bake it. I would not however taste any of the crop, but resolved to preserve it against next season, and in the mean while
use my best endeavours to provide myself with
other food.

But where were my labours to end? The want
of a plough to turn up the earth, or shovel to dig
it, I conquered by making me a wooden spade:
the want of a harrow, I supplied myself with dragging over the corn a great bough of a tree. When
it was growing I was forced to fence it; when
ripe to mow it, carry it home, thresh it, part it
from the chaff, and save it. And after all, I wanted a mill to grind it, sieve to dress it, yest and
salt to make it into bread, and an oven to bake it.
This set my brains on work to find some expedient for every one of these necessaries against the
next harvest.

And now having more seed, my first care was
to prepare me more land. I pitched upon two
large flat pieces of ground near my castle for that
purpose, in which I sowed my seed, and fenced it
with a good hedge. This took me up three months;
by which time the wet season coming on, and the
rain keeping me within doors, I found several oc-

F

casions

cafions to employ myfelf; and while at work, ufed to divert myfelf with talking to my parrot, learning him to know and fpeak his own name *Poll*, the firft welcome word I ever heard fpoke in the ifland. I had been a long time contriving how to make earthen veffels, which I wanted extremely; and when I confidered the heat of the climate, I did not doubt but if I could find any fuch clay, I might botch up a pot, ftrong enough when dried in the fun to bear handling, and to hold any thing that was dry, as corn, meal, and other things.

To be fhort, the clay I found; but it would occafion the moft ferious perfon to finile to fee what aukward ways I took, and what ugly mifhapen things I made; how many either fell out or cracked by the violent heat of the fun, and fell in pieces when they were removed; fo that I think it was two months time before I could perfect any thing; and even then but too clumfey things in imitation of earthen jars. Thefe however I very gently placed in wicker balkets, made on purpofe for them, and between the pot and the balkets, ftuffed it full of rice and barely ftraw: and thefe I prefumed would hold my dried corn, and perhaps the meal when the corn was bruifed. As for the fmaller things, I made them with better fuccefs; fuch as little round pots, flat difhes, pitchers, and pipkins, the fun baking them very hard.

Yet ftill I wanted one thing abfolutely neceffary, and that was an earthen pot, not only to hold my liquid, but alfo to bear the fire, which none of thefe could do. It once happened, that as I was putting out my fire, I found therein a broken piece of one of my veffels burnt hard as a rock, and red as a tile. This made me think of burning fome pots; and having no notion of kiln, or of glazing them with lead, I fixed three large pipkins, and two or three pots in a pile one upon another.

The

The fire I piled round the outſide, and dry-wood
on the top, till I ſaw the pots in the inſide red
hot, and found that they did not crack at all ; and
when I perceived them perfectly red, I let one of
them ſtand in the fire about five or ſix hours, till
the clay melted by the extremity of the heat, and
would have run to glaſs, had I ſuffered it ; upon
which I ſlacked my fire by degrees till the redneſs
abated; and watching them till the morning, I
found I had three very good pipkins, and two
earthen pots, as well burnt and fit for my turn as
I could deſire.

No joy could be greater than mine at this diſcovery. For after this, I may ſay; I wanted for
no ſort of earthen ware. I filled one of my pipkins with water to boil me ſome meat, which it
did admirably well, and with a piece of kid I made
me ſome good broth, as well as my circumſtances
would afford me at that time.

The next concern I had was to get me a ſtone-
mortar to beat ſome corn in, inſtead of a mill to
grind it.   Here indeed I was at a great loſs, as not
being fit for a ſtone-cutter; and many days I ſpent
to find out a great ſtone big enough to cut hollow
and make fit for a mortar, and ſtrong enough to
bear the weight of a peſtil, that would break the
corn without filling it with ſand. But all the ſtones
of the iſland being of a mouldering nature, rendered my ſearch fruitleſs; and then I reſolved to
look out a great block of hard wood; which having
ſoon found, I formed it with my axe and hammer,
and then with infinite labour made a hollow in it,
juſt as the Indians of Braſil make their canoes.
When I had finiſhed this, I made a great peſtil of
iron wood, and then laid them up againſt my ſucceeding harveſt.

My next buſineſs was to make me a ſieve, to
ſift my meal, and part it from the bran and huſk.

F 2   Having

Having no fine thin canvas to search the meal
through, I could not tell what to do. What linen
I had was reduced to rags: I had goats hair enough,
but neither tools to work it, nor did I know how
to spin it: At length I remembered I had some
neckcloths of callico or muslin of the sailors, which
I had brought out of the ship, and with these I
made three small sieves, proper enough for the
work.

I come now to consider the baking part. The
want of an oven I supplied by making some earthen
pans very broad, but not deep. When I had a
mind to bake, I made a great fire upon the hearth,
the tiles of which I made myself; and when the
wood was burnt into live coals, I spread them
over it, till it became very hot; then sweeping
them away, I set down my loaves, and whelming
down the earthen pots upon them, drew the ashes
and coals all around the outside of the pots to continue the heat; and in this manner I baked my
barley loaves, as well as if I had been a complete
pastry-cook, and also made of the rice several
cakes and puddings.

It is no wonder, that all these things took me
up the best part of a year, since what intermediate time I had was bestowed in managing my new
harvest and husbandry; for in the proper season I
reaped my corn, carried it home, and laid it up in
the ear in my large baskets, till I had time to rub,
instead of threshing it. And now indeed my corn
increased so much, that it produced me about
twenty bushels of barley, and as much of rice,
that I not only began to use it freely, but was
thinking how to enlarge my barns, and resolved
to sow as much at a time as would be sufficient for
me for a whole year.

All this while, the prospect of land, which I
had seen from the other side of the island, ran in
my

my mind. I still meditated a deliverance from this
place, though the fear of greater misfortunes
might have deterred me from it. For allowing
that I had attained that place, I run the hazard of
being killed and eaten by the devouring cannibals;
and if they were not so, yet I might be slain, as
other Europeans had been, who fell into their
hands. Notwithstanding all this, my thoughts ran
continually upon that shore. I now wished for
my boy Xury, and the long boat, with the shoulder of mutton sail: I went to the ship's boat, that
had been cast a great way on the shore in the late
storm. She was removed but a little; but her
bottom being turned up by the impetuosity and
fury of the waves and wind, I fell to work with
all the strength I had, and with levers and rollers
I had cut from the wood, to turn her, and repair
the damages she had sustained. This work took
me up three or four weeks, when finding my little strength all in vain, I fell to undermining it by
digging away the sand, and so make it fall down,
setting pieces of wood to thrust and guide it in the
fall. But after this was done, I was still unable
to stir it up, or to get under it, much less to move
it forwards towards the water, and so I was forced to give it over.

This disappointment however did not frighten
me. I began to think whether it was not possible
for me to make a canoe or Periagua, such as the
Indians make of the trunk of a tree. But here I
lay under particular inconveniencies, want of tools
to make it, and want of hands to move it in the
water when it was made. However, to work I
went upon it, stopping all the inquiries I could
make, with this very simple answer I made to myself,
Let's first make it, I'll warrant I'll find some way
or other to get it along when it is done.

I first cut down a cedar-tree, which was five

feet

feet ten inches diameter at the lower part next the ftump, and four feet eleven inches diameter at the end of twenty-two feet, after which it leffened for a fpace, and then parted into branches. Twenty days was I hacking and hewing this tree at the bottom, fourteen more in cutting off the branches and limbs, and a whole month in fhaping it like the bottom of a boat. As for the infide, I was three weeks with a mallet and chiffel, clearing it in fuch a manner, as that it was big enough to carry 26 men, much bigger than any canoe I ever faw in my life, and confequently fufficient to tranfport me and all my effects to that wifhed-for fhore I fo ardently defired.

Nothing remained now, but indeed the greateft difficulty, to get into the water, it lying about 100 yards from it. To remedy the firft inconvenience, which was a rifing hill between this boat and the creek, with wonderful pains and labour I dug into the furface of the earth, and made a declivity. But when this was done, all the ftrength I had was as infufficient to move it, as it was when I attempted to move the boat. I then proceeded to meafure the diftance of ground, refolving to make a canal, in order to bring the water to the canoe, fince I could not bring the canoe to the water. But as this feemed to be impracticable to myfelf alone, under the fpace of eleven or twelve years, it brought me into fome fort of confideration : fo that I concluded this alfo to be impoffible, and the attempt altogether vain. I now faw, and not before, what ftupidity it is to begin work before we reckon its cofts, or judge rightly our own abilities to go through with its performance.

In the height of this work, my fourth year expired, from the time I was caft upon this ifland. At this time I did not forget my anniverfary; but kept it with rather greater devotion than before.

For

For now my hopes being fruftrated, I looked upon
this world as a thing I had nothing to do with;
and very well might I fay, as father Abraham faid
unto Dives, *Between me and thee there is a gulph
fixed.* And indeed I was feparated from its wickednefs too, having neither the luft of the flefh,
the luft of the eye, nor the pride of life; I had
nothing to covet, being lord, king, and emperor
over the whole country I had in my poffeffion,
without difpute, and without control: I had load-
ings of corn, plenty of turtles, timber in abundance, and grapes above meafure. What was all
the reft to me? The money I had by me lay as
defpicable drofs, which I would freely have given
for a grofs of tobacco pipes, or a hand-mill to
grind my corn: in a word, the nature and experience of thefe things dictated to me this juft reflection; That the good things of this world are
no farther good to us, than they are for our ufe;
and that whatever we may heap up to give others,
we can but enjoy as much as we ufe, and no more.

These thoughts rendered my mind more eafy
than ufual. Every time I fat down to meat, I did
it with thankfulnefs, admiring the providential
hand of God who in this wildernefs had fpread a
table to me. And now I confidered what I enjoyed, rather than what I wanted; compared my prefent condition with what I at firft expected it fhould
be; how I fhould have done, if I had got nothing
out of the fhip; That I muft have perifhed before
I had caught fifh or turtles; or lived, had I found
them, like a mere favage, by eating them raw,
and pulling them in pieces with my claws, like a
beaft. I next compared my ftation to that which
I deferved; how undutiful I had been to my parents; how deftitute of the fear of God; how void
of every thing that was good; and how ungrateful for thofe abundant mercies I had received from
Heaven,

Heaven, being fed, as it were, by a miracle, even as great as Elijah's being fed by ravens; and cast on a place where there were no venomous creatures to poison or devour me; in short, making God's tender mercies matter of great confolation, I relinquished all fadnefs, and gave way to contentment.

As long as my ink continued, which with water I made laft as long as I could, I ufed to minute down the days of the month, on which any remarkable thing happened. And,

First, I obferved, that the fame day I forfook my parents and friends, and ran away to Hull, in order to go to fea, the fame day afterwards in the next year I was taken and made a flave by the Sallee rovers:

That the very day I efcaped out of the wreck of the fhip in Yarmouth roads, a year after, on the fame day, I made my efcape from Sallee in my patron's fifhing-boat.

And that on the 30th of September, being the day of the year I was born on, on that day twenty-fix years after, was I miraculoufly faved, and caft afhore on this ifland.

The next thing that wafted after my ink, was the bifcuit which I had brought out of the fhip; and though I allowed myfelf but one cake a-day for above a twelvemonth, yet I was quite out of bread for near a year, before I got any corn of my own.

In the next place, my cloaths began to decay, and my linen had been gone long before. However, I had preferved about three dozen of the failors chequered fhirts, which proved a great refrefhment to me, when the violent beams of the fun would not fuffer me to bear any of the feamens heavy watch-coats; which made me turn failor, and, after a miferable botching manner,

convert

convert them to jackets. To preferve my head, I made me a cap of goat-fkins, with the hair outwards to keep out the rain; which indeed ferved me fo well, that afterwards I made me a waiftcoat and open kneed-breeches of the fame: And then I contrived a fort of an umbrella, covering it with fkins, which not only kept out the heat of the fun, but the rain alfo. Thus being eafy and fettled in my mind, my chiefeft happinefs was to converfe with God, in moft heavenly and comfortable ejaculations.

For five years after this I cannot fay any extraordinary thing occurred to me. My chief employment was to cure my raifins, and plant my barley and rice, of both which I had a year's provifion before-hand. But though I was difappointed in my firft canoe, I made it, at intermediate times, my bufinefs to make a fecond, of much inferior. fize; and it was two years before I finifhed it. But as I perceived it would nowife anfwer my defign of failing to the other fhore, my thoughts were confined to take a tour round the ifland, to fee what further difcoveries I could make. To this intent, after having moved her to the water, and tried how fhe would fail, I fitted up a little maft to my boat, and made a fail of the fhip's fail that lay by me. I then made lockers or boxes at the end of it, to put in neceffaries, provifions, and ammunition, which would preferve them dry either from rain, or the fpray of the fea; and in the infide of the boat, I cut me a long hollow place to lay my gun, and to keep it dry made a flag to hang over it. My umbrella I fixed in a ftep in the ftern, like a maft, to keep the heat of the fun off me. And now refolving to fee the circumference of my little kingdom, I victualled my fhip for the voyage, putting in two dozen of my barley-bread loves, an earthen pot full of parched rice,

a little

a little bottle of rum, half a goat, powder and
fhot, and two watch-coats. It was the 6th of November, in the fixth year of my reign, or captivity, that I fet out on this voyage, which was much
longer than I expected, being obliged to put farther out, by reafon of the rocks that lay a great
way in the fea. And indeed fo much did thefe rocks
furprife fne, that I was for putting back, fearing
that if I ventured farther, it would be out of my
power to return: in this uncertainty I came to an
anchor juft off fhore, to which I waded with my
gun on my fhoulder, and then climbing up a hill,
which overlooked that point, I faw the full extent
of it, and fo I refolved to run all hazards.

In this profpect from the hill, I perceived a violent current running to the eaft, coming very clofe
to the point; which I the more carefully obferved,
thinking it dangerous, and that when I came to it,
I might be drove into the fea by its force, and not
able to return to the ifland; and certainly it mu ft
have been fo, had I made this obfervation; for on
the other fide was the like current, with this difference, that it fet off a greater diftance; and I
perceived there was a ftrong eddy under the land;
fo that my chief bufinefs was to work out of the
firft current, and conveniently get into the eddy.
Two days I ftaid here, the wind blowing very
brifkly E. S. E. which being contrary to the current, leaves a great breach of the fea upon the
point; fo it was neither fit for me to keep too near
the fhore on account of the breach; nor ftand at
too great a diftance, for fear of the ftreams. That
night the wind abating, it grew fo calm, that I
ventured out; and here I may be a monument to
all rafh and ignorant pilots: For I was no fooner
come to the point, and not above the boat's length
from fhore, but I was got into a deep water with
a current like a mill, which drove my boat along

fo

so violently, that it was impossible for me to keep
her near the edge of it, but forced me more and
more out from the eddy to the left of me; and
all I could do with my padlers was useless, there
being no wind to help me.

Now I began to look upon myself as quite lost,
since as the current ran on both sides of the island,
I was very certain they must join again, and then
I had no hopes but of perishing for want in the
sea, after what provision I had was spent, or before, if a storm should happen to arise.

Who can conceive the present anguish of my
mind at this calamity? With longing eyes did I
look upon my little kingdom, and thought the island
the pleasantest place in the universe. Happy, thrice
happy desart, said I, shall I never see thee more?
Wretched creature! whither am I going? Why
did I murmur at my lonesome condition, when now
I would give the whole world to be thither again?
While I was thus complaining, I found myself to
be driven about two leagues into the sea; however, I laboured till my strength was far spent, to
keep my boat as far north as possibly I could, to
that side of the current where the eddy lay on.
About noon I perceived a little breeze of wind
spring up from the S. S. E. which overjoyed my
heart; and I was still more elated, when, in about
half an hour, it blew a gentle fine gale. Had any
thick weather sprung up, I had been lost another
way; for having no compass on board, I should
never have found the way to steer towards the
island, if once it had disappeared; but it proving
the contrary, I set up my mast again, spread my
sail, and stood away northward as much as I could
to get rid of the current. And no sooner did the
boat begin to stretch away, but I perceived by the
clearness of the water, a change of the current
was near: for where it was strong, the water was

foul

foul: and where it was clear, the current abated. To the eaſt I ſoon ſaw, about half a mile, a breach of the ſea upon ſome rocks, which cauſed it again to ſeparate; and as the main force of it drove away more ſouthwardly, leaving the rocks to the north-eaſt, ſo the other came back by the repulſe of the rocks, making a ſharp eddy, which returned back again to the north-weſt with a very ſwift ſtream.

They who have experienced what it is to be reprieved upon the ladder, or to be ſaved from thieves juſt going to take away their lives, or ſuch as have been in the like calamities with my own, may gueſs my preſent exceſs of joy, how heartily I run my boat into the ſtream of this eddy, and how joyfully I ſpread my ſail to the refreſhing wind, ſtanding chearfully before it, with a ſmart tide under foot. By the aſſiſtance of this eddy, I was carried above a league home again, when being in the wake of the iſland, betwixt the two currents, I found the water to be in a ſort of a ſtand About four o'clock in the afternoon, I reached within a league of the iſland, and perceived the points of the rock, which cauſed this diſaſter, ſtretching out, as I obſerved before, to the ſouthward, which throwing off the current more ſouthwardly, had occaſioned another eddy to the north. But having a fair briſk gale, I ſtretched acroſs this eddy, and in an hour came within a mile of the ſhore, where I ſoon landed, to my unſpeakable comfort; and after an humble proſtration, thanking God for my deliverance, with a reſolution to lay all thoughts of eſcaping aſide, I brought my boat ſafe to a little cove, and laid me down to take a welcome repoſe. When I awoke, I was conſidering how I might get my boat home; and coaſting along the ſhore, I came to a good bay, which ran up to a rivulet or brook, where finding a ſafe harbour, I ſtowed her as ſafe as if ſhe had been in a dry dock made on purpoſe for her.

I now perceived myfelf not far from the place where before I had travelled on foot; fo taking nothing with me except my gun and umbrella, I began my journey, and in the evening came to my bower, where I again laid me down to reft. I had not flept long before I was awakened in great furprife, by a ftrange voice that called me feveral times, *Robin, Robin, Robin Crufoe, poor Robin! Where are you, Robin Crufoe? where are you? where have you been?*

So faft was I afleep at firft, that I did not awake thoroughly, but half afleep and half awake, I thought I dreamed that fomebody fpoke to me. But as the voice repeated *Robinfon Crufoe* feveral times, being terribly affrighted, I ftarted up in the utmoft confufion; and no fooner were my eyes fully open, but I beheld my pretty Poll fitting on the top of the hedge, and foon knew that it was he that called me; for juft in fuch bewailing language I ufed to talk and teach him; which he fo exactly learned, that he would fit upon my finger, and lay his bill clofe to my face, and cry, *Poor Robinfon Crufoe, where are you? where have you been? how came you here?* and fuch like prattle I had conftantly taught him. But even tho' I knew it to be the parrot, it was a great while before I could adjuft myfelf; being amazed how the creature got thither, and that he fhould fix about that place, and no where elfe. But now, being affured it could be no other than my honeft Poll, my wonder ceafed; and reaching out my hand, and calling familiarly *Poll*, the creature came to me, and perched upon my thumb, as he was wont, conftantly pratting to me, with *Poor Robinfon Crufoe, and how did I come here, and where had I been?* as if the bird was overjoyed to fee me; and fo I took him home along with me.

I was now pretty well cured of my rambling to

fea;

sea; yet I could wish my boat, which had cost me so much trouble and pains, on this side the island once more, but which indeed was impracticable. I therefore began to lead a very retired life, living near a twelve-month in a very contented manner, wanting for nothing except conversation. As to mechanic labours, which my necessities obliged me to, I fancied I could upon occasion make a tolerable carpenter, were the poor tools I had to work withal but good. Besides as I improved in my earthen ware, I contrived to make them with a wheel, which I found much easier and better; making my work shapely, which before was rude and ugly. But I think I was never so elevated with my own performance or project, than for being able to make a tobacco-pipe; which tho' it proved an aukward clumsy thing, yet it was very sound, and carried the smoke perfectly well, to my great satisfaction.

I also improved my wicker-ware, making me abundance of necessary baskets, which, though not very handsome, were very handy and convenient to fetch things home in, as also for holding my stores, barley, rice, and other provisions.

My powder beginning to fail, made me examine after what manner I should kill the goats or birds to live on, after it was all gone. Upon which I contrived many ways to ensnare the goats, and see if I could catch them alive, particularly a she-goat with young. At last I had my desire: for making pit-falls and traps baited with barley and rice, I found one morning in one of them an old he-goat, and in the other three kids, one male, the other two females.

So boisterous was the old one, that I could not bring him away. But I forgot the old proverb, *That hunger will tame a lion:* for had I kept him three or four days without victuals, and then given

en him some water with a little corn, he would
have been as tame as a young kid. The other creatures I bound with strings together; but I had great
difficulty before I could bring them to my habitation. It was some time before they would feed;
but throwing them sweet corn, it so much tempted
them that they began to be tamer; from hence I
concluded, that if I designed to furnish myself with
goats flesh, when my ammunition was spent, the
tamely breeding them up, like a flock of sheep, a-
bout my settlement, was the only method I could
take. I concluded also I must separate the wild
from the tame, or else they would always run
wild as they grew up; and the best way for this,
was to have some inclosed piece of ground well
fenced, either with hedge or pale, to keep them so
effectually, that those within might not break out,
or those without break in. Such an undertaking
was very great for one pair of hands; but as there
was an absolute necessity for doing it; my first care
was to find a convenient piece of ground where
there was likely to be herbage for them to eat,
water to drink, and cover to keep them from the
sun.

Here again I gave another instance of my ignorance and inexperience, pitching upon a piece of
meadow land so large, that had I inclosed it, the
hedge or pale must have been at least two miles a-
bout. Indeed had it been ten miles, I had time
enough to do it in: but then I did not consider
that my goats would be as wild in so much compass, as if they had had the whole island, and consequently as difficult for me to catch them. This
thought came into my head, after I had carried it
on, I believe, about fifty yards: I therefore altered my scheme, and resolved to inclose a piece
of ground about 150 yards in length, and 100 in
breadth, sufficient enough for as many as would

main-

maintain me till such time as my flock increased, and then I could add more ground. I now vigorously prosecuted my work, and it took me about three months in hedging the first piece; in which time I tethered the three kids in the best part of it, feeding them as near me as possible, to make them familiar: and indeed I very often would carry some ears of barley, or a handful of rice, and feed them out of my hand; by which they grew so tame, that when my inclosure was finished, and I had let them loose, they would run after me for a handful of corn. This indeed answered my end; and in a year and a half's time I had a flock of about twelve goats, kids and all; and in two years after, they amounted to forty-three, besides what I had taken and killed for my sustenance. After which I inclosed five several pieces of ground to feed them in, with pens to drive them into, that I might take them as I had occasion.

In this project I likewise found additional blessings, for I not only had plenty of goats flesh, but milk too, which in my beginning I did not so much as think of. And indeed, though I never had milked a cow, much less a goat, or seen butter or cheese made, yet, after some essays and miscarriages, I made me both, and never afterwards wanted.

How mercifully can the Omnipotent Power comfort his creatures, even in the midst of their greatest calamities? How can he sweeten the bitterest providences, and give us reason to magnify him in dungeons and prisons? What a bounteous table was here spread in a wilderness for me, where I expected nothing at first but to perish for hunger?

Certainly a Stoic would have smiled to have seen me at dinner. There sat my royal majesty, an absolute prince and ruler of my kingdom, attended by my dutiful subjects, whom, if I pleased, I could
either

either hang, draw, quarter, give them liberty, or
take it away. When I dined, I feemed a king,
eating alone, none daring to prefume to do fo till
I had done. Poll, as if he had been my principal
court-favourite, was the only perfon permitted to
talk with me' .My old but 'faithful dog, now
grown exceeding crazy, and who had found no
fpecies to multiply his kind upon, continually fat
on my right hand; while my two cats.fat on each
fide of the table, expecting a bit from my hand, as
a principal mark of my royal favour. Thefe
were not the cats I had brought from the fhip ;
they had been dead long before, and interred near
my habitation by mine own hand. But one of them,
as I fuppofe, generating with a wild cat, a couple
of their young I had made tame; the reft run
wild into the woods, and in time grew fo impudent as to return. and plunder me of my ftores,
till fuch time as I fhot a great many, and the reft
left me without troubling me any more. In this
plentiful manner did I live, wanting for nothing
but converfation. One thing indeed concerned
me, the want of my boat ; I knew not which way
to get her round the ifland. One time I refolved to
go along the fhore by land to her.; but had any
one in England met fuch a figure, it would either
have affrighted them, or made them burft into.
laughter : nay, I could not but fmile myfelf at
my habit, which I think in this place will be very
proper to defcribe.

 The cap I wore upon my head was great, high,
and fhapelefs, made of a goat's fkin, with a flap
or pent-houfe hanging down behind, not only to
keep the fun from me; but to fhoot the rain off
from running into my neck, nothing being more
pernicious than the rain falling upon the flefh in
thefe climates. I had a fhort jacket of goats fkin,
whofe hair hung down fuch a length on either fide,
G 3

that

that it reached down to the calves of my legs. As
for shoes and stockings, I had none, but made a
resemblance of something; I know not what to
call them; they were made like buskins, and laced
on the sides like spatterdashes, barbarously shaped
like the rest of my habit. I had a broad belt of
goats skin dried, girt round me with a couple of
thongs, instead of buckles; on each of which, to
supply the deficiency of sword and dagger, hung
my hatchet and saw. I had another belt, not so
broad yet fastened in the same manner, which hung
over my shoulder, and at the end of it, under my
left arm hung two pouches, made also of goats
skin, to hold my powder and shot. My basket I
carried on my back, and my gun on my shoulder;
and over my head a great clumsey ugly goat-skin
umbrella, which, however next to my gun, was
the most necessary thing about me. As for my
face, the colour was not so swarthy as the Mulat-
toes, or as might have been expected from one
who took so little care of it, in a climate within
nine or ten degrees of the Equinox. At one time
my beard grew so long that it hung down above a
quarter of a yard; but as I had both razors and
scissars in store, I cut it all off, and suffered none
to grow, except a large pair of Mahometan whis-
kers, the like of which I had seen worn by some
Turks at Sallee, not long enough indeed to hang
a hat upon, but of such a monstrous size, as would
have amazed any in England to have seen.

But all this was of no consequence here, there
being none to observe my behaviour or habit. And
so without fear, and without control, I proceeded
on my journey, the prosecution of which took me
up five or six days. I first travelled along the sea-
shore, directly to the place where I first brought
my boat to an anchor, to get upon the rocks; but
having now no boat to take care of, I went over
land

land a nearer way to the same height that I was
before upon; when looking forward to the point
of the rock, which lay out, and which I was forced to double with my boat, I was amazed to see
the sea so smooth and quiet, there being no ripling
motion, nor current any more than in other places.
This made me ponder some time to guess the reason of it, when at last I was convinced, that the
ebb setting from the west, and joining with the
current of water from some great river on shore,
must be the occasion of these rapid streams; and
that consequently, as the winds blew more west-
wardly, or more southwardly, so the current came
the nearer, or went the farther from shore. To
satisfy my curiosity, I waited there till evening,
when the time of ebb being made, I plainly perceived from the rock the current again as before,
with this difference, that it ran farther off, near
half a league from the shore; whereas, in my expedition, it set close upon it, furiously hurrying
me and my canoe along with it, which at another
time it would not have done. And now I was
convinced, that, by observing the ebbing and flowing of the tide, I might easily bring my boat round
the island again. But when I began to think of
putting it in practice, the remembrance of the late
danger struck me with such horror, that I changed
my resolution, and formed another, which was
more safe, though more laborious; and this was
to make another canoe, and so have one for one
side of the island, and one for the other.

I had now two plantations in the island; the
first my little fortification, fort, or castle, with
many large and spacious improvements: for by
this time I had enlarged the cave behind me with
several little caves, one within another, to hold
my baskets, corn, and straw. The piles with
which I made my wall were grown so lofty and

great

great as obfcured my habitation. And near this
commodious and pleafant-fettlement, lay my well
cultivated and improved corn fields, which kindly
yielded me its fruit in the proper feafon. My fecond plantation was that near my country-feat, or
little bower, where my grapes flourifhed, and
where having planted many ftakes, I made inclofures for my goats, fo ftrongly fortified by labour
and time, that it was much ftronger than a wall,
and confequently impoffible for them to breakthro'.
As for my bower itfelf, I kept it conftantly in repair, and cut the trees in fuch a manner as made
them grow thick and wild, and form a moft delightful fhade. In the centre of this ftood my tent.
thus erected: I had driven four piles in the ground,
fpreading over it a piece of the fhip's fail; beneath which I made me a fort of couch with the
fkins of the creatures I had flain, and other things;
and having laid thereon one of the failor's blankets, which I had faved from the wreck of the fhip,
and covering myfelf with a great watch-coat, I
took up this place for my country retreat.

Very frequently from this fettlement did I ufe
to vifit my boat, and kept her in very good order.
And fometimes I would venture in her a caft or
two from fhore, but no farther, left either a ftrong
current, a fudden ftormy wind, or fome unlucky accident, fhould hurry me from the ifland, as before.
But now I intreat your attention, whilft I proceed to inform you of a new, but moft furprifing
fcene of life which here befell me.

You may eafily fuppofe, that, after having been
here fo long, nothing could be more amazing than
to fee a human creature. One day it happened,
that going to my boat, I faw the print of a man's
naked foot on the fhore, very evident on the fand, as
the toes, heels, and every part of it. Had I feen an
apparition in the moft frightful fhape, I could not
have

have been more confounded. My willing ears
gave the ftricteft attention, I caft my eyes around,
but could fatisfy neither the one or the other. I
proceeded alternately to every part of the fhore,
but with equal effect; neither could I fee any o-
ther mark, tho' the fand about it was as fufcepti-
ble to take impreffion, as that which was fo plainly
ftamped. Thus ftruck with confufion and horror,
I returned to my habitation, frightened at every
bufh and tree, taking every thing for men; and poffeffed with the wildeft ideas! That night my eyes
never clofed. I formed nothing but the moft difmal imaginations, concluding it muft be the mark
of the devil's foot which I had feen. For otherwife how could any mortal come to this ifland?
Where was the fhip that tranfported them? and
what figns of any other footfteps? Though thefe
feemed very ftrong reafons for fuch a fuppofition,
yet (thought I) why fhould the devil make the print
of his foot to no purpofe, as I can fee, when he
might have taken other ways to have terrified me?
Why fhould he leave his mark on the other fide of
the ifland, and that too on the fand, where the
furging waves of the ocean might foon have erafed
the impreffion. Surely this action is not confiftent with the fubtilty of Satan, faid I to myfelf, but
rather muft be fome dangerous creature, fome
wild favage of the main land over-againft me, that
venturing too far in the ocean, has been driven
here, either by the violent currents or contrary
winds; and not caring to ftay on this defolate
ifland, has gone back to fea again.

Happy indeed, thought I to myfelf, that none of
the favages had feen me in that place: yet I was
not altogether without fear, left, having found my
boat, they fhould return in numbers and devour
me, or at leaft carry away all my corn, and deftroy my flock of tame goats: in a word, all my
religious

religious hopes vanished, as though I thought God could not now protect me by his power, who had so wonderfully preserved me so long.

What various chains of providence are there in the life of man? How changeable are our affections, according to different circumstances? We love to-day what we hate to-morrow; we shun one hour what we seek the next. This was evident in me in the most conspicuous manner: for I, who before had so much lamented my condition, in being banished from all human-kind, was now even ready to expire, when I considered that a man had set his foot on this desolate island. But when I considered my station of life, decreed by the infinitely wise and good providence of God; that I ought not to dispute my Creator's sovereignty, who had an undoubted right to govern and dispose of his creatures as he thinks convenient; and that his justice and mercy could either punish or deliver me: I say, when I considered all this, I comfortably found it my duty to trust sincerely in him, pray ardently to him, and humbly resign myself to his divine will.

One morning, lying on my bed, these words of the sacred writings came again into my mind, *Call upon me in the day of trouble, and I will deliver thee, and thou shalt glorify me.* Upon this sentence, rising more chearfully from my bed, I offered up my prayers in the most heavenly manner: and when I had done, taking up my Bible to read, these words appeared first in my sight: *Wait on the Lord, and be of good cheer, and he shall strengthen thy heart: Wait, I say, on the Lord.* Such divine comfort did this give me, as to remove all cause of sadness upon that occasion.

Thus, after a world of apprehensions and fears, for three days and nights, I at last ventured out of my castle, and milked my goats, one of which

was almoſt ſpoiled for want of it. I next (though
in great fear) viſited my bower, and milked my
flocks there alſo; when growing bolder, I went
down to the ſhore again, and meaſuring the print
of the foot to mine, to ſee perhaps whether I myſelf had not occaſioned that mark, I found it much
ſuperior in largeneſs; and ſo returned home, now
abſolutely convinced, that either ſome men had
been aſhore, or that the iſland muſt be inhabited;
and therefore that I might be ſurpriſed before I
was aware.

I now began to think of providing for my ſecurity, and revolved in my mind many different
ſchemes for that purpoſe: I firſt propoſed to cut
down my incloſures, and turn my tame cattle
wild into the woods, that the enemy might not
find them, and frequent the iſland in hopes of killing the ſame. *Secondly*, I was for digging up my
corn-fields for the very ſame reaſon. And, *Laſtly*,
I concluded to demoliſh my bower, leſt ſeeing a
place of human contrivance, they might come farther, and find out and attack me in my little caſtle.

Such notions did the fear of danger ſuggeſt to
me; and I looked, I thought, like the unfortunate
king Saul, when not only oppreſſed by the Phili-
ſtines but alſo forſaken by God himſelf. And it is
ſtrange, that a little before, having entirely reſigned myſelf to the will of God, I ſhould now have ſo
little confidence in him, fearing thoſe more who
could kill this fading body, than he who could de-
ſtroy my immortal ſoul.

Sleep was an utter ſtranger to my eyes that
night; yet nature ſpent and tired, ſubmitted to a
ſilent repoſe the next morning. And then, joining reaſon with my fear, I conſidered, that this
delightful and pleaſant iſland might not be ſo entirely forſaken as I might think; but that the inhabitants from the other ſhore might ſail either
. with

with defign, or from neceffity, by crofs winds; and if the latter circumftance, I had reafon to believe they would depart the firft opportunity. However, my fear made me think of a place for retreat upon an attack. I now repented that I had made my door to come out beyond my fortification; to remedy which, I refolved to make me a fecond one: I fell to work, therefore, and drove betwixt that double row of trees, which I planted about twelve years before, feveral ftrong piles, thickening it with pieces of timber and old cables, and ftrengthening the foot of it with earth which I dug out of my cave; I alfo made me feven holes, wherein I planted my mufkets like cannon, fitting them into frames refembling carriages. This being finifhed with indefatigable induftry, for a great way every where, I planted fticks of ofier like a wood, about twenty thoufand of them, leaving a large fpace between them and my wall, that I might have room to fee an enemy, and that they might not be fheltered among the young trees, if they offered to approach the outer wall. And indeed fcarce two years had paffed over my head, when there appeared a lovely fhady grove, and in fix years it became a thick wood perfectly impaffible. For my fafety I left no avenue to go in or out; inftead of which I fet two ladders, one to a part of the rock which was low, and then broke in; leaving room to place another ladder upon that; fo that when I took thofe down, it was impoffible for any man to defcend without hurting himfelf; and if they had, they would ftill be at the outfide of my outer wall. But while I took all thefe meafures of human prudence for my own prefervation, I was not altogether unmindful of other affairs. To preferve my flock of tame goats, that the enemy fhould not take all at once, I looked out for the moft retired part of the ifland, which was the

place

place where I had loft myfelf before mentioned, and there finding a clear piece of land, containing three acres, furrounded with thick woods, I wrought fo hard, that, in lefs than a month's time, I fenced it fo well round, that my flocks were very well fecured in it, and I put therein two he goats and ten fhe ones.

All this labour was occafioned purely by fearful apprehenfions, on account of feeing the print of a man's foot. And not contented yet with what I had done, I fearched for another place towards the weft point of the ifland, where I might alfo retain another flock. Then wandering on this errand more to the weft of the ifland than ever I had yet done, and cafting my eyes towards the fea, methought I perceived a boat at a great diftance; but could not poffibly tell what it was for want of my perfpective glafs. I confidered that it was no ftrange thing to fee the print of a man's foot; and, concluding them cannibals, bleffed God for my being caft on the other fide of the ifland, where none of the favages, as I thought, ever came. But when I came down the hill to the fhore, which was the S. W. point of the ifland, I was foon confirmed in my opinion; nor can any one defcribe my horror and amazement, when I faw the ground fpread with fculls, hands, feet, and bones of human bodies; and particularly I perceived a fpace like a circle, in the midft of which had been a fire, about which I conjectured thefe wretches fat, and unnaturally facrificed and devoured their fellowcreatures.

The horror and loathfomenefs of this dreadful fpectacle, both confounded my fenfes, and made me difcharge from my ftomach in an exceffive manner. I then returned towards my habitation; and in my way thither fhedding floods of tears, and falling down on my bended knees, gave God thanks

H for

for making my nature contrary to thefe wretches, and delivering me fo long out of their hands.

Though reafon and my long refidence here had affured me, that thefe favages never came up to the thick woody parts of the country, and that I had no reafon to be apprehenfive of a difcovery; yet fuch an abhorrence did I ftill retain, that for two years after I confined myfelf only to my three plantations; I mean my caftle, country feat, and inclofure in the woods. And though in procefs of time, my dreadful apprehenfions began to wear away, yet my eyes were more vigilant for fear of being furprifed, and I was very cautious of firing my gun, left being heard by thofe creatures, they fhould proceed to attack me. I refolved, however, manfully to lofe my life if they did, and went armed with three piftols ftuck in my girdle; which, added to the defcription I have given of myfelf before, made me look with a very formidable appearance.

Thus my circumftances for fome time remained very calm and undifturbed; and when I compared my condition to others, I found it was far from being miferable. And indeed would all perfons compare their circumftances, not with thofe above them, but with thofe innumerable unhappy objects beneath them, I am fure we fhould not hear thofe daily murmurings and complainings that are in the world. For my part, I wanted but few things. Indeed the terror which the favages had put me in, fpoiled fome inventions for my own conveniencies. One of my projects was to brew me fome beer; a very whimfical one indeed, when it is confidered, that I had neither cafks fufficient, nor could I make any to preferve it in; neither had I hops to make it keep, yeft to make it work, nor a copper or kettle to make it boil. Perhaps, indeed, after fome years, I might bring this to

bear,

bear, as I had done other things. But now my inventions were placed another way; and day and night I could think of nothing but how I might deftroy fome of thefe cannibals, when procceding to their bloody entertainments; and fo faving a victim from being facrificed, that he might after become my fervant. Many were my contrivances for this purpofe, and as many more objections occurred, after I had hatched them. I once contrived to dig a hole under the place where they made their fire, and put therein five or fix pounds of gun-powder, which would confequently blow up all thofe that were near it; but then I was loath to fpend fo much upon them, left it fhould not do that certa'n execution I could defire; and but only affright, and not kill them. Having laid this defign afide, I again propofed to myfelf to lye privately in ambufh, in fome convenient place, with my three guns double loaded, and let fly at them in the midft of their dreadful ceremony; and having killed two or three of them at every fhot, fall upon the reft fuddenly with my three piftols, and not let one mother's fon efcape. This imagination pleafed my fancy fo much, that I ufed to dream of it in the night-time. To put my defign in execution, I was not long feeking for a place very convenient for my purpofe, where unfeen I might behold every action of the favages. Here I placed my two mufkets, each of which was loaded with a brace of flugs, and four or five fmaller bullets about the fize of piftol bullets; the fowling-piece was charged with near a handful of the largeft fwan fhot; and in every piftol were about four bullets. And thus all things being prepared, no fooner would the welcome light fpread over the element, but *like a giant refrefhed with wine*, as the fcripture has it, would I iffue forth from my caftle, and from a lofty hill, three miles

H 2

distant,

diſtant, view if I could ſee any invaders approach unlawfully to my kingdom. But having waited in vain two or three months, it not only grew very tireſome to me, but brought me into ſome conſideration, and made me examine myſelf, what right I had to kill theſe creatures in this manner :——

If (argued I to myſelf) this unnatural cuſtom of theirs be a ſin offenſive to Heaven, it belongs to the Divine Being, who alone has the vindictive power in his hands, to ſhower down his vengeance upon them. And perhaps he does ſo, in making them become one another's executioners. Or, if not, if God thinks theſe doings juſt, according to the knowledge they conceive, what authority have I to pretend to thwart the decrees of Providence, which has permitted theſe actions for ſo many ages, perhaps from almoſt the beginning of the creation ? They never offended me, what right have I then to concern myſelf in their ſhedding one another's blood ? And indeed I have ſince known, they value no more to kill and devour a captive taken in war, then we do to kill an ox, or eat mutton. I then concluded, it neceſſarily followed, that theſe people were no more murderers than Chriſtians, who many times put whole troops to the ſword, after throwing down their arms. Again I conſidered, that if I fell upon them, I ſhould be as much in the wrong as the Spaniards, who had committed the greateſt barbarities upon theſe people who never had offended them in their whole lives ; as if the kingdom of Spain was eminent for a race of men without common compaſſion to the miſerable, a principal ſign of the moſt generous temper. Theſe conſiderations made me pauſe, and brought me to think I had taken wrong meaſures in my reſolution ; I now argued with myſelf, that it was better for me never to attack, but to remain undiſcovered as long as poſſibly I could ; that an oppoſite

posite conduct would certainly prove destructive; for as it was scarcely to be supposed I could kill them all, I might either be overpowered by the remaining, or that some escaping, might bring thousands to my certain destruction. And indeed religion took their part so much as to convince me how contrary it was to my duty to be guilty of shedding human blood, innocent as to my particular, whatever they are to one another; that I had nothing to do with it, but leave it to the God of all power and dominion, as I said before, to do therein what seemed convenient to his heavenly wisdom. And therefore on my knees I thanked the Almighty for delivering me from blood-guiltiness, and begged his protection that I might never fall into their hands.

Thus giving over an attempt which I had rashly begun, I never ascended the hill on that occasion afterwards; I only removed my boat, which lay on the other side of the island; and every thing that belonged to her, towards the east, into a little cove, that there might not be the least shadow of discovery of any boat near, or habitation upon the island. My castle then became my cell, keeping always retired in it, except when I went out to milk my she-goats, and order my little flock in the wood; which was quite out of danger; for sure I was, that these savages never came here with expectations to find any thing, and consequently never wandered from the coast: however, as they might have several times been on shore as well before as after my dreadful apprehensions, I looked back with horror to think in what state I might have been, had I suddenly met them slenderly armed, with one gun only loaded with small shot; and how great would have been my amazement, if instead of seeing the print of one man's foot, I had perceived fifteen or twenty savages, who having

once fet their eyes upon me, by the the fwiftnefs
of their feet, would have left me no poffibility of
efcaping? Thefe thoughts would fink my very foul,
fo that I would fall into a deep melancholy, till
fuch time as the confideration of my gratitude to
the Divine Being moved it from my heart. I then
fell into a contemplation of the fecret fprings of
providence; and how wonderfully we are delivered, when infenfible of it; and when intricated in
uncertain mazes or labyrinths of doubt or hefita-
tion, what fecret hint directs us in the right way,
when we intended to go out of it; nay, perhaps,
contrary to our bufinefs, fenfe, or inclination. U-
pon which, I fixed within me this as a certain rule,
never to difobey thofe fecret impreffions of mind
to the acting or not acting any thing that offered,
for which I yet could affign no reafon. But let
it be how it will, the advantage of this conduct
very eminently appeared in the latter part of my
abode on this ifland: I am a ftranger in determin-
ing whence thefe fecret intimations of Providence
derive· yet methinks they are not only fome proof
of the converfe of fpirits, but alfo of the fecret
communications they are fuppofed to have with
thofe that have not paffed through the gloomy vale
of death.

These anxieties of mind, and the care of my
prefervation, put a period to all future inventions
and contrivances, either for accommodation or convenience; I now cared not to drive a nail, chop a
ftick, fire a gun, or make a fire, left either the
noife fhould be heard, or the fmoke difcover me.
And on this account I ufed to burn my earthen
ware privately in a cave which I found in the
wood, and which I made convenient for that purpofe; the principal caufe that brought me here was
to make charcoal, fo that I might bake and drefs
my bread and meat without any danger. At that
time

time a curious accident happened me, which I
fhall now relate.

While I was cutting down fome wood for making my charcoal, I perceived a cavity behind a
very thick branch of underwood. Curious to look
into it, I attained its mouth, and perceived it fufficient for me to ftand upright in it. But when I
had entered, and took a further view, two rolling
fhining eyes, like flaming ftars, feemed to dare
themfelves at me; fo that I made all the hafte out
that I could, as not knowing whether it was the devil or a monfter that had taken his refidence in that
place. When I recovered a little from my furprife,
I called myfelf a thoufand fools, for being afraid
to fee the devil one moment, who had now almoft
lived twenty years in the moft retired folitude.
And therefore refuming all the courage I l ad, I
took up a flaming fir e-brand, and in I rufhed again.
I had not proceeded above three fteps when I was
more affrighted than before; for then I heard a very loud figh, like that of a human creature in the
greateft agony, fucceeded with a broken noife, refembling words half expreffed, and then a broken
figh again. Stepping back, Lord! (thought I to
myfelf,) where am I got? Into what inchanted
place have I plunged myfelf, fuch as are reported
to contain miferable captives, till death puts an
end to their forrow? And indeed, in fuch a great
amazement was I, that it ftruck me into a cold
fweat; and had my hat been on my head, I believe
my hair would have moved it off. But again encouraging myfelf with the hopes of God's protection, I proceeded forward, and, by the light of
my firebrand, perceived it to be a monftrous he-
goat, lying on the ground gafping for life, and
dying of mere old age. At firft I ftirred him, thinking to drive him out, and the poor ancient creature ftrove to get upon his feet, but was not able;

fo

fo I e'en let him lie ftil, to affright the favages
fhould they venture into this cave. I now looked round me, and found the place but fmall and
fhapelefs.. At the farther fide of it I perceived a
fort of an entrance, yet fo low, as muft oblige me
to creep on my hands and knees to it; fo, having
no candle, I fufpended my enterprife till the next
day, and then I came provided with two large ones
. of my own making.

Having crept upon my hands and feet through
this ftrait, I found the roof rofe higher up, I think
about twenty feet. But furely never mortal faw
fuch a glorious fight before! The roof and walls
of this cave reflected a hundred thoufand lights to
me from my two candles, as though they were in-
dented with fhining gold, precious ftones, or fparkling diamonds. And indeed it was the moft dolight-
ful cavity or grotto of its kind that could be defired, though entirely dark. The floor was dry
and level, and had a kind of gravel upon it; no
naufeous venomous creatures to be feen there,.
neither any damp or wet about it. I could find no
fault but in the entrance, and I began to think
that even this might be very neceffary for my defence, and therefore refolved to make it my moft
principal magazine. I brought hither two fowling pieces, and three mufkets, leaving only five
pieces at my caftle, planted in the nature of cannon. In a barrel of gun-powder, which I took up
out of the fea, I brought away about fixty pounds
of good powder, which were not damaged; and
thefe, with a great quantity of lead for bullets, I
removed from my caftle to this retreat, now fortified both by art and nature.

I fancied myfelf now like one of the giants of
old, who were faid to live in caves and holes a-
mong the rocks, inacceffible to any but themfelves,
or, at leaft, moft dangerous to attempt. And now,
                                    I defpifed

I defpifed both the cunning and ftrength of the favages, either to find me out, or to hurt me.

But I muft not forget the old goat, who caufed my late dreadful amazement. The poor creature gave up the ghoft the day after my difcovery; and it being very difficult to drag him him out, I dug his grave, and honourably intombed him in the fame place where he departed, with as much cere-mony as any Welch-goat that has been interred a-bout the high mountain *Penmenmoure*.

I think I was now in the twenty-third year of my reign, and my thoughts much eafier than for-merly, having contrived feveral pretty amufe-ments and diverfions to pafs away the time in a pleafant manner. By this time my pretty Poll had learned to fpeak Englifh, and pronounce his words very articulately and plain; fo that for many hours we ufed to chat together after a very familiar man-ner, and he lived with me no lefs than twenty-fix years. My dog, who was nineteen years old, fix-teen of which he lived with me, died fometime a-go of mere old age. As for my cats, they multi-plied fo faft, that I was forced to kill or drive them into the woods, except two or three, which became my particular favourites. Befides thefe, I continually kept two or three houfehold kids a-bout me, whom I did learn to feed out of my hand, and two more parrots who could talk indifferent-ly, and call Robinfon Crufoe, but not fo excel-lently as the firft, as not taking that pains with them. I had alfo feveral fea-fowls which I had wounded and cut their wings; and growing tame, they ufed to breed among the low trees about my caftle walls; all which made my abode very agree-able.

But what unforefeen events fuddenly deftroy the enjoyments of this uncertain ftate of life, when we leaft expect them! It was now the month of
December,

December, in the fouthern folftice, and particular time of my harveft, which required my attendance in the fields; when going out pretty early one morning, before it was day-light, there appeared to me, from the fea-fhore, a flaming light, about two miles from me, at the eaft end of the ifland, where I had obferved fome favages had been before, not on the other fide, but to my great affliction it was on my fide of the ifland.

Struck with a terrible furprife, and my ufual apprehenfions, that the favages would perceive my improvements, I returned directly to my caftle; pulled up the ladder after me, making all things look as wild and natural as poffibly I could. In the next place, I put myfelf in a pofture of defence, loading my mufkets and piftols, and committing myfelf to God's protection, I refolved to defend myfelf till my laft breath. Two hours after, impatient for intelligence, I fet my ladder up to the fide of the hill, where there was a flat place, and then pulling the ladder after me, afcended to the top, where laying myfelf on my belly, with my perfpective glafs I perceived no lefs than nine naked favages fitting round a fmall fire, eating, as I fuppofed, human flefh, with their two canoes haled on fhore, waiting for the flood to carry them off again. You cannot eafily exprefs the confternation I was in at this fight, efpecially feeing them near me; but when I perceived their coming muft be always with the current of the ebb, I became more eafy in my thoughts, being very fully convinced, that I might go abroad with fecurity all the time of flood, if they were not before landed. And indeed this proved juft as I imagined; for no fooner did they all take boat and paddle away, but the tide made N. W. Before they went off they danced, making ridiculous poftures and geftures, for above an hour, all ftark naked; but

whether

whether men or women, or both, I could not perceive. When I faw them gone, I took two guns upon my fhoulders, and placing a couple of piftols in my belt, with my great fword hanging by my fide, I went to the hill, where at firft I made a difcovery of thefe cannibals, and then faw there had been three canoes more of the favages on fhore at that place, which, with the reft, were making over to the main land.

But nothing could be more horrid to me, when going to the place of facrifice, the blood, the bones, and o'her mangled parts of human bodies appeared in my fight: and fo fired was I with indignation, that I was fully refolved to be revenged on the firft that came there, though I loft my life in the execution. It then appeared to me, that the vifits which they make to this ifland are not very frequent, it being fifteen months before they came again : but ftill I was very uneafy, by reafon of the difmal apprehenfions I had of their furprifing me unawares : nor dared I offer to fire a gun on that fide of the ifland, where they ufed to appear, left taking the alarm, the favages might return with many hundred canoes, and then God knows in what manner I fhould have made my end. Thus was I a year or more before I faw any of thefe devouring cannibals again.

But to wave this, the following accident, which demands attention, for a while, eluded the force of my thoughts in revenging myfelf on thofe Heathens.

On the 16th of May (according to my wooden calender) the wind blew exceeding hard, accompanied with abundance of lightening and thunder all day, and fucceeded by a very ftormy night. The feeming anger of the heavens made me have recourfe to my Bible: Whilft I was ferioufly pondering upon it, I was fuddenly alarmed with the

noife

noife of a gun, which I conjectured was fired upon
the ocean.   Such an unufual furprife made me ftart
up in a minute, when with my ladder afcending the
mountain as before, that very moment a flafh of
fire prefaged the report of another gun, which I
prefently heard, and found it was from that part
of the fea where the current drove me away.   I
could not but then think, that this muft be a fhip
in diftrefs, and that thefe were the melancholy fignals for a fpeedy deliverance. Great indeed was my
forrow upon this occafion; but my labours to affift
them muft have proved altogether vain and fruit-
lefs.   However, I brought together all the dry
wood that was at hand, and making a pretty large
pile, fet it on fire on the hill.   I was certain they
plainly perceived it, by their firing another gun
as foon as it began to blaze, and after that feveral more from the fame quarter.   All night long
I kept up my fire: and when the air cleared up, I
perceived fomething a great way at fea, directly E.
but could not diftinguifh what it was, even with
my glafs, by reafon the weather was fo very fog-
gy out at fea.   However, keeping my eyes directly fixed upon it, and perceiving it not to ftir, I
prefently concluded it muft be a fhip at anchor, and
fo very hafty I was to be fatisfied, that taking my
gun, I went to the S. E. part of the ifland, to the
fame rocks where I had been formerly drove away
by the current; in which time the weather being
perfectly cleared up, to my great forrow, I perceived the wreck of a fhip caft away upon thofe
hidden rocks I found when I was out with my boat;
and which, by making a kind of an eddy, were the
occafion of my prefervation.

   Thus, what is one man's fafety is another's ruin; for undoubtedly this fhip had been driven on
them in the night, the wind blowing ftrong at E.
N. E. Had they perceived the ifland, as I now
guessed

guessed they had not, certainly, instead of having fired their guns for help, they would rather have ventured in their boat, and saved themselves that way. I then thought, that perhaps they had done so, upon seeing my fire, and were cast away in the attempt; for I perceived no boat in the ship. But then again I imagined, that perhaps they had another vessel in company, which, upon signal, saved their lives, and took the boat up; or that the boat might be driven into the main ocean, where these poor creatures might be in the most miserable condition. But as all these conjectures were very uncertain, I could do no more than commiserate their distress, and thank God for delivering me, in particular, when so many perished in the raging ocean.

When I considered seriously every thing concerning this wreck, and could perceive no room to suppose any of them saved, I cannot explain by any possible force of words, what longings my soul felt upon this sight, often breaking out in this manner: O that there had been but two or three, nay even one person saved, that we might have lived together, conversed with, and comforted one another! And so much were my desires moved, that when I repeated these words, " Oh! that there had been but one!" my hands would so clinch together, and my fingers press the palms of my hands so close, that, had any soft thing been between, it would have crushed it involuntarily, while my teeth would strike together, and set against each other so strong, that it required some time for me to part them.

'Till the last year of my being on this island, I never knew whether or not any had been saved out of this ship. I had the affliction some time after, to see the corpse of a drowned boy come on shore, at the end of the island which was next the

I

ship-

shipwreck: there was nothing on him but a seaman's waistcoat, a pair of open-kneed linen drawers, and a blue linen shirt; but no particular mark to guess what nation he was of. In his pocket were two pieces of eight, and a tobacco pipe, the last of which I preferred much more than I did the first. And now the calmness of the sea tempted me to venture out in my boat to this wreck, not only to get something necessary out of the ship, but perhaps some living creature might be on board, whose life I might preserve. This had such an influence upon my mind, that immediately I went home, and prepared every thing necessary for the voyage, carrying on board my boat provisions of all sorts, with a good quantity of rum, fresh water, and a compass: so putting of, I paddled the canoe along the shore, till I came at last to the north east part of the island, from whence I was to launch into the ocean; but here the currents ran so violently, and appeared so terrible, that my heart began to fail me; foreseeing, that if I was driven into any of these currents, I might be carried not only out of the reach or sight of the island but even inevitably lost in the boiling surges of the ocean.

So oppressed was I at these troubles, that I gave over my enterprise, sailing to a little creek on the shore, where stepping out, I sat me down on a rising hill, very pensive and thoughtful. I then perceived that the tide was turned, and the flood came on, which made it impracticable for me to go out for so many hours. To be more certain how the sets of the tides or currents lay when the flood came in, I ascended a higher piece of ground, which overlooked the sea both ways; and here I found, that as the current of the ebb set out close by the south-point of the island, so the current of the
flood

flood fet in clofe by fhore of the north fide; and all that I had to do, was to keep to the north of the ifland in my return.

That night I repofed myfelf in my canoe, covered with my watch-coat inftead of a blanket, the heavens being my tefter. I fet out with the firft of the tide full north, till I felt the benefit of the current, which carried me at a great rate eaftward, yet not with fuch impetuofity as before, as to take from me all government of my canoe; fo that in two hours time I came up to the wreck, which appeared to me a moft melancholy fight. It feemed to be a Spanifh veffel by its building, ftuck faft between two rocks; her ftern and quarter beaten to pieces by the fea; her mainmaft and foremaft were brought off by the board; that is, broken fhort off. As I approached nearer I perceived a dog on board, who feeing me coming, yelped and cried; and no fooner did I call him, but the poor creature jumped into the fea, out of which I took him up, almoft famifhed with hunger and thirft; fo that when I gave him a cake of bread, no ravenous wolf could devour it more greedily: and he drank to that degree of frefh water, that he would have burft himfelf, had I fuffered him.

The firft fight I met with in the fhip, were two men drowned in the cook-room or forecaftle, inclofed in one another's arms: hence I very probably fuppofed, that when the veffel ftruck in the ftorm, fo high and inceffantly did the waters break in and over her, that the men not being able to bear it, were ftrangled by the conftant rufhing in of the waves. There were feveral cafks of liquor, whether wine or brandy I could not be pofitive, which lay in the lower hold, as were plainly perceptible by the ebbing out of the water, yet were too large for me to pretend to middle with: likewife I perceived feveral chefts, which I fuppofed to belong to the

I 2

feamen,

feamen, two of which I got into my boat, without
examining what was in them.   Had the ftern of
the fhip been fixed, and the fore part broken off,
I fhould have made a very profperous voyage;
fince, by what I after found in thefe two chefts, I
could not otherwife conclude, but that the fhip muft
have abundance of wealth on board; nay, if I muft
guefs by the courfe fhe fteered, fhe muft have
been bound from the Buenos Ayrès, or the Rio
de la Plata, in the fouthern part of America, beyond the Brazils to the Havannah, in the gulph
of Mexico, and fo perhaps to Spain.   What became of the reft of her failors, I could not certainly
tell; and all her riches fignified nothing at that
time to any body.

Searching farther, I found a cafk, containing a-
bout twenty gallons, full of liquor, which, with
fome labour, I got into my boat; in a cabin were
feveral mufkets, which I let remain there; but took
away with me a great powder-horn, with about
four pounds of powder in it.   I took alfo a fire-
fhovel and tongs, two brafs kettles, a copper pot
to make chocolate, and a grid-iron; all which were
extremely neceffary to me, efpecially the fire-fho-
vel and tongs.   And, fo with this cargo, accompanied with my dog, I came away, the tide ferving
for that purpofe; and the fame evening, about an
hour within night, I attained the ifland, after the
greateft toil and fatigue imaginable.

That night I repofed my wearied limbs in the
boat, refolving the next morning to harbour what
I had gotten in my new-found fubterraneous grotto; and not carrying my cargo home to my ancient caftle.   Having refrefhed myfelf, and got all
my effects on fhore, I next proceeded to examine
the particulars; and fo tapping the cafk, I found
the liquor to be a kind of a rum, but not like what
we had at the Brafils, nor indeed near fo good.

At

At the opening of the cheſt, ſeveral things appeared very uſeful to me; for inſtance, I found in one a very fine caſe of bottles, containing the fineſt and beſt ſorts of cordial waters; each bottle held about three pints, curiouſly tipt with ſilver. I found alſo two pots full of the choiceſt ſweatmeats, and two more which the water had utterly ſpoiled. There were likewiſe ſeveral good ſhirts, exceeding welcome to me, and about one dozen and a half of white linen handkerchiefs and coloured neckcloths, the former of which were abſolutely neceſſary for wiping my face in a hot day; and in the till, I found three bags of pieces of eight, about eleven hundred in all, in one of which, decently wrapt up in a piece of paper, were ſix doubloons of gold, and ſome ſmall bars and wedges of the ſame metal, which I believe might weigh near a pound. In the other cheſt, which I gueſſed to belong to the gunner's mate, by the mean circumſtances that attended it, I only found ſome clothes of very little value, except about two pounds of fine glazed powder, in three flaſks, kept, as I believe, for charging their fowling-pieces on any occaſion; ſo that, on the whole, I had no great advantage by this voyage. The money was indeed as mere dirt to me, uſeleſs and unprofitable, all which I would have freely parted with for two or three pair of Engliſh ſhoes and ſtockings, things that for many years I had not worn, except lately thoſe which I had taken off the feet of thoſe unfortunate men I had found drowned in the wreck, yet not ſo good as Engliſh ſhoes, either for eaſe or ſervice. I alſo found in the ſeamen's cheſt about fifty pieces of eight in rials, but no gold; ſo concluded that what I took from the firſt belonged to an officer, the latter appearing to have a much inferior perſon for its owner. However, as deſpicable as the money ſeemed, I likewiſe lugged it to

my

my cave, laying it up fecurely, as I did the reft of my cargo; and after I had done all this I returned back to my boat, rowing or paddling her along till I came to my old harbour, where I carefully laid her up, and fo made the beft of my way to my caftle. When I arrived there, every thing feemed fafe and quiet: fo that now my only bufi-- nefs was to repofe myfelf after my wonted manner, and take care of my domeftic affairs. But tho' I might have lived very eafy, as wanting for nothing abfolutely needful, yet ftill I was more vigilant than ufual upon account of the favages, never go- ing much abroad; or, if I did, it was to the eaft part of the ifland, where I was well affured that the favages never came, and where I might not be troubled to carry that heavy load of weapons for my defence, as I was obliged to do if I went the other way.

Two years did I live in this anxious condition in all which time, contrary to my former refolu- tions, my head was filled with nothing but projects and defigns, how I might efcape from this ifland; and fo much were my wandering thoughts bent on a rambling difpofition, that had I had the fame boat that I went from Sallee in, I fhould have ven- tured once more to the uncertainty of the raging ocean.

I cannot however but confider myfelf as one of the unhappy perfons, who make themfelves wretch- ed by their diffatisfaction with the ftations which God has placed them in; for, not to take a review of my primitive condition and my father's excel- lent advice, (the going contrary to which was, as I may fay, my *original fin*), the following miftakes of the fame nature certainly had been the means of my prefent unhappy ftation. What bufinefs had I to leave a fettled fortune, and well ftocked plantation, improving and increafing, where, by
this

this time, I might have been worth a hundred thoufand moidores, to turn *fupercargo to Guinea*, to
fetch negroes, when time and patience would have
fo much enlarged my ftock at home, as to be able
to employ thofe whofe more immediate bufinefs it
was to fetch them home, even to my own door?

But as this is commonly the fate of young heads;
fo a ferious reflection upon the folly of it ordinarily attends the exercife of future years, when
the dear bought experience of time teaches us repentance. Thus was it with me; but notwithftanding the thoughts of my deliverance ran fo
ftrongly in my mind, that it feemed to check all the
dictates of reafon and philofohy. And now to ufher
in my kind reader with great pleafure to the remaining part of my relation, I flatter myfelf it will
not be taken amifs, to give him an account of my
firft conceptions of the manner of efcaping, and
upon what foundation I laid my foolifh fchemes.

Having retired to my caftle, after my late voyage to the fhip, my frigate laid up and fecured, as
ufual, and my condition the fame as before, except
being richer, though I had as little occafion for
riches as the Indians of Peru had for gold, before
the cruel Spaniards came among them: one night
in March, being the rainy feafon, in the four and
twentieth year of my folitude, I lay down to fleep,
very well in health, without diftemper, pain, or
uncommon uneafinefs, either of body or mind;
yet notwithftanding, I could not compofe myfelf
to fleep all the night long. All this tedious while,
it is impoffible to exprefs what innumerable thoughts
came into my head. I traced quite over the whole
hiftory of my life in miniature, from my utmoft
remembrance of things till I came to this ifland;
and then proceeded to examine every action and
paffage that had occurred fince I had taken poffeffion of my kingdom. In my reflections upon the
                                    latter,

latter, I was comparing the happy posture of my affairs in the beginning of my reign, to this life of anxiety, fear, and concern, since I had discovered the print of a foot in the sand, that while I continued without apprehension, I was incapable of feeling the dread and terror I now suffered. How thankful rather ought I to have been for the knowledge of my danger, since the greatest happiness one can be possessed of is to have sufficient time to provide against it? How stupendous is the goodness of Providence, which sets such narrow bounds to the sight and knowledge of human nature, that while men walk in the midst of so many dangers, they are kept serene and calm, by having the events of things hid from their eyes, and knowing nothing of those many dangers that surround them, till perhaps they are dissipated and vanish away.

When I came more particularly to consider of the real danger had for so many years escaped; how I had walked about in the greatest security and tranquillity, at a time, perhaps, when even nothing but the brow of the hill, a great tree, or the common approach of night, had interposed between me and the destructive hands of the cannibals, who would devour me with as good an appetite, as I would a pigeon or curlieu; surely all this, I say, could not but make me sincerely thankful to my great Preserver, whose singular protection I acknowledged with the greatest humility, and without which I must inevitably have fallen into the cruel hands of those devourers.

Having thus discussed my thoughts in the clearest manner, according to my weak understanding, I next proceeded to consider the wretched nature of these destroying savages, by seeming, though with great reverence, to inquire, why God should give up any of his creatures to such inhumanity, even to brutality itself, to devour its own kind?

But

But as this was rather matter of abstruse speculation, and as my miserable situation made me think this of mine the most uncomfortable situation in the world, I then began rather to inquire what part of the world these wretches lived in; how far off the coast was from whence they came; why they ventured over so far from home; what kind of boats conveyed them hither; and why I could not order myself and my business so, that I might be as able to attain their country, as they were to come to my kingdom?

But then, thought I, how shall I manage myself when I come thither; what will become of me if I fall into the hands of the savages? or how shall I escape from them, if they make an attempt upon me? and supposing I should not fall into their power, what will I do for provision, or which way shall I bend my course: These counter-thoughts threw me into the greatest horror and confusion imaginable; but then, I still looked upon my present condition to be the most miserable that possibly could be, and that nothing could be worse, except death. For (thought I) could I but attain the shore of the main, I might perhaps meet with some relief, or coast it along, as I did with my boy Xury, on the African shore, till I came to some inhabited country, where I might meet with some relief, or fall in with some Christian ship that might take me in; and if I failed, why then I could but meet with death, which would put an end to all my miseries. These thoughts I must confess, were the fruit of a distempered mind, an impatient temper, made desperate, as it were, by long continuance of the troubles and the disappointments I had met with in the wreck, where I hoped to have found some living person to speak to, by whom I might have known what place I was, and of the probable means of my deliverance. Thus, while

my

my thoughts were agitated, my refignation to the
will of heaven was intirely fufpended! fo that I
had no power to fix my mind to any thing, but to
the project of a voyage to the main land. And
indeed fo much was I inflamed upon this account,
that it fet my blood into a ferment, and my pulfe
beat high, as though I had been in a fever, till
nature being, as it were, fatigued and exhaufted
with the very thoughts of it, made me fubmit
myfelf to a filent repofe.

In fuch a fituation it is very ftrange, that I did
not dream of what I was fo intent upon; but, inftead of it, my mind roved on a quite different
thing, altogether foreign. I dreamed, that as I
was iffuing from my caftle, one morning, as cu-
ftomary, I perceived upon the ftore, two canoes,
and eleven favages, coming to land, who had
brought with them another Indian, whom they defigned to make a facrifice of, in order to devour;
but juft as they were going to give the fatal blow,
methought the poor defigned victim jumped away,
and ran directly into my little thick grove before
my fortification, to abfcond from his enemies;
when perceiving that the others did not follow him
that way, I appeared to him; that he humbly
kneeled down before me, feeming to pray for my
affiftance; upon which I fhewed him my ladder,
made him afcend, carried him to my cave, and he
became my fervant; and when I had gotten this
man, I faid to myfelf, Now furely I may have
fome hopes to attain the main-land; for this fellow will ferve me as a pilot, tell me what to do,
and where I muft go for provifions; what places
to fhun, what to venture to, and what to efcape.
But when I awaked, and found all thefe inexpref-
fible impreffions of joy entirely vanifhed, I fell into the greateft dejection of fpirit imaginable.

Yet this dream brought me to reflect, that one

fure

sure way of escaping was to get a savage; that after I had ventured my life to deliver him from the bloody jaws of his devourers, the natural sense he might have of such a preservation, might inspire him with a lasting gratitude and most sincere affection. But then this objection reasonably interposed: How can I effect this (thought I) without I attack a whole caravan of them, and kill them all? Why should I proceed on such a desperate attempt, which my scruples before had suggested to be unlawful; and indeed my heart trembled at the thoughts of so much blood, though it were a means to procure my deliverance. 'Tis true, I might reasonably enough suppose these men to be real enemies to my life, men who would devour me, was it in their power, so that it was self-preservation in the highest degree to free myself by attacking them in my own defence, as lawfully as if they were actually assaulting me: though all these things, I say, seemed to me to be of the greatest weight, yet, as I just said before, the dreadful thoughts of shedding human blood, struck such a terror to my soul, that it was a long time before I could reconcile myself to it.

But how far will the ardency of desire prompt us on? For, notwithstanding the many disputes and perplexities I had with myself, I at length resolved, right or wrong, to get one of these savages into my hands, cost what it would, or even though I should lose my life in the attempt. Inspired with this firm resolution, I set all my wits at work, to find out what methods I should take to answer my design: this indeed was so difficult a task, that I could not pitch upon any probable means to execute it: I therefore resolved continually to be in a vigilant posture, to perceive when the savages came on shore, and to leave the

rest

reft to the event, let the opportunities offer as they would.

Such were my fixed refolutions; and accordingly I fet myfelf upon the fcout, as often as I could, till fuch time as I was heartily tired of it. I waited for above a year and a half, the greateft part of which time I went out to the weft and fouth-weft corner of the ifland, almoft every day, to look for canoes; but none appeared. This was a very great difcouragement; yet, though I was very much concerned, the edge of my defire was as keen as ever, and the longer it feemed to be delayed, the more eager was I for it: in a word I never before was fo careful to fhun the loathing fight of thefe favages, as I was now eager to be with them: and I thought myfelf fufficiently able to manage one, two, or three favages, if I had them, fo as to make them my entire flaves, to do whatfoever I fhould direct them, and prevent their being able at any time to do me a mifchief. Many times did I ufe to pleafe myfelf with thefe thoughts, with long and ardent expectations; but nothing prefenting, all my deep projected fchemes, and numerous fancies, vanifhed away, as tho', while I retained fuch thoughts, the decree of Providence was fuch, that no favages were to come near me.

About a year and a half after, when I was ferioufly mufing of fundry other ways how I fhould attain my end, one morning early I was very much furprifed by feeing no lefs than five canoes all on fhore together on my fide the ifland, and the favages that belonged to them all landed, and out of my fight. Such a number of them difconcerted all my meafures; for feeing fo many boats, each of which could contain fix, and fometimes more, I could not tell what to think of it, or how to order my meafures, to attack twenty or thirty men fingle handed: upon which,

which, much difpirited and perplexed, I lay ftill
in my caftle: which however I put in a proper
pofture for an attack; and having formerly provided all that was neceffary, was foon ready to enter upon an engagement, fhould they attempt it.
Having waited for fome time, my impatient temper would let me bear it no longer; I fet my guns
at the foot of my ladder, and, as ufual, afcended
up to the top of the hill at two ftages, ftanding
however in fuch a manner that my head did not
appear above the hill, fo that they could not eafily perceive me: and here, by the affiftance of my
perfpective glafs, I obferved no lefs than thirty in
number around a fire, feafting upon what meat
they had dreffed: how they cooked it, or what it
was, I could not then perfectly tell; but they were
all dancing and capering about the flames, ufing
many frightful and barbarous geftures.

But while, with a curious eye, I was beholding
thefe wretches, my fpirits funk within me, when
I perceived them drag two miferable creatures,
from the boats, to act afrefh the dreadful tragedy,
as I fuppofed they had done before. It was not
long before one of them fell upon the ground,
knocked down, as I fuppofe, with a club or wood-
en fword, for that was their manner; while two
or three others went immediately to work, cutting
him open for their cookery, and then fell to devour him as they had done the former; while the
laft unhappy captive was left by himfelf till fuch
time as they were ready for him. The poor creature looked round him with a wifhful eye, trembling at the thoughts of death; yet feeing himfelf
little at liberty, nature that very moment, as it
were, infpired him with hopes of life: he ftarted
away from them, and ran with incredible fwiftnefs
along the fands, directly to that part of the coaft
where my ancient and venerable caftle ftood.

K

You

You may well imagine I was dreadfully affrighted upon this occasion, when, as I thought, they pursued him in a whole body, all running towards my palate. And now, indeed, I expected that part of my dream was going to be fulfilled, and that he would certainly fly to my grove for protection, but for the rest of my dream, I could depend nothing on it, that the savages would pursue him thither and find him there. However, my spirits beginning to recover, I still kept upon my guard; and I now plainly perceived there were but three men out of the number that pursued him. I was infinitely pleased with what swiftness the poor creature ran from his pursuers, gaining so much ground of them, that I plainly perceived, could he thus hold it for half an hour, there was not the least doubt but he would save his life from the power of his enemies.

Between them and my castle there was a creek, the very same which I sailed into with all my effects from the wreck of the ship, on the steep banks of which I very much feared the poor victim would be taken, if he could not swim for his escape: but soon was I out of pain for him, when I perceived he made nothing of it, though at full tide; but with an intrepid courage, spurred on by the sense of danger, he plunged into the flood, swimming over in about thirty strokes, and then landing, ran with the same incredible strength and swiftness as before. When the three pursuers came to the creek, one of them, who I perceived could not swim (happily for his part,) returned back to his company; while the others, with as equal courage, but much less swiftness, attained the other side, as though they were resolved never to give over their pursuit. And now, or never, I thought was the time for me to procure me a servant, companion, or assistant; and that I was

decreed

R Crusoe Releves his man Friday P.97

decreed by Providence to be the instrument that should save this poor creature's life. I immediately descended my two ladders with the greatest expedition; I took up my two guns, which I said before were at the bottom of them; and getting up again with the same haste towards the hill, I made nearer the sea. In a word, taking a short cut down the hill, I interposed between the pursuers and pursued, hallooing aloud to the latter, who venturing to look back, was no doubt at first as much terrified at me as I at them. I beckoned to him with my hand to return back, in the mean time advancing towards the pursuers, and rushing on the foremost, I knocked him down with the stock of my piece, and laid him flat on the ground. I was very unwilling to fire, lest the rest should hear, though at that distance I questioned whether they could or no; and being out of sight of the smoke, they could not easily have known what to make of it. The other savage seeing his fellow fall, stopped as if he had been amazed; when, advancing towards him, I could perceive him take his bow from his back, and fixing an arrow to it, was preparing to shoot at me, and without dispute might have lodged the arrow in my breast; but, in this absolutely necessary case of self-preservation, I immediately fired at him, and shot him dead, just as his hand was going to draw the fatal string. All this while the savage who had fled before stood still, and had the satisfaction to see his enemies killed, as he thought; who designed to take away his life: so affrighted was he with the fire and noise of my piece, that he stood as it were like Lot's wife, fixed and immoveable, without either sense or motion. This obliged me to halloo to him again, making the plainest signs I could to him to draw nearer. I perceived he understood these tokens by his approaching to me a little way, when,

as if afraid I should kill him too, he stopped again.
Several times did he advance, and as often stop in
this manner, till, coming more to my view, I perceived him trembling, as if he was to undergo the
same fate. Upon which I looked upon him with
a smiling countenance, and still beckoning to him;
at length he came close to me, and kneeled down,
kissed the ground, laid his head upon it, and taking
me by my foot, set the same upon his head: and
this, as I understood afterwards, was a token of
swearing to be my slave for ever. I took him up,
and making much of him, encouraged him in the
best manner I could. But my work was not yet
finished; for I perceived the savage whom I knocked down, was not killed, but stunned with the
blow, and began to come to himself. Upon which
I pointed to my new servant, and shewing him that
his enemy was not yet expired, he spoke some
words to me, but which I could not understand;
yet being the first sound of a man's voice I had
heard for above twenty-five years, they were very
pleasing to me. But there was no time for reflection now, the wounded savage recovering himself
so far as to sit upon the ground, which made my
poor prisoner as much afraid as before; to put
him out of which fear, I presented my other gun
at the man, with an intent to shoot him, but my
savage, for so I must now call him, prevented my
firing, by making a motion to me, to lend him my
sword which hung naked in a belt by my side. No
sooner did I grant his request, but away he ran
to his enemy, and at one blow cut off his head as
dexterously as the most accomplished executioner
in Germany could have done; for it seems these
creatures make use of wooden swords made of
hard wood, which will bear edge enough to cut off
heads and arms at one blow. When this valorous
exploit was done, he came to me, laughing, as a

token

token of triumph, delivered me my sword again, with abundance of surprising gestures, laying it along, with the blooding and ghastly head of the Indian at my feet.

The greatest astonishment that my new servant conceived, was the manner of killing the savage at such a distance, without a bow and arrow: and such was his longing desire to know it, that he first pointed to the dead carcase, and then made signs to me to grant him leave to go to him. Upon which I bid him go, and as well as I could, made him sensible I granted his request. But when he came there, how wonderfully was he struck with amazement! First he turned him on one side, then on another, wondering he could perceive no quantity of blood, he bleeding inwardly: and after sufficiently admiring the wound the bullet had made in his breast, he took up his bow and arrows, and came back again; upon which I turned to go away, making many signs to him to follow, left the rest missing their companions, might come in pursuit of him. And this I found he understood very well, by his making me to understand that his design was to bury them, that they might not be seen if it happened; and which by signs again I made him sensible I very much approved of. Immediately he fell to work, and never was grave-digger more dexterous in the world than he was; for in an instant, as I might say he scraped a large hole in the sands with his hands, sufficient to bury the first in; there he dragged him, and without any ceremony he covered him over; in like manner he served the other: so that I am sure no undertaker could be more expert in his business; for all this was done in less than a quarter of an hour. I then called him away, and instead of carrying him directly to my castle at first, I conveyed him to my cave, on the further part of the island;

and

and so my dream was not fulfilled in that particular, that my grove should prove an asylum or sanctuary to him.

Weary and faint, hungry and thirsty, undoubtedly must this poor creature be, supported chiefly by that vivacity of spirit, and uncommon transports of joy that his deliverance occasioned. Here I gave him bread, and a bunch of raisins to eat, and water to drink, on which he fed very chearfully, to his exceeding refreshment. I then made him a convenient bed, with a parcel of rice straw, and a blanket upon it, (a bed which I used myself sometimes,) and then pointing to it, made signs for him to lye down to sleep, upon which the poor creature went to take a welcome repose.

Indeed he was a very comely handsome young fellow, extremely well made, with straight long limbs, not too large, tall and well shaped, and, as near as I could reckon, about twenty-six years of age. His countenance had nothing in it fierce or surly, but rather a sort of majesty in his face; and yet, especially when he smiled, he had all the sweetness and softness of an European. His hair was not curled like wool, as many of the blacks are, but long and black, with the most beautiful, yet careless, tresses spreading over his shoulders. He had a very high and large forehead, with a great vivacity and sparkling sharpness in his eyes. His skin was not so tawny as the Virginians, Brasilians, or other Americans, but rather of a bright dun olive colour, that had something agreeable in it, though not very easy to give a description of. His face was round and plump, with a small nose, very different from the flatness of the negroes, a pretty small mouth, thin lips, fine teeth, very well set, and white as the driven snow. In a word, such handsome features, and exact symmetry in every part, made me consider, that I had saved the

life

life of an Indian prince, no less graceful and accomplished than the great Oroonoko, whose memorable behaviour and unhappy contingencies of life have charmed the world, both to admiration of his person, and compassion to his sufferings.

But let him be either prince or peasant, all my happiness centered in this, that I had now got a good servant or companion, to whom, as he deserved, I was resolved to prove a kind master and lasting friend. He had not, I think, slept above an hour, when he awakened again, and while I was milking my goats hard by, out he runs from the cave towards me in my inclosure, and laying himself down on the ground in the lowest prostration, made all the antic gestures imaginable, to express his thankfulness to me for being his deliverer. I confess, though the manner of his behaviour seemed to be ludicrous enough to occasion laughter, yet I was very much moved at his affection, so that my heart melted within me, fearing he might die away in excess of joy, like reprieved malefactors; especially as I was incapable either to let him blood, or administer physic. It were to be wished, that Christians would take example by this Heathen, to have a lasting remembrance of the benefits and deliverances they have received, by the kind mediation and powerful interposition of their benefactors and deliverers: and it would likewise be happy for mankind, were there no occasion to blame many, who, instead of thankfully acknowledging favours and benefits, rather abuse and contemn those who have been the instruments to save them from destruction.

But, leaving these just reflections, I return to the object that occasioned them; for my man, to conclude the last ceremony of obedience, laid down his head again on the ground, close to my foot, and set my other foot upon his head, as he

had

had done before, making all the figns of fubjec-
tion, fervitude, and fubmiffion imaginable, to let
me underfland he would ferve me as long as his
life endured. As I underftood him in many things,
I made him fenfible I was very well pleafed with
him; and in a little time I began to fpeak to him,
and learn him how to talk to me again. In the
firft place, I made him underftand his name was
to be Friday, becaufe it was upon that day I faved
his life: then I taught him to fay Mafter, which
I made him fenfible was to be my name. I likewife taught him to fay Yes and No, and to know
what they meant. I gave him fome milk in an
earthen pot, making him view me while I drank
it before him, and foaked my bread in it; I gave
him a cake of bread, and caufed him foak it likewife, to which he readily confented, making figns
of the greateft fatisfaction imaginable.

All that night did I keep him there; but no
fooner did the morning light appear, when I ordered him to arife, and come along with me, with
certain tokens that I would give him fome clothes
like mine, at which he feemed very glad, being
ftark naked, without the leaft covering whatever.
As we paffed by the place where the two men had
been interred, my man pointed directly to their
graves, fhewing me the marks that he had made
to find them again, giving me to underftand, by
figns, that he would dig them up, and devour
them. At this I appeared extremely difpleafed, expreffed my utmoft abhorrence, as if I would vomit
at the apprehenfions of it, beckoning with my
hand to come away, which he did with the greateft
reverence and fubmiffion. After this I conducted
him to the top of the hill, to view if the reft of
the favages were yet remaining there; but when
I looked through my perfpective glafs, I could fee
no appearance of them, nor of their canoes; fo
that

that it was very evident they never minded their deceafed companions whom I had flain; which, if they had, they would furely have fearched for, or left one boat behind for them to follow, after they returned from their purfuit.

Curiofity, and a defire of fatisfaction, animating me with courage to fee this fcene of barbarity, I took my man Friday with me, putting a fword into his hand, with the bow and arrows at his back, which I perceived he could ufe very dexteroufly, caufing him to carry one gun for me, and I two for myfelf; and thus equipped againft all attacks, away we marched directly to the place of their bloody entertainment. But when I came there, I was ftruck with the utmoft horror at fo dreadful a fpectacle, whilft Friday was no way concerned about it, being no doubt in his turn one of thefe devourers. Here lay feveral human bones, there feveral pieces of mangled flefh, half eaten, mangled and fcorched, whilft ftreams of blood ran promifcuoufly as waters from a fountain. As I was mufing on this dreadful fight, Friday took all the pains he could, by particular figns, to make me underftand, that they had brought over four prifoners to feaft upon, three of whom they had eaten up, and that he was the fourth, pointing to himfelf: that there having been a bloody battle between them and his great king, in the juft defence of whom he was taken prifoner, with many others; all of thefe were carried off to different places, to be devoured by their conquerors; and that it was his misfortune to be brought hither by thefe wretches for the fame purpofe.

After I was made fenfible of thefe things, I caufed Friday to gather thefe horrid remains, and lay them together upon a heap, which I ordered to be fet on fire, and burnt them to afhes: my man, however, ftill retained the nature of a cannibal,
having

having a hankering stomach after some of the flesh; but such an extreme abhorrence did I express at the least appearance of it, that he durst not but conceal it: for I made him very sensible, that if he offered any such thing, I would certainly shoot him.

This being done, I carried my man with me to my castle, and gave him a pair of linen drawers, which I had taken out of the poor gunner's chest before mentioned; and which, with a little alteration, fitted him very well: in the next place, I made him a jerking of goat-skin, such as my skill was able to manage, and indeed I thought myself then a tolerable good tailor. I gave him also a cap, which I made of a hare's skin, very convenient and fashionable. Thus being cloathed tolerable well, my man was no less proud of his habit, than I was in seeing him in it. Indeed he went very aukwardly at first, the drawers being too heavy on his thighs, not used to bear any weight, and the sleeves of the waistcoat galled his shoulders, and the inside of his arms; but by a little easing where he complained they hurt him, and by using himself to them, at length he took to them very well.

My next concern was, where I should lodge him: and that I might do well by him, and yet be perfectly easy myself, I erected a tent for him in the vacant place between my two fortifications, in the inside of the last, and the outside of the first: and as there was an entrance or door into my cave, I made a formal framed door-case, and a door to open on the inside; I barred it up in the night-time, taking in my ladders too; so that, was my man to prove treacherous, there could be no way to come at me in the inside of my innermost wall, without making so much noise in getting over, that it must needs waken me; for my first wall had now

a conta complete roof over it of long poles, fpreading over my tent, and leaning up to the fide of the mountain; which was again laid crofs with fmaller fticks inftead of laths, and thatched over a great thicknefs with rice ftraw, which was as ftrong as reeds: and at the hole of the place, left on purpofe to go in or out by the ladder, I had placed a kind of a trap-door, which, if it had been attempted on the outfide, would not have opened at all, but have fallen down, and made a great noife; and as to my weapons, every night I took them all to my bed-fide.

But there was no occafion for this precaution; for furely never mafter had a more fincere, faithful, and loving fervant than Friday proved to me. Without paffion, fullennefs, or defign, perfectly obliging and engaging, his affections were as much tied to me, as thofe of a child to his parents: and I might venture to fay, he would have facrificed his life for the faving mine, upon any occafion whatfoever. And indeed the many teftimonies he gave me of this, fufficiently convinced me that I had no occafion to ufe thefe precautions. And here I could not but reflect, with great wonder, that however it has pleafed the Almighty in his providence, and in the government of the creation, to take from fo great a part of the world of his creatures, the nobleft ufes to which their faculties, and the powers of their fouls are adapted, yet that he has beftowed upon them the fame reafon, affections, fentiments of kindnefs, and obligation, paffions of refentment, fincerity, fidelity, and all the capacities of doing and receiving good that he has given us; and that when he is gracioufly pleafed to offer them occafions of exerting thefe, they are as ready, nay, more ready, to apply them to the proper ufes for which they were beftowed, than we often are. Thefe thoughts
would

would make me melancholy, especially when I considered how mean a use we make of all these, even though we have these powers enlightened by the Holy Spirit of God, and by the knowledge of his word, as an addition to our understanding; and why it has pleased the heavenly Wisdom to conceal the like saving knowledge from so many millions of souls, who could certainly make a much better use of it than generally mankind do at this time. These reflections would sometimes lead me so far, as to invade the sovereignty of providence, and, as it were, arraign the justice of such an arbitrary disposition of things, that should obscure that light from some, and reveal it to others, and yet expect a like duty from all. But I closed it up, checking my thoughts with this conclusion; *first*, That we were ignorant of that right and law by which these should be condemned; but that as the Almighty was necessarily, and by the nature of his essence, infinitely just and holy; so it could not be otherwise, but that if these creatures were all destined to absence from himself, it was on account of sinning against that light, which, as the scripture says, was a law to themselves, and by such rules as their consciences would acknowledge to be just, though the first foundation was not discovered to us. And, *secondly*, That still as we were the clay in the hand of the potter, no vessel could thus say to him, Why hast thou fashioned me after this manner?

I had not been above two or three days returned to my castle, but my chief design was, how I should bring Friday off from his horrid way of feeding; and to take from him that inhuman relish he by nature had been accustomed to, I thought it my duty to let him taste other flesh, which might the rather tempt him to the same abhorrence I so often expressed against their accursed way of living.

ing. Upon which one morning I took him out with me, with an intention to kill a kid out of the flock, and bring it home, and drefs it. As I was going, I perceived a fhe-goat lying down in the fhade, and two young kids fitting by her. Immediately I catched hold of my man Friday, and bidding him fland ftill and not ftir, I prefented my piece, and fliot one of the kids. My poor fervant, who had at a diftance perceived me kill his adverfary, and yet did not know by what means, or how it was done, ftood trembling and furprifed, and looked fo amazed, that I thought he would have funk into the earth. He did not fee the kid I aimed at, or beheld I had killed it, but ripped up his waiftcoat to fee if he was not wounded, thinking my refolution was to kill him; for coming to me, he fell on his knees earneftly pronouncing many things which I did not underftand the meaning of; which at length I perceived was, that I would not take away his life.

Indeed I was much concerned to fee him in that condition, where nature is upon the fevereft trial, when the immediate hand of death is ready to put for ever a period to this mortal life: and indeed fo much compaffion had I to this creature, that it was with difficulty I refrained from tears. But however, as another fort of countenance was neceffary, and to convince him that I would do him no harm, I took him, fmiling, by the hand, then laughed at him, and pointing to the kid which I had flain, made figns to him to fetch it, which accordingly he did. No lefs curious was he in viewing how the creature was killed, than he had been before in beholding the Indian; which, while he was admiring at, I charged my gun again, and prefently perceived a great fowl like a hawk, perching upon a tree within fhot; and, therefore, to let Friday underftand what I was going to do, I called him to

L

me

me again, pointing at the fowl, which I found to be a parrot. I made him underſtand that I would ſhoot and kill that bird; accordingly I fired, and bid him look, when immediately he ſaw the parrot fall down. Again he ſtood like one amazed, notwithſtanding all I had ſaid to him; and the more confounded he was, becauſe he did not perceive me put any thing into my gun. Undoubtedly a thing ſo utterly ſtrange, carrying death along with it, far or near, either to man or beaſt, muſt certainly create the greater aſtoniſhment to one who had never heard of ſuch a thing in his whole life: and really his amazement continued ſo long, that had I allowed it, he would have proſtrated himſelf before me and my gun, with the greateſt worſhip and adoration. As for the gun in particular, he would not ſo much as ſuffer his fingers to touch it for ſeveral days after; but would come and communicate his thoughts to it, and talk to it, as if the ſenſeleſs piece had underſtood and anſwered him: all this I could perceive him do, when he thought my back was turned, the chief intent of which was, to deſire it not to kill him, as I afterwards came to underſtand.

I never ſtrove to prevent his admiration, nor hinder him from thoſe comical geſtures he uſed on ſuch occaſions; but when his aſtoniſhment was a little over, I made tokens to him to run and fetch the parrot that I had ſhot; which he accordingly did, ſtaying ſome time longer than uſual, by reaſon the bird, not being quite dead, had fluttered ſome way farther from the place where ſhe fell. In the mean time, as he was looking for her, I took the advantage of charging my gun again, that ſo I might be ready for any other mark that offered; but nothing more occurred at that time. So I brought home the kid, and the ſame evening took off the ſkin, and divided the carcaſe as well as I
could.

could. Part of this flesh I stewed and boiled, in a
pot I had for this purpose. And then spreading
my table, I sat down, giving my man some of it
to eat, who was wonderfully pleased, and seemed
to like it very well; but what was most surprising
to him was to see me eat salt with it: upon which
he made me to understand, the salt was very bad
for me; when putting a little into his mouth he
seemed to nauseate it in such a manner, as to spit
and sputter at it, and then washed his mouth with
fresh water: but to shew him how contrary his
opinion was to mine, I put some meat into my
mouth without salt, and feigned to spit and sputter as much for the want of it, as he had done at
it: yet all this proved of no signification to Friday; and it was a long while before he could endure salt in his meat or broth, and even then but
a very small quantity.

Thus, having fed him sufficiently with boiled
meat and broth at that time, the next day I was
resolved to feast him with a roasted piece of the
kid. And having no spit to fasten it, nor jack to
turn it, I made use of that common artifice which
many of the people of England have, that is, to
set two poles upon each side of the fire, and one
cross on the top, hanging the meat thereon with
a string, and so turning round continually, roast
it in the same manner as we read bloody tyrants
of old cruelly roasted the holy martyrs. This
practice caused great admiration in my man Friday,
being quite another way than that to which the
savages were accustomed. But when he came to
taste the sweetness and tenderness of the flesh, he
expressed his entire satisfaction above a thousand
different ways. And as I could not but understand
his meaning, you may be sure I was as wonderfully pleased, especially when he made it also very

 plain.

plain to me, that he would never, while he lived, eat man's flesh more.

It is now high time I should set my servant to work; so next day I put him to beat out some corn, and sift it in the same manner as I had done before. And really the fellow was very quick and handy in the execution of any thing I ordered him to go about. I made him understand it was to make bread for us to eat, and afterwards let him see me bake it. In short, he did every thing as I ordered him in a little time as well as I could perform it myself.

But now considering I had two mouths to feed instead of one, it was necessary that I must provide more ground for my harvest, and plant a larger quantity of corn than I commonly used to do; upon which I marked out a larger piece of land, fencing it in, in the same manner as I had done before; in the execution of which I must give Friday this good word, that no man could work more hardy, or with better will than he did: and when I made him sensible that it was for bread to serve him as well as me, he then very passionately made me understand, that he thought I had much more labour on his account, than I had for myself; and that no pains or diligence should be wanting in him, if I would but direct him in those works wherein he might proceed.

I must certainly own, that this was the most pleasant year I ever had in the island; for after some time Friday began to talk pretty well, and understand the names of those things which I was wont to call for, and the places where I used to send him. So that my long silent tongue, which had been useless so many years, except in an exolamatory manner, either for deliverance or blessings, now began to be occupied in teaching, and talking to my man Friday; for indeed I had such

a singular

a singular satisfaction in the fellow himself, so innocent did his simple and unfeigned honesty appear more and more to me every day, that I really began entirely to love him, and for his part, I believe there was no love lost, and that his nature had been more charmed with my exceeding kindness, and his affections more placed upon me, than any other object whatsoever among his own countrymen. I once had a great mind to try if he had any hankering inclination to his own country again: and by this time having learned him the English so well, that he could give me tolerable answers to any question which I demanded, I asked him, whether that nation to which he belonged ever conquered in battle? This question made Friday to smile, and to which he answered, *Yes, yes, We always fight the better;* as much as to say, they always got the better in fight. Upon which we proceeded on the following discourse. You say, said I, that you always fight the better; why then, Friday, how came you to be taken prisoner?

Friday. But for all that, my nation beat much.

Master. How, say you, beat! if your nation beat them, how came you to be taken?

Friday. They more many mans than my nation in the place where me was, they take one, two, three, and me: my nation much overbeat them in the yonder place where me now was, there my nation mans beat one, two, three, great tousauds.

Master. Then why did not your men recover you from the hands of your enemies?

Friday. They run one, two, or three, and me; they make all go in the canoo; my nation have no canoo that time.

Master. 'Tis very well, Friday; but what does your nation do with the prisoners they take? Do they

they

they carry them away and eat them as thefe have done?

Friday. Yes, yes, my nation eat mans too, eat up all.

Mafter. To what place do they carry them to be devoured.

Friday. Go to other nations where they think.

Mafter. Do they bring them hither?

Friday. Yes, come over hither, come over other place.

Mafter. And have you been with them here Friday?

Friday. Yes, me been here, (*pointing to the north weft of the ifland, being the fide where they ufed to land.*)

Thus having got what account I could from my man, I plainly underftood, that he had been as bad as any of the reft of the cannibals, having been formerly among the favages who ufed to come on fhore on the fartheft part of the ifland, upon the fame bloody occafion as he was brought hither for: and fometime after I carried him to that place where he pointed; and no fooner did he come there, but he prefently knew the ground, fignify-ing to me that he was once there when they ate up twenty men, two women, and a young child; but as he could not explain the number in *Englifh*, he did it by fo many ftones in a row, making a fign to me to count them.

This paffage I have the rather mentioned, be-caufe it led to things more important and ufeful for me to know: for after I had this fatisfactory difcourfe with him, my next queftion was, how far it was from the ifland to the fhore, and whe-ther the canoes were not often loft in the ocean? To which he anfwered, there was no danger; that no canoes were ever loft; but that after a little way out to the fea, there was a ftrong current,

and

and a wind always one way in the afternoon. This I thought at firſt to be no more than the ſets of the tide, of going out or coming in; but I afterward underſtood it was occaſioned by the great draught and reflux of the mighty river Oroonoko, in the mouth or gulf of which I imagined my kingdom lay; and that the land which I perceived to the W. and N. W. muſt be the great iſland Trinidad, on the north of the river. A thouſand queſtions (if that would ſatisfy me) did I aſk Friday about the nature of the country, the ſea, the coaſts, the inhabitants, and what nations were neareſt them; to which queſtions the poor fellow declared all he knew, with the greateſt openneſs and utmoſt ſincerity. When I demanded of him the particular names of the various nations of his ſort of people, he could only anſwer me in general, that they were called *Carabe*. Hence it was I conſidered that theſe muſt be the Caribbees, ſo much taken notice of by our maps, to be on that part of America, which reaches from the mouth of the river Oroonoko to Guiania, and ſo on to St. Martha. Then Friday proceeded to tell me, that up a great way beyond the moon, as much as to ſay, beyond the ſetting of the moon, which muſt be W. from their country, there dwelt white-bearded men ſuch as I, was, pointing to my whiſkers, and that they kill *much mans*. I was not ignorant with what barbarity the Spaniards treated theſe creatures; ſo that I preſently concluded it muſt be them, whoſe cruelties had ſpread throughout America, to be remembered even to ſucceeding generations.

Well, you may be ſure, this knowledge, which the imperfect information of my man had led me to, was very comfortable to me, and made me ſo curious as to aſk him, how I might depart from this iſland, and get among thoſe white men? He
told

told me, *Yes, yes, I might go in two canoes.* In two canoes, thought I what does my man mean; Surely he means one for himself, and another for me; and if not, how muft two canoes hold me without being joined, or one part of my body being put in one, and another in the other ? And indeed it was a long while before I underftood his meaning, which was, that it muft be a large boat, as big as two canoes, able to bear with the waves, and not fo liable to be overwhelmed as one muft be.

I believe there is no ftate of life but what may be happy, if people would but endeavour for their part to make it fo. He is not the happieft man that has the moft riches, but he that is content with what he hath. Before I had my fervant, I thought myfelf miferable till I had him; and now that I enjoyed the happy benefits of him, I ftill complained, and begged a deliverance from a place of retirement, eafe, and plenty, where Providence had fufficiently bleffed me. In a word, from this time I entertained fome hopes, that one time or other I might find an opportunity to make my efcape from this ifland, and that this poor favage might be a great furtherance thereto

All the time fince my man became fo intelligent as to underftand and fpeak to me, I fpared no pains nor diligence to inftruct him, according to my poor fhare of knowledge, in the principles of religion, and the adoration that he ought to pay to the *True God.* One time, as I very well remember, I afked him who made him ? At firft the innocent creature did not underftand what I meant; but rather thought I afked him who was his father; upon which I took another way to make him fenfible, by demanding from him an anfwer to this queftion. Friday, faid I, who is it that made the fea, this ground whereon we walk, and

all

all thefe hills and woods which we behold? And here indeed I did not mifs of my intention; for he told me, it was old Benamuckee (the god whom I fuppofed thefe favages adored) who lived a great way beyond all. But as for his attributes, poor Friday was an utter ftranger. He could defcribe nothing of this great perfon; and all that he could fay was, that he was very old, much older than the fea and land, the moon, or the ftars. Friday, (faid I again,) if this great and old perfon has made all things in the world, how comes it to pafs, that all things, as you in particular, do not adore and worfhip him? Upon this, looking very grave, with a perfect fweet look of innocence, he replied, *Mafter, all things fay O to him*, by which it may reafonably be fuppofed he meant adoration. And where, faid I, do the people of your country go when they die? He anfwered, they all go to *Benamuckee*. What, and thofe people that are eaten up, do they go there? *Benamuckee*, faid he, *love 'em dearly; me pray to Benamuckee in de canoe, and Benamuckee wou'd love me when dey eat a me all up.*

Such difcourfes as thefe had I with my man, and fuch made me fenfible, that the true God is worfhipped, though under imperfect fimilitude; and that the falfe adoration which the Heathens give to their imaginary deity, is as great an argument of the divine effence, as the moft learned Atheift *(falfly fo called)* can bring againft it: for God will be glorified in his works, let the denomination be what it will; and I cannot be of that opinion which fome conceive, that God fhould decree men to be damned for want of a right notion of faith, in a place where the wifdom of the Almighty has not permitted it to be preached; and therefore cannot but conclude, that fince obedience is the beft facrifice, thefe poor creatures, acting by that
light

light and knowledge which they are poffeffed with, may nndoubtedly obtain a happy falvation, tho' not that enjoyment with Chrift, as his faints, confeffors, and martyrs muft enjoy.

But laying thefe determinations afide, more fit for divines than me to difcufs, I began to inftruct my fervant in the faving knowledge of the true Deity, in which the directions of God's Holy Spirit affifted me. I lifted up my hands to heaven, and pointing thereto, told him, that the great Maker of heaven and earth lived there: that as his infinite power fafhioned this world out of a confufed chaos, and made it in that beautiful frame which we behold, fo he governs and preferves it by his unbounded knowledge, fovereign greatnefs, and peculiar providence; that he was omnipotent, could do every thing for us, give every thing to us, and take every thing away from us: that he was a rewarder and punifher of good and evil actions: that there was nothing but what he knew, no thoughts fo fecret but what he could bring to light; and thus, by degrees, I opened his eyes, and defcribed to him the manner of the creation of the world, the fituation of paradife, the tranfgreffion of our firft parents, the wickednefs of God's peculiar people, and the univerfal fins and abominations of the whole earth. When thefe things were implanted in his mind, I told him, that as God's juftice was equal to his mercy, he refolved to deftroy this world, till his Son Jefus Chrift interpofed in our behalf; and, to procure our redemption, obtained leave of his heavenly Father to come down from heaven into the world, where he took human nature upon him, inftructed us in our way to eternal life, and died as a facrifice for our fins; that he was now afcended into heaven, mediating for our pardon, delivering our petitions, and obtaining all thofe good benefits

which

which we afk in his name, by humble and hearty prayers, all which were heard at the throne of heaven. As very frequently I ufed to inculcate things into his mind, Friday one day told me, that if our great God could hear us beyond the fun, he muft furely be a greater God than their *Benamuckee*, who lived but a little way off, and yet could not hear them till they afcended the great mountains where he dwelt, to fpeak to him. What, faid I, Friday, did you go thither to fpeak to him too? He anfwered, No, they never went that were young men, none but old men called their *Oowakakee*, meaning the Indian priefts, who went to fay O, (fo he called faying their prayers,) and they returned back, and told them what *Benam..ckee* faid. From hence I could not but obferve how happy we Chriftians are, who hath God's immediate revelation for our certain guide; and that our faith is neither mifled, nor our reafon impofed upon, by any fet of men fuch as thefe Indian impoftors.

But, to clear up this palpable cheat to my man Friday, I told him, that the pretence of their ancient men going up to the mountain to fay O to their god *Benamuckee* was an impofture, and that their bringing back an anfwer was all a fham, if not worfe; for that if there was any fuch thing fpoken to them, furely it muft proceed from an infernal fpirit. And here I thought it neceffary to enter into a long difcourfe with him, which I did after this manner:

Friday, (faid I,) you muft know that before this world was made, there was an almighty power exifting, by whofe power all things were made, and whofe majefty fhall have no end. To be glorified and adored by beings of a heavenly nature, he created angels and arch-angels, that is, glorious fpirits refembling himfelf, to encompafs his throne,

eternally

eternally finging forth his praife in the moft heavenly founds and divine harmony. And, among this heavenly choir, Lucifer bore a great fway, as being then one of the peculiar favourites of thefe celeftial abodes; but he, contrary to that duty he owed his heavenly fovereign, with unbounded ingratitude to his divine Creator, not only envied him that adoration which was his due, but thought to ufurp that throne which he had neither power to keep, nor title to pretend to. He raifed a diffenfion and civil war in heaven, and had a number of angels to take his part. Unbounded folly! ftupendous pride! thus to hope for victory, and afpire above his powerful Creator! the Deity, not fearful of fuch an enemy, yet juftly provoked at this rebellion, commiffions his arch-angel Michael to lead forth the heavenly hoft, and give him battle; the advantage of which was quickly perceived, by Satan's being overthrown, and the prince of the air (for fo the devil was called) with all his fallen angels, driven headlong into a difmal place, which is called *Hell*.

The recital of this truth made my man give the greateft attention, and he expreffed a great fatisfaction by his geftures, that God had fent the devil into the deep hole. And then I defired him to give great heed to what I had further to fay.

No fooner (proceeded I) was God freed from, and the heavens clear of this arch-traitor, but the Father fpeaks to the Son and Holy Spirit, who belonged to his effence, and were equal to him in power and glory, *Come let us make man*, (faid he) *in our own image, after our own likenefs*, Gen. i. 26. to have dominion over the creatures of the world which we have created. And thefe he intended fhould glorify him in heaven, according to their obedience in this ftate of probation on earth which was, as it were, to be the fchool to train

them

them up for those heavenly mansions. Now Satan seeing himself foiled, yet that God had not taken the power from him as prince of the air, which power Heaven defigned he should retain, whereby his creatures might be tried; in revenge for the difgrace he had received, he tempts Adam's wife Eve to tafte of the tree of knowledge of good and evil, which God had forbidden. He appears to her in the fhape of a ferpent, then a moft beautiful creature, and tells her, that it was no better than an impofition which God had put upon her and her hufband, not to eat of that fair fruit which he had created; that the tafte thereof would make them immortal like God himfelf; and confequently as great and powerful as he. Upon which fhe not only eat thereof herfelf, but made her hufband eat alfo, which brought them both under the heavenly difpleafure.

Here Friday expreffed a great concern; *Ah, poor mans!* (cried he) *naughty womans! naughty devil! make God not love de mans, make mans like devil himfelf.*

Friday, faid I, God ftill loved mankind; and though the devil tempted human nature fo far, he would not fuffer him to have an abfolute power over them. I have told you before of his tender love to his people, till they, like Lucifer, difobeyed his commands and rebelled againft him; and even then, how Jefus Chrift, his only Son, came to fave finners. But ftill every man that lives in the world is under temptation and trial. The devil has yet a power, as prince of the air, to fuggeft evil cogitations into our minds, and prompt us on to wicked actions, that he might glory in our deftruction. Whatever evil thoughts we have proceed from him; fo that God, in this our diftrefs, expects we fhould apply ourfelves to him by forvent prayer for fpeedy redrefs. He is not like

Bena-

Benamuckee, to let none come near him but *Oowa-kakee*, but suffers the people as well as priests to offer themselves at his feet, thereby to be delivered from the power and temptation of the devil.

But though at first my man *Friday* expressed some concern at the wickedness of *Lucifer*, I found it not so easy to imprint the right notions of him in his mind, as it was about the divine essence of God: for their nature assisted me in all my arguments, to shew to him plainly the necessity of a great first cause, and over-ruling governing power, of a secret directing Providence, and of the equity and reasonableness of paying adoration to our Creator; whereas there appeared nothing of all this in the notion of an evil spirit, of his first beginning, his nature, and above all, of his inclination to evil actions, and his power to tempt us to the like. And indeed this unlearned *Indian*, by the mere force of nature, puzzled me with one particular question, more than ever I could have expected.

I had, it seems, one day been talking to him of the omnipotent power of God, and his infinite abhorrence of sin, insomuch that the scriptures styled him *a consuming fire* to all the workers of iniquity ; and that it was in his power, whenever he pleased, to destroy all the world in a moment, the greater part of which are continually offending him.

When, with a serious attention, he had listened a great while to what I said, after I had been telling him how the devil was God's enemy in the hearts of men, and used all his malice and skill to defeat the good design of Providence, and destroy the kingdom of Christ in the world, and so forth: Very well, master, *(said Friday,)* you say God is so strong, so great, is he not much strong, much mightier than the naughty devil ? To be sure, *Fri-*
day,

day, said I, God is more wise, and stronger than the serpent : he is above the devil, which makes us pray to him, that he would tread down *Satan* under our feet, enable us to resist his violent temptations, and quench his fiery darts. *Why then,* answered *Friday* quickly, *if God, as you say, has much strong, much might as the devil, why God no kill devil, make no more tempt, no more do wicked?*

You may be certain I was strangely surprised at this question of my man's; and tho' an old man, I was but a young doctor, and consequently very ill qualified for a casuist, or a resolver of intricate doubts in religion. And as it required some time for me to study for an answer, I pretended not to hear him, nor to ask him what he said : but so earnest was he for an answer, as not to forget his question, which he repeated in the very same broken words as above. When I had recovered myself a little, *Friday*, said I, *God will at last punish him severely, being reserved for judgment, and is to be cast into the bottomless pit, to remain in fire everlasting.* But all this did not satisfy *Friday;* for returning upon me, he repeated my words, RESERVE AT LAST, *me no understand; but why not kill devil now, not kill devil, great, great while ago ? Friday*, said I, you may as well ask me why God does not kill you and me, when by our wicked actions we so much offend his Divine Majesty ? He gives us time to repent of our sins, and thereby we may obtain pardon. At these words, *obtain pardon, Friday* mused a great while; and at last looking me stedfastly in the face; *Well well,* said he, *that's very well; so you, I, devil, all wicked mans, all preserve, repent God, pardon all.*

Indeed here I was run down to the last extremity, when it became very evident to me, how mere natural notions will guide reasonable creatures to the knowledge of a Deity, and to the homage due

to the fupreme being of a God; but however, nothing but divine revelation can form the knowledge of Jefus Chrift, and of a redemption pur-
chafed for us, of the Mediator of the new cove-
nant, and of an Interceffor at the footftool of
God's throne; and therefore the gofpel of our
Lord and Saviour Jefus Chrift, that is, the Word
and Spirit of God, promifed for the guide and
fanctifier of his people, are the moft neceffary in-
ftructors of the fouls of men, in the faving knowledge of the Almighty, and the means to attain
eternal happinefs.

And now I found it neceffary to put an end to
this difcourfe between my man and me; for which
purpofe I rofe up haftily, and made as if I had
fome occafion to go out, fending *Friday* for fomething that was a good way off. I then fell on my
knees, and befeeched God that he would infpire
me fo far as to guide the poor favage in the knowledge of Chrift, to anfwer his queftions more clearly, that his confcience might be convinced, his
eyes opened, and his foul faved. When he returned again, I entered into a very long difcourfe with
him, upon the fubject of the world's redemption
by the Saviour of it, and the doctrine of repentance preached from heaven, together with an holy faith in our bleffed Redeemer Jefus Chrift: and
then I proceeded to explain to him, according to
my weak capacity, the reafon why our Saviour
took not on him the nature of angels, but rather
the feed of *Abraham*; and how the fallen angels
had no benefit by that redemption; and, laftly,
that he came only to the loft fheep of the houfe of
Ifrael, and the like. God knows I had more fincerity than knowledge in all the ways I took for
this poor *Indian*'s inftruction; and I muft acknowledge, what I believe every body that acts upon
the fame principle will find, that in laying heavenly

ly truths open before him, I informed and instruct-
ed myself in many things, that either I did not
know, or had not perfectly confidered before; fo
that however this poor creature might be improved, by my inftruction, certain it is, that I myself
had great reafon to be thankful to Providence for
fending him to me. His company allayed my grief,
and made my habitation comfortable; and when I
reflected, that the folitary life to which I had been
fo long confined that made me to look further towards heaven, by making me the inftrument, under Providence, to fave the life, and for aught I
know, the foul of this poor favage, by bringing
him to the knowledge of Jefus Chrift, it caufed a
fecret joy to fpread through every part of my foul;
and I frequently rejoiced, that ever I was brought
into this place, which I once thought the moft miferable part of the world.

In this thankful frame of mind did I afterwards
continue, while I abode on the ifland; and for
three years did my man and I live in the greateft
enjoyment of happinefs. Indeed I believe the favage was as good a Chriflian as I; and I hope we
were equally penitent; and fuch penitents as were
comforted and reftored by God's Holy Spirit; for
now we had the word of the Lord to inftruct us
in the right way, as much as if we had been on
the Englifh fhore.

By the conftant application I made of the Scriptures, as I read them to my man Friday, I earneftly endeavoured to make him underftand every
part of it, as much as lay in my power. He
alfo, on the other hand, by his very ferious queftions and inquiries, made me a much better pro-
ficient in fcripture-knowledge than I fhould have
been by my own private reading and ftudy. I muft
not omit another thing, proceeding from the experience I had in my retirement: it was that in-

finite and inexpreſſible bleſſing, the knowledge of
God through Jeſus Chriſt, which was, ſo plain and,
eaſy to be underſtood, as immediately to direct me
to carry on the great work of ſincere repentance
for my ſins, and laying hold of a Saviour for eternal life, to a practical ſtated reformation, and obedience to all God's inſtitutions, without the aſſiſtance of a reverend and orthodox divine; and eſpecially by this ſame inſtruction, ſo to enlighten this
ſavage creature; as to make him ſo good a Chriſtian as very few could exceed him. And there
was only this great thing wanting, that I had no authority to adminiſter the holy ſacrament, that heavenly participation of Chriſt's body and blood;
yet however we reſted ourſelves content, that God
would accept our-deſires, and according to our
faith have mercy on us.

But what we wanted one way was made up in
another; and that was univerſal peace in our little church. We had no diſpures and wranglings
about the nature and quality of the holy, bleſſed,
and undivided Trinity, no niceties in doctrine, or
ſchemes of church-government; no ſour and mo-
roſe diſſenters to impoſe more ſublimated notions
upon us, no pedant ſophiſters to confound us with
unintelligible myſteries: but, inſtead of all this,
we enjoyed the moſt certain guide to Heaven, that
is, the word of God; beſides which, we had the
comfortable views of his Spirit leading us to the
truth, and making us both willing and obedient to
the inſtruction of his word. As the knowledge
and practice of this are the principal means of ſalvation, I cannot ſee what it avails any Chriſtian
church, or man, in the world, to amuſe himſelf
with ſpeculations and opinions, except it be to diſ-
play their particular vanity and affectation.

You may well ſuppoſe, that, by the frequent
diſcourſe we had together, my man and me became

came moſt intimately acquainted, and that there was but very little that I could ſay, but what Friday underſtood: and indeed he ſpoke very fluently, though it was but broken Engliſh. I now took a particular pleaſure in relating all my adventures, eſpecially thoſe that occurred ſince my being caſt on this iſland. I made him underſtand that wonderful myſtery, as he conceived, of gun-powder and bullet, and taught him how to ſhoot. I alſo preſented to him a knife, which pleaſed him exceedingly, making him a belt, with a frog hanging thereto, like thoſe in which we wear hangers in England; and inſtead of a hanger to put in the frog, I gave him a hatchet, which was not only a good, but even a better weapon upon many occaſions. In a word, my man thus accoutered, looked upon himſelf as great as Don Quixote, when that celebrated champion went to combat the windmill.

I next gave him a very particular deſcription of the territories of Europe, and in a particular manner of Old England, the place of my nativity. I laid before him the manner of our worſhipping God, our behaviour one to another, and how we trade in ſhips to every part in the univerſe. I then told him my misfortunes in being ſhipwrecked, ſhowing him, as near as I could, the place where the ſhip lay, which had been gone long before: but I brought him to the ruins of my boat, which before my whole ſtrength could not move, but now was almoſt rotten, and fallen to pieces. I obſerved my man Friday to view this boat with an uncommon curioſity; which when he had done, he ſtood pondering a great while, and ſaid nothing. At laſt, ſaid I, Friday, what makes you ponder ſo much? He replied, *O Maſter, me ſee like boat come to peace at my nation.*

It was ſome time indeed before I underſtood

what

what my man meant; but examining ſtrickly into
it, I plainly found, that ſuch another boat reſembling mine had come upon the country where
he dwelt; that is to ſay, by his farther explanation, that the boat was driven there through violent ſtorms and ſtreſs of weather. It then came
into my mind, that ſome European ſhip having been
caſt away, the poor diſtreſſed creatures were forced to have recourſe to the boat to ſave their lives;
and being all, as I thought, drowned, I never concerned myſelf to aſk any thing concerning them,
but my only inquiry was about the boat, and what
deſcription my man could give of it.

Indeed Friday anſwered my demands very well,
making every thing very plain to my underſtanding; but beyond meaſure was I ſatisfied, when he
told me, with great warmth and ardour, *O Maſter,
we ſave white mans from drown;* upon which I
immediately aſked him, if there were any *whitemans,* as he called them, in the boat; *Yes, yes,*
ſaid he, *the boat full, very full of white mans.* How
many, Friday? ſaid I, hereupon he numbered his
fingers, and counted ſeventeen.   And when I aſked him what became of them all, and whether they
lived or not? he replied, *Yes maſter, they all live,
they be live among my nation.*   This information
put freſh thoughts into my head, that theſe muſt be
thoſe very men who before I concluded had been
ſwallowed up in the ocean after they had left their
ſhip, that had ſtruck upon the rocks of my kingdom, and after eſcaping the fury of the deep, landed upon the wild ſhore, and committed themſelves
to the fury of theſe devouring Indians.

The manner of their cruelties to one another,
which conſequently, as I thought, muſt be acted
with greater barbarity to ſtrangers, created in me
a great anxiety, and made me ſtill more curious
to aſk Friday concerning them; he told me he was
ſure.

fure they ftill lived there, having refided among them above four years, and that the favages gave them victuals to live upon. But pray, Friday, faid I, whence proceeded all this good nature and generofity? How came it to pafs that they did not kill and eat them, to pleafe their devouring appetites; and occafion fo fplendid an entertainment among them? *No, no* faid Friday, *they not kill 'em, they make brother with 'em;* by which I underftood there was a truce between them. And then I had a more favourable opinion of the Indians, upon Friday's uttering thefe words. *My nation, t'other nation no eat mans, but when mans make war fight;* as though he had faid, that neither thofe of his kingdom, nor any other nations that he knew of, ever ate their fellow-creatures, but fuch as their law of arms allowed to be devoured; that is, thofe miferable captives, whofe misfortune it fhould be to be made prifoners of war.

Some confiderable time after, upon a very pleafant day, in moft ferene weather, my man and I ftood up on the top of a hill, on the eaft fide of the ifland, whence I had once before beheld the continent of America. I could not tell immediately what was the matter; for fuddenly Friday fell a jumping and dancing as if he had been mad; and upon my demanding the reafon of his behaviour, *O joy,* faid he, *O glad! there fee my country, there my nation, there live white mans gether.* And indeed fuch a rapturous fenfe of pleafure appeared in his countenance, that his eyes had an uncommon fparkling and brightnefs, and fuch a ftrange eagernefs, as if he had a longing defire to be in his own country again. This made me not fo well fatisfied with my man Friday as before; for, by this appearance, I made no difpute, but that if he could get back thither again, he would not only be unmindful of what religion I had taught him,

but

but likewife of the great obligation he owed me for his wonderful deliverance : nay, that he would not only inform his country-men of me, but accompany hundreds of them to my kingdom, and make me a miferable facrifice like thofe unhappy wretches taken in battle.

Indeed I was very much to blame to have thefe cruel and unjuft fufpicions, and muft freely own I wronged the poor creature very much, who was of a quite contrary temper. And had he had that difcerning acutenefs which many Europeans have, he would certainly have perceived my coldnefs and indifference, and alfo have been very much concerned upon that account; as I was now more circumfpected, I had much leffened my kindnefs and familiarity with him, and while this jealoufy continued, I ufed that artful way (now too much in fafhion, the occafion of ftrife and diffention) of pumping him daily, thereby to difcover whether he was deceitful in his thoughts and inclinations : but certainly he had nothing in him but what was confiftent with the beft principles, both as a religious Chriftian and a grateful friend.; and indeed I found every thing he faid was fo ingenuous and innocent, that I had no room for fufpicion ; and, in fpite of all uneafinefs, he not only made me entirely his own again, but alfo caufed me much to lament that I ever conceived one ill thought of him.

As we were walking up the fame hill another day, when the weather was fo hazy at fea, that I could not perceive the continent, Friday, faid I, don't you wifh yourfelf to be in your own country, your own nation, among your old friends and acquaintances? *Yes*, faid he, *me much O glad to be at my own nation.* And what would you do there, Friday? Would you turn wild again eat man's flefh, and be a favage as you were formerly? *No*
no,

no, (anſwered he, full of concern, and ſhaking his head,) *Friday now tell them to live good, tell them pray God, tell them to eat corn bread, cattle fleſh, milk, no eat man again.* But ſurely, replied I, if you ſhould offer to do all this, they will kill you, and to manifeſt their contempt of ſuch inſtruction, eat you up when they have done. He then put on a grave, yet innocent and ſmooth countenance, ſaying, *No, they no kill me, they willing love learn :* that is, that they would be very willing to learn : adding withal, *that they had learned much of the bearded mans that come in the boat.* Will you, ſaid I, go back again, Friday ? He ſmiled at that, and told me, that he could not ſwim ſo far. But, ſaid I, I will make a canoe for you : *Yes, Maſter,* ſaid he, *me go if you go, me no go if you ſtay.* I go, Friday ! why, would you have them eat me up, and devour your kind maſter ? *No, no,* ſaid he, *me make them not eat maſter, me make they much love you ;* that is, he would tell them how I had ſlain his enemies, and thereby ſaved his life, for which reaſon he would make them love me : and then he related to me, as well as he was able, how exceeding kind thoſe of his nation were to the white, or bearded men, as he called them, who, in their great calamity, were driven into their country.

It was from this time, indeed, I had ſtrong inclinations to venture over, and uſe my utmoſt efforts, if poſſible, to join theſe white-bearded men, who undoubtedly were Spaniards or Portugueſe; for thought I, it muſt be certainly a better and ſafer way to eſcape when there is a good company, than for me alone, from an iſland forty miles off the ſhore, and without any aſſiſtance. Some days after, Friday and I being at work, as uſual, at the ſame time diverting ourſelves with various diſcourſes, I told him I had a boat which I would beſtow

upon

upon him, whenever he pleafed to return to his own nation : and to convince him of the truth of what I faid, I took him with me to the other fide of the ifland, where my frigate lay, and then taking it from under the water, (for I always kept it funk for fear of a difcovery) we both went into it to fee how it would manage fuch an expedition.

And really never could any be more dexterous in rowing than my faithful fervant, making the boat go as faft again as I could. Well, now, Friday, faid I, fhall we now go to your fo much defired nation ? But inftead of meeting with that chearfulnefs I expected, he looked very dull and melancholy at my faying fo ; which indeed at firft furprifed me, till he made me fenfible, that his concern was about the boat's being too fmall to go fo far a voyage. Upon which I let him underftand I had a much bigger ; and accordingly the next day went to the place where the firft boat lay, which I had made, when all the ftrength I had, or art I could ufe, failed me in my attempt to get it into the water; but now it having lain in the fun two and twenty years, and no care being taken of it all that while, it became in a manner rotten. My man told me, that fuch a boat would do very well to the purpofe, fufficient to carry *enough vittle, dring, bread*, for that was his manner of talking. In fhort, my mind being ftrongly fixed upon my defign of going over with him to the continent, I very plainly told him, that we would both go and make a boat full as big, and more proportionable than that, wherein he might fafely return to his own nation.

Thefe words made Friday look fo very penfive, that I thought he would have fallen at my feet. It was fome time before he could fpeak a word, which made me afk him what was the matter with

him ?

him? He replied in a very soft and moving tone, *What has poor Friday done? why are you angry mad with poor servant? What me done, O what me done?* Friday, said I, you never yet have offended me; what makes you think I am angry with you, when I am not angry at all? *You no angry, no angry,* said he several times; *if you be no angry, why den send Friday over great water to my own nation?* Why, surely, Friday, answered I, did not you wish to be there when from a mountain you beheld the place where you was born? and is it not to satisfy your desires that I am willing to give you leave to return thither? *Yes, yes, said Friday, me wish be there sure 'nough, but me den wish master there too; no wish Friday there, no master there.* In short, he could not endure the thoughts of going there without me. I go there, Friday, said I, what shall I do there?——He answered very quickly, *O master you do great deal much good, you teach all de wild mans to be good tame mans; you learn dem to be sober, live good life, to know God and pray God.* Alas! poor Friday, said I, what can I do against their priests of Benamuckee, or indeed what good can I make your nation sensible of, when I myself am but a poor ignorant man? *No, no, master said he, you be no ignorant, you teachee me good, you teachee dem good.* You shall go without me, Friday, said I, for I don't care to accompany you thither; I would rather live in this solitude than venture among such inhuman savages. Go your way, since you desire it, and leave me alone by myself, as I was before I saved your life.

Never was any creature more thunder-struck than *Friday* was at these words. *Go me away, leave master away,* said he, after a long silence; *no, no, Friday die, Friday live not, master gone;* as though he had said, I neither can nor will live,

if

if my mafter fends me from him. And here I cannot but take notice of the ftrong ties of friendfhip which many times furpafs thofe of confanguinity: for often we find a great difagreement among kindred; and when there is any feeming regard for each other, it is very feldom true, and fcarce ever lafting, if powerful intereft does not bear the fway; and that alone is often the occafion of the greateft hatred in the world, which is to defire the death of parents and relations, for the fake of acquiring their fortunes: but there was no fuch thing between my fervant and me: inftead of which there was the greateft gratitude, and the moft fincere love; he found me not only his deliverer, but his preferver and comforter; not a fevere and cruel tyrant, but a kind, loving, and affable friend. He wanted for no manner of fuftenance; and when he was ill, or out of order, I was his phyfician, not only for his body, but his foul; and therefore no wonder was it, that fuch an innocent creature, long fince divefted of his former natural cruelty, fhould have an uncommon concern at fo cruel a feparation from me, which pierced him to the very foul, and made him defire even to die, rather than live without me.

After I had told *Friday*, in a very carelefs manner, that he fhould be at his liberty as foon as the boat was made, the language of his eyes expreffed all imaginable confufion; when immediately running to one of his hatchets, which he ufed to wear as a defenfive weapon, he gives it into my hand, with a heart fo full, that he could fcarcely fpeak. *Friday*, faid I, what is it you mean? what muft I do with this? *Only kill Friday*, faid he, *Friday care not live long.* But what muft I kill you for? replied I again. *Ah! dear mafter, what made you Friday fave from eat a me up, fo keep long Friday, make Friday love God and not love Benamuckee,*
and

and now Friday send away, never see Friday more.
As though the poor creature had said, Alas, my
dearest kind master, how comes it to pass, that
after having ventured your precious life to save
me from the jaws of the devouring cannibals like
myself, after such a tender regard to provide for
me such a comfortable nourishment, and continuing so long a kind master, and a most sincere
friend; and after making me forsake the false notion of an Indian Deity, and worship the true
God in spirit and in truth: after all this, how
comes it now, that you are willing to send me a-
way to my former course of living, by which means
undoubtedly we shall be dead to each other; but
greater must be my misfortune, that I shall never
behold my best friend I have in the world any more.
And this undoubtedly, though he could not express
himself so clearly, must be his sentiments; for the
tears ran down his cheeks in such a plentiful manner, that I had much ado to refrain from weeping
also when I beheld the poor creature's affection;
so that I was forced to comfort him in the best
manner I could, which I did, by telling him, if
he was content to abide with me, I should be ever
willing to keep him.

After Friday's grief was something abated, more
fully to convince me of his affection, he said, *U
master, me not care to be in my nation, leave you
here; me desire nation learn good, that's all;*
meaning, that his desire was for the conversion of
that barbarous people. But as I had no apostolic
mission, nor any concern about their salvation, so
I had not the least intention or desire of undertaking it: and the strength of my inclination, in
order to escape, proceeded chiefly from my late
discourse with Friday, about these seventeen white
bearded men that had been driven upon the barbarian coast, whom I designed to join, as the on-

ly means to further our escape. To which intent my man and I went to search for a proper tree to fell, whereof we might make a large periagua or canoe, to undertake the voyage: and indeed we were not long in finding one fit for our purpose, there being enough of wood in the island to have built a fleet of large vessels, but the thing we principally wanted was, to get one so near the water, that we might launch it after it was finished, and not commit so horrid a mistake as I had done once before.

Well, after a great search for what was best and most convenient, Friday at last, whose judgment in such affairs was much superior to mine, pitches upon a kind of wood the most fitting for it. To this day I cannot tell the name of the tree, nor describe it any other way, than only by saying, that it is very like what we call *fustic*, or betwixt that and the Nicaragua wood, being much of the same colour and smell. But though my man exceeded me in the knowledge of the most proper tree, yet I shewed him a much better and cleaner way to make a canoe than ever he knew before: for he was for burning the hollow or cavity of the tree, in order to make this boat; but I then told him how we might do it with tools, learning him at the same time how to use them, which indeed he did very dexterously; so that in a month's labour we finished it, making it very handsome, by cutting the outside into the true shape of a boat. After this it took us a full fortnight before we could get her into the water, which we did, as it were, inch by inch, upon great rollers: but when she was in, she would have carried twenty men, with all the ease imaginable.

As I was very well pleased, you may be sure, at the launching of this man of war of mine, I was no lefs amazed to behold with what dexterity my man would manage her, turn her, and paddle her along. Well, Friday, faid I, what do you think of it now? Do you think this will carry us over? *Yes, Mafter*, faid he, *me venture over well, though great blow wind*. But my defign was yet farther, which he was infenfible of; and that was to make a maft and fail, and to provide her with an anchor and cable. As to a maft, that was no difficult thing at all to procure; fo I fixed upon a ftraight young cedar-tree, which I found near the place, great plenty of it abounding in the ifland; and fetting Friday to cut it down, I gave him particular directions how to fhape and order it; but as to the fail, that I managed myfelf. I very well knew I had fome old ones, or pieces of fails enough, which had lain fix and twenty years by me; but not begin careful to preferve them, as thinking I fhould have no occafion to ufe them any more, when I came to look them over, I found them almoft all rotten, except two; and with thefe I went to work, and after a great deal of pains and awkward tedious ftitching for want of needles, at length I finifhed three cornered ugly thing, like what we call in England a fhoulder of mutton fail, to go with a boom at bottom, and a little fmall fprit at the top, like thofe which our longboats ufe, and which I very well knew how to manage: efpecially fince it was like that which I had in my patron's fifhing boat, when with my boy Xury I made my efcape from the Barbarian fhore.

It was near two months, I think, before I compleated this work, that is, the rigging, and fitted my maft and fails; and indeed they were nicely done, having made a fmall ftay, and a fail, or forefail to it, to affift, if we fhould turn to the weftward; and, which was ftill more, I fixed a rudder to the ftern of her, to fteer with; and though L was but a very indifferent ſhipwright, yet, as I was ſenſible of the great uſefulneſs and abſolute neceſſity of a thing like this, I applied myſelf to it with ſuch a conſtant application, that at laſt I accompliſhed my deſign: but what with the many dull contrivances I had about it, and the failure of many things, it coſt me as much pains in ordering as in making the boat. Beſides, when all this was done, I had my man to teach what belonged to its navigation; for though he very well underſtood how to paddle a canoe along, he was an utter ſtranger to a ſail and rudder, and was amazed when he ſaw me work the boat to and again in the ſea, by them, and how the ſail gibbed and filled this way or that way, as the courſe we ſailed changed. After ſome time, and a little uſe, I made all theſe things very familiar to him, ſo that he became an expert ſailor, except in relation to the compaſs, and that I could make him underſtand but little of. But as it hapenned, there was ſeldom occaſion for it, there being but little cloudy weather, and ſcarce ever any fog in thoſe parts; the ſtars were always viſible in the night, and the ſhore perſpicuous by day, except in the rainy ſeaſon, which confined every one to his habitation.

Thus entered in the ſeven and twentieth year of my reign, or captivity, which you pleaſe, (the laſt three of which, bleſſed with the company of my man Friday, ought not to be reckoned,) I kept the anniverſary of my landing here, with the ſame thankfulneſs to God, for his tender mercies, as I did before; and certainly, as I had great cauſe for a thankful acknowledgment for my deliverance at firſt, I had much greater now, for ſuch ſingular and additional teſlimonies of the care of Providence over me, in all my diſtreſſes, both of body and mind, and the great hopes I had of being effectually and ſpeedily delivered; for I had a ſtrong impreſſion upon my mind,

mind, that I should not be another year in this island. But, however, I still continued on with my husbandry, digging, planting, and fencing, as usual ; gathering and curing my grapes, and doing all other things that were necessary.

And now the rainy season beginning to come on, obliged me to keep the longer within doors ; but before this, I brought my new vessel into the creek, where I had landed my rafts from the ship, and haling her up to the shore, I ordered my man Friday to dig a dock sufficient to hold her in, and deep enough to give her water, wherein she might float ; and then, when the tide was out, we made a strong dam cross the end of it, to keep out the water ; by which means she lay dry, as to the tide from the sea ; and to keep the rain from her, we thatched her over, as it were, with boughs of trees, like a house ; and so we waited for the months of November and December, in which I designed to venture over the ocean.

No sooner did the seasonable weather begin to draw near, but so much was I elevated with this new designed adventure, that I daily prepared for the voyage.   The first thing I thought on was, to lay by a certain quantity of provisions, as a sufficient store for such an expedition, intending in a week or fortnight's time to open the dock, and launch out the boat for that purpose. But one morning as I was very busy upon something necessary for this occasion, I called Friday to me, and bid him go to the sea-shore, and see if he could find a turtle or tortoise, a thing which we commonly had once a week, as much upon account of the eggs, as for the sake of the flesh. He had not been long gone, but he came running back, as though he was pursued for life, and as it were flew over my outward wall, or fence, like one that felt not the ground, or steps, he set his feet on ;

and

and before I had time to enquire the reason of his precipitation, he cries out, *O dear master, O sorrow! sorrow! Bad! O bad!* Why, what's the matter, *Friday?* said I. *O yonder, yonder,* said he, *there be one, two, or three canoes! two, three.* Surely (thought I) there must be six, by my man's way of reckoning; but, on a stricter inquiry I found there were but three. Well, Friday, said I, don't be terrified, I warrant you we will not only defend ourselves against 'em, but kill the most of these cruel savages. But though I comforted him in the best manner I could, the poor creature trembled so, that I scarce knew what to do with him: *O master,* said he, *they come look* Friday, *cut pieces* Friday, *cut a me up.* Why, Friday, said I, they will eat me up as well as you, and my danger is as great as yours. But since it is so, we must resolve to fight for our lives. What say you? can you fight, Friday? Yes said he very faintly, *me shoot, me kill what I can, but there come great many number.* That's no matter, said I again, our guns will terrify those that we do not kill: I am very willing to stand by you to the last drop of my blood? now tell me, if you will do the like by me, and obey my orders in whatsoever I command? Friday then answered, *O master, me lose life for you, me die when you bid die.* Thus concluding all questions concerning his fidelity, immediately I fetched him a good dram of rum, (of which I had been a very good husband,) and gave it him to comfort his heart. After he had drank it, I ordered him to take the two fowling pieces, which we always carried, and load them with large swan shot, as big as small pistol bullets; then I took four muskets, and loaded them with two slugs, and five small bullets each, charging my two pistols each with a brace. I hung my great sword, as customary, naked to my side, and gave Friday

his

his hatchet, as a most excellent weapon for defence.

Thus prepared, I thought as well of myself as any knight-errant that ever handled a sword and spear. I took my perspective glass, and went up to the side of the hill, to see what I could discover; and I perceived very soon, by the glass, that there were one and twenty savages, three prisoners, and three canoes; and that their chief concern seemed to be the triumphant banquet upon the three poor human bodies; a thing which by this time I had observed was very common with them. I also remarked, that they did not land at that place from whence Friday made his escape, but nearer to the creek, where the shore was low, and where a thick wood came very close to the sea. My soul was then filled with indignation and abhorrence at such inhuman wretches, which put a period to all my former thoughts in their vindication: neither would I give myself time to consider their right of conquest, as I had done before; but descending from the mountain, I came down to Friday, and told him, I was resolved to go speedily to them and kill them all; asking him again, in the same breath, if he would stand by me? When by this time being recovered from his fright, and his spirit much cheered with the dram I had given him, he was very pleasant, yet seriously telling me, as he did before, *When I bid die, he would die.*

And now it was, having fixed my resolution in so strong a manner, that nothing could divest my breast of its uncommon fury, I immediately divided the loaded arms betwixt us. To my man Friday I gave a pistol to stick in his girdle, with three guns upon his shoulder, a weight too great I confess to bear; but what must a poor king do, who had but one soldier in the world? But to shew I made him bear no more than what I would

lay

lay on myself, I stuck the other pistol in my girdle, and other three guns upon my shoulders; nay something more, but that was like Æsop's burden, a small bottle of rum, which was soon lightened to our exceeding refreshment. Thus we marched out, under a ponderous load of armour, like two invincible champions, with a quantity of powder and bullets to stand our battle, and load again, when the pieces were discharged. And now my orders being to be obeyed, I charged Friday to keep close behind me, and not to stir, or shoot, or attempt any thing till I commanded him; and, in the interim, not to speak so much as one word. It was in this order I fetched a compass to the right hand, of near a mile, as well to get over the creek, as to attain the wood; by this I thought to come within shot of them before I could be discerned; as I found by my glass would not be difficult to accomplish.

But how fickle and wavering is the mind of men, even in our greatest fury and strongest inclination? For while I was taking this march, my resolution began to abate, not through fear of their numbers, who were a parcel of naked unarmed wretches, but those reflections occurred to my thoughts; What power was I commissioned with, or what occasion or necessity had I to go and imbrue my hands in human blood, and murder people that had neither done nor intended to do me any wrong? They were innocent in particular as to me; and their barbarous custom was not only their misfortune, but a sign that God had left them in the most immense stupidity; but yet did not warrant me to be a judge of their actions, much less an executioner of his righteous judgments; that, on the contrary, whenever he thought fit, he would take vengeance on them himself, and punish them in a national way, according to their

national

national crimes; but that was nothing at all to me, who had no concern with them. Indeed my man *Friday* might juftify himfelf, becaufe they were his declared enemies, of that very fame nation that went to facrifice him before, and indeed it was lawful for him to attack them, which I could not fay was fo with refpect to me. So warmly did thefe things prefs upon my thoughts all the way I went, that I only refolved to place myfelf fo as to behold their bloody entertainment, without falling upon them, except fomething more than ordinary, by God's fpecial direction, fhould oblige me thereto.

Thus fixed in my refolution, I entered in the thick wood, (my man *Friday* following me clofe behind,) when with all poffible wearinefs and filence I marched till I came to the fkirt of it, on that fide which was the neareft to them; for only one end of the wood interpofed between me and them. Upon which I called very foftly to *Friday*, and fhewing him a great tree, that was juft at the corner of the wood, I ordered him to repair thither, and bring me word, if he could plainly perceive their actions: Accordingly, he did as I commanded him, and came back with this melancholy ftory, that they were all about their fire, eating the flefh of one of their prifoners; and that another lay bound upon the fand, a little diftant from them, which they defigned for their next facrifice; and this, he told me, was not one of their nation, but one of thofe very bearded men, who was driven by a ftorm into their country, and of whom he had fo often talked to me about. You may be fure, that upon hearing this, my foul was ready to fink within me; when afcending up into a tree, I faw plainly by my glafs, a white man, who lay upon the beach of the fea, with his hands and feet ty'd with flags, or things refembling rufhes, being

ing, covered with cloaths, and feemed to be an *European*. From the tree where I took this pro-fpect, I perceived another tree, and a thicket be-yond it, about fifty yards nearer to them, than where I was; which, by taking a fmall circle round, I might come at undifcovered, and then I fhould be within half a fhot of thefe devourers. And this confideration alone, to be more per-fectly revenged upon them, made me with-hold my paffion, though I was enraged to the higheft de-gree imaginable; when going back about twenty paces, I got behind fome bufhes, which held all the way till I came to the other tree; and then I a-fcended to a little rifing ground, not above eigh-teen yards diftance, and there I had a full view of thefe creatures, and I could perceive all their ac-tions.

Such a fight did then appear, as obliged me not to lofe a moment's time. No lefs than nineteen of thefe dreadful wretches fat upon the ground, clofe huddled together, expreffing all the delight imaginable at fo barbarous an entertainment; and they had juft fent other two to murder this poor unhappy *Chriftian*, and bring him limb by limb to their fire; for they were juft then going to untie the bands from his feet, in order for death, as fet-ters are knocked off the feet of malefactors before they go to the place of execution. Hereupon, immediately turning to my man, Now, *Friday*, faid I, mind what I fay, fail in nothing, but do exactly as you fee me do. All which he promifing he would perform, I fet down one of my mufkets, and the fowling-piece upon the ground, and *Friday* did the fame by his; and with the other mufket I took my aim at the favages, bidding him do the like: Are you ready, faid I? *Yes, mafter*, faid he. Why then fire at them, faid I; and that very mo-ment I gave fire likewife.

I only

I only killed one, and wounded two; but my man *Friday*, taking his aim much better than I, killed two, and wounded three. You may be sure they were in a dreadful consternation, at such an unexpected disaster; and those who yet had escaped our penetrating shot, immediately jumped upon their feet, but were in such confusion, that they knew not which way to run or look, not knowing from whence their destruction came. We then threw down our pieces, and took up others, giving a second dreadful volley; but as they were loaded only with swan-shot, or small pistol bullets, we perceived only two of them fall; though many were wounded, who run yelling and screaming about like mad creatures. Now *Friday*, said I, lay down your piece, and take up the musket, and follow me. He did so, with great courage, when shewing ourselves to the savages, we gave a great shout, and made directly to the poor victim, who would have been sacrificed, had not our first fire obliged the butchers, with three others, to jump into a canoe. By my order, *Friday* fired at them, at which shot I thought he had killed them all, by reason of their falling to the bottom of the boat; however, he killed two, and mortally wounded a third. In the mean time, I cut the flags that tied the hands and feet of the poor creature, and lifting him up, asked him in the *Portuguese* tongue, *What he was?* He answered me in *Latin, Christianus*; but so very weak and faint, that he could scarce stand or speak. Immediately I gave him a dram, and a piece of bread to cherish him, and asked him what countryman he was? He said, *Espaniola*, and then uttered all the thankfulness imaginable for his deliverance. *Signior*, (said I with as much *Spanish* as I was master of,) let us talk afterwards, but fight now; here, take this sword and pistol, and do what you can. And indeed he did

O

so

ſo with ſuch courage and intrepidity, that he cut two of them to pieces in an inſtant, the ſavages not having the power to fly for their lives. I ordered *Friday* to run for thoſe pieces we had left at the tree, which he brought me with great ſwiftneſs, and then I gave him my muſket, while I loaded the reſt. But now there happened a fierce encounter between the *Spaniard* and one of the ſavages, who had made at him with one of their wooden ſwords; and though the former was as brave as could be expected, having twice wounded his enemy in the head; yet, being weak and faint, the *Indian* had thrown him upon the ground, and was wreſting my ſword out of his hand, which the *Spaniard* very wiſely quitting, drew out his piſtol, and ſhot him through the body before I could come near him, though I was running to his aſſiſtance. As to *Friday*, he purſued the flying wretches with his hatchet, diſpatching three, but the reſt were too nimble for him. The *Spaniard* taking one of the fowling-pieces, wounded two, who running into the wood, *Friday* purſued and killed one; but the other, notwithſtanding his wounds, plunged himſelf into the ſea, and ſwam to thoſe two who were left in the canoe, which, with one wounded, were all that eſcaped out of one and twenty. The account is as follows:

Killed at firſt ſhot from the tree,	3	*Killed or died of their wounds*		4
At the ſecond ſhot	2	*Eſcaped in the boat, whereof one wounded, if not ſlain*		4
By Friday *in the boat*	2			
Ditto of thoſe firſt wounded	2			
Ditto in the wood	1	Total		21
By the Spaniard	3			

The ſavages in the canoe worked very hard to
get

get out of our reach, and *Friday* was as eager in pursuing them; and indeed I was no less anxious about their escape, lest after the news had been carried to their people, they should return in multitudes, and destroy us. So being resolved to pursue them, I jumped into one of their canoes, and bid *Friday follow* me; but no sooner was I in, than, to my surprise, I found another poor creature, bound hand and foot for the slaughter, just as the *Spaniard* had been, with very little life in him. Immediately I unbound him, and would have helped him up; but he could neither stand nor speak, but groaned so piteously, as thinking he was only unbound in order to be slain. Hereupon I bid *Friday* speak to him and tell him of his deliverance; when pulling out my bottle, I made the poor wretch drink a dram, which, with the joyful news he had received, so revived his heart, that he sat up in the boat. As soon as *Friday* began to hear him speak, and look more fully in his face, it would have moved any one to tears to perceive his uncommon transports of joy; for he kissed, embraced him, hugged him, cried, laughed, hallooed, jumped about, danced, sung, then cried again, wrung his hands, beat his face and head, then sung and jumped about again, like a distracted creature: so that it was a great while before I could make him speak to me, or tell me what was the matter with him: but when he came to the liberty of his speech, at last he told me it was his father.

Here indeed I was infinitely moved to see that dutiful and tender affection this poor savage had to his aged parent. He would sit down by him in the boat, open his breast, and hold his father's head close to his bosom, half an hour together, to cherish it; then he took his arms and ancles, which were stiff and numbed with binding, and

chaffed

chaffed and rubbed them with his hands; by which means perceiving what the cafe was, I gave him fome rum, which proved of great benefit to him.

While we were bufy in this action, the favages had gotten almoft out of fight; and happy it was we did not purfue them; for there arofe from the north-weft, which continued all night long, fuch a violent ftorm, that I could not fuppofe otherwife but that they were all drowned. After this, I called *Friday* to me, and afked him if he had given his father any bread? He fhook his head, and faid, *None, not one bit, me eat a up all?* fo I gave him a cake of bread out of a little pouch I carried for this end. I likewife gave him a dram for himfelf, and two or three bunches of raifins for his father. Both thefe he carried to him, for he would make him drink the dram to comfort him.

Away he then runs out of the boat as if he was bewitched, with fuch an extraordinary fwiftnefs, that he was out of fight as it were in an inftant; but at his return I perceived him flacken his pace, becaufe he had fomething in his hand. And this I found to be, as he approached nearer, an earthen jug with fome water to his father, with two more cakes of bread, which he delivered into my hands. Being very thirfty myfelf, I drank fome of the water, of which when his father had drank fufficiently, it more revived his fpirits than all the rum I had given him.

I then called *Friday* to me, and ordered him to carry the *Spaniard* one of the cakes, and fome water, who was repofing himfelf upon a green place under the fhade of a tree, but fo weak, that though he exerted himfelf, he could not ftand upon his feet. Upon which I ordered *Friday* to rub and bathe his ancles with rum, as he did his father's. But every minute he was employed in this, he would caft a wifhful eye towards the boat, where

he

he left his father fitting; who fuddenly difappear-
ing, he flew like lightning to him, and finding he only laid himfelf down to eafe his limbs, he returned back to me prefently; and then I fpoke to the
Spaniard to let *Friday* help him, and lead him to
the boat, in order to be conveyed to my dwelling,
where I would take care of him. Upon which,
Friday took him upon his back, and fo carried him
to the canoe, fetting him clofe by his father; and
prefently ftepping out again, launched the boat off,
and paddled it along the fhore fafter than I could
walk, though the wind blew very hard too: and
having brought them fafe to the creek, away he
runs to fetch the other canoe; which he brought
to the creek almoft as foon as I got to it by land;
when wafting me over, he took our new guefts
out of the boat; but fo weak were they, that I
was forced to make a kind of a hand-barrow; and
when I came to my caftle, not being willing to
make an entrance into my wall, we made them a
handfome tent, covered with old fails, and boughs
of trees, making two good beds of rice-ftraw,
with blankets to lye upon and cover them. Thus,
like an abfolute king, over fubjects who owed
their lives to me, I thought myfelf very confiderable, efpecially as I had now three religions in
my kingdom, my man *Friday* being a Proteftant,
his father a Pagan, and the *Spaniard* a Papift:
but I gave *liberty of confcience* to them all.

To get provifions for my poor weak fubjects, I
ordered *Friday* to kill me a yearling goat; which,
when he had done, I cut off the hinder quarters,
and chopping it into fmall pieces, boiled and ftewed it, putting barley and rice into the broth.
This I carried into their tent, fet a table, dined
with them myfelf, and encouraged them. *Friday*
was my interpreter to his father, and indeed to
the *Spaniard* too, who fpoke the language of the

favages

savages pretty well. After dinner I ordered *Friday* to fetch home all our arms from the field of battle, and the next day to bury the dead bodies, which he did accordingly.

And now I made *Friday* inquire of his father whether he thought thofe favages had efcaped the late ftorm in their canoe; and if fo, whether they would not return with a power too great for us to refift? He anfwered, that he thought it im-poffible they could outlive the ftorm; or if they were driven fouthwardly, they would come to a land where they would as certainly be devoured, as if they were drowned in the fea. And fuppofe they had attained their own country, the ftrange-nefs of their fatal and bloody attack, would make them tell their people, that the reft of them were killed by thunder and lightning; not by the hand of man, but by two heavenly fpirits (meaning, *Friday* and me) who were fent from above to de-ftroy them. And this, he faid, he knew, becaufe he heard them fay the fame to one another. And indeed he was in the right on't; for I have heard fince, that thefe four men gave out, that whoever went into that inchanted ifland, would be deftroy-ed by fire from the gods.

No canoes appearing fome time after, as I ex-pefted, my apprehenfion ceafed: Inftead of which my former thoughts of a voyage took place, efpe-cially when *Friday's* father affured me I fhould have good ufage in his nation. As to the *Spani-ard*, he told me, that fixteen more of his country-men, and *Portuguefe*, who had been fhipwrecked, made their efcape thither; that though they were in union with the favages, yet they were very miferable for want of provifion and other necef-faries. When I afked him about the particulars of his voyage, he anfwered, that their fhip was bound from *Rio de la Plata* to the *Havannah*;

that

that when the ship was lost, only five men perished in the ocean; the rest having saved their lives
in the boat, were now landed on the main continent. And what do they intend to do there? said
I. He replied, they have concerted measures to
escape, by building a vessel, but that they had neither tools nor provisions, so that all their designs
came to nothing. Supposing (said I) I should make
a proposal, and invite them here, would they not
carry me prisoner to *New Spain?* He answered,
No: for he knew them to be such honest men, as
would scorn to act such inhuman baseness to their
deliverer: That if I pleased, he and the old savage would go over to them, talk with them a-
bout it, and bring me an answer: That they should
all swear fidelity to me as their leader, upon the
holy sacrament: and for his part, he would not
only do the same, but stand by me to the last drop
of his blood, should there be occasion.

Thefe solemn assurances made me resolve to
grant them relief, and to send these two over for
that purpose: but when every thing was ready, the
Spaniard raised an objection, which carried a great
deal of weight in it: *You know, Sir,* said he, *that
having been some time with you, I cannot but be
sensible of your stock of rice and corn, sufficient
perhaps, for us at present, but not for them, should
they come over presently; much less to victual a
vessel for an intended voyage. Want might be as
great an occasion for them to disagree and rebel,
as the children of* Israel *did against God himself,
when they wanted bread in the wilderness. And
therefore, my advice is to wait another harvest, and
in the mean time cultivate and improve some more
land, whereby we may have plenty of provisions,
in order to execute our design.*

This advice of the *Spaniard's* I approved extremely; and so satisfied was I of his fidelity, that,
I esteemed

I esteemed him ever after. And thus we all four went to work upon some more land, and against seed-time we had gotten so much cured and trimmed up, sufficient to sow 22 bushels of barley on, and 16 jars of rice, which was in short all the seed we had to spare.

As we were four in number, and by this time all in good health, we feared not a hundred Indians, should they venture to attack us; and while the corn was growing, I pitched upon some trees, fit to build us a large vessel, in case the *Spaniards* came over; which being marked, I ordered *Friday* and his father to cut them down, appointing the *Spaniard*, who was now my privy counsellor, to oversee and direct the work. I likewise increased my flocks of goats, by shooting the wild dams, and bringing home their kids to my inclosure: nor did I neglect the grape-season, but cured them as usual, though I had such a quantity now, as would have filled 80 barrels with raisins. And thus all of us being employed, they in working, and I in proving for them, till harvest came, God Almighty blessed the increase of it so much, that from twenty-two barrels of barley, we threshed out two hundred and twenty, and the like quantity of rice, sufficient to victual a ship fit to carry me and all the Spaniards to any part of America.

Thus the principal objection being answered by a sufficient stock of provision, I sent my two ambassadors over to the main-land, with a regal authority to administer the oaths of allegiance and fidelity, and have an instrument signed under their hands, though I never asked whether they had pen, ink or paper: when giving each of them a musket, eight charges of powder and ball, and provision enough for eight days, they sailed away with a fair gale, on a day when the moon was at full.

Scarce

Scarce a fortnight had passed over my head, but, impatient for their return, I laid me down to sleep one morning, when a strange accident happened, which was ushered in by my man's coming running to me, and calling aloud, *Master, master, they are come, they are come.* Upon which, not dreaming of any danger, out I jumped from my bed, put on my cloths, and hurried through my little grove; when looking towards the sea, I perceived a boat about a league and a half distant, standing in for the shore, with the wind fair. I beheld they did not come from the side where the land lay on, but from the southermost end of the island. So these being none of the people we wanted, I ordered *Friday* to lie still, till such time as I came down from the mountain, which with my ladder I now ascended, in order to discover more fully what they were; and now, with the help of my perspective glass, I plainly perceived an English ship, which I concluded it to be, by the fashion of its long boat; and which filled me with such uncommon transports of joy, that I cannot tell how to describe; and yet some secret doubts hung about me, proceeding from I know not what cause, as though I had reason to be upon my guard. And indeed I would have no man contemn the secret hints, and intimations of danger, which very often are given, when he may imagine there is no possibility of its being real: had not I been warned by this silent admonition, I had been in a worse situation than before, and perhaps inevitably ruined.

Not long it was, before I perceived the boat to approach the shore, as though they looked for a place where they might conveniently land; and at last they ran their boat on shore upon the beach, about half a mile's distance; which proved so much the happier for me, since, had they come into the creek,

creek, they had landed juſt at my door, and might not only have forced me out of my caſtle, but plundered me of all I had in the world. Now I was fully convinced they were all Engliſhmen, three of which were unarmed and bound; when immediately the firſt four or five leapt on ſhore and took thoſe three out of the boat as priſoners; one of whom I could perceive uſed the moſt paſſionate geſtures of intreaty, affliction, and deſpair, while the others, in a leſſer degree, ſhewed abundance of concern.

Not knowing the meaning of this, I was very much aſtoniſhed, and I beckoned to *Friday*, who was below, to aſcend the mountain, and likewiſe view this ſight. *O Maſter*, ſays he to me, *you ſee* Engliſh *mans eat priſoners as well as* Savage *mans*. And do you think they will eat them, *Friday ?* ſaid I, *Yes,* ſaid *Friday, they eat a all up.* No, ho, ſaid I, *Friday*, I am much more concerned left they murder them; but as for eating them up, that I am ſure they will never do.

And now I not only lamented my misfortune, in not having the Spaniard and Savage with me, but alſo that I could not come within ſhot of them unperceived, (they having no fire arms among them,) and ſave theſe three men, whom I thought they were going to kill with their ſwords. But ſome comfort it was to me, that I perceived they were ſet at liberty to go where they pleaſed, the raſcally ſeamen ſcattering about as though they had a mind to ſee the place: and ſo long did they negligently ramble, that the tide had ebbed ſo low, as to leave the boat aground. Nor were the two men that were in her more circumſpect: for having drunk a little too much liquor, they fell faſt aſleep; but one of them waking before the other, and perceiving the boat too faſt a-ground for his ſtrength to move it, he hallooed out to the reſt,

who

who made all poſſible expedition to come to him:
but, as Providence ordered it, all their force was
ineffectual to launch her, when I could hear them
ſpeak to one another, *Why, let her alone, Jack,
can't ye, ſhe'll float next tide;* by which words I
was fully convinced they were my own countrymen. All this while I lay very quiet, as being
fully ſenſible it could be no leſs than ten hours
before the boat would be afloat, and then it would
be ſo dark, as that they could not eaſily perceive
me, by which means I ſhould be at more liberty to
hear their talk, and obſerve all their motions: not
but that I prepared for my defence: yet as I had
now another ſort of enemies to combat with, I
acted with more caution. I took two fuſees on
my ſhoulders, and gave *Friday* three muſkets;
beſides, my formidable goat-ſkin coat, and mon-
ſtrous cap, made me look as fierce and terrible
as *Hercules* of old, eſpecially when two piſtols
were ſtuck in my belt, and my naked ſword hanging by my ſide.

It was my deſign at firſt not to make any attempt till it was dark, but it being now two o'-
clock, in the very heat of the day, the ſailors
were all ſtraggling into the woods, and undoubtedly were lain down to ſleep. The three poor
diſtreſſed creatures, too anxious to get any repoſe, were, however, ſeated under the ſhade of
a great tree, about a quarter of a mile from me.
Upon which, without any more ado, I approached towards them, with my man following behind
me, and, before I was perceived, I called aloud
to them in *Spaniſh, What are ye, Gentlemen?*

At theſe words they ſtarted up in great confuſion,
when they beheld the ſtrange figure I made, they
returned no anſwer, but ſeemed as if they would
fly from me; *Gentleman,* (ſaid I in *Engliſh,*) *don't
be afraid, perhaps you have a friend nearer than*
you

you expect. He muſt be from Heaven *ſaid one of them, gravely pulling off his hat, for we are paſt all help in this world. All help is from Heaven,* ſaid I : *but, Sir, as I have perceived every action between you and theſe brutes ſince your landing, only inform me how to aſſiſt you, and I will do it to the utmoſt of my power.*

Am I talking with God or man? ſaid he, in melting tears. Are you of human kind, or an angel? Sir, ſaid I, *my poor habit may tell you I am a man, and an* Engliſhman, *willing to aſſiſt you, having but this ſervant only : here are arms and ammunition : tell freely your condition, can we ſave you?* The ſtory, ſaid he, is too long to relate, ſince our butchers are ſo near : but, Sir, I was maſter of that ſhip, my men have mutinied, and it is a favour they have put my mate, this paſſenger and me, on ſhore, without murdering us, though we expect nothing but periſhing here. *Are your enemies gone?* ſaid I. No, replied he, (pointing to a thicket,) there they lye, while my heart trembles, leſt, having ſeen and heard us, they ſhould murder us all. *Have they fire-arms?* ſaid I. They have but two pieces, ſaid he, one of which is left in the boat. He alſo told me, there were two enormous villains among them, that were the authors of this mutiny, who, if they were killed or ſeized, might induce the reſt to return to their obedience. Well, well, ſaid I, let us retire farther under the covering of the woods ; and there it was I made theſe conditions with him :

I. That while they ſtaid in the iſland, they ſhould not pretend to any authority ; but ſhould entirely conform to my orders, and return to me the arms which I ſhould put into their hands.

II. That if the ſhip was recovered, they ſhould afford Friday and myſelf our paſſage *gratis* to England.   When

When he had given me all the satisfaction I could
desire, I gave him and his two companions each
of them a gun, with powder and ball sufficient,
advising them to fire upon them as they lay sleep-
ing.   The captain modestly said, that he was sor-
ry to kill them; though, on the other hand, to let
these villains escape, who were the authors of his
misery, might be the ruin of us all.   Well, said
he, do as you think fit: and so accordingly I fired, killing one of the captain's chiefest enemies,
and wounding the other, who eagerly called for
assistance; but the captain (who had reserved his
piece) coming up to him, *Sirrah*, said he, *'tis too
late to call for assistance, you should rather cry to
God to pardon your villainy*; and so knocked him
down with the stock of his gun: three others were
also slightly wounded, who at my approach cried
out for mercy.   This the captain granted, upon
condition that they would swear to be true to him
in recovering the ship, which they solemnly did:
however, I obliged the captain to keep them bound.
After which I sent Friday and the captain's mate
to secure the boat, and bring away the oars and
sails; when, at their return, three men coming
back, and seeing their late distressed captain now
their conqueror, submitted to be bound also.   And
then it was, that having more liberty, I related
the adventures of my whole life, which he heard
with a serious and wonderful attention.   After
this I carried him and his two companions into my
little fortified castle, shewed them all my conveniencies, and refreshed them with such provisions
as I could afford.   When this was over, we began to consider about regaining the ship: he said,
that there were twenty-six hands on board, who
knowing their lives were forfeited by the law, for
conspiracy and mutiny, were so very hardened,
that it would be dangerous for our small company

to attack them. This was a reasonable inference indeed; but something we must resolve on, and immediately put in execution: we therefore heaved the boat upon the beach so high, that she could not shoot off at high water mark, and broke a hole in her not easily to be stopped; so that all the signals they gave for the boat to come on board were in vain. This obliged them to send another boat ashore, with ten men armed, whose faces the captain plainly descried, the boatswain being the chief officer; but he said there were three honest lads among them, who were forced into the conspiracy. Hereupon I gave him fresh courage, (for I had perceived he was in concern;) in the mean while securing our prisoners, except two, whom we took to our assistance, we thought ourselves able enough to adventure a battle. When the sailors landed, and beheld their boat in that condition, they not only halooed, but fired for their companions to hear, yet they received no answer. This struck them with horror and amazement, thinking their companions were murdered, they made as if they would return to the ship. I could perceive the captain's countenance change at this, till of a sudden three men were ordered to look after the boat, while the other seven leapt on shore, in order to search for their companions: and indeed they came to the brow of the hill, near my ancient castle, from whence they could see to a great distance in the woods, and there shouting and hallooing till tired and weary, they at length seated themselves under a spreading tree. My opinion was, that nothing could be done till night, when I might use some artifice to get them all out of the boat; but of a sudden they started up, and made to the sea-side; hereupon I ordered Friday and the captain's mate to go over the creek, and halloo as loud as they could, and so decoying them

into

Into the woods, come round to me again. And
this indeed had a good effect; for they followed
the noife, till coming weftward to the creek, they
called for their boat to carry them over, and taking one of the men out of her, left two to look
after her, having faftened her to the ftump of a
little tree on fhore. Hereupon immediately the
captain and our party paffing the creek, out of
their fight, we furprifed them both, by the captain's knocking down one, and ordering the other
to furrender upon pain of death, and who, being
the honefteft of them all, fincerely joined with us.
By this time it was pretty late; when the reft returning to their boat, which they found aground
in the creek, the tide out, and the men gone, they
ran about wringing their hands, crying it was an
inchanted ifland, and that they fhould be all murdered by fpirits or devils. My men would willingly
have fallen upon them, but I would not agree to
hazard any of our party. But to be more certain, Friday and the captain crawled upon their
hands and feet as near as poffible; and when the
boatfwain approached in fight, fo eager was the
captain, that he fired, and killed him on the fpot:
Friday wounded the next man, and a third ran a-
way. Hereupon I advanced with my whole army,
and it being dark, I ordered the men we had furprifed with the boat, to call them by their names,
and to parley with them. Accordingly he called
out aloud, *Tom Smith, Tom Smith?* He anfwered,
Who's that? Robinfon, anfwered the other, for
God's fake, Tom, *furrender immediately, or you're
all dead men.* Who muft we furrender to, fays
Smith. *To our captain and fifty men here, who
have taken me prifoner, wounded* Will Fryes, *and
killed the boatfwain.* Shall we have quarters then?
faid he. Hereupon the captain calls out, *You,
Smith, you know my voice, furrender immediately,*
P 2

and

and you shall all have your lives granted except
Will Atkins. Hereupon *Atkins* cries out, *What
have I done, Captain, more than the rest, who have
been as bad as me ?* but that was a lie, for he was
the person that laid hold of him, and bound him.
However, he was ordered to submit to the governor's mercy, for such was I called. And so
laying down their arms, we bound them all, and
seized on their boat.

After this, the captain expostulated with them,
telling them, that the governor was an Englishman, who might execute them there; but he
thought they would be sent to England, except
Will Atkins, who was ordered to prepare for
death next morning. Hereupon Atkins implored
the captain to intereede for his life, and the rest begged that they might not be sent to England. This answered our project for seizing the ship. For after sending Atkins, and two of the worst, fast bound to the
cave, and the rest being committed to my bower, I
sent the captain to treat with them in the governor's
name, offering them pardon if they would assist in
recovering the ship. Upon which they all promised to
stand by him till the last drop of their blood; and whoever acted treacherously, should be hanged in chains
upon the beach. They were all released on these
assurances; and then the captain repaired the other
boat, making his passenger captain of her, and
gave him four men well armed; while himself, his
mate, and five more, went in the other boat. By
midnight they came within call of the ship, when
the captain ordered Robinson to hail her, and tell
them, that with great difficulty they had found the
men at last. But while they were discoursing, the
captain, his mate, and the rest entered, and knocked down the second mate and carpenter, secured
those that were upon the deck, by putting them
under hatches, while the other boat's crew entered

ed

ed and fecured the forecaftle; they then broke into the round-houfe, where the mate, after fome refiftance, fhot the pirate captain through the head,
upon which all the reft yielded themfelves prifoners.   And thus the fhip being recovered, the joyful fignal was fired, which I heard with the greaf-
eft joy imaginable: nor was it long before he brought
the fhip to an anchor at the creek's mouth, where,
coming to me unawares, *There*, fays he, *my deareft friend and deliverer, there is your fhip, and we
are your feruants;* a comfort fo unfpeakable, as
made me fwoon in his arms, while, with gratitude
to Heaven, we were tenderly embracing each o-
ther.

Nothing now remained, but to confult what we
fhould do with the prifoners, whom he thought it
was not fafe to take on board.   Hereupon, con-
certing with the captain, I dreffed myfelf in one
of his fuits, and fending for them, told them, that
as I was going to leave the ifland with all my people, if they would tarry there, their lives fhould
be fpared; if not, they fhould be hanged at the firft
port they came at.   They agreed to ftay.   Hereupon I told them my whole ftory, charging them
to be kind to the Spaniards that were expected,
gave them all my arms, and informing them of e-
very thing neceffary for their fubfiftence, I and
my man Friday went on board.   But the next
morning two of the men came fwimming to the
fhip's fide, defiring the captain to take them on
board, though he hanged them afterwards, complaining mightily how barbaroufly the others ufed
them.   Upon which I prevailed with the captain
to take them in, and being feverely whipt and
pickled, they proved more honeft for the future.
And fo I bid farewel to this ifland, carrying along
with me my money, my parrot, umbrella, and
goat-fkin cap; fetting fail December 12th 1686, af-

ter twenty-eight years, two months, and nineteen days refidence, that fame day and month that I efcaped from Sallee, landing in England, June 11 1687, after five and thirty years abfence from my own country, which rendered me altogether a ftranger there.

Here I found my firft captain's widow alive, who had buried a fecond hufband, but in very mean circumftances, and whom I made mighty eafy upon my account. Soon after I went down to Yorkfhire, where all my family were expired, except two fifters, and as many of one of my brother's children. I found no provifion had been made for me, they concluded I had been long fince dead; fo that I was but in a very flender ftation. Indeed the captain did me a great kindnefs, by his report to the owners, how I had delivered their fhip on the defolate ifland, upon which they made me a prefent of 200l. Sterling. I next went to Lifbon, taking my man Friday with me, and there arriving in April, I met the Portuguefe captain, who had taken me on board on the African coaft; but being ancient, he had left off the fea, and refigned all his bufinefs to his fon, who followed the Brazil trade. So altered both of us were, that we did not know each other at firft, till I difcovered myfelf more fully to him. After a few embraces, I began to inquire of my concerns; and then the old gentleman told me, that it was nine years fince he had been at Brazil, where my partner was then living, but my truftees were both dead; that he believed I fhould have a good account of the product of my plantation; that the imagination of my being loft had obliged my truftees to give an eftimate of my fhare to the procurator-fifcal, who, in cafe of my not returning, he had given one third to the King, and the reft to the monaftery of St. Auguftine; but if I put in my claim, or any one for

me,

me, it would be returned, except the yearly product, which was given to the poor. I then desired him to tell me what improvement he thought had been made of my plantation, and whether he imagined it was worth my while to look after it? He answered, he did not know how much it was improved; but this he was certain of, that my partner was grown vastly rich upon his half of it; and that he had been informed, that the king had 200 moidores *per annum* for his third part. He added, that the survivors of my trustees were persons of an ingenuous character; that my partner could witness my title, my name being registered in the country, by which means I should indisputably recover a considerable sum of money. But, answered I, how could my trustees dispose of my effects, when I made you only my heir? This he said was true; but their being no affidavit made of my death, he could not act as my executor. However, he had ordered his son (then at Brasil) to act by procuration upon my account, and he had taken possession of my sugar-house, having accounted himself for eight years with my partner and trustees for the profits, of which he would give me a very good account.

And indeed this he performed very faithfully in a few days, making himself indebted to me 470 moidores of gold, over and above what had been lost at sea, after I had left the place. And then he recounted to me what misfortunes he had gone through, which forced my money out of his hands, to buy part in a new ship: *but*, says he, *you shall not want, take this, and when my son returns, every farthing shall be paid you.* Upon which he put into my hand a purse of 150 moidores in gold, as likewise the instrument containing the title to the ship which his son was in, and which he offered as security for the remainder. But really when I

saw

saw so much goodness, generosity, tenderness, and real honesty, I had not the heart to accept it; for fear he should straiten himself upon my account. *It is true*, said he, *it may be so; but then the money is yours, and you may have the greatest occasion for it.* However, I returned fifty of them back again, promising that I would freely give him the other hundred when I got my effects in my hands, and that I designed to go myself for that purpose. But he told me he could save me that trouble, and so caused me to enter my name, with a publick notary, as likewise my affidavit, with a procuration affixed to it; and this he ordered me to send in a letter to one of his acquaintance, a merchant in Brazil: and indeed nothing could be more faithfully and honourably observed; for in seven months time I had a very faithful account of all my effects, what sums of money were raised, what expended, and what remained for my use: in a word, I found myself to be worth 5000l. Sterling, and 1000l. *per annum*. Nor was this all, for my partner congratulated me upon my being alive, telling me how much my plantation was improved, what negroes were at work, and how many *Ave Marias* he had said to the virgin Mary for my preservation; desiring me to accept kindly some presents he had sent me, which I found shewed the greatest generosity.

No sooner did the ship arrive, but I rewarded my faithful captain, by returning him the hundred moidores; and not only forgiving him all he owed me, I allowed him yearly a hundred more, and fifty to his son, during their lives. And now being resolved to go to England, I returned letters of thanks to the prior of St. Augustine, and in particular to my old partner, with very suitable presents. By the captain's advice I was perswaded to go by land to Calais, and there take passage for
England;

England; when, as it happened, I got a young
English gentleman, a merchant's son at Lisbon, to
accompany me, together with two English, and
two Portuguese gentlemen; so that with a Portuguese servant, an English sailor, and my man Friday, there were nine of us in number.

Thus armed and equipped, we set out, and
came to Madrid, when the summer decaying, we
hasted to Navarre; where we were informed, that
there was scarcely any passing, by reason of the prodigious quantity of snow; so that we were obliged to
abide near twenty days at Pampeluna, and at last to
take a guide to conduct us safe towards Tholouse.
And now twelve other gentlemen joining with us,
together with their servants, we had a very jolly
company. Away our guide led us by the frightful mountains, and through so many intricate
mazes and windings, that we insensibly passed them,
which, as we travelled along, ushered us into the
prospect of the fruitful and charming provinces of
Languedoc and Gascogne.

But now came on two adventures, both tragical and comical. First, our guide was encounter-
ed by three wolves and a bear, who set upon him
and his horse, and wounded him in three places: upon which my man riding up to his assistance, shot one of them dead upon the spot, which
made the others retire to the woods But the
pleasantest adventure was, to behold my man attack the bear. 'Tis such a creature, that if you
let him alone, he will never meddle with you: and
this my man very well knew, and so begging leave
of me in broken English, he told us *he would make
good laugh*. Why, you silly fool, said I he'll eat
you up at a mouthful. *Eatee me up*, replied he,
by way of scorn, *me not only eatee him, but make
much good laugh*. Upon which, pulling off his boots,
he claps on his pumps, and running after the monstrous

ftrous beaft, he called out, that he wanted to difcourfe with him, and then throwing ftones on purpofe to incenfe him, the beaft turns about in a fury,
and with prodigious ftrides fhuffles after him. But
though he was not fwift enough to keep up pace
with Friday, who made up to us as it were for
help, yet being angry, *You dog*, faid I, *immediately take horfe, and let us fhoot the creature*. But
he cried, *Dear Mafter, no fhoot, me make you laugh
much*. And fo he turned about making figns to
follow, while the bear ran after him, till coming
to a great oak, he afcended in a minute, leaving
his gun at the bottom of it. Nor did the bear
make any difficulty of it, but afcended like a cat,
though his weight was very great. You muft confider I was not a little amazed at the folly of my
man, as not perceiving any thing to occafion our
laughter, till fuch time as we rode up nearer, and
beheld the beaft mounted upon the oak, on the beginning of the fame branch, to which Friday clung
at the farther end, where the bear durft not come.
Hereupon Friday cried out, *Now mafter, me make
much laugh; me make de bear dance*. Upon which
he fell a-fhaking the bough, which made the creature look behind him, to fee how he could retreat.
Then, as if the bear had underftood his ftammer-
ing Englifh: *Why you no come farther, Mr Bear*,
faid he, *pray, Mr Bear, come farther:* and then
indeed we all burft into laughter, efpecially when
we perceived Friday drop like a fquirrel upon the
ground, leaving the beaft to make the beft of his
way down the tree. And now thinking it the
moft convenient time to fhoot the creature, Friday
cried out, *O dear mafter, no fhoot, me fhoot by and
by;* when taking up the gun, *Me no fhoot yet*, faid
he, *me make once more much laugh*. And accordingly he was as good as his word; for the creature
defcending backwards from the tree very leifure-

ly,

ly, before he could lay one foot on the ground, Friday fhot him through the ear, ftone dead: and looking to fee whether we were pleafed, he burft out into a hearty laughter, faying, *So we kill de bear in my country, not with the gun but with much long arrows.* Thus ended our diverfion, to our great fatisfaction; efpecially in a place where the terrible howlings ftruck us with a continual terror. But the fnows now growing very deep, particularly on the mountains, the ravenous creatures were obliged to feek for fuftenance in the villages, where, coming by furprife on the country people, they killed feveral of them, befides a great number of their fheep and horfes.

Our guide told us, we had yet one more dangerous place to pafs by; and if there were any more wolves in the country, there we fhould find them. This was a fmall plain, encompaffed with woods, to get through a long lane, to the village where we were to lodge. When we entered the wood, the fun was within half an hour of fetting; and a little after it was fet, we came into the plain, which was not above two furlongs over, and then we perceived five great wolves crofs the road, without taking notice of us, and fo fwift as though they were purfuing after their prey. Hereupon our guide believing there were more coming, defired us to be upon our guard. Accordingly our eyes were very circumfpect, till about half a league farther, we perceived a dead horfe and near a dozen of wolves devouring its carcafe. My man Friday fain would have fired at them, but I would not permit him; nor had we gone half over the plain, but we heard dreadful howlings in a wood on our left, when prefently we faw an hundred come up againft us, as though they had been an experienced army. This obliged us to form ourfelves in the beft manner; and then I ordered that every other

man

man ſhould fire, that thoſe who did not might be ready to give a ſecond volley ſhould they advance upon us and then, every man ſhould make uſe of his piſtols.   But there was no neceſſity for this; for the enemy being terrified, ſtopped at the noiſe of the fire; four of them were ſhot dead, and ſeveral others being wounded, went bleeding away, as we could very plainly diſcover by the ſnow.   And now remembring what had been often told me, that ſuch was the majeſty of man's voice, as to ſtrike terror even into the fierceſt creatures, I ordered all our companions to halloo as loud as poſſible; and in this notion I was not altogether miſtaken, for they immediately turned about upon the firſt halloo, and began to retire; upon which ordering a ſecond volley in their rear, they galloped into the woods with great precipitation.

Thus we had ſome ſmall time to load our pieces again, and then made all the haſte we could on our way; but we had not rode far, before we were obliged to put ourſelves in a poſture of defence as before, being alarmed with a very dreadful noiſe in the ſame wood, on our left hand, the ſame way as we were to paſs, only that it was at ſome diſtance from us.   By this time the darkſome clouds began to ſpread over the elements, and the night growing very duſky, made it ſo much the more to our diſadvantage; but ſtill the noiſe increaſing, we were fully aſſured, that it was the howling and yelling of thoſe ravenous creatures; when preſently three troops of wolves, on our front, appeared to our ſight, as though a great number of them had a deſign to ſurround us and devour us in ſpite of fate.   But as they did not fall upon us immediately, we proceeded on our journey in as ſwift a manner as the roads would permit our horſes, which was only a large trot. It was in this manner we travelled, till ſuch time

as

as we difcovered another wood, and had the profpect of its entrance through which we were to
pafs, at the fartheft fide of the plain. But furely
none can exprefs the terror we were in, when,
approaching the lane, we perceived a confufed
number of the fierceft wolves ftanding, and as it
were guarding its entrance. Nor were we long
in this amazement, before another occafion of horror prefented itfelf; for fuddenly we heard the report of a gun at another opening into the wood,
and looking that way, out ran a horfe bridled and
faddled, flying with the greateft fwiftnefs, and no
lefs than fixteen or feventeen wolves purfuing after him, in order to devour the poor creature;
and unqueftionably they did fo, after they had run
him down, not being able to hold out that fwiftnefs with which he at firft efcaped them.

When we rode up to that entrance from whence
the horfe came forth, there lay the carcafes of another horfe and two men, mangled and torn by
thefe devouring wolves: and undoubtedly one of
thefe men was the perfon who fired the gun which
we had heard, for the piece lay by him; but alas!
moft of the upper part of his body and his head
were entombed in the bowels of thefe ravenous
creatures.

What courfe to take, whether to proceed or retreat, we could not tell; but it was not long before the wolves themfelves made us come to a refolution: for fuch numbers furrounded us, every
one of whom expected their prey, that, were our
bodies to be divided among them, there would not
be half a mouthful a-piece. But happy, very happy it was for us that but a little way from the entrance, there lay fome very large timber trees.
which I fuppofed had been cut down and laid there
for fale; amongft which I drew my little troop,
placing ourfelves in a line behind one long tree,

Q

which

which ferved us for a breaſt-work, when defiring them to alight, we ſtood in a triangle, or three fronts, incloſing our horſes in the centre, the only place where we could preſerve them.

Never certainly was there a more furious charge than what the wolves made upon us in this place; and the fight of the horſes, which was the principal thing they aimed at, provoked their hunger, and added to their natural fierceneſs. They came on us with a dreadful noiſe, that made the woods to ring again; and beginning to mount the pieces of timber, I ordered every other man to fire as before directed, and indeed ſo well did they take their aim, that they killed ſeveral of the wolves at the firſt volley; but ſtill we were obliged to keep a continual firing, by reaſon they came on like devils, puſhing one another with the greateſt fury. But our ſecond volley ſomething abated their courage, when ſtopping a little, we hoped they would have made the beſt of their way; however, it did not prove ſo, for others made a new attempt upon us: and though in four firings we killed ſeventeen or eighteen of them, laming twice as many, yet they ſeveral times ſucceſſively came on, as though they valued not their lives for the ſake of their prey.

Unwillingly was I to ſpend our laſt ſhot too ſuddenly, and therefore called my other ſervant, and giving him a horn of powder, bid him lay a large train quite along the timber, which he did, while *Friday* was charging my fuſee and his own, with the greateſt dexterity. By this time the wolves coming up the timber, I ſet fire to the train, by ſnapping a diſcharged piſtol cloſe on the powder. This ſo ſcorched and terrified them, that ſome fell down, and others jumped in among us; but theſe we immediately diſpatched, when all the reſt frighted with the light, which the darkſome night cauſed to appear more dreadful, began at length to retire;

tire; upon which, ordering our laſt piſtols to be fired at once, giving at the ſame time, a great ſhout, the wolves were obliged to have recourſe to their ſwiftneſs, and turn tail; and then we ſallied out upon twenty lame ones, cutting them in pieces with our ſwords, which obliged them to howl lamentably, to the terror of their fellows, who reſigned to us the field as victorious conquerors. And indeed I queſtion whether *Alexander* king of *Macedonia*, in any of his conqueſts, had more occaſion for triumph than we had; for he was but attacked by numerous armies of ſoldiers; whereas our little army was obliged to combat a legion of devils, as it were, worſe than the cannibaſl, who, the ſame moment, had they ſlain us would have ſacrificed us, to ſatisfy their voracious appetites.

Thus ended our bloody battle with the beaſts, having killed threeſcore of them, and ſaved our lives from their fury. We ſtill had a league farther to go, when, as we went, ours ears were ſalutde with their moſt unwelcome howlings, and we expected every moment another attack. But in an hour's time we arrived at the town where we were to lodge; and here we found the place ſtrictly guarded, and all in terrible confuſion, as well they might, for fear of the bears and wolves breaking into the village, in order to prey upon their cattle and people. The next morning we were obliged to take a new guide, by reaſon the other fell very bad of his wounds, which he had received, as before mentioned. After he had reached *Thoulouſe*, we came into a warm, pleaſant, and fruitful country, not infeſted with wolves, or any ſort of ravenous creatures : and when we told our ſtory there, they much blamed our guide, for conducting us through the foreſt at the foot of the mountains, in ſuch a ſevere ſeaſon, when the ſnow obliged the

 wolves

wolves to feek for fhelter in the woods. When we informed them in what manner we placed our-felves, and the horfes in the centre, they exceed-ingly reprehended us, and told us, it was an hun-dred to one, but we had all been deftroyed; for that it was the very fight of the horfes, their fo much defired prey, that made the wolves more ragingly furious than they would have been, which was evident, by their being at other times really afraid of a gun; but then being exceeding hungry and furious, upon that account, their eagernefs to come at the horfes made them infenfible of their danger; and that if we had not by a continual fire, and at laft by the cunning ftratagem of the train of powder, got the better of them, it had been great odds if their number had not over-powered us; befides, it was a great mercy we alight-ed from our horfes, and fought them with that courage and conduct, which, had we failed to do, every man of us, with our beafts, had been de-voured: and indeed this was nothing but truth; for never in my life was I fo fenfible of danger, as when three hundred devils came roaring upon us, to fhun whofe unwelcome company, if I was fure to meet a ftorm every week, I would rather go a thoufand leagues by fea.

I think I have nothing uncommon in my paffage through France to take notice of, fince other tra-vellers of greater learning and ingenuity have gi-ven a more ample account than my pen is able to fet forth. From Thouloufe I travelled to Paris, from thence to Calais, where I took fhipping, and landed at Dover the 14th of January, in a very cold feafon.

Thus, come to the end of my travels, I foon difcovered my new found eftate, and all the bills of exchange I had brought were currently paid. The good ancient widow, my only privy counfel-

lor,

lor, thought no pains nor care great enough to procure my advantage; nor had I ever occasion to blame her fidelity, which drew from me an ample reward. I was for leaving my effects in her hands, intending to set out for Lisbon, and so to the Brasils; but as in the *Desolate Island* I had some doubts about the Romish religion, so I knew there was little encouragement to settle there, unless I would apostatize from the orthodox faith, or live in continual fear of the inquisition. Upon this account I resolved to sell my plantation; and for that intent I wrote to my old friend at Lisbon, who returned me an answer to my great satisfaction; which was, that he could sell it to good account: however, if I thought it convenient to give him liberty to offer it in my name to the two merchants, the survivors of my trustees, residing at the Brasils, who consequently understood its intrinsic value, having lived just upon the spot, and who I was sensible were very rich, and therefore might be the more willing to purchase it; he did not in the least doubt, but that I should make four or five thousand pieces of eight more of it, than I could do, if I disposed of it in any other manner whatsoever.

You may be sure I could not but agree with this kind and ingenious proposal; and immediately I sent him an order to offer it to them, which he accordingly did; so that, about eight months after, the ship being in that time returned, he gave me a satisfactory account, that they not only willingly accepted the offer, but that they had also remitted 33,000 pieces of eight to a correspondent of their own at Lisbon, in order to pay for the purchase.

Hereupon in return I signed the instrument of sale according to form, which they had sent from Lisbon, and returned it again to my old friend, he having sent me for my estate, bills of three

Q 3

hundred

hundred twenty-eight thousand pieces of eight, reserving the payment of one hundred moidores per
annum, which I had allowed him during life, likewise fifty to his son during his life also, according
to my faithful promise, which the plantation was
to make good as a rent-charge.

And thus having led my reader to the knowledge of the first part of my life, so remarkable
for the many peculiar providences that attended
it, floating in an ocean of uncertainty and disappointment, of adversity and prosperity, beginning
foolishly, and yet ended happily, methinks now that
I am come to a safe and pleasant haven, it is time
to cast out my anchor, and laying up my vessel,
bid for a while adieu to foreign adventures. I
had no other concerns to look after, but the care
of my brother's two sons, which, with the good
widow's persuasions, obliged me to continue at
home seven years. One of these children I bred
up a gentleman, and the other an experienced
sailor, remarkable for his courage and bravery.
Besides this, I married a virtuous young gentlewoman, of a very good family, by whom I had
two sons and one daughter. But my dear and tender wife leaving this earthly stage, (as in the second part of my life you will hear,) which rent
my soul as it were asunder, my native country
became weary and tiresome to me: and my nephew happening to come from the sea, tempted
me to venture another voyage to the East Indies,
which I did in the year 1694, at which time I vi-
sited my island, and informed myself of every thing
that happened since my departure.

One might reasonably imagine, that what I had
suffered, together with an advanced age, and the
fear of losing, not only what I had gotten, but my
life also, might have choked up all the seeds of
youthful ambition and curiosity, and put a lasting
                                        period

period to my wandering inclinations. But as nothing but death can fully allay the active part of
my life, no lefs remarkable for the many various
contingencies of it; you will next perceive how
I vifited my little kingdom, faw my fucceffors the
Spaniards, had an account of the ufage they met
with from the Englifhmen, agreeing and difagree-
ing, uniting and feparating, till at laft they were
fubjected to the Spaniards, who yet ufed them very
honourably, together with the wonderful and fuc-
cefsful battles over the Indians, who invaded, and
thought to have conquered the ifland, but were
repelled by their invincible courage and bravery,
having taken eleven men and five women prifoners, by which at my return I found about twenty
young children on my little kingdom. Here I
ftaid twenty days, left them fupplies of all neceffary things, as alfo a carpenter and fmith, and
fharing the ifland into parts, referving the whole
property to myfelf. Nor will you be infenlible,
by the account of thefe things, of feveral new adventures I have been engaged in, the battles I have
fought, the deliverances I have met with: and
while, in the furprifing relation of fuch remarkable occurrences, I fhall defcribe many of God's
kindeft providences to me in particular, no lefs
confpicuous in the fame goodnefs, power and majefty of our great Creator, fhewn, one way or
other, over the face of the earth, if duly advert-
ed to.

The further adventures of Robinson Crusoe, *where-in are contained several strange and surprising accounts of his travels, and the most remarkable transactions both by sea and land; with his wonderful vision of the* Angelic World.

WHEN we consider the puissant force of Nature, and what mighty influence it has many times over the temper of the mind, it will be no such great wonder to think, that my powerful reason should be overcome by a much stronger inclination. My late acquired kingdom ran continually in my thoughts all the day, and I dreamed of it in the night; nay, I made it the continual subject of my talk, even to impertinence, when I was awake. I had such vapours in my head, that I actually supposed myself at my castle; that I not only perceived Friday's father, but the old Spaniard, and the wicked sailors, but that I talked and discoursed with them about their manner of living; that I heard these things related to me, which I found afterwards to be but too true: and that I executed my judgments with the greatest severity upon the offenders. And indeed, this anticipating all the pleasing joys of my life, scarcely afforded me one pleasant hour: my dear and tender wife could not but take notice of it, which drew these affectionate speeches from her: *My dear,* said she, *I am really persuaded that some secret impulse from heaven occasions in you a determination to see the island again: nor am I less sensible, but your being engaged to me, and these dear children, is the only hindrance of your departure. I know, my dear, if I was in the grave, you would not long continue at home; prevent not your happiness upon my account, whose only comfort centers in you. All that I can object is, that such an hazardous undertaking is no way consistent with a person of your*

years;

years; but if you are refolved to go, added fhe, weeping, *only permit me to bear you company, and that is all that I defire.* Such endearing tendernefs, graced with the moft innocent, and yet moft powerful charms, brought me infenfibly into my right underftanding; and when I confidered all the tranfactions of my life, and particularly my new engagement; that I had now one child already born, and my wife big of another; and that I had no occafion to feek for more riches, who already was bleffed with fufficiency, with much ftruggling I altered my refolutions at laft, refolving to apply myfelf to fome bufinefs or other, which might put a period to fuch wandering inclinations. Hereupon I bought a little farm in the county of Bedford, with a refolution to move thither: upon this there was a pretty convenient houfe, furrounded with land, very capable of improvement, which fuited my temper as to planting, managing, and cultivating. Nor was I long before I entered upon my new fettlement, having bought ploughs, harrows, carts, waggons, horfes, cows, and fheep; fo that I now led the life of a country gentleman, and as happy in my retirement as the greateft monarch in the world. And what made me think my happinefs the greater was, that I was in that *middle ftate of life,* which my father had fo often recommended, much refembling the felicity of a rural retirement, which is elegantly defcribed by the poet in thefe lines:

Free from all vices, free from care,
Age has no pain, and youth no fnare.

But, in the midft of this my happinefs, I was fuddenly plunged into the greateft forrows that I could poffibly endure: for, when I leaft expected it, my dear and tender wife was forced to fubmit to the irrefiftible power of death, leaving this tranfitory life for a better. It is impoffible for me to exprefs the beauties of her mind, or the lovelinefs of her perfon ; neither can I too much lament her lofs, which my lateft breath fhall record : her influence was greater over me than the powers of my own reafon, the importunities of friends, the inftructions of a father, or the melting tears of a tender and difconfolate mother : in a word, fhe was the fpirit of all my affairs, and the centre of my enterprifes. But now, fince the cruel hand of death had clofed my deareft's eyes, I feemed in my thoughts a ftranger to the world ; my privy counfellor being gone, I was like a fhip without a pilot, that could only run before the wind. And when I looked around me in this bufy world, one part labouring for bread, and the other fquandering away their eftates, this put me in mind how I had lived in my little kingdom, where both reafon and religion dictated to me, that there was fomething that certainly was the reafon and end of life, which was far fuperior to what could be hoped for on this fide the grave. My country delights were now as infipid and dull, as mufic or fcience to thofe who have neither tafte nor ingenuity. In fhort, refolving to leave off houfekeeping, I left my farm, and in a few months returned to London.

But neither could that great city, fo famous for its variety of entertainment, afford me any agreeable delight : a ftate of idlenefs I found to be the very dregs of life, and moft hurtful to body and foul. It was now the beginning of the year 1694, at which time my nephew (who, as I before obferved, had been brought up to the fea, and advanced to be captain of a fhip) was returned from a fhort voyage to Bilboa, the firft he had made in that ftation. He comes to me one morning, telling

ling me, that some merchants of his acquaintance had proposed to him to go a voyage for them, to the East Indies and China, in the manner of private traders : and now, *uncle*, said he, *if you'll accompany me thither, I'll engage to land you upon your old island, to visit the state of your little kingdom.*

Just before he came in, my thoughts were fixed to get a patent for its possession, and then to fill it with inhabitants. After I had paused a little while, and looked stedfastly on him, *What devil, or spirit*, said I, *sent you with this unlucky errand ?* He started at first, but recovering himself, when he perceived I was not offended, Sir, replied he, what I have proposed cannot, I hope, be styled unlucky, since certainly you must be desirous to see your little territory, where you reigned with more content than any of your brother-kings in the universe. Nephew, said I, if you will leave me there, and call for me as you come back, I care not if I give my consent : but he answered, that the merchants would not allow their vessel, loaden with an infinite value, to return there again, which was a month's sail out of the way : besides, Sir, said he, if I should miscarry, was your request granted, why then you would be locked up as before. This indeed carried a great deal of reason in it, but we found out a remedy, and that was, to carry a framed sloop on board, ready to be set up in the island, by the assistance of some carpenters, which we should carry with us, that might be fitted in a few days to go to sea. I was not long in forming my resolution, which over-swayed my good friend the widow's persuasions, and the natural affection I bore to my young children. I made my will, and settled my estate in such a manner, that I was perfectly sure that my poor infants would have justice done them. The
good

good widow not only undertook to make proviſion for my voyage, but alſo took the charge of my domeſtic affairs, and to provide for my children's education; and indeed no mother could take more care, or underſtood that office better; for which I lived to reward, and return her my hearty thanks.

The beginning of January 1694-5, my nephew being ready to ſail, I and Friday went on board in the Downs on the 8th, having, beſide that ſloop already mentioned, a very conſiderable cargo for my new colony. *Firſt*, I had ſome ſervants, whom I propoſed to leave there, as inhabitants, or to work while I ſtaid there, as they ſhould appear willing: there were two carpenters, a ſmith, and a very ingenious fellow who was Jack of all trades; for he was not only a cooper by trade, but alſo he was dexterous at making wheels and hand mills to grind corn, likewiſe a good turner, and a good pot-maker. I alſo carried a taylor, who conſented to ſtay in my plantation, and proved a moſt neceſſary fellow in the iſland. As to my cargo, it conſiſted of a ſufficient quantity of linen, and Engliſh ſtuffs, for cloathing the Spaniards that I expected to find there; as likewiſe gloves, hats, ſhoes, ſtockings; together with beds, bedding, and houſehold ſtuff, eſpecially kitchen utenſils, with pots, kettles, pewter, braſs, &c. alſo nails, tools of all ſorts, ſtaples, hooks, hinges, and all other things neceſſary; all which, I think, coſt me about three hundred pounds. Nor was this all; for I carried an hundred ſpare-arms, muſkets and fuſees, beſides ſome piſtols, a conſiderable quantity of ſeveral ſorts of ſhot, two braſs cannon, beſides ſwords, cutlaſſes, and the iron part for ſome pikes and halberts. I made my nephew take with us two ſmall quarter deck guns, more than he had occaſion for in his ſhip, to leave behind, if there was a neceſſity; that ſo we might build a fort there,

there, and man it againſt all oppoſers whatſoever.

Well, we put out to ſea; and though I can't ſay this voyage was ſo unproſperous as my others had been, yet contrary winds drove us ſo far northward, that we were obliged to put in at Galway in Ireland, where we lay wind-bound two and twenty days. Here indeed, our proviſions were very cheap, and we added to our ſhip's ſtores, by taking in ſeveral live hogs, two cows and calves, which I then reſolved to put on ſhore in my iſland, if our neceſſities did not call for them. On the 5th of February we ſailed from Ireland, with a very fair gale, which laſted for ſome days; and I think it was about the 20th of the ſame month, late in the evening, when the mate informed us, that he ſaw a flaſh of fire, and heard a gun fired; and when he was ſpeaking, a boy came in, and told us, that the boatſwain had heard another. Upon which we all ran to the quarter deck, from whence in a few moments we perceived a terrible fire at a diſtance. We had immediately recourſe to our reckonings, in which we were all of opinion, that there could be no land that way, it appearing to be at N. N. W. Hereupon we concluded that ſome ſhip had taken fire at ſea, and that it could not be far off, by the report of the guns which we had heard. We made up directly to it, and in half an hour's time, the wind being fair, we could plainly perceive a great ſhip on fire in the middle of the ſea. Touched with this unhappy diſaſter, and conſidering my former circumſtances, when the Portugueſe captain took me up, I immediately ordered five guns to be fired, that the poor creatures, not ſeeing us, it being dark, (though we could perceive their flame,) might be ſenſible there was deliverance at hand, and conſequently might endeavour to ſave themſelves in their boat. Nor was it long before the ſhip blew up in the

R   air,

air, and the fire was extinguished in the ocean.
But supposing them all to be in their boats, we
hung out our lanterns, and kept firing till eight
o'clock in the morning; when, with our perspec-
tives, we beheld two boats, full of people, making
towards us, though the tide was against them;
then spreading out our ancient, and hanging out
a waft, as a signal for them to come on board, in
half an hour's time, we came up to them, and took
them all in, there being no less than sixty-four
men, women and children.. It was a French merchant ship of 300 tons, homeward bound from
Quebeck in the river of Canada. The master informed me how, by the negligence of the steers-
man, the steerage was set on fire; that, at his
outcry for help, the fire was, as they thought, totally extinguished; but that some sparks getting
between the timber, and within the ceiling, it
proceeded into the hold, where there was no re-
sisting it; that then they got into their boats, as
creatures in the last extremity, with what provision they had, together with oars, sails, and a
compass, intending to go back to Newfoundland,
the wind blowing at S. E. and by E. though there
were several chances against them, as storms to
overset and founder them, rains and colds, to
benumb and perish their limbs, and contrary winds
to keep them back and starve them: but, said he,
in this our great distress, we heard the welcome
report of your guns, when, with unspeakable
joy, taking down our masts and sails, we were
resolved to lye by till morning; but perceiving
your light, we set our oars at work to keep our
boat a-head, the sooner to attain your ship, the
happy instrument of our deliverance.

Indeed no one can express the joy of these poor
creatures on this occasion; fear and grief are easily set forth; sighs and tears, with a few motions
of

of the hands and head, are all the demonstrations
of these passions; but an excess of joy carries in
it a thousand extravagancies; especially, I think,
amongst the French, whose temper is allowed to be
more volatile, passionate, sprightly, and gay, than
that of other nations. Some were weeping, tear-
ing themselves in the greatest agonies of sorrow,
and running stark mad about the ship; while the
rest were stamping with their feet, wringing their
hands, singing, laughing, swooning away, vomit-
ing, fainting, with a few returning hearty thanks
to the Almighty, and crossing themselves. I think,
if I am not mistaken, our surgeon was obliged to
let thirty of them blood. But among the passengers, there were two priests, the one an old, and
the other a young man; but what amazed me
more, was, that the oldest was in the worst plight;
for no sooner did he perceive himself freed from
danger, but he dropt down, as it were without
life, and, to every one's appearance, quite dead;
but the surgeon, chaffing and rubbing his arm, opened a vein, which at first dropped, and then flowing more freely, the old man began to open his
eyes, and in a quarter of an hour was well again.
But soon remembering his happy change, the joy
of which whirled his blood about faster than the
vessels could convey it, he became so feverish, as
made him more fit for bedlam than any other place;
but the surgeon giving him a sleepy dose, he was
perfectly composed the next morning.

Remarkable indeed was the behaviour of the
young priest. At his entrance on board the ship,
he fell on his face in the most humble prostration
to the Almighty. I thought indeed he had fallen
into a swoon, and so ran to help him up; but he
modestly told me, he was returning his thanks to
the Almighty, desiring me to leave him a few moments, and that, next to his Creator, he would

return me thanks alfo. And indeed he did fo, about three minutes after, with great ferioufnefs and affection, while the tears ftood in his eyes, which convinced me of the gratitude of his foul. Nor did he lefs fhew his piety and wifdom, in applying himfelf to his country people, and labouring to compofe them, by the moft powerful reafons, arguments, and perfuafions. And when, indeed, thofe people had taken their night's repofe, in fuch lodgings as our fhip would allow, we found nothing but the beft of manners, and the moft civil acknowledgments, for which the French are eminently remarkable. The next day the captain, and one of the priefts, defired to fpeak with me, and my nephew, the commander. They told us, that they had faved fome money, and valuable things out of the ruined veffel, which was at our fervice; only that they defired to be fet on fhore fome where in our way. At the firft my nephew was for accepting the money; but I (who knew how hard my cafe would have been, had the Portuguefe captain ferved me fo) perfuaded him to the contrary; and therefore told them, that as we had done nothing but what we were obliged to do, by nature and humanity, and what we ourfelves might expect from others in fuch calamity; fo we took them up to fave them, not to plunder them, or leave them naked upon the land, to perifh for want of fubfiftence, and therefore would not accept their money: but as landing them, that was a great difficulty; for, being bound to the Eaft Indies, it was impoffible wilfully to change our voyage upon their particular account, nor could my nephew (who was under charter-party to purfue it by way of Brafil) anfwer it to the freighters. All that we could do, was to put ourfelves in the way of meeting fome fhips homeward bound from the Weft Indies, that if poffible they might get a

paffage

passage to France or England. Indeed they were very thankful for our first kindness; but were under great concern, especially the passengers, at their being carried to the East Indies. They begged therefore I would keep on the banks of Newfoundland, where probably they might meet with some ship or sloop to carry them to Canada, whence they came. As this was but a reasonable request, I was inclined to grant it, since it was no breach of charter-party, and that the laws of God and nature obliged us to do what good we could to our fellow-creatures; and besides, the danger we ourselves should be in for want of provisions; so we consented to carry them to Newfoundland, if wind and weather would permit; if not, that we should carry them to Martinico in the West Indies. But as it happened, in a week's time, we made the banks of Newfoundland, where the French people hired a bark to carry them to France. But the young priest being desirous to go to the East Indies, I readily agreed to it, because I liked his conversation, and two or three of the French sailors also entered themselves on board our ship.

Now directing our course for the West Indies, steering S. and S. by E. about twenty days, with little wind, another adventure happened to exercise our humanity. In the latitude of 27 degrees 5 min. north, the 19th of March, 1694-5, we perceived a sail, (our course S. E. and by S.) which bore up to us, and then she appeared to be a large vessel, having lost her main-top-mast, fore-mast, and boltsprit; when firing a gun as a signal of distress, wind N. N. W. we soon came to speak with her. She was a ship of Bristol, bound home from Barbadoes, out of which road she had been forced by a hurricane to the westward, in which they lost their masts.

They told us, their expectations were to see

the Bahama iflands, but were driven away by a
ftrong wind at N. N. W. and having no fails to
work the fhip with, but the main courfe, and a
kind of fquare fail upon a jury foremaft, becaufe.
they could not come near the land, were endea-
vouring to ftand for the Canaries; nay, what was
worfe, befides all their fatigue, they were almoft
ftarved for want of provifion, having ate nothing .
for eleven days; all that they had aboard was fugar, a barrel of frefh water, and feven cafks of
rum.   In this fhip were three paffengers, a youth,
his mother, and a maid-fervant, who were in a
moft deplorable condition for want of food.   If I
had not gone on board their fhip, the knowledge
of their mifery had been concealed from me, and
they would have inevitably perifhed, though indeed their fecond mate (who was captain, by reafon the true captain was not on board when the
hurricane happened) had before informed me that
there were fuch perfons on-board, whom he fuppofed to be dead, being afraid to inquire after
them, becaufe he had nothing to give them for
relief.   Hereupon we refolved to let them have
what we could fpare, ordering the mate to bring
fome of his men on board us, which he did accordingly; as he and they looked like fkeletons, when
meat was fet before them, I ordered them to eat
fparingly.   But, however they foon fell fick;
which obliged the furgeon to mix fomething in their
broth, which was to be to them both food and
phyfic.   When they were fed, we ordered our
mate to carry them a fack of bread, and four or
five pieces of beef; but the furgeon charged them
to fee it boiled, and to keep a guard on the cook-
room, to prevent the men from eating it raw, and
confequently killing themfelves with what was defigned for their relief.   But particularly I defired
the mate to fee what condition the poor paffengers
                                      were

were in, and the furgeon gave him a pitcher of the
fame broth which he had prepared for the men.
And being curious to fee this fcene of mifery myfelf, I took the captain (as we called the mate of
the fhip) in our own boat, and failed after them.
    Here was a fad fight indeed! fcarce were the
victuals half boiled in the pot, but they were ready to break open the cook-room door. To ftay
their ftomachs, the mate gave them bifcuits, which
were dipped in, and foftened with the liquor of
the meat, which they call *Breuife*; telling them,
it was for their own fafety, that he was obliged
to give them but a little at a time : and fo feeding
them gradually, their bellies were comfortably
filled, and the men did very well again. But when
they came to the poor gentlewoman in the cabin,
who for feveral days had continued without food,
giving what fhe had to her fon, they found her as
it were in the arms of death. She was fitting upon the floor of the deck, with her back up againft
the fides, between two chairs, which were lafhed-
faft, and her head fhrunk between her fhoulders,
like a fenfelefs corpfe. Nothing was wanting in
my mate to revive and encourage her; opening
her lips, and putting fome broth into her mouth
with a fpoon. But not having ftrength to fpeak,
fhe lifted up her head with much difficulty, intimating that it was now too late! at the fame time
pointing to the youth her fon, as though fhe defired him to do what he could to fave the lad; and
in a little after fhe died.
    The youth indeed was not fo far gone, yet lay
ftretched out in a cabin bed, like one that had
fcarce any life. In his mouth was a piece of an
old glove, the reft of which he had ate up. At
firft he vomited what the mate had given him; but
at length began fenfibly to revive, though in the
greateft

greateſt concern for the death of his tender mother.

As to the poor maid, ſhe lay by her miſtreſs, like one in the laſt pangs of death: her limbs were diſtorted, one of her hands was claſped round the frame of a chair, which ſhe gripped ſo hard, that it was with ſome difficulty we ſeparated her from it: her other arm lay over her head, and her feet lay both together ſet faſt againſt the frame of the cabin table: not only being ſtarved with hunger, but overcome with grief for the loſs of her miſtreſs, whom ſhe loved moſt tenderly. It was a great while before the ſurgeon could bring her to life, and a much longer time before ſhe came to her ſenſes.

After we had ſailed with them ſome days, we ſent them five barrels of beef, one of pork, two hogſheads of biſcuit, with peaſe, flower, and other things, taking three caſks of ſugar, ſome rum, and ſome pieces of eight for ſatisfaction, we left them, but took the youth and maid with us, with all their goods. The lad was about ſeventeen years old, very handſome, modeſt, ſenſible, and well-bred, but mightily concerned for the loſs of his honoured mother, having loſt his father at Barbadoes but a few months before. He beſeeched the ſurgeon to intercede with me to take him out of the ſhip; for that the ſailors, not ſparing a ſmall ſuſtenance, had ſtarved his mother. But hunger has no bounds, no right, and conſequently is incapable of any compaſſion. When the ſurgeon told him, that our voyage might put him in bad circumſtances, and farther from his friends, he anſwered, he did not care, ſo he was delivered from that terrible crew: that as the captain (meaning me) had ſaved him from death, ſo he was ſure he would do him no harm; and as for the maid, when ſhe was reſtored to her ſenſes, ſhe would.

would be no lefs thankful, let us carry them where we would. And indeed the furgeon fo reprefented their cafe to me, that I confented, and took them on board with all their goods, except eleven hogfheads of fugar; but the youth having a bill of lading, I made the commander oblige himfelf to deliver a letter and the deceafed widow's goods to Mr. Rogers, a merchant in Briftol; but I believe the fhip was loft at fea, for we could never hear what became of her afterwards. We were now in the latitude of 19 deg. 32 min. having as yet a tolerable good voyage. But, paffing by feveral little incidents relating to wind and weather, I fhall relate what is more remarkable concerning my little kingdom, to which I was then drawing near. I had great difficulty in finding it; for as I came to, and went from it before, on the fouth and eaft fide of the ifland, as coming from the Brafils; fo now approaching between the main and the ifland, not having any chart for the coaft, nor land-mark, it obliged us to go on fhore on feveral iflands in the mouth of the river O-roonoko, but to no purpofe. This I percei-ved, that what I thought was a continent before, was no fuch thing, but a long ifland, or rather a ridge of fands. On one of thefe iflands I found fome Spaniards, but they belonged to the ifle de Trinidad, who came hither in a floop to make falt, and to try to find fome pearl mufles. But at length I came fair on the fouth fide of my ifland, and then I prefently knew the countenance of my little kingdom, fo we brought the fhip fafe to an anchor, broadfide within the little creek, where ftood my ancient and venerable caftle.

No fooner did I fee the place, but calling for Friday, I afked him where he was? But when he looked a little, he clapped his hands, crying, *O joys, O there, O yes, O there!* pointing to our old
abode,

abode, and then fell a dancing and capering as if
he was mad, and I had much ado to keep him from
jumping into the sea, to swim ashore. Friday,
said I, what do you think, shall we go see your
father? At the mentioning his father's name the
poor affectionate creature fell a weeping : *No no,
says he, me see him no more, never see poor father
more ! he long ago die, die long ago ; he much old
man.* You don't know that, Friday, said I, but
shall we see any body else ? He looks about, and
pointing to the hill above my house, cries out,
We see, we see, there much men and there ! which,
though I could not perceive them with my perspective glass, was true, by what the men themselves told me the next day.

When the English ancient was spread, and three
guns fired as a signal of friendship, we perceived
a smoke rise from the creek ; upon which I ordered the boat out, taking Friday with me, and hanging out a white flag of truce, I went on shore, accompanied also by the young friar, to whom I had
related the history of the first part of my life : besides we had sixteen men well armed, in case we
had met with any opposition.

After we had rowed directly into the creek, the
first man I fixed my eye upon, was the Spaniard
whose life I had saved, and whose face I perfectly
well knew. I ordered them all to stay in the boat
for a while ; but Friday, perceiving his father at
a distance, would have jumped into the sea, had
they not let the boat go. No sooner was he on
shore, but he flew like a swift arrow out of a bow,
to embrace his aged father. Certainly it would
melt a man of the firmest resolution, into the soft-
est tears, to see with what uncommon transports
of joy he saluted him : he first kissed him, then
stroked his face, took him in his arms, laid him
under a shady tree, sat down by him, then looked

as earneft at him as one would do at a picture, for a quarter of an hour together. After this, he would lye upon the ground, ftroke his legs, and kifs them, then get up and ftare at him, as though he was bewitched: but the next day one could not forbear laughter to fee his behaviour, for he would walk feveral hours with his father along the fhore, leading him by the hand, as though he was a lady; while, every now and then he would run to the boat, to get fomething for him, as a lump of fugar, dram, bifcuit, or fomething or other that was good. His frolios ran in another channel in the afternoon; for when he fet old Friday on the ground, he would dance round him, making comical poftures and geftures: and all this while would be telling him one ftory or other of his travels and adventures.

It was on the 10th of April, *anno* 1695, that I fet my foot upon the ifland a fecond time. When my faithful Spaniard, accompanied by one more, approached the boat, he little knew who I was, till I difcovered myfelf to him: Signior, faid I, in Portuguefe, don't you know me? he fpoke never a word, but giving his mufket to his attendant, extended his arms, and faying fomething in Spanifh, that I did not then underftand, he came forward and embraced me, faying, he was inexcufeable, not to know his deliverer; who, like an angel fent from heaven, had faved his life. He then beckoned to the man to call out his companions, afking me, if I would walk to my own habitation, and take poffeffion, where I fhould find fome mean improvements: but indeed they were extraordinary ones; for they had planted fo many trees fo clofe together, that the place was like a labyrinth, which none could find out, except themfelves, who knew its intricate windings. I afked him the meaning of all thefe fortifications;

he

he told me he would give me a large account of
what had paffed fince my departure to this time,
and how he had fubdued fome Englifh, who thought
to be their murderers, hoping I would not be difpleafed, fince neceffity compelled them to it. As
I knew they were wicked villains, fo I told him,
that I was not only far from finding fault with it,
but was rather heartily glad that they had fubdued them. While we were thus talking, the man
whom he had fent returned, accompanied by eleven more, but in fuch habits, that it was impoffible to tell what nations they were of. He firft
turned to me, and pointing to them; Thefe, Sir,
faid he, are fome of the gentlemen who owe their
lives to your goodnefs; then turning-to them, and
pointing to me, he made them fenfible who I was:
and then indeed they faluted me one by one; not
as ordinary men, but as though they had been
ambaffadors or noblemen, and I a triumphant conqueror; for their behaviour not only agreed with
a manlike, majeftic gravity, but at the fame time
was fo obliging and courteous, as made them ad-
mirable to the laft degree.

Before I relate the hiftory of the tranfactions
of my kingdom, as I had it from the Spaniard's
own mouth, I muft here infert what I omitted in
my former relation. The matter is this: Juft before we weighed anchor to fet fail, there happened a quarrel on board the fhip, which had like to
have occafioned a fecond mutiny, till fuch time as
the courageous captain taking two of the moft refractory prifoners, laid them in irons, threatening,
as they were concerned in the former diforders,
to have them hanged in England for running a-
way with the fhip. This frightened fome of the
reft, as thinking the captain would ferve them in
the fame manner, though he feemed to give them
good words for the prefent. But the mate having
                              intelligence

intelligence of this, made me acquainted with their
fears; so that, to make them more easy, and ourfelves more fafe from their confpiracies, I was o-
bliged to go down, and pafs my honour's word
for it, that, upon their good behaviour, all that
was paft fhould be pardoned; in teftimony of which
I ordered the two men's irons to be taken off, and
themfelves forgiven. But as this had brought us
to an anchor that night, in which there was a
calm, the two men that had been in irons, ftole
each of them a mufket, and fome other weapons,
and taking the fhip's pinnace, not yet haled up,
ran away to their brother rogues. The next
morning we fent the long-boat, with men to purfue them; but all in vain: the mate, in revenge,
would have demolifhed my little caftle, burnt its
furniture, and deftroyed their plantations; but
having no orders for it, he did not put it in execution. And thus there were five Englifhmen in
the ifland, which caufed great differences, as my
faithful Spaniard gave me a perfect account of, in
the following manner:

You cannot, Sir, but remember the embaffy you
fent me about, and what a difappointment we met
with, by your abfence, at our return. There is
but little variety in the relation of our voyage,
being bleffed with calm weather, and a fmooth fea.
Great indeed was the joy of my countrymen, to
fee me alive, having acted as the principal man
on board, the captain of the fhipwrecked veffel
dying before; nor was their furprife lefs, as knowing I was taken prifoner by the favages of another nation, they thought me long fince entombed
in their monftrous bowels. But when I fhewed
them the arms, ammunition, and provifions I had
brought for them, they looked upon me as a fecond Jofeph advanced in Pharoah's court, and immediately prepared to come along with me. In-

S

deed

deed they were obliged to trespass upon their friendly savages by borrowing two of their canoes, under a pretext for fishing: and they came away
the next morning, but without any provisions of
their own, except a few roots, which served them
instead of bread. After three weeks absence, we
arrived at your habitation. Here we met with
three English sailors, who, I confess, gave us provisions, and that letter of direction you had left
for us, which informed us how to bring up tame
goats, plant corn, cure grapes, make pots ; and
in short, every thing that was necessary for our
use ; as, in particular, I knew your method best,
so taking Friday's father to assist me, we managed
all the affairs ; nor were the rest of the Spaniards
wanting in their kind offices, dressing food for the
Englishmen, who did nothing but ramble and divert themselves in the woods, either shooting parrots, or catching tortoises.   But we had not been
long ashore, before we were informed of two more
Englishmen, unnaturally turned out of their common place of residence by the three others above
mentioned: this made my Spaniards and me (whom
they now looked upon as their governor in your
absence) endeavour to persuade them to take them
in, that we might be as one family ; but all our
intreaties were in vain, so that the poor fellows,
finding nothing to be done without industry, pitched there tents on the north side of the island, a
little inclining to the west, for fear of savages.
Here they built two huts, one to lodge, and the
other to lay their stores in ; for my good natured
Spaniards giving them some seeds, they dug and
planted as I had done, and began to live prettily.
But while they were thus comfortably going on,
the three unnatural brutes, their countrymen, in
a mere bullying humour, insulted them, by saying, the governor (meaning you) had given them
possession

poſſeſſion of the iſland, and d—mn' 'em, they ſhould build no houſes upon their ground, without paying rent. The two honeſt men (for ſo let me now diſtinguiſh them) thought their three countrymen only jeſted, and one of them invited them in, to ſee their fine habitations; while the other facetiouſly told them, that ſince they built tenements, with great improvements, they ſhould, according to the cuſtom of landlords, give them a longer leaſe; at the ſame time deſiring them to fetch a ſcrivener to draw the writings. One of the wretches ſwearing he ſhould pay for the jeſt, ſnatches up a firebrand, and clapping it to the outſide of their hut, very fairly ſet it on fire, which would ſoon have conſumed it, had not the honeſt man thruſt him away, and trod it out with with his feet. Hereupon the fellow returns with a pole, with which he would have ended his days, had not the poor man avoided the blow; when fetching his muſket, he knocked down the villain that began the quarrel. The other two coming to aſſiſt their fellow, obliged the honeſt man to take his muſket alſo, and both of them preſenting their pieces, bid the villains ſtand off; and if they did not lay down their arms, death ſhould decide the diſpute one way or other. This brought them to a parley, in which they agreed to take their wounded man and be gone; but they were in the wrong that they did not diſarm them when they had the power, and then make their complaint to me and my Spaniards for juſtice, which might have prevented their farther deſigns againſt them. And indeed ſo many treſpaſſes did they afterwards commit, by treading down their corn, ſhooting their young kids and goats, and plaguing them night and day, that they reſolved to come to my caſtle, challenge all the three, and decide their right by one plain battle, while the Spaniards ſtood by to ſee

fair

fair play. One day it happened, that two of my
Spaniards (one of whom underſtood Engliſh) being in the woods, were met by one of the honeſt
men, who complained how barbarous their countrymen had been in deſtroying their corn, killing
their milk-goat, and three kids, which deprived
them of their ſubſiſtence; that if we did not grant
them relief, they muſt be inevitably ſtarved; and,
ſo they parted: but when my Spaniards came home
at night, and ſupper being on the table, one of
them began to reprehend the Engliſhmen, but in
a very mannerly way; which they reſenting, replied, what buſineſs had their countrymen there
without leave, when it was none of their ground?
Why, ſaid my Spaniard, calmly, _Ingleſe_, they muſt
not ſtarve; but they replied, Let them ſtarve
and be d—nn'd, they ſhould neither plant nor build,
and d—mn them they ſhould be their ſervants,
and work for them, for the iſland was theirs, and
they would burn all the huts they ſhould find in
the land. By this rule, ſaid my Spaniard, ſmiling,
we ſhall be your ſervants too. Aye, by G—d,
and ſo you ſhall, replied the impudent raſcal. U-
pon which, ſtarting up, Will Aitkins cries, Come,
Jack, let's have t'other bruſh with them; who
dare to build in our dominions? Thus leaving us
ſomething heated with juſt paſſion, away they
trooped, every man having a gun, piſtol, and
ſword, muttering ſome threatning words, that we
could then but imperfectly underſtand. That night
they deſigned to murder their two companions,
and ſlept till midnight in the bower, thinking to
fall upon them in their ſleep; nor were the honeſt
men leſs thoughtful concerning them; for at this
juncture they were coming to find them out, but
in a much fairer way. As ſoon as the villains came
to the huts, and found no body there, they concluded that I and my Spaniards had given them
notice,

notice, and therefore fwore to be revenged on us. Then they demolifhed the poor men's habitation; not by fire, as they attempted before, but pulled down their houfes, limb from limb, not leaving ftick nor ftone on the ground where they ftood, broke their houfehold ftuff in pieces, tore up their trees, fpoiled their inclofures; and, in fhort, quite ruined them of every thing they had. Had thefe people met together, no doubt but there would have been a bloody battle; but Providence ordered it for the better; for juft as the three were got thither, the two were at our caftle; and when they left us, the three came back again, but in a great rage, fcoffingly telling us what they had done; when one taking hold of a Spaniard's hat, twirls it round, faying, *And you, Seignior,* Jack Spaniard, *fhall have the fame fauce; if you don't mend your manners.* My Spaniard, a grave, but courageous man, knocked him down with one blow of his fift; at which another villain fired his piftol, and narrowly miffed his body, but wounded him a little in the ear. Hereat enraged, the Spaniard takes up the fellow's mufket whom he had knocked down, and would have fhot him, if I and the reft had not come out, and taken their arms from every one of them.

Thefe Englifhmen perceiving they had made all of us their enemies, began to cool; but notwithftanding their better words, the Spaniards would not return them their arms again, telling them, they would do them no manner of harm, if they would live peaceably; but if they offered any injury to the plantation or caftle, they would fhoot them as they would do ravenous beafts. This made them fo mad, that they went away raging like furies of hell. They were no fooner gone, but in came the two honeft men, fired with the jufteft rage, if fuch can be, having been ruined as aforefaid.

aforefaid. And indeed it was very hard, that nineteen of us fhould be bullied by three villains continually offending with impunity.

It was a great while, Sir, before we could perfuade the two Englifhmen from purfuing, and undoubtedly killing them with their fire-arms ; but we promifed them juftice fhould be done them, and in the mean time they fhould refide with us in our habitation. In about five days after, thefe three vagrants, almoft ftarved with hunger, drew near our grove, and perceiving me, the governor, and two others, walking by the fide of the creek, they very fubmiffively defired to be received into the family again. We told them of their great incivility to us, and of their unnatural barbarity to their countrymen ; but yet we would fee to what the reft agreed to, and in half an hour's time would bring them word. After fome debate, we called them in, where their two countrymen laid a heavy charge againft them, for not only ruining, but defigning to murder them, which they could not deny. But here I was forced to interpofe as a mediator, by obliging the two Englifhmen not to hurt them, being naked and unarmed ; and that the other three fhould make them reftitution, by building their two huts, and fencing their ground in the fame manner as it was before. Well, being in a miferable condition, they fubmitted to this at-prefent, and lived fome time regularly enough, except as to the working part, which they did not care for, but the Spaniards would have difpenfed with that, had they continued eafy and quiet. Their arms being given them again, they fcarce had them a week, when they became as troublefome as ever ; but an accident happening foon after, obliged us to lay afide private refentments, and look to our common prefervation.

One night, Sir, I went to bed, perfectly well,
in

in health, and yet by no means could I compose myself to sleep: upon which being very uneasy, I got up, and looked out; but it being dark, I could perceive nothing but the trees around our castle; I went to bed again, but it was all one, I could not sleep; when one of my Spaniards hearing me walk about, asked who it was up? I answered, it is I. When I told him the occasion; Sir, said he, such things are not to be slighted; for certainly there is some mischief plotting near us. Where are the Englishmen? said I. He answered, in their huts; for they lay separate from us, Sir, since the last mutiny. Well, said I, some kind spirit gives this information for our advantage. Come let us go abroad, and see if any thing offers to justify our fears. Upon which, I and some of my Spaniards went up the mountain, not by the ladder, but through the grove; and then we were struck with a panic fear on seeing a light, as though it were a fire, at a very little distance, and hearing the voice of several men. Hereupon we retreated immediately, and missing the rest of our forces, made them sensible of the impending danger: but, with all my authority, I could not make them stay where they were, so earnest were they to see how things went. Indeed the darkness of the night gave them opportunity enough to view them (by the light of their fire) undiscovered. As they were in different parties, and straggling over the shore, we were much afraid that they should find out our habitations, and destroy our flocks of goats; to prevent which, we sent an Englishman and two Spaniards to drive the goats into the valley where the cave lay; or, if there was occasion, into the cave itself. As to ourselves, resuming our native courage, and prudent conduct, had we not been divided, we durst venture to attack a hundred of them; but before it was yet light, we resolved to

send

fend out Friday's father as a fpy, who immediately ftripped himfelf naked, gets among them undifcovered, and in two hours time brings word, that
they were two parties of two different nations,
who lately having a bloody battle with one another, happened to land by mere chance in the fame
ifland, to devour their miferable prifoners: that
they were entirely ignorant of any perfon's inhabiting here; but rather being filled with rage and
fury againft one another, he believed, that as foon
as day-light appeared, there would be a terrible
engagement. Old Friday had fcarce ended his relation when we heard an uncommon noife, and
perceived that there was a horrid engagement between the two armies.

Such was the curiofity of our party, efpecially
the Englifhmen, that they would not lye clofe,
though Old Friday told them their fafety depended upon it; and that if we had patience, we fhould
behold the favages kill one another. However,
they ufed fome caution, by going further into the
woods, and placing themfelves in a convenient
place to behold the battle.

Never could there be a more bloody engagement, nor men of more invincible fpirits, and prudent conduct, according to their way and manner
of fighting. It lafted near two hours, till that
party which was neareft to our caftle began to de-
cline, and at laft to fly from their conquerors.
We were undoubtedly put into a great confternation on this account, left they fhould run into our
grove, and confequently bring us into the like
danger. Hereupon we refolved to kill the firft
that came, to prevent difcovery; and that too
with our fwords, and the butt end of our mufkets, for fear the report of our guns fhould be
heard.

And fo indeed, as we thought, it happened:
for

for three of the vanquished army crossing the creek, ran directly to the place, as to a thick wood for shelter; nor was it long before our scout gave us notice of it; as also, that the victors did not think fit to pursue them. Upon this I would not suffer them to be slain, but had them surprised and taken by our party: and afterwards they proved very good servants to us, being stout young creatures, and able to do a great deal of work. The remainder of the conquered savages fled to their canoes, and put out into the ocean, while the conquerors joining together, shouted by way of triumph, and about three in the afternoon they also embarked for their own nation. Thus we were freed at once from the savages and our fears, not perceiving any of these creatures for some considerable time after. We found two and thirty men dead in the field of battle; some were slain with long arrows, which we found sticking in their bodies; and the rest were killed with great unwieldy wooden swords, which denoted their vast strength, and of which we found seventeen, besides bows and arrows: but we could not find one wounded creature among them alive; for they either kill their enemies quite, or carry those wounded away with them.

This terrible fight tamed the Englishmen for some time, considering how unfortunate they might have been, had they fallen into their hands, who would not only kill them as enemies, but also for food, as we do cattle; and indeed so much did this nauseate their stomachs, that it not only made them very sick, but more tractable to the common necessary business of the whole society, planting, sowing, and reaping, with the greatest signs of amity and friendship; so that being now all good friends, we began to consider of circumstances in general; and the first thing we thought of, was,

was, whether, as we perceived the savages haunted that side of the island, and there being more retired parts of it, and yet as well suited to our manner of living, and equally to our advantage, we ought not rather to move our place of residence, and plant it in a much safer place, both for the security of our corn and cattle.

After a long debate on this head, it was resolved, or rather voted *nemine contradicente*, not to remove our ancient castle, and that for this very good reason, that some time or other we expected to hear from our supreme governor (meaning you Sir,) whose messengers not finding us there, might think the place demolished, and all his subjects destroyed by the savages.

As to the next concern relating to our corn and cattle, we consented to have them removed to the valley where the cave was, that being most proper and sufficient for both. But yet, when we considered further, we altered one part of our resolution; which was, to remove part of our cattle hither, and plant only part of our corn there: so that in case one part was destroyed, the other might be preserved. Another resolution we took, which really had a great deal of prudence in it; and that was, in not trusting the three savages whom we had taken prisoners, with any knowledge of the plantations which we had made in the valley, of what number of cattle we had there, much less of the cave, wherein we kept several arms, and two barrels of powder you left for us, at your departure from this island. But though we would not change our habitation, we resolved to make it more fortified and more secret. To this end, Sir, as you had planted trees at some distance before the entrance of your palace; so we, imitating your example, planted and filled up the whole space of ground, even to the banks of the
creek,

creek, nay, into the very ooze, where the tide flowed, not leaving a place for landing: and among thofe I had planted, they had intermingled fo many fhort ones, all of which growing wonderfully faft and thick, a little dog fcarcely could find a paffage through them. Nor was this fufficient, as we thought; for we did the fame to all the ground, to the right and left hand of us, even to the top of the hill, without fo much as leaving a paffage for ourfelves except by the ladder: which being taken down, nothing but what had wings or witchcraft could pretend to come near us. And indeed this was exceedingly well contrived, efpecially to ferve that occafion, for which we afterwards found it neceffary.

Thus we lived two years in a happy retirement, having all this time not one vifit from the favages. Indeed one morning we had an alarm, which put us in fome amazement; for a few of my Spaniards being out very early, perceived no lefs than twenty canoes, as it were coming on fhore; upon which, returning home, with great precipitation, they gave us the alarm, which obliged us to keep at home all that day and the next, going out only in the night-time to make our obfervation: but as good luck would have it, they were upon another defign, and did not land that time upon the ifland.

But now there happened another quarrel between the three wicked Englifhmen, and fome of my Spaniards. The occafion was this: One of them being enraged at one of the favages, whom he had taken prifoner, for not being able to comprehend fomething which he was fhewing him, fnatched up a hatchet in a great fury, not to correct, but to kill him; yet miffing his head, gave him fuch a barbarous cut in the fhoulder, that he had like to have ftruck off his arm; at which one
of

of my good-natured Spaniards interpofed between the Englifhman and favage, befeeched the former not to murder the poor creature; but this kindnefs had like to have coft the Spaniard his life, for the Englifhman ftruck at him in the fame manner, which he nimbly and wifely avoiding, returned fuddenly upon him with his fhovel (being all at work about their corn-land,) and very fairly knocked the brutifh creature down. Hereupon another Englifhman, coming to his fellow's affiftance, laid the good Spaniard on the earth; when immediately two others coming to his relief, were attacked by the third Englifhman, armed with an old cutlafs, who wounded them both. This uproar foon reached our ears, when we rufhing out upon them, took the three Englifhmen prifoners; and then our next queftion was, what fhould be done to fuch mutinous and impudent fellows, fo furious, defperate, and idle, that they were mifchievous to the highelt degree, and confequently not fafe for the fociety to let them live among them.

Now, Sir, as I was governor in your abfence, fo I alfo took the authority of a judge; and having them brought before me, I told them, that if they had been of my country, I would have hanged every mother's fon of them; but fince it was an Englifhman (meaning you, kind Sir,) to whom we were indebted for our prefervation and deliverance, I would in gratitude ufe them with all poffible mildnefs; but at the fame time leaving them to the judgment of the other two Englifhmen, who, I hoped, forgetting their refentments, would deal impartially by them.

Hereupon one of his countrymen ftood up: *Sir,* faid he, *leave it not to us, for you may be fenfible we have reafon to fentence them to the gallows: befides, Sir, this fellow,* Will Atkins *and the two others, propofed to us, that we might murder you*

all

*all in your sleep, which we would not confent to ;
but knowing their inability, and your vigilance, we
did not think fit to difcover it before now.*

How Seignior, faid I, do you hear what is al-
ledged againft you ? what can you fay to juftify
fo horrid an action, as to murder us in cold blood ?
So far, Sir, was the wretch from denying it, that
he fwore, d-mn him but he would do it ftill. But
what have we done to you Seignior Atkins, faid I,
or what will you gain by killing us ? What fhall
we do to prevent you ? muft we kill you, or you
kill us : Why will you, Seignior Atkins, (faid I
fmiling,) put us to fuch an unhappy dilemma, fuch
a fatal neceffity ? But fo great a rage did my fcof-
fing, and yet fevere jeft, put him into, that he
was going to fly at me, and undoubtedly had attempted to kill me if he had been poffeffed of weapons, and had not been prevented by three Spaniards. This unparalleled and villainous carriage, made us ferioufly confider what was to be
done. The two Englifhmen and the Spaniard,
who had faved the poor Indian's life mightily petitioned me to hang one of them, for an example
to the others, which fhould be him that had twice
attempted to commit murder with his hatchet, it
being at that time thought impoffible the poor flave
fhould recover. But they could never gain my
confent to put him to death, for the reafons above-
mentioned, fince it was an Englifhman (even yourfelf) who was my deliverer, and as merciful coun-
fels are moft prevailing, when earneftly preffed,
fo I got them to be of the fame opinion as to clemency. But, to prevent their doing us any further mifchief, we all agreed, that they fhould have
no weapons, as fword, gun, powder, or fhot, but
be expelled from the fociety, to live as they pleafed, by themfelves ; that neither the two Englifhmen, nor the reft of the Spaniards, fhould have

T

converfation

converſation with them upon any account whatſoever: that they ſhould be kept from coming within a certain diſtance of our caſtle; and if they dared to offer us any violence, either by ſpoiling,
burning, killing, or deſtroying any of the corn,
plantings, buildings, fences, or cattle belonging
to the ſociety, we would ſhoot them as freely as
we would do beaſts of prey, in whatſoever places
we ſhould find them.

This ſentence ſeemed very juſt to all but themſelves; when, like a merciful judge, I called out
to the two honeſt Engliſhmen, ſaying, You muſt
conſider they ought not to be ſtarved neither;
and ſince it will be ſome time before they can raiſe
corn and cattle of their own, let us give them
ſome corn to laſt them eight months, and for ſeed
to ſow, by which time they'll raiſe ſome for themſelves: let us alſo beſtow upon them ſix milk-
goats, four he-ones, and ſix kids, as well for their
preſent ſupport, as for a further increaſe; with
tools neceſſary for their work, as hatchets, an axe,
ſaw, and other things convenient to build them
huts: all which were agreed to; but before they
took them in poſſeſſion, I obliged them ſolemnly
to ſwear, never to attempt any thing againſt us
or their countrymen for the future. Thus diſ-
miſſing them from our ſociety, they went away,
ſullen and refractory, as though neither willing to
go nor ſtay: however, ſeeing no remedy, they
took what proviſion was given them, propoſing,
to chuſe a convenient place, where they might live
by themſelves.

About five days after, they came to thoſe limits
appointed, in order for more victuals, and ſent me
word by one of my Spaniards, whom they called
to, where they had pitched their tents, and marked themſelves out an habitation and plantation, at
the N. E. and moſt remote part of the iſland. And
indeed

indeed there they built themselves two very handsome cottages, resembling our little castle, being
under the side of a mountain, with some trees already growing on three sides of it, so that planting a few more, it would be obscured from sight,
unless particularly sought for. When these huts
were finished, we gave them some dry goat-skins
for bedding and covering; and upon their giving
us fuller assurances of their good behaviour for
the future, we gave them some pease, barley, and
rice for sowing, and whatever tools we could spare.

Six months did they live in this separate condition, in which they got their first harvest in, the
quantity of which was but small, because they had
planted but little land: for indeed, all their plantations being to form, made it the more difficult,
especially as it was a thing out of their element:
and when they were obliged to make their boards
and pots, &c. they could make little or nothing
of it. But the rainy season coming on, put them
into a greater perplexity for want of a cave to
keep their corn dry, and prevent it from spoiling:
and so much did this humble them, that they begged of my Spaniards to help them, to which the
good-natured men readily consented, and in four
days space worked a great hole in the side of the
hill for them, large enough for their purpose, to
secure their corn and other things from the rain,
though not comparable to ours, which had several
additional apartments.

But a new whim possessed these rogues about
three quarters of a year after, which had like to
have ruined us and themselves too: for, it seems
being tired and weary of this sort of living, which
made them work for themselves, without hopes of
changing their condition, nothing would serve
them, but they would make a voyage to the continent, and try if they could seize upon some of

the favages, and bring them over as flaves, to do their drudgery, while they lived at eafe and pleasure.

Indeed the project was not fo prepofterous, if they had not gone farther; but they neither did, nor propofed any thing, but what had mifchief in the defign, or the event. One morning thefe three fellows came down to the limited ftation, and humbly defired to be admitted to talk with us: which we readily granted; they told us, in fhort, that being tired of their manner of living, and the labour of their hands, in fuch employments, not being fufficient to procure the neceffaries of life, they only defired one of the canoes we came over in, with fome arms and ammunition, for their defence, and they would feek their fortunes abroad, and never trouble us any more. To be fure, we were glad enough to get rid of fuch wretched plagues; but yet honefty made us ingenuoufly reprefent to them, by what we ourfelves had fuffered, the certain deftruction they were running into, either of being ftarved to death, or murdered by the favages. To this they very audacioufly replied, that they neither could nor would work; and confequently, that they might as well be ftarved abroad as at home: and as to their falling into the hands of the favages, why, if they were murdered, that was nothing to us, there was an end of them, neither had they any wives or children to cry after them; nay, fo intent were they upon their voyage, that if the Spaniards had not given them arms, fo they had but the canoe, they would have gone without them.

Though we could not well fpare our fire-arms, rather then they fhould go like naked men, we let them have two mufkets, a piftol, a cu lafs, and three hatchets, which were thought very fufficient: we gave them alfo goats flefh, a great bafket full

of

of dried grapes, a pot of fresh butter, a young live kid, and a large canoe sufficient to carry twenty men. And thus, with a mast made of a long pole, and a sail of six large goats skins dried, having a fair breeze, and a flood tide with them, they merrily sailed away, the Spaniards calling after them, *Bon veyajo*, no man ever expecting to see them more.

When they were gone, the Spaniards and Englishmen would often say one to another, *O how peaceable do we now live, since those turbulent fellows have left us?* Nothing could be farther from their thoughts, than to behold their faces any more; and yet scarce two and twenty days had passed over their heads, but one of the Englishmen, being abroad a-planting, perceived at a distance, three men well armed, approaching towards him. Away he flies with speed to our castle, and tells me and the rest, that we were all undone, for that strangers were landed upon the island, and who they were he could not tell; but added, that they were not savages, but men habited, bearing arms. Why then, said I, we have the less occasion to be concerned, since, if they are not Indians, they must be friends; for I am sure there is no Christian people upon earth, but what will do us good rather than harm. But while we were considering of the event, up came the three Englishmen, whose voices we quickly knew, and so all our admiration of that nature ceased at once. And our wonder was succeeded by another sort of inquiry, which was, what could be the occasion of their returning so quickly to the island, when we little expected, and much less desired their company? But as this was better to be related by themselves, I ordered them to be brought in, when they gave me the following relation of their voyage:

After two days sail, or something less, they

T 3

reached

reached land, where they found the people coming
to give them another fort of reception than what
they expected or defired : for as the favages were
armed with bows and arrows, they durft not venture on fhore, but fteered northward, fix or feven
hours, till they gained an opening, by which they
plainly perceived, that the land that appeared from
this place was not the main land, but the ifland.
At their entrance into the opening of the fea,
they difcovered another ifland, on the right hand
northward, and feveral more lying to the weftward; but being refolved to go on fhore fome-
where or other, they put over to one of the wef-
tern iflands. Here they found the natives very
courteous to them, giving them feveral roots and
dried fifh; nay, even their women too were as
willing to fupply them with what they could procure them to eat, bringing it a great way to them
upon their heads. Among thefe hofpitable Indians
they continued fome days, inquiring by figns and
tokens, what nations lay around them; and were
informed, that there were feveral fierce and terrible people lived every way, accuftomed to eat
mankind: but for themfelves, they never ufed
fuch diet, except thofe that were taken in battle,
and of them they made a folemn feaft.

The Englifhmen inquired how long it was fince
they had a feaft of that kind? They anfwered, a-
bout two moons ago, pointing to the moon; and
then to two fingers; that, at this time, their king
had two hundred prifoners, which were fattening
up for the flaughter. The Englifhmen were mighty
defirous of feeing the prifoners, which the others
miftaking, thought they wanted fome of them for
their own food: upon which they beckoned to
them, pointing to the rifing, and then to the fetting of the fun; meaning, that by the time it appeared in the eaft next morning, they would bring
them

them some: and indeed they were as good as their word; for by that time they brought eleven men and five women, just as so many cows and oxen are brought to sea-port towns, to victual a ship. But as brutish as these Englishmen were, their stomachs turned at the sight. What to do in this case, they could not tell: to refuse the prisoners, would have been the highest affront offered to the savage gentry; and to dispose of them, they knew not in what manner: however, they resolved to accept them, and so gave them, in return, one of their hatchets, an old key, a knife, and six or seven of their bullets: things which though they were wholly ignorant of, yet seemed entirely contented with; and dragging the poor wretches into the boat, with their hands bound behind them, delivered them to the Englishmen. But this obliged them to put off as soon as they had these presents, lest the donors should have expected two or three of them to be killed, and to be invited to dinner the next day: and so taking leave with all possible respect and thanks, though neither of them understood what the other said, they sailed away back to the first island, and there set eight of the prisoners at liberty. In their voyage they endeavoured to comfort, and have some conversation with the poor captives; but it was impossible to make them sensible of any thing; and nothing they could say, or give, or do for them, could make them otherwise persuaded, but that they were unbound only to be devoured: if they give them any food, they thought it was only to fatten them for the slaughter; or looked at any one more particularly, the poor creature supposed itself to be the first sacrifice: and even when we brought them to our island, and began to use them with the greatest humanity and kindness, yet they expected every day that their new masters would devour them.

And

And thus, Sir, did thefe three ftrange wanderers conclude their unaccountable relation of their voyage, which was both amazing and entertaining. Hereupon I afked them, where their new family was? They told me, they had put them into one of their huts, and they came to beg fome victuals for them. This, indeed, made us all long to fee them; and fo taking Friday's father with us, leaving only two at our caftle, we came down to behold thofe poor creatures.

When we arrived at the hut, (they being bound again by the Englifhmen, for fear of efcaping,) we found them ftark naked, expecting their fatal tragedy: there were three lufty men, well fhaped, with ftraight and fair limbs, between thirty and five and thirty years old; and five women, two of them might be from thirty to forty, two more, not above four and twenty; and the laft a comely tall maiden of about feventeen. Indeed, all the women were very agreeable, both in their proportion and features, except that they were tawny, which their modeft behaviour and other graces made amends for, when they afterwards came to be cloathed.

This naked appearance, together with their miferable circumftances, was no very comfortable fight to my Spaniards, who, for their parts, I may venture, Sir, without flattery, to fay, are men of the beft behaviour, calmeft tempers, and fweeteft nature, that can poffibly be; for they immediately ordered Friday's father to fee if he knew any of them, or if he underftood what they could fay. No fooner did the old Indian appear, but he looked at them with great ferioufnefs; yet, as they were not of his nation, they were utter ftrangers to him, and none could underftand his fpeech or figns, but one woman. This was enough to anfwer the defign, which was to affure them they

would

would not be killed, being fallen into the hands
of Chriſtians, who abhorred ſuch barbarity. When
they were fully ſatisfied of this, they expreſſed
their joy, by ſuch ſtrange geſtures, and uncommon tones, as it is not poſſible for me to deſcribe.
But the woman, their interpreter, was ordered
next to inquire, whether they were content to
be ſervants, and would work for the men, who
had brought them hither to ſave their lives? Hereupon (being at this time unbound) they fell a capering and dancing, one taking this thing upon her
ſhoulders, and the other that, intimating, that
they were willing to do any thing for them. But
now, Sir, having women among us, and dreading
that it might occaſion ſome ſtrife, if not blood, I
aſked the three men what they would do, and how
they intended to uſe theſe creatures, whether as
ſervants or women ? One of them very pertly
and readily anſwered, they would uſe them as
both. Gentlemen, ſaid I, as you are your own
maſters, I am not going to reſtrain you from that ;
but, methinks, for avoiding diſſenſion among you,
I would only deſire you to engage, that none of
you will take more than one for a woman or a
wife, and that having taken this one, none elſe
ſhould preſume to touch her ; for though we have
not a prieſtly authority to marry you, yet it is
but reaſonable, that whoever thus takes a woman,
ſhould be obliged to maintain her, ſince nobody
elſe has any thing to do with her : and this indeed
appeared ſo juſt to all preſent, that it was unani-
mouſly agreed to. The Engliſhmen then aſked my
Spaniards, whether they deſigned to take any of
them ? but they all anſwered, No ; ſome decla-
ring they had already wives in Spain ; and others,
that they cared not to join with infidels. On the
reverſe, the Engliſhmen took each of them a tem-
porary wife, and ſo ſet up a new method of living.

As

As to Friday's father, the Spaniards, and the three favage fervants we had taken in the late battle, they all lived with me in our ancient caftle; and indeed we fupplied the main part of the ifland with food, as neceffity required. But the moft remarkable part of the ftory is, how thefe Englifhmen, who had been fo much at variance, fhould agree about the choice of thefe women; yet they took a way good enough to prevent quarrelling among themfelves. They fet the five women in one of their huts, and going themfelves to the other, drew lots which fhould have the firft choice. Now, he that had the firft lot went to the hut, and fetched out her he chofe, and it is remarkable, that he took her that was the moft homely and eldeft of the number, which made the reft of the Englifhmen exceeding merry. The Spaniards themfelves could not but finile at it: but, as it happened, the fellow had the beft thought, in chufing one fit for application and bufinefs: and indeed fhe proved the beft wife of all the parcel.

But when the poor creatures perceived themves placed in a row, and feparated one by one, they were again feized with an unfpeakable terror, as now thinking they were going to be flain in earneft: and when the Englifhmen came to take the firft, the reft fet up a lamentable cry, clapt their arms around her neck, and hanging about her, took their laft farewell, as they thought, in fuch trembling agonies, and affectionate embraces, as would have foftened the hardeft heart in the world, and made the dryeft eyes melt into tears; nor could they be perfuaded, but that they were going to die, till fuch time as Friday's father made them fenfible that the Englifhmen had chofen them for their wives, which ended all their terror and concern upon this occafion.

Well, after this, the Englifhmen went to work,
and

and being affifted by my good-natured Spaniards,
in a few hours they erected every one of them a
new hut or tent, for their feparate lodging, fince
thofe they had already were filled with tools,
houfehold ftuff, and provifion. They all continued on the north fhore of the ifland, but feparate
as before; the three wicked ones pitching farther
off, and the two honeft men nearer our caftle; fo
that the ifland feemed to be peopled in three places, three towns beginning to be built for that
purpofe. And here I cannot but remark, what is
very common, that the two honeft men had the
worft wives, (I mean as to induftry, cleanlinefs,
and ingenuity,) while the three reprobates enjoyed women of quite contrary qualities.

But another obfervation I made was, in favour
of the two honeft men, to fhew what difparity
there is between a diligent application to bufinefs
on the one hand, and a flotliful, negligent, and
idle temper, on the other. Both of them had the
fame parcel of ground laid out, and corn to fow,
fufficient for them; but both did not make the fame
improvements, either in their cultivation, or in
their planting. The two honeft men had a multitude of young trees planted about their habitations,
fo that when you approached near them, nothing
appeared but a wood, very pleafing and delightful. Every thing they did profpered and flourifhed; their grapes planted in order, feemed as tho'
managed in a vineyard, and were infinitely preferable to any of the others. Nor were they
wanting to find out a place of retreat, but dug a
cave in the moft retired part of a thick wood, to
fecure their wives and children, with their provifion and chiefeft goods, furrounded with innumerable ftakes, and having a moft fubtle entrance,
in cafe any mifchief fhould happen either from
their fellow-countrymen, or the devouring favages.

As to the reprobates, (though I muſt own they were much civilized than before,) inſtead of a delightful wood ſurrounding their dwelling we found the words of King *Solomon* too truly verified ; *I went by the vineyard of the ſlothful, and it was all overgrown with thorns.* In many places their crop was obſcured with weeds ; the hedges having ſeveral gaps in them, the wild goats had got in, and eaten up the corn, and here and there was a dead buſh, to ſtop in thoſe gaps for the preſent, which was no more than ſhutting the ſtable-door after the ſteed was ſtolen away. But as to their wives, they (as I obſerved before) were more diligent, and cleanly enough, eſpecially in their victuals, being inſtructed by one of the honeſt men, who had been a cook's mate on board a ſhip: and very well it was ſo ; for as he cooked himſelf, his companions and their families lived as well as the idle buſbands, who did nothing but loiter about, fetch turtles eggs, catch fiſh and birds, and do any thing but work, and lived accordingly, while the diligent lived very handſomely and plentifully, in the moſt comfortable manner. And now, Sir, I come to lay before your eyes a ſcene quite different from any thing that ever happened us before, and perhaps ever befel you in all the time of your reſidence on this iſland. I ſhall inform you of its original in the following manner :

One morning, Sir, very early, there came five or ſix canoes of Indians on ſhore, indiſputably upon their old cuſtom of devouring their priſoners. All that we had to do upon ſuch an occaſion, was to lye concealed, that they, not having any notice of inhabitants, might depart quietly, after performing their bloody execution : whoever firſt diſcovered the ſavages, was to give notice to all the three plantations to keep within doors, and then a proper ſcout was to be placed to give intelligence of their departure. But, not-withstanding these wise measures, an unhappy dis-aster discovered us to the savages, which was like to have caused the desolation of the whole island: for, after the savages were gone off in their canoes, some of my Spaniards and i looking abroad, and being inflamed with a curiosity to see what they had been doing, to our great amazement, beheld three savages fast asleep on the ground, who, either being gorged, could not awake when the others went off, or having wandered too far into the woods, did not come back in time.

What to do with them at first we could not tell; as for slaves, we had enough of them already; and as to kill them, neither Christianity nor hu-manity would suffer us to shed the blood of per-sons who never did us wrong. We perceived they had no boat left them to transport them to their own nation; and that by letting them wander about, they might discover us, and inform the first savages that should happen to land upon the same bloody occasion, which information might entirely ruin us; and therefore I counselled my Spaniard to secure them, and set them about some work or other, till we could better dispose of them.

Hereupon we all went back, and making them awake, took them prisoners. It is impossible to express the horror they were in, especially when bound, as thinking they were going to be murder-ed and eaten, but we soon eased them of their fear as to that point. We first took them to the bower where the chief of our country-work lay, as keeping goats, planting corn, &c. And then carried them to the two Englishmen's habita-tion, to help them in their business; but happy it was for us all, we did not carry them to our cas-tle, as by the sequel will appear. The English-men indeed found them work to do ; but whe-

U

ther

ther they did not guard them ſtrictly, or that they thought they could not better themſelves, I can-not tell; but certainly one of them ran away in-to the woods, and they could not hear of him for a long time after.

Undoubtedly there was reaſon enough to ſup-poſe he got home in ſome of the canoes, the ſa-vages returning in about four weeks time, and going off in the ſpace of two days. You may be certain, Sir, this thought could not but terrify us exceedingly, and make us juſtly conclude that this ſavage would inform his countrymen of our abode in the iſland, how few and weak we were in compariſon to their numbers; and we expected it would not be long before the Engliſhmen would be attacked in their habitations; but the ſavages had not ſeen their places of ſafety in the woods, nor our caſtle, which it was a great happineſs they did not know.

Nor were we miſtaken in our thoughts upon this occaſion; for about eight months after this, ſix canoes, with about ten men in each canoe, came ſailing by the north ſide of the iſland, which they never were accuſtomed to before, and land-ed about an hour after ſun riſe, near a mile from the dwelling of the two Engliſhmen, who, it ſeems, had the good fortune to diſcover them about a league off: ſo that it was an hour before they could attain the ſhore, and ſome longer time be-fore they could come at them. And now being confirmed in this opinion, that they were certain-ly betrayed, they immediately bound the two ſlaves which were left, cauſing two of the three men, whom they brought with the women, and who proved very faithful, to lead them with their wives, and other conveniencies, into their retired cave in the wood, and there to bind the two fel-lows hand and foot, till they had further orders.

They

They then opened their fences, where they kept
their milk goats, and drove them all out, giving
the goats liberty to ramble in the woods, to make
the favages believe that they were wild ones; but
the flave had given a truer information, which
made them come to the very inclofures. The two
frighted men fent the other flave of the three who
had been with them by accident, to alarm the Spaniards, and defire their affiftance; in the mean
time, they took their arms and ammunition, and
made to the cave, where they had fent their wives,
and fecuring their flave, feated themfelves in a
private place, from whence they might behold all
the actions of the favages. Nor had they gone
far, when afcending a rifing ground, they could
fee a little army of Indians approaching to their
beautiful dwelling, and, in a few moments more,
perceive the fame, and their furniture, to their
unfpeakable grief, burning in a confuming flame:
and when this was done, they fpread here and
there, fearching every bufh and place for the people, of whom, it is very evident, they had information. Upon which the two Englifhmen, not
thinking themfelves fecure where they ftood, retreated about half a mile higher in the country,
rightly concluding, that the farther the favages
ftrolled, there would be leffer numbers together:
upon which they next took their ftand by the trunk
of an old tree, very hollow and large, whence
they refolved to fee what would offer: but they
had not ftood long there before two favages came
running directly towards them, as though having
knowledge of their being there, who feemed refolved to attack them; a little farther were three
more, and five more behind them again, all running the fame way. It cannot be imagined what
perplexity the poor men were in at this fight,
thinking, that if affiftance did not fpeedily come,.

their cave in the wood would be difcovered, and confequently all therein loft: fo they refolved to refift them there; and when overpowered, to af-cend to the top of the trees, where they might defend themfelves as long as their ammunition lafted, and fell their lives as dear as poffible to thofe devouring favages. Thus fixed in their re-folution, they next confidered, whether they fhould fire at the firft two, or wait for the three, and fo take the middle party, by which the two firft and the five laft would be feparated. In this regula-tion the two favages alfo confirmed them, by turn-ing a little to another part of the wood; but the three, and the five after them, came directly to-wards the tree. Hereupon they refolved to take them in a direct line, as they approached nearer, becaufe perhaps the firft fhot might hit them all three; and upon this occafion, the man who was to fire, charged his piece with three or four bul-lets. And thus, while they were waiting, the fa-vages came on, one of them was the runaway, who had caufed all the mifchief: fo they refolved he fhould not efcape, if they both fired at once. But however, though they did not fire together, they were ready charged; when the firft that let fly was too good a markfman to mifs his aim; for he killed the formoft outright, the fecond (who was the runaway Indian) fell on the ground, being fhot through the body, but not dead, and the third was a little wounded on the fhoulder, who, fitting down on the ground, fell a fcreaming in a moft fearful manner. The noife of the guns, which not only made the moft refounding echoes, from one fide to another, but raifed the birds of all forts, fluttering with the moft confufed noife, fo much terrified the five favages behind, that they ftood ftill at firft, like fo many inanimate images. But when all things were in profound filence, they

came

came to the place where their companions lay: and thefe, being not fenfible that they were liable to the fame fate, ftood over the wounded man, undoubtedly inquiring the occafion of this fad calamity; and 'tis as reafonable to fuppofe, he told them, that it came by thunder and lightning from the gods, having never feen nor heard of a gun before, in the whole courfe of their lives. By this time, the Englifhmen having loaded their pieces, fired both together a fecond time, when feeing them all fall immediately upon the ground, they thought they had killed every creature of them. This made them come up boldly before they had charged their guns, which indeed was a wrong ftep; for when they came to the place, they found four alive, two of them very little wounded, and one not at all, which obliged them to fall upon them with their mufkets: they firft knocked the runaway favage on the head, and another that was but a little wounded in the arm, and then put the other languifhing wretches out of their pain; while he that was not hurt, with bending knees, and uplifted hands, made piteous moans, and figns to them to fpare his life: nor indeed were they unmerciful to the poor wretches, but pointed to them to fit down at the root of a tree hard by; and then one of the Englifhmen, with a piece of rope twine he had in his pocket by mere chance, tying his two feet together, and his two hands behind him, they left him there, making all the hafte they could after the other two, fearing they fhould find out their cave: but though they could not overtake them, they had the fatisfaction to perceive them, at a diftance, crofs a valley towards the fea, a quite contrary way to their retreat; upon which they returned to the tree, to look after their prifoner; but when

U. 3.   they

they came there he was gone, leaving the piece of rope-yarn wherewith he was bound behind him.

Well, now they were as much concerned as ever, as not knowing how near their enemies might be, or in what numbers: immediately they repaired to their cave, to see if all was well there, and found every thing safe, except the women, who were frighted upon their husbands account, whom now they loved entirely. They had not been long here, before seven of my Spaniards came to assist them; while the other ten, their servants, and Friday's father, were gone to defend their bower, corn, and cattle, in case the savages should have rambled so far. There accompanied the seven Spaniards, one of the three savages that had formerly been taken prisoners; and with them also that very Indian whom the Englishmen had a little before left under the tree; for it seems, they passed by that way where the slaughter was made, and so carried along with them that poor wretch that was left bound. But so many prisoners now becoming a burden to us, and fearing the dreadful consequence of their escaping, most of the Spaniards and English urged the absolute necessity there was of killing them for our common preservation: but, Sir, the authority I bore as a governor, over-ruled that piece of cruelty; and then I ordered them to be sent prisoners to the old cave in the valley, bound hands and feet, with two Spaniards to guard them.

So much encouraged were the Englishmen at the approach of the Spaniards, and so great was their fury against the savages, for destroying their habitations, that they had not patience to stay any longer; but, taking five Spaniards along with them, armed with four muskets, a pistol, and a quarter-staff, away they went in pursuit of their enemies. As they passed by the place where the

savages

favages were flain, it was very eafy to be perceived that more of them had been there, having attempted to carry off their dead bodies, but found
it impracticable. From a r'fing ground, our party
had the mortification to fee the fmoke that proceeded from the ruins; when coming farther in
fight of the fhore, they plainly perceived that the
favages had embarked in their canoes, and were
putting out to fea. This they were very forry
for, there being no coming at them to give them
a parting falute; but, however, they were glad
enough to get clear of fuch unwelcome guefts.

Thus the two honeft, but unfortunate Englifhmen, being ruined a fecond time, and their improvements quite deftroyed; moft of my good natured Spaniards helped them to rebuild, and we
all affifted them with needful fupplies; nay, what
is more remarkable, their three mifchievous countrymen, when they heard it, (which was after all
thefe difafters were over, they living remote eaftward,) very friendly fympathifed with them, and
worked for them feveral days: fo that in a little
time their habitation was rebuilt, their neceffities
fupplied, and themfelves reftored to their former
tranquillity

Though the favages had nothing to boaft of in
this adventure, (feveral canoes being driven a-
fhore, followed by two drowned creatures, having
undoubtedly met with a ftorm at fea that very
night they departed,) yet it was natural to be fuppofed, that thofe, whofe better fortune it was to
attain their native fhore, would inflame their nation to another ruinous attempt, with a greater
force, to carry all before them. And indeed fo it
happened; for, about feven months after, our
ifland was invaded with a moft formidable navy,
no lefs than eight and twenty canoes full of favages, armed with wooden fwords, monftrous clubs,
bows,

bows, and arrows, and fuch like inftruments of war, landing at the eaft fide of the ifland. You may well, Sir, imagine, what conflernation our men were in upon this account, and how fpeedily they were to execute their refolution, having only that night's time allowed them. They knew that fince they could not withftand their enemies, concealment was the only way to procure their fafety: and therefore they took down the huts that were built for the two Englifhmen, and drove their flock of goats, together with their own at the bower, to the old cave in the valley, leaving as little appearance of inhabitants as poffible; and then potted themfelves with all their force, at the plantation of the two men. As they expected, fo it happened; for early the next morning, the Indians, leaving their canoes at the eaft end of the ifland, came running along the fhore, about two hundred and fifty in number, as near as could be guefled. Our army was but little indeed; and what was our greateft misfortune, we had not arms fufficient for them. The account, as to the men, Sir, is as follows:

<table>
<tr><td>17 Spaniards.</td><td rowspan="9">To arm thefe they had</td><td>11 Mufkets.</td></tr>
<tr><td>5 Englifhmen.</td><td>5 Piftols.</td></tr>
<tr><td>1 Old Friday.</td><td>3 Fowling-pieces.</td></tr>
<tr><td>3 The three favages ta-</td><td>2 Swords.</td></tr>
<tr><td>ken with the women,</td><td>3 Old halberts.</td></tr>
<tr><td>who proved faithful</td><td>5 Mufkets, or fowling-</td></tr>
<tr><td>fervants.</td><td>pieces, taken from</td></tr>
<tr><td>3 Other flaves, living</td><td>the failors whom you</td></tr>
<tr><td>with the Spaniards.</td><td>reduced.</td></tr>
</table>

As to our flaves, we gave three of them halberts, and the other three long ftaves, with great iron fpikes at the end of them, with hatchets by their fides: we alfo had hatchets flicking in our girdles,
befides

befides the fire arms: nay, two of the women, infpired with Amazonian fortitude, could not be
diffuaded from fighting along with their deareft
hufbands, and if they died, to die with them.
Seeing their refolution, we gave them hatchets
likewife; but what pleafed them beft, were the
bows and arrows (which they dexteroufly knew
how to ufe) that the Indians had left behind them,
after their memorable battle one againft another.

Over this army, which, though little, was of
great intrepidity, I was conftituted chief general
and commander; and knowing *Will. Atkins*, tho'
exceeding wicked, yet a man of invincible courage,
I gave him the power of commanding under me:
he and fix men, with their mufkets loaded, with
fix or feven bullets apiece, were planted juft behind a fmall thicket of bufhes, as an advanced
guard, having orders to let the firft pafs by; and
then, when he fired into the middle of them, make
a nimble retreat round part of the wood, and fo
come in the rear of the Spaniards, who were fha-
ded by a thicket of trees; for though the favages
came on with the fiercenefs of lions, yet they
wanted the fubtilty of foxes, being out of all
manner of order, and ftraggling in heaps every
way: and indeed when Will. Atkins, after fifty
of the favages had paffed by, had ordered three of
his men to give fire, fo great was their confternation, to fee fo many men killed and wounded, and
hear fuch a dreadful noife, and yet not know
whence it came, that they were frightened to the
higheft degree; and when the fecond volley was
given, they concluded no lefs but that their companions were flain by thunder and lightning from
heaven. In this notion they would have continued, had Will. Atkins and his men retired as foon
as they fired, according to order; or had the reft
been near them, to pour in their fhot continually,

there

there might have been a complete victory obtained; but staying to load their pieces again, discovered the whole matter. They were perceived by
some of the scattering savages at a distance, who
let fly their arrows among them, wounded Atkins
himself, and killed his fellow Englishman, and one
of the Indians taken with the women. Our party
did not fail to answer them, and in their retreat
killed about twenty savages. Here I cannot but
take notice of our poor dying slave, who, though
stopt from his retreat by a fatal arrow, yet with
his staff and hatchet desperately and gallantly af-
sailed the pursuers, and killed five of the savages,
before his life submitted to a multiplicity of wounds.
Nor is the cruelty or malice of the Indians to be
less remarked, in breaking the arms, legs, and
heads of the two dead bodies with their clubs and
wooden swords, after a most wretched manner.
As Atkins retreated, our party advanced, to in-
terpose between him and the savages; but after
three volleys, we were obliged to retreat also:
for they were so numerous and desperate, that they
came up to our very teeth, shot their arrows like
a cloud, and their wounded men, enraged with
cruel pain, fought like madmen. They did not,
however, think fit to follow us, but drawing themselves up in a circle, they gave two triumphant
shouts in token of victory, though they had the
grief to see several of their wounded men bleed to
death before them.

After I had, Sir, drawn up our little army together upon a rising ground, Aitkins, wounded as
he was, would have had us attack the whole body
of the savages at once. I was extremely well
pleased with the gallantry of the man; but upon
consideration I replied, *You perceive, Seignior,
Aitkins, how their wounded men fight; let them
alone till morning, when they will be faint, stiff,*
and

*and fore, and then we shall have fewer to combat
with.* To which, *Will. Aitkins,* smiling, replied,
*That's very true, Seignior, and so shall I too ; and
that's the reason I would fight them, now I am warm.*
We all answered, Seignior Aitkins, for your part,
you have behaved very gallantly ; and if you are
not able to approach the enemy in the morning,
we will fight for you ; till then we think it convenient to wait ; and so we tarried.

By the brightness of the moon that night, we
perceived the savages in great disorder about their
dead and wounded men. This made us change our
resolution, and resolve to fall upon them in the
night, if we could give them one volley undifcovered. This we had a fair opportunity to do,
by one of the two Englishmen's leading us round,
between the woods and the sea-side westward, and
turning short south, came privately to a place
where the thickest of them were. Unheard and
unperceived, eight of us fired among them, and
did dreadful execution ; and in half a minute after,
eight more of us let fly, killing and wounding a-
bundance of them ; and then dividing ourselves into three bodies, eight persons in each body, we
marched from among the trees to the very teeth
of the enemy, sending forth the greatest shouts
and acclamations. The savages hearing a different noise from three quarters at once, stood in
the utmost confusion ; but coming in sight of us,
let fly a volley of arrows, which wounded poor
old Friday, yet happily it did not prove mortal.
We did not however give them a second opportunity, but rushing in among them, we fired three
several ways, and then fell to work with our
swords, staves, hatchets, and the butt-end of our
muskets, with a fury not to be resisted ; so that,
with the most dismal screaming and howling, they
had recourse to their feet, to save their lives by a

speedy

speedy flight. Nor must we forget the valour of the two women; for they exposed themselves to the greatest dangers, killed many with their arrows, and valiantly destroyed several more with their hatchets.

In fighting these two battles, we were so much tired, that we did not then trouble ourselves to pursue them to their canoes, in which we thought they would presently put to the ocean: but there happening a dreadful storm at sea, which continuing all that night, it not only prevented their voyage, but dashed several of their boats to pieces against the beach, and drove the rest so high upon the shore, that it required infinite pains to get them off. After our men had taken some refreshment and a little repose, they resolved early in the morning to go towards the place of their landing, and see whether they were gone off, or in what posture they remained. This necessarily led them to the place of battle, where several of the savages were expiring; a sight no way pleasing to generous minds, to delight in their misery, though obliged to conquer them by the law of arms: but our own Indian slaves put them out of their pain, by dispatching them with their hatchets. At length, coming in view of the remainder of their army, we found them leaning upon their knees, which were bended towards their mouth, and the head between the two hands. Hereupon, coming within musket-shot of them, I ordered two pieces to be fired without ball, in order to alarm them, that we might plainly know whether they had the courage to venture another battle, or were utterly dispirited from such an attempt, that so we might accordingly manage them. And indeed the project took very well; for no sooner did the savages hear the first gun, and perceive the flash of the second, but they suddenly started upon their feet, in the greatest

greateſt conſternation ; and when we approached towards them, they ran yowling and ſcreaming a-way up the hill into the country.

We could rather, at firſt, have wiſhed, that the weather had permitted them to have gone off to the ſea ; but when we conſidered that their eſcape might occaſion the approach of multitudes, to our utter ruin and diſſolution, we were very well pleaſed the contrary happened : and Will. Atkins (who, though wounded, would not part from us all this while) adviſed us not to let ſlip this ad-vantage, but clapping between them and their boats, deprive them of the capacity of ever re-turning to plague the iſland : *I know,* (ſaid he,) *there is but one objection you can make, which is, that theſe creatures, living like beaſts in the wood, may make excurſions, riffle the plantations, and de-ſtroy the tame goats : but then conſider, we had bet-ter to do with an hundred men, whom we can kill, or make ſlaves of, at leiſure, than with an hundred nations, whom it is impoſſible we ſhould ſave our-ſelves from, much leſs ſubdue.* This advice, and theſe arguments being approved of, we ſet fire to their boats ; and though they were ſo wet that they would not burn entirely, yet we made them incapable for ſwimming in the ſeas. As ſoon as the Indians perceived what we were doing, many of them ran out of the woods, in ſight of us, and kneeling down piteouſly cried out, *Oa, Oa, Wa-ramakoa,* intimating, I ſuppoſe, that if we would but ſpare their canoes, they would never trouble us again.

But all their complaints, ſubmiſſions, and in-treaties, were in vain : for ſelf-preſervation obli-ging us to the contrary, we deſtroyed every one of them that had eſcaped the fury of the ocean. When the Indians perceived this, they raiſed a la-mentable cry, and ran into the woods, where they

X

con-

continued running about, making the woods ring with their lamentation. Here we fhould have con-fidered, that making thefe creatures thus defperate, we ought, at the fame time, to have fet a fuffici-ent guard upon the plantations: for the favages, in their ranging about, found out the bower, de-ftroyed the fences, trod the corn down under their feet, and tore up the vines and grapes. It is true, we were always able to fight thefe creatures; but as they were too fwift for us, and very numerous, we durft not go out fingle, for fear of them; though that too was needlefs, they having no weapons, nor any materials to make them; and indeed their extremity appeared in a little time af-ter.

Though the favages, as already mentioned, had deftroyed our bower, and all our corn, grapes, &c. yet we had ftill left our flock of cattle in the val-ley by the cave, with fome little corn that grew there, and the plantation of Will. Aitkins and his companions, one of whom being killed by an ar-row, they were now reduced to two: it is re-markable, that this was the fellow who cut the poor Indian with his hatchet, and had a defign to murder me and my countrymen the Spaniards. As our condition was fo low, we came to the re-folution to drive the favages up to the farther part of the ifland, where no Indians landed: to kill as many of them as we could, till we had reduced their number; and then to give the remainder fome corn to plant, and to teach them how to live by their daily labour. Accordingly we purfued them with our guns, at the hearing of which, they were fo terrified, that they would fall to the ground. Every day we killed and wounded fome of them, and many we found ftarved to death, fo that our hearts began to relent at the fight of fuch miferable objects. At laft, with great difficulty,

taking

taking one of them alive, and using him with kindness and tenderness, we brought him to Old Friday, who talked to him, and told him how good we would be to them all, giving them corn and land to plant and live in, and present nourishment, provided they would keep within such bounds as should be allotted them; and not do prejudice to others: *Go then,* said he, *and inform your countrymen of this; which, if they will not agree to, every one of them shall be slain.*

The poor creatures, thoroughly humbled, being reduced to about thirty-seven, joyfully accepted the offer, and earnestly begged for food; hereupon we sent twelve Spaniards and two Englishmen, well armed, together with Old Friday, and three Indian slaves, who marched to the place where they were. The slaves were loaded with a large quantity of bread, and rice cakes, with three live goats: and the poor Indians being ordered to sit down on the side of the hill, they ate the victuals very thankfully, and have proved faithful to the last, never trespassing beyond their bounds, where at this day they quietly and happily remain, and where we now and then visit them. They are confined to a neck of land about a mile and a half broad, and three or four in length on the south-east corner of the island, the sea being before, and lofty mountains behind them, free from the appearance of canoes; and indeed their countrymen have never made any inquiry after them. We gave them twelve hatchets, and three or four knives; have taught them to build huts, make wooden spades, plant corn, make bread, breed tame goats, and milk them, as likewise to make wicker-works, in which, I must ingenuously confess, they infinitely outdo us, having made themselves several pretty necessaries and fancies, as baskets, sieves, bird cages, and cup-boards, as

X 2

stools,

ftools, beds, and couches, no lefs ufeful than delightful : and now they live the moft innocent and inoffenfive creatures that ever were fubdued in the world, wanting nothing but wives to make them a nation.

Thus, kind Sir, have I given you, according to my ability, an impartial account of the various tranfactions that have happened in the ifland fince your departure, to this day : and we have great reafon to acknowledge the kind providence of Heaven in our merciful deliverance. When you infpect your little kingdom, you will find in it fome little improvement, your flocks increafed, and your fubjects augmented: fo that from a defolate ifland, as this was before your wonderful deliverance upon it, here is a vifible profpect of its becoming a populous and well governed little kingdom, to your immortal fame and glory.

The end of the Spanifh governor's relation.

✿✿✿✿✿✿✿✿✿✿✿✿✿✿✿✿✿✿✿✿✿✿

The continuation of the life of Robinfon Crufoe ; both of thofe paffages that happened during the time of his continuance on the ifland, and after his departure, till he arrived again in his native country.

THere is no doubt to fuppofe, but that the precedent relation of my faithful Spaniard was very agreeable, and no lefs furprifing to me, to the young prieft, and to all who heard it: nor were thefe people lefs pleafed with thofe neceffary utenfils that I brought them, fuch as the knives, fciffars, fpades, fhovels, and pick axes, with which they now adorn their habitations. So much had they addicted themfelves to wicker-work prompted

by

by the ingenuity of the Indians, who affifted them,
that when I viewed the Englifhmen's colonies,
they feemed at a diftance as though they had lived
like bees in a hive: for Will. Aitkins, who was
now become a very induftrious and fober man, had
made himfelf a tent of bafket-work round the outfide; the walls were worked in as a bafket, in
pannels or ftrong fquares of thirty-two in number, ftanding about feven feet high: in the middle was another, not above twenty paces round,
but much ftronger built, being of an octagonal
form, and in the eight corners ftood eight ftrong
pofts, round the top of which he laid ftrong pieces,
pinned with wooden pins, from which he raifed a
pyramid for the roof, mighty pretty, I affure you,
and joined very well together with iron fpikes,
which he made himfelf; for he had made him a
forge, with a pair of wooden bellows and charcoal for his work, forming an anvil out of one of
the iron-crows, to work upon, and in this manner
would he make himfelf hooks, ftaples, fpikes, bolts,
and hinges. After he had pitched the roof of his
innermoft tent, he made it fo firm between the
rafters with bafket-work, thatching that over a-
gain with rice ftraw, and over that a large leaf of
a tree, that his houfe was as dry as if it had been
tiled or flated. The outer circuit was covered as
a lean-to quite round this inner apartment, laying
long rafters from the thirty-two angles, to the
top-pofts of the inner houfe, about twenty feet
diftance: fo that there was a fpace like a wall betwixt the outer and inner wall, near twenty feet
in breadth. The inner place he partitioned off
with the fame wicker-work, dividing it into fix
neat apartments, every one of which had a door,
firft into the entry of the main tent, and another
into the fpace and walk that was round it, not only convenient for retreat, but for circle, there

X 3   was.

was a paffage directly to the door of the inner
houfe; on either fide was a wicker partition, and
a door, by which you go firft into a large room
twenty-two feet wide, and about thirty long, and
through that into another of a fmaller length, fo
that in the outward circle were ten handfome
rooms, fix of which were only to be come at thro'
the apartments of the inner tent, ferving as retiring rooms to the refpective chambers of the
inner circle, and four large warehoufes, which
went in through one another, two on either hand
of the paffage that led through the outward door
to the inner tent. In fhort, nothing could be built
more ingenioufly, kept more neat, or have better
conveniencies; and here lived the three families,
Will. Aitkins, his companion, their wives and
children, and the widow of the deceafed As to
religion, the men feldom taught their wives the
knowledge of God, any more than the failors
cuftom of fwearing by his name. The greateft
improvement their wives had, was, they taught
them to fpeak Englifh, fo as to be underftood.

None of their children were then above fix years
old; they were all fruitful enough; and, I think,
the cook's mate's wife was big of her fixth child.

When I inqu'red of the Spaniards about their
circumftances while among the favages, they told
me, that they abandoned themfelves to defpair,
reckoning themfelves a poor and miferable people,
that had no mean put into their hands, and confequently muft foon be ftarved to death. They
owned, however, that they were in the wrong to
think fo, and for refufing the affiftance that reafon
offered for their fupport, as well as future deliverance, confeffing that grief was a moft infigni-
ficant paffion, as it looked upon things as without
remedy, and having no hope of good things to
come; all which verified this noted proverb,

In-

In trouble to be troubled,
Is to have your trouble doubled.

Nor did his remarks end here; for making ob-
fervations upon my improvements, and on my
condition at firft, infinitely worfe than theirs, he
told me, that Englifhmen had, in their diftrefs,
greater prefence of mind than thofe of any other
country that he had met with; and that they and
the Portuguefe were the worft men in the world
to ftruggle under misfortunes. When they landed
among the favages, they found but little provifion,
except they would turn cannibals, there being but
a few roots and herbs, with little fubftance in
them, and of which the natives gave them but
very fparingly. Many were the ways they took
to civilize and teach the favages, but in vain:
for they would not own them to be their inftruc-
tors, whofe lives were owing to their bounty.
Their extremities were very great, many days
being entirely without food, the favages there
being more indolent and lefs devouring than thofe
who had better fupplies. When they went out to
battle, they were obliged to affift thefe people; in
one of which my faithful Spaniard being taken,
had like to have been devoured. They had loft
their ammunition, which rendered their fire arms
ufelefs; nor could they ufe the bows and arrows
that were given them, fo that while the armies
were at a diftance, they had no chance, but when
clofe, then they could be of fervice with halberts
and fharpened fticks, put into the muzzles of their
mufkets. They made themfelves targets of wood,
covered with the fkins of wild beafts; and when
one happened to ke knocked down, the reft of the
company fought over him till he recovered; and
then ftanding clofe, in a line, they would make
their way through a thoufand favages. At the
return

return of their friend, who they thought had been entombed in the bowels of their enemies, their joy was inconceivable. Nor were they lefs furprifed at the fight of the loaves of bread I had fent them, things that they had not feen for feveral years, at the fame time croffing and bleffing it, as though it was manna fent from heaven: but when they knew the errand, and perceived the boat which was to carry them to the perfon and place from whence fuch relief came, this ftruck them with fuch a furprife of joy as made fome of them faint away, and others burft out into tears.

This was the fummary account that I had from them. I fhall now inform the reader what I next did for them, and in what condition I left them. As we were all of opinion that the favages would fcarce trouble them any more, fo we had i o apprehenfions on that fcore. I told them I was come purely to eftablifh, and not to remove them; and, upon that occafion, had not only brought them neceffaries for convenience and defence, but alfo artificers, and other perfons, both for their neceffary employments, and to add to their number. They were all together when I thus talked to them; and before I delivered to them the ftores I had brought, I afked them one by one, if they had entirely forgot their firft animofities, would engage in the ftricteft friendfhip, and fhake hands with one another? On this, Will. Atkins, with abundance of good humour, faid, they had afflictions enough to make them all fober, and enemies enough to make them all friends: as for himfelf, he would live and die among them, owning, that what the Spaniards had done to him, his own mad humour had made neceffary for them to do. Nor had the Spaniards occafion to juftify their proceeding to me; but they told me, that, fince Will. Atkins had behaved himfelf fo villiantly in fight, and

at

at other times fhewed fuch a regard to the common intereft of them all, they had not only forgotten all that was paft, but thought he ought as much to be trufted with arms and neceffaries as any of them, which they teftified by making him next in command to the governor: and they moft heartily embraced the occafion of giving me this folemn affurance, that they would never feparate their intereft again as long as they lived.

After thefe kind declarations of friendfhip, we appointed all of us to dine together the next day; upon this I caufed the fhip's cook and his mate come on fhore for that purpofe, to affift in dreffing our dinner. We brought from the fhip fix pieces of beef, and four of pork, together with our punch-bowl, and materials to fill it; and in particular, I gave them ten bottles of French claret, and ten of Englifh beer, which was very acceptable to them. The Spaniards added to our feaft five whole kids, which being roafted, three of them were fent as frefh meat to the failors on board, and the other two we ate ourfelves. After our merry and innocent feaft was over, I began to diftribute my cargoe among them. Firft, I gave them linen fufficient to make every one of them four fhirts, and at the Spaniards requeft made them up fix. The thin Englifh ftuffs I allotted to make every one a light coat like a frock agreeable to the climate, and left them fuch a quantity, as to make more upon their decay; as alfo pumps, fhoes, hats, and ftockings. It is not to be expreffed the pleafing fatisfaction which fat upon the countenances of thefe poor men, when they perceived what care I took of them, as if I had been a common father to them all; and they all engaged never to leave the ifland, till I gave my confent for their departure. I then prefented to them the people I brought, to-wit, the tailor, fmith, and

and the two carpenters ; but my Jack of all trades was the moſt acceptable preſent I could make them. My tailor fell immediately to work, and made every one of them a ſhirt ; after which, he learned the women how to ſew and ſtitch, thereby to become the more helpful to their huſbands. Neither were the carpenters leſs uſeful, taking in pieces their clumſy things, inſtead of which they made convenient and handſome tables, ſtools, bedſteads, cupboards, lockers and ſhelves. But when I carried them to ſee Will. Atkin's baſket-houſe, they owned they never ſaw ſuch a piece of natural ingenuity before: *I am ſure*, ſaid one of the carpenters, *the man that built this has no need of us ; you need, Sir, do nothing, but give him tools.*

I divided the tools among them in this manner : to every man I gave a digging-ſpade, a ſhovel, and a rake, as having no harrows or ploughs ; and to every ſeparate place a pick-axe, a crow, a broad axe, and a ſaw, with a ſtore for a general ſupply, ſhould any be broken or worn out. I left them alſo nails, ſtaples, hinges, hammers, chiſſels, knives, ſciſſars, and all ſorts of tools and iron work ; and for the uſe of the ſmith, gave them three tons of unwrought iron for a ſupply : and as to arms and amunition, I ſtored them even to profuſion, or at leaſt to equip a ſufficient little army againſt all oppoſers whatſoever.

The young man (whoſe mother was unfortunately ſtarved to death,) together with the maid, a pious and well educated young woman, ſeeing things ſo well ordered on ſhore (for I made them accompany me,) and conſidering they had no occaſion to go ſo far a voyage as to the Eaſt Indies, they both deſired of me, that I would leave them there, and enter them among my ſubjects. This I readily agreed to, ordering them a plat of ground, on which were three little houſes erected, environ-

ed

ed with basket-work, pallisadoed like Atkins', and adjoining to his plantation. So contrived were their tents, that each of them had a room apart to lodge in, while the middle tent was not only their storehouse, but their place for eating and drinking. At this time the two Englishmen removed their habitation to their former place; so that now the island was divided into three colonies; *first*, Those I have just now mentioned, *secondly*, That of Will. Aitkins, where there were four families of Englishmen, with their wives and children, the widow and her children: the young man, and the maid, who, by the way we made a wife of before our departure; three savages, who were slaves; the taylor, smith, (who served also as a gunsmith,) and my other celebrated person called *Jack of all trades*. *Thirdly*, My chief colony, which consisted of the Spaniards, with Old Friday, who still remained at my old habitation, which was my capital city: and surely never was there such a metropolis, it now being hid in so obscure a grove, that a thousand men might have ranged the island a month, and looked purposely for it, without being able to find it, though the Spaniards had enlarged its boundaries, both without and within, in a most surprising manner.

But now I think it high time to speak of the young French priest of the order of St. *Benedict*, whose judicious and pious discourses, upon sundry occasions, merit an extraordinary observation: nor can his being a French Papist priest, I presume, give offence to any of my readers, when they have this assurance from me, that he was a person of the most courteous disposition, extensive charity, and exalted piety. His arguments were always agreeable to reason, and his conversation the most acceptable of any person that I had ever yet met with in my life.

Sir,

Sir, faid he to me one day, *fince under God (at* the fame time crofling his breaft) *you have not only faved my life, but, by permitting me to go this voyage, have granted me the happinefs of free converfation, I think it my duty, as my profeffion obliges me, to fave what fouls I can, by bringing them to the knowledge of fome Catholic doctrine,—neceffary to falvation; and fince thefe people are under your immediate government, in gratitude, juftice, and decency for what you have done for me, I offer no farther points in religion, than what fhall merit your approbation.* Being pleafed with the modefty of his carriage, I told him he fhould not be the worfe ufed for being of a different perfuafion, if, upon that very account, we did not differ in points of faith, not decent in a part of the country, where the poor Indians ought to be inftructed in the knowledge of the true God and his Son Jefus Chrift. To this he replied, that converfation might eafily be feparated from difputes; that he would difcourfe with me rather as a gentleman, than a religious: but that if he did enter upon religious arguments, upon my defiring the fame, I would give him liberty to defend my own principles. He farther added, that he would do all that became him in his office, as a prieft as well as a Chriftian, to procure the happinefs of all that was in the fhip: that though he could not pray with, he would pray for us, on all occafions: and then he told me feveral extraordinary events of his life, within a few years paft, but particularly in this laft, which was the moft remarkable: that in this voyage he had the misfortune to be five times fhipped and unfhipped: his firft defign was to have gone to Martinico, for which taking fhip at St. Malo, he was forced into Lifbon by bad weather, the veffel running aground in the mouth of the Tagus: that from thence he went on board a Portuguefe tuguese ship, bound to the Maderas, whose master being but an indifferent mariner, and out of his reckoning, they were drove to Fial, where selling their commodity, which was corn, they resolved to take in their loading at the isle of May, and to sail to Newfoundland; at the banks of which, meeting a French ship bound to Quebec, in the river of Canada, and from thence to Martinico; in this ship he embarked, the master of which dying at Quebec, that voyage was suspended: and lastly, shipping himself for France, this last ship was destroyed by fire, as before has been related.

At this time we talked no further: but another morning he comes to me, just as I was going to visit the Englishmen's colony, and tells me, that as he knew the prosperity of the island was my principal desire, he had something to communicate, agreeable to my design, by which perhaps he might put it, more than he yet thought it was, in the way of the benediction of Heaven. How, Sir? said I, in a surprise, are we not yet in the way of God's blessing, after all these signal providences and deliverances, of which you have had such an ample relation? He replied, I hope, Sir, you are in the way, and that your good design will prosper: but still there are some among you that are not equally right in their actions: and remember, I beseech you, Sir, that *Achan*, by his crime, removed God's blessing from the camp of the children of Israel; that though six and thirty were entirely innocent, yet they became the objects of divine vengeance, and bore the weight of the punishment accordingly.

So sensible was I touched with this discourse, and so satisfied with that ardent piety that inflamed his soul, that I desired him to accompany me to the Englishmen's plantations, which he was very glad of, by reason these were the subjects of what he

Y

designed

designed to discourse with me about; and while we walked on together, he began in the following manner:

Sir, said he, I must confess it is a great unhappiness that we disagree in several doctrinal articles of religion; but surely both of us acknowledge this, that there is a God, who having given us some stated rules for our service and obedience, we ought not willingly and knowingly to offend him, either by neglecting what he has commanded, or by doing what he has forbidden us. This truth every Christian owns, that whenever any one presumptuously sins against God's command, the Almighty then withdraws his blessing from him; every good man therefore, ought certainly to prevent such neglect of, or sin against God and his commands. I thanked the young priest for expressing so great a concern for us, and desired him to explain the particulars of what he had observed, that, according to the parable of *Achan*, I might remove the accursed thing from among us. Why then, Sir, said he, in the first place, you have four Englishmen, who have taken savage women to their wives, by whom they have several children, though none of them are legally married, as the law of God and man requires; they, I say, Sir, are no less than adulterers, and as they still live in adultery, are liable to the curse of God. I know, Sir, you may object the want of a priest, or clergyman of any kind; as also, pen, ink, and paper, to write down a contract of marriage, and have it signed between them. But neither this, nor what the Spanish governor has told you of their chusing by consent, can be reckoned a marriage, nor any more than an agreement to keep them from quarrelling among themselves; for, Sir, the essence or sacrament of matrimony (so he called it) not only consists in mutual con-

- sent,

sent, but in the legal obligation which compels them to own and acknowledge one another to abstain from other persons, the men to provide for their wives and children, and the women to the same and like conditions, *mutatis mutandis* on their side: whereas, Sir, these men, upon their own pleasure, on any occasion, may forsake those women, and marry others, and by disowning their children suffer them utterly to perish. Now, Sir, added he, can God be honoured in such an unlawful liberty as this? how can a blessing succeed the best endeavours, if men are allowed to live in so licentious a way? I was indeed struck with the thing myself, and though that they were much to blame, that no formal contract had been made, though it had been but breaking a stick between them, to engage them to live as man and wife, never to separate; but love, cherish, and comfort one another all their lives? yet, Sir, said I, when they took these women, I was not here; and if it is adultery, it is past my remedy, and I cannot help it. *True, Sir,* answered the young priest, *you cannot be charged with that part of the crime which was done in your absence ; but I beseech you, don't flatter yourself, that you are under no obligation now to put a period to it; which, if you neglect to do, guilt will be entirely on you alone, since it is certainly in nobody's power but yours to alter their condition.* I must confess, I was so dull, that I thought he meant I should part them, and knowing that this would put the whole island in confusion, I told him I could not consent to it upon any account whatsoever. *Sir,* said he, in a great surprise, *I do not mean that you should separate, but marry them, by a written contract, signed by both man and woman, and by all the witnesses present, which all the* European *laws decree to be of sufficient efficacy.* Amazed with such true piety and

Y 2

since-

sincerity, and considering the validity of a written contract, I acknowledged all that he said to be very just and kind; and that I would discourse with the men about it; neither could I see what reason they could have not to let him marry them, whose authority in that affair is owned to be as authentic, as if they were married by any of our clergymen in England.

The next complaint he had to make to me, was this; that though these English subjects of mine had lived with these women seven years, and tho' they were of good understanding, and capable of instruction, having learned not only to speak, but to read English, yet all this while they had never taught them any thing of the Christian religion, or the knowledge of God, much less in what manner he ought to be served. *And is not this an unaccountable neglect?* said he, warmly. *Depend upon it, God Almighty will call them to account for such contempt. And though I am not of your religion, yet I should be glad to see these people released from the devil's power, and be saved by the principles of the Christian religion, the knowledge of God, of a Redeemer, the resurrection, and of a future state. But as it is not too late, if you please to give me leave to instruct them, I doubt not but I shall supply this great defect, by bringing them into the great circle of Christianity, even while you continue in the island.*

I could hold no longer, but embracing him, told him, with a thousand thanks, I would grant whatever he requested, and desired him to proceed in the third article, which he did in the following manner:

Sir, said he, it should be a maxim among all Christians, *That Christian knowledge ought to be propagated by all possible means, and on all occasions.* Upon this account our church sends missionaries into

into Perſia, India, and China, men who are willing to die for the ſake of God and the Chriſtian faith, in order to bring poor infidels into the way of ſalvation. Now, Sir, as here is an opportunity to convert ſeven and thirty poor ſavages, I wonder how you can paſs by ſuch an occaſion of doing good, which is really worth the expence of a man's whole life.

I muſt confeſs I was ſo confounded at this diſcourſe, that I could not tell how to anſwer him. *Sir, ſaid* he, ſeeing me in diſorder, *I ſhall be very ſorry if I have given you offence*, No, Sir, ſaid I, I am rather confounded; and you know my circumſtances, that being bound to the Eaſt Indies in a merchant ſhip, I cannot wrong the owners ſo much, as to detain the ſhip here, the men lying on victuals and wages on their account. If I ſtay above twelve days, I muſt pay 3 l. Sterling *per diem* demurrage, nor muſt the ſhip ſtay above eight days more; ſo that I am unable to engage in this work, unleſs I would leave the ſhip, and be reduced to my former condition. The prieſt, though he owned this was hard upon me, yet laid it to my conſcience, whe her the bleſſing of ſaving ſeven and thirty ſouls was not worth venturing all that I had in the world? Sir, ſaid I, it is very true : but as you are an eccleſiaſtic, it naturally falls into your profeſſion: why therefore don't you rather offer to undertake it yourſelf, than preſs me to it? Upon this he turned about, making a very low bow, I moſt humbly thank God and you, Sir, ſaid he, for ſo bleſſed a call; and moſt willingly undertake ſo glorious an office, which will ſufficiently compenſate all the hazards and difficulties I have gone through in a long and uncomfortable voyage.

While he was thus ſpeaking, I could diſcover a rapture in his face, by his colour going and coming;

ming; at the same time his eyes sparkled like fire, with all the signs of the most zealous transports. And when I asked whether he was in earnest; Sir, said he, it was to preach to the Indians, I consented to come along with you; these infidels, even in this little island, are infinitely of more worth than my poor life : if so that I should prove the happy instrument of saving these poor creatures souls, I care not if I never see my native country again. One thing I only beg of you more, is, that you would leave Friday with me, to be my interpreter, without whose assistance neither of us will understand each other.

This request very sensibly troubled me, first upon Friday's being bred a protestant, and secondly, for the affection I bore to him for his fidelity : but immediately the remembrance of Friday's father coming into my head, I recommended him to him as having learned Spanish, which the priest also undrestood, and so was thorougly satisfied with him.

When we came to the Englishmen, after I had told them what necessary things I had done for them, I talked to them of the scandalous life they led, told them what notice the clergyman had taken of it, and asked them if they were married men or batchelors ? They answered, two of them were widowers, and the other three single men. But, said I, with what conscience can you call these your wives, by whom you have so many children, and yet are not lawfully married ? They all said, that they took them before the governor as such, having nobody else to marry them, which they thought as legal as if they had had a parson. No doubt, said I, but in the eye of God you are so : but unless I am assured of your honest intention never to desert these poor creatures, I can do nothing more for you, neither can you expect

God's

God's blessing while you live in such an open course of adultery. Hereupon Will Atkins, who spoke for the rest, told me, That they believed their wives the most innocent and virtuous creatures in the world; that they would never forsake them while they had breath: and that if there was a clergyman in the ship, they would be married to them with all their heart. I told you before, said I, that I have a minister with me, who shall marry you to-morrow morning, if you are willing; so I would have you consult to-night, with the rest about it. I told him, the clergyman was a Frenchman, and knew not a word of English, but that I would act as a clerk between them. And indeed this business met with such speedy success, that they all told me, in a few minutes after, that they were ready to be formally married as soon as I pleased; with which informing the priest, he was exceedingly rejoiced.

Nothing now remained, but that the women should be made sensible of the meaning of the thing; with which being well satisfied, they with their husbands attended at my apartment the next morning: there was my priest, habited in a black vest, something like a cassoc with a sash round it, much resembling a minister, and I was his interpreter. But the seriousness of his behaviour, and the scruples he made of marrying the women, who were not baptized, gave them an exceeding reverence for his person: nor indeed would he marry them at all, till he obtained my liberty to discourse both with the men and women, and then he told them, That in the sight of all indifferent men, and in the sense of the laws of society, they had lived in open adultery, which nothing now but their consent to marry, or final separation, could put an end to; and even here was a difficulty with respect to the laws of Christian matrimony, in marrying a profeſſed Chriſtian to a heathen idolater, unbaptized; but yet there was time enough to make them profeſs the name of Chriſt, without which nothing could be done: that, beſides, he believed themſelves very indifferent Chriſtians; and conſequently had not diſcourſed with their wives upon that ſubject; and that unleſs they promiſed him to do ſo, he could not marry them, as being expreſsly forbidden by the laws of God.

All this they heard attentively, and owned readily, *But, Lord, Sir!* ſaid *Will Atkins* to me, *how ſhould we teach them religion, who know nothing of it ourſelves? How can we talk to our wives of God,* Jeſus Chriſt, *heaven and* hell ? *why, they would only laugh at us, who never yet have practiſed religion, but on the contrary, all manner of wickedneſs.* Will Atkins, ſaid I, cannot you tell your wife, ſhe is in the wrong, and that her gods are idols, which can neither hear, ſpeak, nor underſtand; but that our God, who has made, can deſtroy all things ; that he rewards the good, and puniſhes the wicked; and at laſt will bring us to judgment ? cannot you tell her theſe things ? That's true, ſaid Atkins, but then ſhe'll tell me, it is utterly falſe, ſince I am not puniſhed and ſent to the devil, who hath been ſuch a wicked creature. Theſe words I interpreted to the prieſt! O! ſaid he, tell him, his repentance will make him a very good miniſter to his ſpouſe, and qualify him to preach on the mercy and long-ſuffering of a merciful Being, who deſires not the death of a ſinner, and even defers damnation to the laſt judgment; this will lead him to the above doctrine, and will make him an excellent preacher to his wife. I repeated this to Atkins, who, being more than ordinarily affected with it, replied, I know all this, Sir, and a great deal more; but how can I have the impudence to talk thus to my

wife,

wife, when my confcience witneffes againft me?
ALAS! faid he, (with tears in his eyes and giving a great figh,) as for repenting, that is for
ever paft me. Paft you! Atkins, faid I, what do
you mean? You know well enough, faid he, what
I mean; *I mean it is too late.*

  When I told the prieft what he faid, the poor
affectionate man could not refrain from weeping;
but recovering himfelf, *Pray, Sir,* faid he, *afk
him if he is contented that it is too late ; or is he
concerned, and wifhes it were not fo?* This queftion I put fairly to Aitkins; who replied in a paffion, *How can I be eafy in a ftate which I know
muft terminate in my ruin? for I really believe,
fome time or other, I fhall cut my throat, to put a
period to my life and to the terrors of my confcience.*

  At this the clergyman fhook his head. *Sir,* faid
he, *pray tell him it is not too late ; Chrift will give
him repentance, if he has recourfe to the merit of
his paffion. Does he think he is beyond the power
of divine mercy? there may indeed be a time when
provoked mercy will no longer ftrive, but nev'r too
late for men to repent in this world.* I told Aitkins
every word the prieft had faid, who then parted
from us to talk to his wife, while we difcourfed
with the reft. But thefe were very ftupid in religious matters, yet all of them promifed to do
their endeavours to make their wives turn Chriftians; and upon which promifes the prieft married the three couple. But as Aitkins was the only fincere convert, and of more fenfe than the
reft, my clergyman was earneftly inquiring after
him: *Sir,* faid he, *let us walk out of this labyrinth, and I dare fay we fhall find this poor man
preaching to his wife already.* And indeed we
found it true; for coming to the edge of the wood,
we perceived Aitkins and his favage wife fitting
under the fhade of a bufh, in very earneft dif-
                                        courfe;

courfe: he pointed to the fun, to the quarters of the earth, to himfelf, to her, the woods, and the trees. Immediately we could perceive him ftart upon his feet, fall down upon his knees, and lift up both his hands; at which the tears ran down my clergyman's cheeks: but our great misfortune was, we could not hear one word that paffed between them. Another time he would embrace her, wiping the tears from her eyes, kiffing her with the greateft tranfports, and then both kneel down for fome minutes together. Such raptures of joy did this occafion in my young prieft, that he could fcarcely contain himfelf: And a little after this, we obferved by her motion, as frequently lifting up her hands, and laying them on her breaft, that fhe was mightily affected with his difcourfe, and fo they withdrew from our fight.

When we came back, we found them both waiting to be called in; upon which we agreed to examine him alone, and fo I began thus to difcourfe him. Prithee, Will. Aitkins, faid I, what education had you, What was your father?

W. A. A better man than ever I fhall be; he was, Sir, a clergyman, who gave me good inftruction, or correction, which I defpifed like a brute, as I was, and murdered my poor father.

Pr. Ha! a murderer!

[Here the prieft ftarted and looked pale, as thinking he had really killed his father.]

R. C. What, did you kill him with your hands?

W. A. No, Sir, I cut not his throat, but broke his heart, by the moft unnatural turn of difobedience to the tendereft and beft of fathers.

R. C. Well, I pray God grant you repentance; I did not afk you to extort a confeffion; but I afked you, becaufe I fee you have more knowledge of what is good than your companions.

W. A. O, Sir, whenever I look back upon my
paft

paſt life, conſcience upbraids me with my father; the ſins againſt our parents make the deepeſt wounds, and their weight lyes the heavieſt upon the mind.

R. C. You talk, Will, too feelingly and ſenſibly for me; I am not able to bear it.

W. A. You bear it, Sir! you know nothing of it.

R. C. But yes, Aitkins, I do; and every ſhore, valley, and tree in this iſland, witneſs the anguiſh of my ſoul for my undutifulneſs to my kind father, whom I have murdered likewiſe: yet my repentance falls infinitely ſhort of yours. But, Will, how comes the ſenſe of this matter to touch you juſt now?

W. A. Sir, the work you have ſet me about has occaſioned it; for talking to my wife about God and religion, ſhe has preached me ſuch a ſermon that I ſhall retain it in laſting remembrance.

R. C. No, no, it is your own moving pious arguments to her, has made conſcience fling them back upon you. But pray, Aitkins, inform us what paſſed between you and your wife, and in what manner did you begin.

W. A. I talked to her of the laws of marriage, the reaſon of ſuch compacts, whereby order and juſtice is maintained; without which men would run from their wives and children, to the diſſolution of families or inheritances.

R. C. Well, and what did ſhe ſay to all this?

W. A. Sir, we began our diſcourſe in the following manner, which I ſhall exactly repeat according to my mean capacity, if you think it worth your while to honour it with your attention.

✿✤✿✤✿✤✿✤✿✤✿✤✿✤✿✤✿✤✿✤✿✤✿✤✿

The DIALOGUE *between* Will. Aitkins *and his
wife in the wood.*

Wife. YOU tell me marriage God appoint; have
you God in your country?

W. A. Yes, child, God is in every nation.

Wife. No; great old Benamuckee god is in my
country, not yours.

W. A. My dear, God is in heaven, which he
made; he also made the earth, the sea, and all that
is therein.

Wife. Why you not tell me much long ago?

W. A. My dear, I have been a wicked wretch,
having a long time lived without the knowledge
of God in the world.

Wife. What, not know great God in own nation; No no good ting? No say O to him? that's
strange!

W. A. But, my dear, many live as if there was
no God in heaven for all that.

Wife. Why God suffer this? why makee not
live well?

W. A. It is our own faults, child.

Wife. But, if he much great, can makee kill,
why no makee kill when to serve him? No be
good mans no cry O to him?

W. A. That's true, my dear, he may strike us
dead, but his abundant mercy spareth us.

Wife. Did not you tell God tankee for that?

W. A. No, I have neither thanked him for his
mercy, nor feared him for his power.

Wife. Then me not believe your God be good,
nor makee kill, when you makee him angry.

W. A. Alas! must my wicked life hinder you
from believing in him?

Wife.

Wife. How can me tink your God live there? *(pointing to heaven.)* Sure he no ken what you do here.

W. A. Yes, yes, my dear, he hears us speak, sees what we do, and knows what we even think.

Wife. Where then makee power strong, when he hears you curse, swear de great damn?

W. A. My dear this shews he is indeed a God and not a man, who has such tender mercy?

Wife. Mercy! what do you call mercy?

W. A. He pities and spares us: as he is our great Creator, so is he also our tender father.

Wife. So God never angry, never kill wicked, then he no good, no great mighty.

W. A. O my dear, don't say so, he is both; and many times he shews terrible examples of his judgement and vengeance.

Wife. Then you makee de bargain with him; you do bad ting, he no hurt you, he hurt other mans.

W. A. No indeed, my sins are all presumptions upon his goodness.

Wife. Well, and yet no makee you dead? and you give him no tankee neither.

W. A. It is true, I am an ungrateful, unthankful dog that I am.

Wife. Why, you say, he makee you, why makee you no much better then.

W. A. It is I alone that have deformed myself, and abused his goodness.

Wife. Pray makee God know me, me no makee him angry, no do bad ting.

W. A. You mean, my dear, that you desire I would teach you to know God: alas! poor dear creature! he must teach thee, and not I. But I'll pray earnestly to him to direct thee, and to forgive me, a miserable sinner. *(Hereupon he went a little distance, and kneeling down, prayed earnest-*

ly

ly to God to enlighten her mind, and to pardon his
sins : when this was done, they continued their dis-
course thus.)

Wife. What you put down knee for ? For what
hold up hand ? Who you speak to ?

W. A. My dear, I bowed in token of submission
to him that made me, and prayed that he would
open your eyes and understanding.

Wife. And can he do that too? And will he
hear what you say ?

W. A. Yes, my dear, he bids us pray, and has
given us promise that he will hear us.

Wife. When did he bid you pray ? What, do you
hear him speak ?

W. A No my dear, but God has spoken formerly to good men from heaven : and by divine revelation they have written all his laws down in a
book.

Wife. O where dat good book ?

W. A. I have it not now by me: but one time
or other I shall get it for you to read. *Then he em-*
braced her with great affection.

Wife. Pray tell a mee did God teachee them write
that book ?

W. A. Yes, and by that rule we know him to
be God.

Wife. What way, what rule you know him ?

W. A. Because he teaches what is good, just,
and holy ; and forbids all wicked and abominable
actions that incur his displeasure.

Wife. O me fain understand that, and if he do
all things you say he do, surely he hear me say O
to him; he makee me good if I wish to be good ;
he no kill me if I love him ; me tink, believe him
great God ; me say O to him, along with you my
dear.

Here the poor man fell upon his knees, and made
her kneel down by him, praying with the greatest
fervency,

fervency, that God would instruct her by his Holy
Spirit : and that God by his providence would send
them a Bible for both their instructions. And such
was the early piety of this new convert, that she
made him promise never to forsake God any more,
lest, being made dead as she called it, she should
not only want her instructor, but himself be misera-
ble in a long eternity.

Such surprising account as this was, proved
very affecting to us both, but particularly to the
young clergyman, who was mightily concerned he
could not talk to her himself. Sir, said he, there
is something more to be done to this woman than
to marry her : I mean, that she ought to be baptized. To this I presently agreed : Pray, said he
again, ask her husband, whether he has ever talked to her of Jesus Christ, the salvation of sinners,
the nature of faith, and redemption in and by him,
of the Holy Spirit, the resurrection, last judgement, and a future state; but the poor fellow
melted into tears at this question, saying, that he
had said something to her of these things, but his
inability to talk of them, made him afraid lest
her knowledge of them should rather make her
contemn religion, than be benefited by it : but
that if I would discourse with her, it would be
very evident my labour would not be in vain. Accordingly I called her in, and placing myself as interpreter between the religious priest and the woman, I intreated him to go on : but surely never
was such a sermon preached by any clergyman in
these latter days, with so much zeal, knowledge,
and sincerity; in short, he brought the woman to
embrace the knowledge of Christ, and of redemption by him, with so surprising a degree of understanding, that she made it her own request to be
baptized.

He then performed his office in the sacrament

of

of baptifm, firft, by faying fome words over to
himfelf in Latin, and then afked me to give her a
name, as being her godfather, and pouring a whole
difh full of water upon the woman's head, he faid
MARY, I baptize thee in the name of the Father,
and of the Son, and of the Holy Ghoft; fo that
none could know of what religion he was. After
this he pronounced the benediction in Latin. Thus
the woman being made a Chriftian, he married
her to Will. Atkins; which being finifhed, he af-
fectionately exhorted him to lead a holy life for
the future; that fince the Almighty, by the convictions of his confcience, had honoured him to
be the inftrument of his wife's converfion, he
fhould not difhonour the grace of God, that while
the favage was converted, the inftrument fhould
be caft away. Thus ended a ceremony, to me
the moft pleafant and agreeable I ever paffed in
my life.

The affairs of the ifland being fettled, I was
preparing to go on board, when the young man
(whofe mother was ftarved) came to me, faying,
that as he underftood I had a clergyman with me,
who had married the Englifhmen with favages,
he had a match to make between two Chriftians,
which he defired might be finifhed before I departed. Thinking that it was he himfelf that had
courted his mother's maid, I perfuaded him not to
do any thing rafhly upon the account of his folitary circumftances; that the maid was an unequal
match for him, both in refpect to fubftance and
years; and that it was very probable he would
live to return to his own country, where he might
have a far better choice. At thefe words, fmiling,
he interrupted me, thanking me for my good advice; that as he had nothing to beg of me, but a
fmall fettlement, with a fervant or two, or fome
few neceffaries; fo he hoped I would not be unmindful

mindful of him when I returned to England, but
give his letters to his friends; and that when he
was redeemed, the plantation and all its improvements, however valuable, should be returned to
me again. But as for the marriage he proposed,
that it was not himself, but that it was between
my Jack of all trades, and the maid Susan.

I was indeed agreeably surprised at the mentioning this match, which seemed very suitable, the
one being a very ingenious fellow, and the other
an excellent, dexterous, and sensible housewife,
fit to be governess of the whole island: so we married them the same day; and as I was her father,
and gave her away, so I gave her a handsome por-
tion, appointing her and her husband a convenient
large space of ground for their plantation. The
sharing out of the land I left to Will. Atkins, who
really divided it very justly to every person's fatisfaction: they only desired one general writing
under my hand for the whole, which I caused to
be drawn up, signed, and sealed to them, setting
out their bounds, and giving them a right to the
whole possession of their respective plantations,
with their improvements, to them and their heirs,
reserving all the rest of the island as my own property, and a certain rent for every particular
plantation after eleven years. As to their laws and
government, I exhorted them to love one another:
and as to the Indians who lived in a nook by themselves, I allotted three or four of them plantations, and the rest willingly chose to become fervants to the other families, by which means they
were employed in useful labour, and fared much
better than they did before. Besides, the savages
being thus mixed with the Christians, the work of
their conversion might be set on foot by the latter,
in the clergyman's absence, to our equal satisfac-
tior. The young priest, however, was a little

anxious

anxious left the Chriftians fhould not be willing
to do their parts in inftructing thofe poor Indians:
I therefore told him, we fhould call them all together; that he fhould fpeak to the Spaniards who
were Papifts, and I to the Englifh who were Pro-
teftants, and make them promife that they would
never make any diftinction in religion, but teach
the general true knowledge of God, and his fou
Jefus Chrift, in order to convert the poor favages: and this indeed they all promifed us accordingly.

When I came to Will Atkin's houfe, I found
his baptized wife, and the young woman newly
married to my Jack of all trades, were become
great intimates, and difcourfing of religion together. O Sir, fays Will. Atkins, when God has
finners to reconcile to himfelf, he never wants an
inftructor: I knew I was unworthy for fo good a
work, and therefore this young woman has been
fent hither as it were from heaven, who is fufficient to convert a whole ifland of favages. The
young woman blufhed, and was going to rife; but
I defired her to fit ftill, and hoped that God would
blefs her in fo good a work: and then pulling out
a bible, (which I brought on purpofe in my pocket for him). Here Atkins, faid I, here is an af-
fiftant that perhaps you had not before. So confounded was the poor man, that it was fome time
before he could fpeak; at laft turning to his wife,
My dear, he faid, did I not tell you that God
could hear what we faid? Here's the book I prayed for, when you and I kneeled under the bufh:
God then heard us, and now has fent it. The
woman was furprifed, and thought really God had
fent that individual book from heaven; but I turned to the young woman, and defired her to explain
to the new convert, that God may properly be
faid to anfwer our petitions, when, in the courfe

of

of his providence, such particular things come to
pass as we petitioned for. This the young woman did effectually; but surely Will. Atkins's joy
cannot be expressed; no man being more thankful
for any thing in the world, than he was for his
Bible, nor desired it from a better principle.

After several religious discourses, I desired the
young woman to give me an account of the anguish she felt when she was starving to death for
hunger; to which she readily consented, and began in the following manner:

" Sir," said she, " all our victuals being gone,
after I had fasted one day, my stomach was very
sickish, and at the approach of night, I was inclined to yawning, and sleepy. When I slept upon
the couch three hours, I awaked a little refreshed;
three hours after my stomach being more and more
sickish, I lay down again, but could not sleep, being very faint and ill. Thus I passed the second
day with a strange variety, first hunger, then sick
again, with reachings to vomit: that night I
dreamed I was at Barbadoes, buying plenty of
provisions, and dined heartily. But when I awaked, my spirits were exceedingly sunk, to find myself in the extremity of famine. There was but
one glass of wine, which being mixed with sugar,
I drank up: but for want of substance to digest
upon, the fumes of it got into my head, and made
me senseless for some time. The third day I was
so ravenous and furious, that I could have eaten
a little child if it had come in my way; during
which time I was as mad as any creature in bedlam. In one of these fits I fell down, and struck
my face against the corner of a pallet bed, where
my mistress lay: the blood gushed out of my nose;
but by my excessive bleeding, both the violence of
the fever, and the ravenous part of the hunger a-
bated. After this I grew sick again, strove to vomit,

mit, but could not; then bleeding a fecond time, I fwooned away as dead; when I came to myfelf I had a dreadful gnawing pain in my ftomach, which went off towards night, with a longing defire for food. I took a draught of water and fugar, but it came up again; then I drank water without fugar, and that ftaid with me. I laid me down on the bed, praying God would take me away; after I had flumbered, I thought myfelf a-dying, therefore recommended my foul to God, and wifhed fome body would throw me into the fea. All this while my departing miftrefs lay by me; the laft bit of bread fhe had, fhe gave it to her dear child, my young mafter. The morning after, I fell into a violent paffion of crying, and after that into hunger. I efpied the blood that came from my nofe in a bafon, which I immediately fwallowed up. At night I had the ufual variations, as pain in the ftomach, fick, fleepy, and ravenous; and I had no thought but that I fhould die before morning. In the morning came on terrible gripings in my bowels. At this time I heard my young mafter's lamentations, by which I underftood his mother was dead: Soon after the failors cried, *A fail, a fail,* hallowing as if they were diftracted, for joy of that relief, which afterwards we received from your hands."

Surely never was a more diftinct account of ftarving to death than this. But to return to the difpofition of things among my people, I did not take any notice to them of the floop that I had framed, neither would I leave them the two pieces of brafs cannon, or the two quarter-deck guns that I had on board, left, upon any difguft, they fhould have feparated, or turned pirates, and fo made the ifland a den of thieves, inftead of a plantation of fober pious people: but leaving them in a flourifhing condition, with a promife to fend

them

them further relief from Brasil, as sheep, hogs, and cows, (being obliged to kill the latter at sea, having no hay to feed them,) I went on board the ship again, the first of May 1695, after having been twenty days among them: and next morning, giving them a salute of five guns at parting, we set sail for the Brasils. The third day, towards evening, there happening a calm, and the current being very strong, we were drove to the N. N. E. towards the land. Some hours after we perceived the sea covered as it were with something very black, not easily at first to be discovered: upon which our chief mate ascending the shrouds a little way, and taking a view with a perspective glass, he cries out, an Army! An army, you fool, said I, what do you mean? Nay, Sir, said he, don't be angry, I assure you it is not only an army, but a fleet too; for I believe there are a thousand canoes paddling along, and making with great haste towards us.

Indeed every one of us were surprised at this relation: and my nephew the captain could not tell what to think of it, but thought we should all be devoured. Nor was I free from concern, when I considered how much we were becalmed, and what a strong current set towards the shore: however, I encouraged him not to be afraid, but bring the ship to an anchor, as soon as we were certain that we must engage them. Accordingly we did so, and furled all our sails; as to the savages, we feared nothing, but only that they might set the ship on fire, to prevent which I ordered them to get their boats out, and fasten them, one close by the head, and the other by the stern, well manned, with skeets and buckets to extinguish the flames, should it so happen. The savages soon came up with us, but there were not so many as the mate had said; for instead of a thousand canoes,

there

there were only one hundred and twenty; too many indeed for us, several of their canoes containing about sixteen or seventeen men.

As they approached us, they seemed to be in the greatest amazement, not knowing what to make of us. They rowed round the ship, which occasioned us to call to the men in the boats not to suffer them to come near them. Hereupon they beckoned to the savages to keep back, which they accordingly did; but at their retreat they let fly about fifty arrows among us, and very much wounded one of our men in the longboat. I called to them not to fire upon any account, but handing them down some deal boards, the carpenters made them a kind of a fence to shield them from the arrows. In half an hour after they came so near astern of us, that we had a perfect sight of them; then they rowed a little farther out, till they came directly alongside of us, and then approached so near us, as they could hear us speak: this made me order all our men to keep close, and get their guns ready. In the mean time I ordered Friday to go out upon deck, and ask them in his language what they meant? No sooner did he do so, but six of the savages, who were in the foremost canoe, stooping down, shewed us their naked backsides, as much as to say in *English*, *kiss our*—: but Friday quickly knew what this meant, by immediately crying out they were going to shoot; unfortunately for him, poor creature! who fell under the cloud of three hundred arrows, not less than seven piercing through his body, killing one of the best servants, and faithfullest of companions in all my solitudes and afflictions.

So enraged was I at the death of poor Friday, that the guns, which before were charged with only powder, to frighten them, I ordered to be loaded with small shot; nor did the gunners fail in their aim, but at this broadside split and over-set, thirteen or fourteen of their canoes, which killed numbers of them, and set the rest a-swimming: the others, frightened out of their wits, little regarding their fellows drowning, scoured away as fast as they could. One poor wretch our people took up, swimming for his life, an hour after. He was very sullen at first, so that he would neither eat nor speak: but I took a way to cure him, by ordering them to throw him into the sea, which they did, and then he came swimming back like a cork, calling in his tongue, as I suppose, to save him. So we took him on board, but it was a long time before we could make him speak or understand English; yet when we had taught him, he told us, they were going with their kings to fight a great battle: and when we asked him, what made them come up to us? he said, *to makee de great wonder look* : where it is to be noted, that those natives, and those of Africa, always add two *e*'s at the end of English words, as *makee, takee*, and the like, from which it is a very difficult thing to make them break off.

Being now under sail, we took our last farewel of poor honest Friday, and interred him with all possible decency and solemnity; putting him into a coffin, and committing him to the deep, at the same time causing eleven guns to be fired for him. Thus ended the life of one of the most grateful, faithful, honest, and affectionate servants, that ever any man was blessed with in the world.

Having now a fair wind for Brasils, in about twelve days time we made land in the latitude of five degrees south of the line. Four days we kept on S. by E. in sight of shore, when we made cape St. Augustine, and in three days we came to an anchor off the *bay of All Saints*. I had great difficulty here to get leave to hold correspondence on shore; for neither the figure of my partner, my
two

two merchant truftees, nor the fame of my wonderful prefervation in the ifland, could procure me the favour, till fuch time as the prior of the monaftery of the Auguftines (to whom I had given 500 moidores) obtained leave from the governor, for me perfonally, with the captain and one more, together with eight failors, to come on fhore; upon this condition, that we fhould not land any goods out of the fhip, or carry any perfon away without licence: I found means however to get on fhore three bales of Englifh goods, fuch as fine broad cloths, ftuffs, and fome linen, which I brought as a prefent for my partner, who had fent me on board a prefent of frefh provifions, wine, and fweetmeats, worth above thirty moidores, including fome tobacco, and three or four fine gold medals.

Here I delivered my partner in goods to the value of 100 l. Sterling, and obliged him to fit up the floop I bought, for the ufe of my ifland, in order to fend them refrefhments: and fo active was he in this matter, that he had the veffel finifhed in a few days, to the mafter of which I gave particular inftructions to find the place. I foon loaded him with a fmall cargo; and one of our failors offered to fettle there, upon my letter to the Spanifh governor, if I would allot him tools and a plantation. This I willingly granted, and gave him the favage we had taken prifoner to be his flave. All things being ready for the voyage, my old partner told me, there was an acquaintance of his, a Brafil planter, who having fallen under the difpleafure of the church, and in fear of the Inquifition, which obliged him to be concealed, would be glad of fuch an opportunity to make his efcape, with his wife and two daughters; and if I would allot them a plantation in my ifland, he would give them a fmall ftock to begin with, for

that

that the officers had already feized his effects and eftate, and ·left him nothing but a little houfhold ftuff, and two flaves. This requeft I prefently granted, concealing him and his family on board our fhip, till fuch time as the floop (where all the effects were) was gone out of the bay, and then we put them on board, who carried fome materials, and plants for planting fugar-canes, along with them. By this floop, among other things, I fent my fubjects 3 milk-cows and 5 calves, about 22 hogs, 3 fows big with pig, 2 mares and a ftone-horfe. I alfo engaged three Portugal women to go for fake of the Spaniards, which, with the perfecuted man's two daughters, were fufficient, fince the reft had wives of their own, though in another country: all which cargo arrived fafe, no doubt, to their exceeding comfort, who, with this addition, were about fixty or feventy people, befides children.

At this place my truly honeft and pious clergyman left me; for a fhip being ready to fet fail for Lifbon, he afked me leave to go thither; but I affure you, it was with the greateft reluctancy I parted from a perfon, whofe virtue and piety merited the greateft efteem.

From the Brafils we made directly over the Atlantic ocean to the Cape of Good-Hope, having a tolerable good voyage, fteering for the moft part S. E. We were on a trading voyage, and had a fupercargoe on board, who was to direct all the fhip's motions after fhe arrived at the Cape; only being limited to a certain number of days, or ftay, by charter-party, at the feveral ports fhe was to go to. At the Cape we only took in frefh water, and then failed for the coaft of Coromandel: we were there informed, that a French man of war of 50 guns, and two large merchant fhips, were

A a

failed

failed for the Indies, but we heard no more of them.

In our paffage we touched at the ifland of Madagafcar, where, though the inhabitants are naturally fierce and treacherous, and go conftantly armed with bows and lances, yet for fome time they treated us civily enough; and, in exchange for knives, fciffars, and other trifles, they brought us eleven good fat bullocks, which we took partly for prefent frefh victuals, and the remainder to falt for the fhip's ufe.

So curious was I to view every corner of the world where I came to, that I went on fhore as often as I could. One evening, when on fhore, we obferved numbers of the people ftanding gazing at us at a diftance. We thought ourfelves in no danger, as they had hitherto ufed us kindly. However, we cut three boughs out of a tree, fticking them at a diftance from us, which, it feems, in that country, is not only a token of truce and amity, but when poles or boughs are fet up on the other fide, it is a fign the truce is accepted. In thefe treaties, however, there is one principal thing to be regarded, that neither party come beyond one another's three poles or boughs; fo that the middle fpace is not only fecure, but is alfo allowed as a market for traffic and commerce: when the truce is thus accepted, they ftick up their javelins and lances at the firft poles, and come on unarmed; but if any violence is offered, away they run to their poles, take up their weapons, and then the truce is at an end. This evening it happened that a greater number of people than ufual, both men and women, traded among us for fuch toys as we had, with fuch great civility, that we made us a little tent of large boughs of trees, fome of the men refolving to lye on fhore all night. But, for my part, I and fome others took our lodging

in the boat, with boughs of trees fpread over it,
having a fail fpread at the bottom to lye upon.
About two o'clock in the morning, we were awakened by the firing of mufkets, and our men crying out for help, or elfe they would all be murdered. Scarce had we time to get the boat afhore,
when our men came plunging themfelves into the
water, with about four hundred of the iflanders
at their heels. We took up feven of the men,
three of them very much wounded, and one left
behind killed, while the enemy poured their arrows fo thick among us, that we were forced to
make a barricade, with boards lying at the fide of
the boat, to fhield us from danger: and having
got ready our fire-arms, we returned them a volley, which wounded feveral of them, as we could
hear by their cries. In this condition we lay till
break of day, and then making fignals of diftrefs
to the fhip, which my nephew the captain heard
and underftood, he weighed anchor and ftood as
near the fhore as poffible, and then fent another
boat with ten hands in her to affift us; but we called to them not to come near, informing them of
our unhappy condition. However, they ventured; when one of the men taking the end of a
tow-line in his one hand, and keeping our boat
between him and our adverfaries, fwam on board
us, and made faft our line to the boat; upon this,
flipping our cables, they towed us out of the reach
of their arrows, and quickly after, a broadfide
was given them from the fhip, which made a moft
dreadful havock among them. When we got on
board, we examined into the occafion of this fray;
the men who fled informed us, that an old woman, who fold milk within the poles, had brought
a young woman with her, who carried roots or
herbs, the fight of whom fo much tempted our
men, that they offered rudenefs to the maid, at

which the old woman fet up a great cry; nor
would the failors part with the prize, but carried
her among the trees, while the old woman went
and brought a whole army down upon them. At
the beginning of the attack one of our men was
killed with a lance, and the fellow, who began
the mifchief, paid dear enough for his miftrefs,
though as yet we did not know what had become
of him; the reft luckily efcaped. The third night
after the action, being curious to underftand how
affairs ftood, I took the fupercargo, and twenty
ftout fellows with me, and landed about two hours
before midnight, at the fame place where thofe
Indians ftood the night before, and there we divided our men into two bodies, the boatfwain
commanding one, and I another. It was fo dark,
that we could fee nobody, neither did we hear
any voice near us: but by and by the boatfwain
falling over a dead body, we agreed to halt till
the moon fhould rife, which we knew would be
in an hour after. We perceived here no fewer
than two and thirty bodies upon the ground,
whereof two were not quite dead. Satisfied with
this difcovery, I was for going on board again;
but the boatfwain, and the reft told me, they
would make a vifit to the Indian town, where
thofe dogs, fo they called them, refided, afking
me at the fame time to go along with them; for
they did not doubt, befides getting a good booty,
but they fhould find Tom Jeffery there, for that
was the unhappy man we miffed. But I utterly
refufed to go, and commanded them back, being
unwilling to hazard their lives, as the fafety of
the fhip wholly depended upon them. Notwithftanding all I could fay to them, they all left me
but one, and the fupercargo: fo we three returned to the boat, where a boy was left, refolving
to ftay till they returned. At parting I told them
I fup-

I supposed most of them would run the same fate
with Tom. Jeffery. To this they replied, *Come
boys, come along, we'll warrant we'll come off safe
enough:* and so away they went, notwithstanding
all my admonitions, either concerning their own
safety, or the preservation of the ship. Indeed
they were gallantly armed, every man having a
musket, bayonet, and a pistol, besides cutlasses,
hangers, pole-axes, and hand-granadoes. They
came to a few Indian houses at first, which not
being the town they expected, they went farther,
and finding a cow tied to a tree, they concluded
that she would be a sufficient guide, and so it proved; for after they untied her, she led them directly to the town, which consisted of above two
hundred houses, several families living in some of
the huts together. At their arrival, all being in
a profound sleep, the sailors agreed to divide themselves into three bodies, and set three parts of
the town on fire at once, to kill those that were
escaping, and plunder the rest of the houses. Thus
desperately resolved they went to work; but the
first party had not gone far, before they called
out to the rest, that they had found Tom. Jaf-
fery; whereupon they all ran up to the place,
and found the poor fellow indeed hanging up naked by one arm, and his throat cut almost from
ear to ear: in a house that was hard by the tree
they found sixteen or seventeen Indians, who had
been concerned in the fray, two or three of them
being wounded, who were not gone to sleep; this
house they set on fire first, and in a few minutes
after, five or six places more in the town appeared in flames. The conflagration spread like wild-
fire, their houses being all of wood, and covered
with flags or rushes. The poor affrighted inhabitants endeavoured to run out to save their lives,
but they were driven back into the flames by the

            sailors,

failors, and killed without mercy. At the firft
houfe above mentioned, after the boatfwain had
flain two with his pole axe, he threw a hand gra-
nade into the houfe, which burfting, made a terrible havock, killing and wounding moft of them;
and their king and moft of his train, who were
then in that houfe, fell victims to their fury every creature of them being either fmothered or
burnt.   All this while they never fired a gun, left
the people fhould awaken fafter than they could
overpower them.   But the fire awakened them
faft enough, which obliged our fellows to keep
together in bodies.   By this time the whole town
was in a flame, yet their fury rather increafed,
calling out to one another to remember Tom
Jeffery.   The terrible light of this conflagration
made me very uneafy, and roufed my nephew the
captain, and the reft of his men, who knew nothing of the matter. When he perceived the dreadful fmoke, and heard the guns go off, he readily
concluded his men were in danger; he therefore
takes another boat, and comes afhore himfelf, with
thirteen men well armed. He was greatly furprifed to fee me and only two men in the boat,
but more fo when I told him the ftory; but tho'
I argued with him, as I did with his men, about
the danger of the voyage, the interefts of the
merchants and owners, and the fafety of the fhip,
yet my nephew, like the reft, declared, that he
would rather lofe the fhip, his voyage, his life,
and all, than his men fhould be loft for want of
help: and fo away he went.   For my part, feeing
him refolved to go, I had not power to ftay behind.   He ordered the pinnace back again for
twelve men more, and then we marched directly
as the flame guided us.   But furely never was
fuch a fcene of horror beheld, or more difmal
cries heard, except when Oliver Cromwell took

Drogheda

Drogheda in Ireland, where he neither fpared man, woman, nor child.

The firft object, I think, we met with, was the ruins of one of their habitations, before which lay four men and three women killed, and two more burnt to death among the fire, which was now decaying. Nothing could appear more barbarous than this revenge: none more cruel than the authors of it. As we went on, the fire increafed, and the cry procceded in proportion. We had not gone much farther, when we beheld three naked women, followed by fixteen or feventeen men, flying with the greateft fwiftnefs from our men, who fhot one of them in our fight. When they perceived, us whom they fuppofed alfo their murderers, they fer up a moft dreadful fhriek, and both of them fwooned away in the fright. This was a fight which might have fof'tened the hardeft heart; and in pity we took fome ways to let them know we would not hurt them, while the poor creatures with bended knees, and lift-up hands, made piteous lamentations to us to fave their lives. I ordered our men not to hurt any of the poor creatures whatfoever; but being willing to underftand the occafion of all this, I went among thefe unhappy wretches, who neither underftood me, nor the good I meant them However, being refolved to put an end to this barbarity, I ordered the men to follow me. We had not gone fifty yards before we came up with the boatfwain, with four of our men at his heels, all of them covered with blood and duft, and in fearch of more people to fatiate their vengeance. As foon as we faw them we called out, and made them underftand who we were; upon which they came up to us, fetting up a halloo of triumph, in token that more help was come. Noble captain, faid he to my Nephew, I'm glad you're come: we have not half

done

done with thefe villanous hell-hound dogs, we'll root out the very nation of them from the earth, and kill more than poor Tom has hairs upon his head : and this he went on till I interrupted him. Blood-thirfty dog ! faid I, will your cruelty never end ? I charge you touch not one creature more ; flop your hands, and ftand ftill, or you're a dead man this moment. Why, Sir, faid he, you neither know whom you are protecting, nor what they have done; but pray come hither, and behold an inftance of compaffion, if fuch can merit your clemency; and with that he fhewed me the poor fellow with his throat cut, hanging upon the tree.

Indeed here was enough to fill their breafts with rage, which however I thought had gone too far, agreeable to thefe words of Jacob to his fons Simeon and Levi : *Curfed be their anger for it was fierce ; and their wrath for it was cruel.* But this fight made my nephew and the reft as bad as they; nay, my nephew declared, his concern was only for his men ; as for the people, not a foul of them ought to live. Upon this the boatfwain and eight more directly turned about, and went to finifh the intended tragedy ; which being out of my power to prevent, I returned back both from the difmal fight, and the piteous cries of thofe unfortunate creatures, who were made victims to their fury. Indeed it was an eggregious piece of folly in me to return to the boat with but one attendant; and I had very near paid for it, having narrowly efcaped forty armed Indians, who had been alarmed by the conflagration; but having paffed the place where they ftood, I got to the boat accompanied with the fupercargo, and fo went on board, fending the pinnace back again, to affift the men in what might happen. When I had got to the boat, the fire was almoft extinguifhed, and the noife was abated; but I had fcarce been half an hour on board

the

the fhip, when I heard another volley given by our failors, and a great fmoke, which, as I afterwards found, was our men falling upon thofe houfes and perfons that flood between them and the fea : but here they fpared the wives and children, and killed only the men, to the number of about fixteen or feventeen. By the time they got to the fhore, the pinnace and the fhip's boat were ready to receive them, and they all got fafe on board, not a man of them having received the leaft hurt, except two, one of whom ftrained his foot, and the other burnt his hand a little; for they met with no refiftance, the poor Indians being unprepared, amazed, and confounded.

I was extremely angry with every one of them, but particularly with the captain, who, inftead of cooling the rage of the men, had prompted them on to farther mifchief, nor could he make me any other excufe, but that as he was a man he could not mafter his paffions, at the fight of one of his men fo cruelly murdered. As for the reft, knowing they were not under my command, they took no notice of my anger; but rather boafted of their revenge. According to all their accounts, they killed or deftroyed about one hundred and fifty men, women, and children, befides burning the town to afhes. They took their companion Tom Jeffery from the tree, covered him with fome of the ruins, and fo left him. But however this action of our men might feem to them juftifiable, yet I always openly condemned it with the appellation of the *Maffacre* of *Madagafcar*. For tho' they had flain this Jeffery, yet certainly he was the firft aggreffor, by attempting to violate the chaftity of a young innocent woman, who ventured down to them on the faith of the public capitulation, which was fo treacheroufly broken.

While we were under fail, the boatfwain would

often

often defend this bloody action, by saying, *that the Indians had broke the truce the night before, by shooting one of our men without provocation; and tho' the poor fellow had taken a little liberty with the wench, he ought not to have been murdered in so villainous a manner: and that they had acted nothing but what the divine laws commissioned to be done to such homicides.* However, I was in the same mind as before, telling them that they were murderers, and bid them depend upon it, that God would blast their voyage for such an unparalleled piece of barbarity.

When we came into the gulf of Persia, five of our men, who ventured on shore, were either killed or made slaves by the Arabians, the rest of them having scarce time to escape to their boat. This made me upbraid them afresh with the just retribution of Heaven for such actions: upon which the boatswain very warmly asked me, whether those men, on whom the tower of Siloam fell were greater sinners than the rest of the Galileans; and besides, Sir, said he, none of these five poor men that are lost were with us at the massacre of Madagascar, as you call it, and therefore your reprehension is very unjust, and your application improper. Besides, added he, you are continually using the men very ill, upon this account, and being but a passenger yourself, we are not obliged to bear it; nor can we tell what ill designs you may have to bring us to judgment for it in England; and therefore if you do not leave this discourse, as also not concern yourself with any of our affairs, I will leave the ship, and not sail among such dangerous company.

All this I heard very patiently; but it being often repeated, I at length told him, the concern I had on board was none of his business; that I was a considerable owner in the ship, and therefore

had

had a right to fpeak in common, and that I was no way accountable to him, nor to any body elfe. As no more paffed for fome time after, I thought all had been over. At this time we were in the road of Bengal, where, going on fhore with the fuper-cargo, one day, in the evening, as I was preparing to go on board, one of the men came to me, and told me, I need not trouble myfelf to come to the boat, for that the cockfwain and others had order-ed him not to carry me on board any more. This infolent meffage much furprifed me; yet I gave him no anfwer to it, but went directly and ac-quainted the fupercargo, intreating him to go on board, and by acquainting the captain with it, prevent the mutiny which I perceived would hap-pen. But before I had fpoken this, the matter was effected on board: for no fooner was he gone off in the boat, but the boatfwain, gunner, car-penter, and all the inferior officers, came to the quarter-deck, defiring to fpeak with the captain; and there the boatfwain made a long harangue, exclaiming againft me, as before mentioned; that if I had not gone afhore peaceably for my own di-verfion, they by violence would have compelled me for their fatisfaction; that as they had fhipped with the captain, fo they would faithfully ferve him; but if I did not quit the fhip, or the captain oblige me to it, they would leave the fhip imme-diately; hereupon, turning his face about by way of fignal, they all cried out, O-vE and ALL, CNE and ALL.

You may be fure, that though my nephew was a man of great courage, yet he could not but be furprifed at their fudden and unexpected behavi-our: and though he talked ftoutly to them, and afterwards expoftulated with them, that in com-mon juftice to me, who was a confiderable owner in the fhip, they could not turn me, as it were,

out

out of my own houfe, which might bring their lives in danger, fhould they ever be taken in England : nay, though he invited the boatfwain on fhore to accommodate matters with me, yet all this, I fay, fignified nothing : they would have nothing to do with me, and they were refolved to go on fhore, if I came on board. Well, faid my nephew, if you are fo refolved, permit me to talk with him, and then I have done : and fo he came to me, giving me an account of their refolution, how one and all defigned to forfake the fhip when I came on board, for which he was mightily concerned. I am glad to fee you, nephew, faid I, and rejoice it is no worfe, fince they have not rebelled againft you : I only defire you to fend my neceffary things on fhore, with a fufficient fum of money, and I will find my way to England as well as I can. Though this grieved my nephew to the heart, yet there was no remedy but compliance ; in fhort, all my neceffaries were fent me, and fo this matter was over in a few hours.

I think I was now near a thoufand leagues farther off England by fea than at my little kingdom, except this difference, that I might travel by land over the Great Mogul's country to Surat, from thence up to Baffora, by fea up the Perfian gulph, then take the way of the caravans over the Arabian defart to Aleppo and Scanderoon, there take fhipping to Italy, and fo travel by land into France, and from thence crofs the fea to England.

My nephew left me two perfons to attend me ; one of them was his fervant, and the other clerk to the purfer, who engaged to be mine. I took lodgings in an Englifh woman's houfe, where feveral French, one Englifh, and two Italian merchants refided. The handfome entertainment I met with here, occafioned me to ftay nine months, confidering what courfe I fhould take. Some Englifh

glifh goods I had with me of great value, befides
a thoufand pieces of eight, and a letter of credence
for more, if there was any fuch neceffity. The
goods I foon difpofed of to advantage, and bought
here feveral good diamonds, which I could eafily
carry about with me. One morning the Englifh
merchant came to me, as being very intimate together, *Countryman*, faid he, *I have a project to
communicate to you, which, I hope, will fuit to both
our advantage. To be fhort, Sir, we are both in a
remote part of the world from our country, but yet
in a place where men of bufinefs may get a great
deal of money. Now, if you will put a thoufand
pounds to my thoufand pounds, we will hire a fhip
to our fatisfaction; you fhall be captain, I will be
merchant, and we'll go a trading voyage to* China;
*for why fhould we lye fill like drons, while the
whole world is in a continual motion.*

This propofal foon got my confent, being very
agreeable to my rambling genius; and the more
fo, becaufe I looked upon my countryman to be a
very fincere perfon; it required fome time before
we could get a veffel to our mind, and failors to
man it accordingly; at length we bought a fhip,
and got an Englifh mate, boatfwain, and gunner,
a Dutch carpenter, and three Portuguefe foremaft-
men; and, for want of others, made fhift with
Indian feamen. We firft failed to Achin, in the
ifland of Sumatra, and then to Siam, where we
bartered our wares for fome arrack and opium,
the laft of which bore a great price among the
Chinefe; in a word, we went up to Sufkan, making a very great voyage; and, after eight months
time, I returned to Bengal, very well fatisfied
with this adventure, having not only got a fufficient quantity of money, but an infight of getting
a great deal more.

The next voyage my friend propofed to me,

B b

was

was to go among the Spice iſlands, and bring home a load of cloves from the Manillas, or thereabouts, iſlands belonging partly to Spain, but where the Dutch trade very conſiderably. We were not long preparing for this voyage, which we made no leſs ſucceſsful than the laſt, touching at Bornea, and ſeveral other places which I do not perfectly remember, and returning home in about five months time. We ſoon ſold our ſpices, which were chiefly cloves, and ſome nutmegs, to the Perſian merchants, who carried them away for the gulph; and, in ſhort, making five to one advantage, we were loaded with money.

Not long after my friend and I had made up our accounts, to our entire ſatisfaction, there came in a Dutch coaſter from Batavia, of about two hundred tons. The crew of this veſſel pretended themſelves ſo ſickly, that there were not hands ſufficient to undertake a voyage, and the captain having given out that he intended to go to Europe, public notice was given that the ſhip was to be ſold. No ſooner did this come to our ears, but we bought the ſhip, paid the maſter, and took poſſeſſion. We would alſo haye very willingly entertained ſome of the men: but they having received their ſhare of booty, were not to be found, being all together fled to Agra, the great city of the Mogul's reſidence; and from thence were to travel to Suraſ, and ſo by ſea to the Perſian gulph. And indeed they had reaſon to fly in this manner: for the truth of it was, the pretended captain was the gunner only, and not the commander: that having been on a trading voyage, they were attacked on ſhore by the Malayans, who killed three men, and the captain: after whoſe death the other eleven men run away with the ſhip to the bay of Bengal, and left the mate and other five men more on ſhore; but of this af-

fair

fair we fhall have occafion to fpeak at more length hereafter.

- However they came by the fhip, we thought we bought it honeftly; neither did we fufpect any thing of the matter; when the man fhewed us a bill of fale for the fhip (undoubtedly forged) to one Emanuel Clofterfhoven, which name he went by. And fo without any more to do, we picked up fome Dutch and Englifh feamen, refolving for another voyage for cloves among the Philippian and Malacca iflands: in fhort, we continued thus five or fix years, trading from port to port with extraordinary fuccefs; in the feventh year we undertook a voyage to China, defigning to touch at Siam, and buy fome rice by the way. In this voyage, contrary winds beat us up and down for a confiderable time among the iflands in the ftraits of Malacca. No fooner were we clear of thofe rugged feas but we perceived our fhip had fprung a leak, which obliged us to put into the river Cambodia, which lyes northward of the gulph, and goes up to Siam.

One day as I was on fhore refrefhing myfelf, there comes to me an Englifhman, who was a gunner's mate on board an Englifh Eaft India fhip, riding up the river, near the city of Cambodia, Sir, faid he, *you may wonder at my bufinefs, having never feen me in your life; but though I am a ftranger, I have fomething to tell you that very nearly concerns you; and indeed it is the imminent danger you are in has moved me to give to you this timely notice.* Danger! faid I, what danger? I know of none, except my fhip being leaky, for which I defign to have run her aground to-morrow morning. *Sir,* faid he, *I hope you will be better employed, when you fhall hear what I have to fay to you. You know the town of Cambodia is about 15 leagues up this river: about three leagues on this*

fide of it, there, lyes two Dutch *and three* Englifh
*fhips. And would you venture here, without confi-
dering what ftrength you have to engage them?* I
knew not what he meant by this difcourfe, and
turning fhort upon him, Sir, faid I, I know no
reafon I have to be afraid either of any Englifh or
Dutch fhips. I am no interloper, and what bufinefs have they then with me? *Well, Sir,* faid the
man, *if you do think yourfelf fecure, all as I can
fay, you muft take your chance; however, I am
very forry you are fo deaf to good advice, but I affure you, if you do not put to fea immediately, you
will be attacked by five long boats full of men, hanged yourfelf for a pirate, if you are taken, and the
particulars examined afterwards. I thought, Sir,
added he, I might have met with better reception
for fuch a fingular piece of fervice.* Sir, faid I,
I never was ungrateful to any man: but pray explain yourfelf, and I'll go on board this minute,
whether the leak be ftopped or no. Why, Sir,
faid he, to be fhort, becaufe time is precious, the
matter is this: *You know well enough that you was
with the fhip at* Sumatra, *where your captain was
murdered by the* Malayans, *with three of his failors, and that either you, or fome who were on board
you, ran away with the fhip, and are fince turned*
pirates at fea. *Now, Sir, this is the fum of what
I had to fay; and I can pofitively affure you, that
if you be taken, you will be executed without much
ceremony; for undoubtedly you cannot but be fenfible
what little law merchant fhips fhew to pirates, whenever they fall into their unmerciful hands.*

Sir, faid I, I thank you for your kind information: and though I am fure no man could come
more honeftly by the fhip than I have done; yet
knowing their enterprife, and being fatisfied of
your honeft intention, Ill be upon my defence.
Prithee Sir, faid the man, *don't talk of being upon*

your

your defence, the best you can make is to be out of danger; and therefore, if you have any regard to your life, and the lives of your men, take the advantage, without fail, of putting out to sea at high water; by which means, as you have a whole tide before you, you will be gone too far out of their reach before they can come down.

I am mighty well satisfied, said I, in this particular, and of your kindness, which merits my greatest esteem? pray, Sir, what amends shall I make you; He replied, *I know not what amends you are willing to make, because you may have some doubts of its certainty; but to convince you of the truth of what I say, I have one offer to make to you. On board one of the English ships, I have nineteen months pay due to me, and this Dutchman that is with me has seven months pay due to him, which if you will make good to us, we will go along with you. If you shall find, that there is nothing in what we have said, then we shall desire nothing; but when you are convinced that we have saved the ship, your life, and the lives of the men, we will leave the whole to your generosity.*

So reasonable did this every way appear, that I immediately consented, and we went directly on board. As soon as we came on board, my partner calls joyfully out, That they had stopped the leak! Well, thank God, said I, but pray let us weigh anchor forthwith. Weigh! said he, what is the meaning of this hurry? Pray ask no questions, said I, but all hands to work, without losing a moment's time: upon which in great surprise, the captain was called, who immediately ordered the anchor to be got up; and though the tide was not quite down, yet being assisted with a little land breeze, we stood out to sea. I then called my partner into the cabin, and related the story at large, which was confirmed, and more

ampli-

amplified by the two men I had brought on board. Scarce had we finished our discourse, upon this head, but a sailor came to the cabin-door, with a message from the captain, that we were chased by five sloops full of armed men. Very well, said I, it is plain now there is something in it. And so going upon deck, I told all the men there was a design for seizing the ship, and of executing us for pirates; and asked them, whether they would faithfully stand by us, and by one another? To which they unanimously replied, that they would fight to their last drop of blood. I then asked the captain, which way he thought best for us to manage the battle? Sir, said he, *the only method is to keep them off with our great shot as long as we are able, and then have recourse to our small arms: and when both these fail us, then retire to close quarters, when perhaps the enemy, wanting materials, can neither break open our bulk heads, nor get in upon us.* Mean time the gunner was ordered to bring two guns to bear fore and aft out of the steerage, and so load them with musket bullets, and small pieces of old iron; and the deck being cleared, we prepared for the engagement, still however, keeping out at sea. The boats followed us with all the sail they could make, and we could perceive the two foremost were English, which outsailed the rest by two leagues, and which we found would come up with us: hereupon we fired a gun without ball, intimating that they should bring to, and we put out a flag of truce, as a signal for parley; but finding them crouding after us, till they came within shot, we took in our white, and hanging out the red flag, immediately fired at them with ball: we then called to them with a speaking trumpet, bidding them at their peril keep off.

But all this signified nothing; for depending upon

on the ftrength that followed them, they were
refolutely bent for mifchief: hereupon I ordered
them to bring the fhip to, by which means, they
laying upon our broadfide, we let fly at them at
once, one of whom carried away the ftern of the
hindermoft boat, and obliged them not only to
take down their fail, but made them all run to the
head of the boat, to keep them from finking; and
fo fhe lay by, having enough of it. In the mean
time we prepared to welcome the foremoft boat
in the fame manner. While we were doing this,
one of the three hindermoft boats came up to the
relief of that which was difabled, and took the
men out of her. We again called to parley with
them; but inftead of an anfwer, one of the boats
came clofe under our ftern; whereupon our gunner let fly his two chace-guns, but miffing, the
men in the boat fhouted, and waving their caps,
came on with greater fury. To repair this feeming difgrace, the gunner foon got ready, and firing
the fecond time, did a great deal of mifchief among
the enemy. We waved again, and bringing our
quarter to bear upon them, fired three guns more,
when we found the boat a-finking, and feveral
men already in the fea; hereupon, manning our
pinnace, I gave orders to fave as many as they
could, and inftantly to come on board, becaufe
the reft of their boats were approaching: accordingly they did fo, and took up three of them, one
of whom was almoft paft recovery; and then
crouding all the fail we could, after our men came
on board, we ftood out farther to fea, fo that the
other three boats gave over their chace, when they
came up to the firft two. Thus delivered from
imminent danger, we changed our courfe to the
eaftward, quite out of the courfe of all European
fhips.

Being now at fea, and inquiring more particularly

larly of the two feamen, the meaning of all this,
the Dutchman, at once, let us into the fecret.
He told us, that the fellow who fold us the fhip,
was an arrant thief, who had run away with her;
that the captain was treacheroufly murdered on
the coaft of Malacca by the natives there, with
three of his men; that he, the Dutchman, and
four more, being obliged to have recourfe to the
woods for their fafety, at length efcaped by means
of a Dutch fhip, in its way to China, which had
fent their boat on fhore for frefh water: That, after this he went to Batavia, where two of the
feamen belonging to the fhip (who had deferted
the reft in their travels) arrived, and there gave
an account that the fellow who ran away with
the fhip had fold her at Bengal to a fet of pirates,
who went a cruifing, and had already taken one
Englifh and two Dutch fhips richly laden.

Now, though this was abfolutely falfe, yet concerning us directly, my partner truly faid, that
our deliverance was to be efteemed fo much the
more by reafon, had we fallen into their hands,
we could have expected nothing from them but
immediate death, confidering our accufers would
have been our judges: and therefore his opinion
was, to return directly to Bengal, where being
known, we could prove how honeftly we came by
the fhip, of whom we bought her, and the like,
and where we were fure of fome juftice; at leaft
would not be hanged firft, and judged afterwards.
I was at firft of my partner's opinion; but when
I had more ferioufly confidered of the matter, I
told him we ran a great hazard in attempting to
return, being on the wrong fide of the ftraits of
Malacca, and that if, upon alarm given, we fhould
be taken by the Dutch off Batavia or Englifh elfe-
where, our running away would be a fufficient
evidence to condemn us. This danger indeed

ftartled

ftartled not only my partner, but likewife all the fliip's company; fo we changed our former refolution, and refolved to go to the coaft of Tonquin, and fo to that of China, where purfuing our firft defign as to trade, we might likewife have an opportunity to difpofe of the fliip fome way or other, and to return to Bengal in any country veffel we could procure. This being agreed to, we fteered away N. N. E. about 50 leagues off the ufual courfe to the eaft, which put us to fome inconveniencies. As the wind blew fteadily againft us, our voyage became very tedious, and we began to be afraid of want of provifion; and what was ftill worfe, we apprehended, that as thofe fhips, from whofe boats we had efcaped, were bound to China, they might get before us and have given frefh information, which might create another vigorous purfuit. Indeed I could not help being grieved, when I confidered that I, who had never wronged or defrauded any perfon in my life, was now purfued like a common thief; and, if taken, to run the greateft danger of being executed as fuch; and, though innocent, I found myfelf under the neceffity of flying for my fafety: and thereby efcape being brought to fliame, of which I was even more afraid than of death itfelf. It was eafy to read my dejection in my countenance. My mind was oppreffed, like thofe unhappy innocent perfons, who, being overpowered by blafphemous and perjured evidences, wickedly refolved to take away their lives, or ruin their reputation, have no other recourfe in this world to eafe their forrow, but fighs, prayers, and tears. My partner feeing me fo concerned, encouraged me as well as he could; and, after defcribing to me the feveral ports of that coaft, he told me, he would either put in on the coaft of Cochinchina, or elfe in the bay of Tonquin,

from

from whence we might go to Macao, a town once possessed by the Portuguese, and where still many European families reside.

To this place we steered, and early next morning came in sight of the coast; but thought it advisible to put into a small river, where we could either over-land, or by the ship's pinnace, know what vessels were in any ports thereabouts. This happy step proved our deliverance; for next morning there came to the bay of Tonquin two Dutch ships, and a third without any colours; and, in the evening, two English ships steered the same course. The river where we were was but small, and run but a few leagues up the country northward: the country was wild and barbarous, and the people thieves, having no correspondence with any other nation, dealing only in fish, oil, and such gross commodities; and one barbarous custom they still retained, that when any vessel was unhappily shipwrecked upon their coast, they make the men prisoners or slaves; so that now we might fairly say we were surrounded by enemies both by sea and land.

As the ship had been leaky, we took the opportunity, in this place, to search her, and to stop up the places which let in the water. We accordingly lightened her, and bringing our guns and other moveable things to one side, we essayed to bring her down, that we might come at her bottom: but, upon second consideration, we did not think it safe to let her lye on dry ground, neither indeed was the place convenient for it. The inhabitants, not used to such a sight as to see a ship lye down on one side, and heel in towards the shore, not perceiving her men, who were at work on her bottom, with stages and boats on the off-side, presently imagined the ship had been cast away, and lay fast on the ground. Agreeable to
this

this fuppofition they furrounded us with ten or twelve large-boats, with a refolution, undoubted-ly, to plunder the fhip, and to carry away thofe they found alive for flaves to their king. But when they perceived our men hard at work on the fhip's bottom and fide, wafhing, graving, and flop-ping her, it filled them all with fuch furprife, that they ftood gazing, as tho' they were confounded. Nor could we imagine what their defign was; however, for fear of danger, we handed down arms and ammunition, to thofe at work, in order to defend themfelves; and indeed this precaution was abfolutely neceffary; for, in a quarter of an hour after, the natives, concluding it was really a fhipwreck, and that we were faving our lives and goods, which they thought belonged to them, came down upon our men, as though it had been in a line of battle. We lay at prefent but in a very unfit pofture to fight; and before the ftages could be got down, or the men in the boat come on board as they were ordered, the Cochinchinefes were upon them, and two of their boats boarding our longboat, they began to lay hold of our men as prifoners. The firft they feized was a ftout Englifh failor, who never fired his mufket, like a fool, as I imagined, but laid it down in the boat; but he knew what he was doing; for by main force he dragged the Pagan out of the boat into ours, by the two ears, and knocked his brains out againft the boat's gunnel: A Dutchman that was next him fnatched up the mufket, and knocked down five more with the butt end of it; however, this was doing very little to their number; but a ftrange unexpected accident, which rather merits laughter than any thing elfe, gave our men a complete vic-tory over them.

It feems the carpenter, who was preparing to grave the outfide of the fhip, as well as to pay

the

the feams, where he caulked, to ftop the leaks,
had gotten two kettles juft let down in the boat,
one filled with boiling pitch, and the other with
rofin, tallow, oil, and fuch ftuff as the fhipwrights
ufe : the carpenter's man had a great iron laddle
with which he ufed to fupply the workmen with
hot ftuff, and as two of the enemies entered the
boat where the fellow ftood, he faluted them with a
full laddle of the hot boiling liquor, which, the poor
creatures being half naked, made them roar out,
and jump into the fea. Well done, Jack, fays the
carpenter, give them the other doze : and fo ftepping forward himfelf, takes a mop, and dipping
it into the pitch-pot, he and his man fo plentifully
flung it among them, as that none efcaped being
fcalded : upon which they all made the beft of
their way, crying and howling in fuch a frightful
manner, that in all my adventures I never heard
the like. And indeed never was I better pleafed
with any conqueft than I was with this, there being fo little bloodfhed, and having an averfion to
killing fuch favage wretches, (more than was neceffary,) as knowing they came on errands, which
their laws and cuftoms made them think were juft
and equitable. By this time all things being in
order, and the fhip fwimming, they found their
miftake, fo they did not venture a fecond attack :
Thus ended our merry fight ; and having got fome
rice, bread, roots, and fixteen good hogs on board
the day before, we fet fail, not daring to go into the bay of Tonquin, but fteered N. E. towards
the ifle of Formofa, or as though we would go to
the Manillas, or Philippine iflands, for fear of
meeting with any European fhips. When we anchored at the ifle Formofa, the inhabitants, not
only courteoufly fupplied us with provifions and
frefh water, but dealt very fairly and honeftly
with us in their bargains and agreements. From
this

this place we steered north, keeping still off the
coast of China, till we were beyond all its ports
where European ships usually come; and at length
being come to the latitude of thirty degrees, we
resolved to put into the first trading port we
should come at; and standing for the shore, a boat
came off two leagues to us with an old Portuguese
pilot on board, who offered his service; we very
gladly accepted him, and sent the boat back again.
And now, having the old man on board, I talked
to him of going to Nanquin, the most northward
part of the coast of China. What will you do
there? said he, smiling, I told him we would sell
our cargo and purchase calicoes, raw and wrought
silks, tea, &c. and so return the same way back.
O, said he, you had better put in at Macao, where
you may buy China wares as cheap as at Nanquin,
and sell your opium at a greater advance. But,
said I, we are gentlemen as well as merchants,
and design to see the great city of Pekin, and the
magnificent court of the monarch of China. Why
then, said he, you should go to Ningpo, where
there is a navigable river that goes through the
heart of that vast empire, two hundred and seven-
ty leagues from the sea, which crosses all the rivers, passes considerable hills, by the help of the
sluices and gates, and goes even up to the city of
Pekin. You may go to Nanquin, if you please,
and travel to Pekin, and there is a Dutch ship just
before bound that way. At the name of a Dutch
or English ship, I was struck with confusion; they
being as great a terror to me in this vessel, as an
Algerine man of war is to them in the Mediter-
ranean. The old man finding me troubled, Sir,
said he, 1 hope the Dutch are not now at war
with your nation: No, said I, but God knows
what liberty they may take when out of the reach
of the law. Why, says he, what occasion is there

for peaceable merchants to fear? For, believe me, they never meddle with any but PIRATES.

At the mentioning of the word *pirates*, my countenance turned to that of fcarlet; nor was it poffible for me to conceal it from the old pilot; who taking notice of it, *Sir*, faid he, *take what courfe you pleafe, I'll do you all the firvice I can.* Signior, faid I, I am a little concerned at your mentioning *pirates*; I hope there are none fuch in thefe feas, becaufe you fee in what a weak condition we are to defend ourfelves. " O, Sir," *faid he,*" " if that's all, don't be concerned, I don't " remember one in thefe feas thefe fifteen years, " except about a month ago one was feen in the " bay of *Siam*, but fhe is gone to the fouth- " ward; neither was fhe built for a privateer, but " was run away with by a reprobate captain, and " fome of his men, the right captain having been " murdered by the *Malayans*."

What! faid I, (as though ignorant of what had happened,) did they kill the captain! "No," *faid he*," " it is generally thought the *Malayans* " murdered him; but perhaps they might procure " them to do it, and therefore they juftly deferve " hanging. The rogues were lately difcovered " in the bay of *Siam*, in the river of *Cambodia*, " by fome *Dutchmen* who belonged to the fhip, " and had much ado to efcape the five boats that " purfued them, but they have all given fuch an " exact defcription of the fhip, that wherever they " find her, they will be fure to know her, and " they have folemnly fwore to give no quarter to " the captain or the feamen, but hang them every " one up at the yard arm, without any formal " bufinefs of bringing them to a court of judica- " ture."

Being fenfible, that, having the old man on board, he was incapable of doing me any mifchief,
Well,

Well, Signior, said I, it is for this very reason I would have you carry us up to Nanquin, where neither Englifh nor Dutch fhips come: and I mufl tell you their captains are a parcel of rafh, proud, infolent rafcals, that neither know what belongs to juftice, nor how to behave themfelves as the laws of God or nature direct. Fellows that would prove murderers to punifh robbers, and take upon them to adjudge innocent men to death, without any proof to prove them guilty; but perhaps I may live to call them to account for it, in a place where they may be taught how juftice is to be executed. And fo I told him all the ftory of buying the fhip, and how we were faved by the means of two men: that the murder of the captain by the Malayans, as alfo the running away with the fhip, I believed to be true; but that we, who bought it, were turned pirates, was a mere fiction, to cover their cowardice and foolifh behaviour, when they attacked us, and the blood of thofe men we kill in our own juft defence, lay to their door, who fent to attack us by furprife.

Sir, faid the old man amazed, " you have ta-
" ken the right courfe to fteer to the north, and,
" if I might advife you, I would have you fell
" your fhip in China, and buy or build another in
" that country; and I'll procure people to buy
" the one and fell the other." Well, but Signior,
faid I, if I fell the fhip in this manner, I may
bring fome innocent perfons into the fame danger
as I have gone through, perhaps, worfe, even
death itfelf, whereby I fhould be as guilty of their
murder as villainous executioners. " That need
" not trouble you," (fays the old man;) " I'll
" find a way to prevent that; for thefe command-
" ers you talk of I know them very well, will in-
" form them rightly of the matter as you have rela-
" ted, and I am perfuaded they will not only believe
C c 2

" me,

" me, but act more cautioufly for the future."
And will you deliver one meffage from me to them ?
" Yes, (faid he,) if you will give it under your
" hand, that I may prove it is not my own pro-
" duction." Hereupon I wrote a large account
of their attacking me in their long-boat, the pretended reafon and unjuft defign of it; that they
had done what they might be afhamed of, and
could not anfwer for at any tribunal in England.
But this letter was written in vain. Providence
ordered things another way. We failed directly
for Nanquin, and in about thirteen days fail, came
to an anchor at the fouth-weft point of the great
gulf of that place, where we learned that two
Dutch fhips were gone the length before us, and
that we fhould certainly fall into their hands. We
were all at a great lofs in this exigency, and would
very gladly have been on fhore almoft any where;
but our old pilot told me, that if I would fail to
the fouthward about two and forty leagues, there
was a little port called Quinchange, where no
European fhips ever came, and where we might
confider what was further to be done. Accordingly we weighed anchor the next day, calling only
twice on fhore by the way to get frefh water. The
country people very courteoufly fold us roots, tea,
rice, fowls, and other provifions. After five days
fail we came to the port, and landed with unfpeakable joy. We refolved to difpofe of ourfelves and effects in any other way poffible, than
enter on board that ill-fated veffel more; for no
ftate can be more miferable than a continued fear,
which is a life of death, a confounder of our un-
derftandings, that fets the imagination at work to
form a thoufand frightful things that may never
happen. And we fcarce flept one night, without
dreaming of halters, yard-arms, or gibbets; of
fighting, being taken, and being killed; nay, fo
violent

violent were our apprehenfions, that we would bruife our hands and heads againft the fides of the cabin, as though actually engaged. The ftory of the Dutch cruelty at Ampona often came into our thoughts when awake; and, for my part, I thought my condition very hard, that, after fo many difficulties, and fuch fignal deliverances, I fhould be hanged in my old age, though innocent of any crime that deferved fuch punifhment; but then religion would feem to reprefent to me, as though the voice of it had faid, Confider, O man! what fins you have been formerly guilty of, which now thou art called to an account for, to expiate with thy blood! And as to thy innocence, what art thou more innocent than thy bleffed Redeemer Jefus Chrift, who fuffered for thy offences, and to whofe providence you ought to fubmit, let what will happen? After this natural courage would infpire me to refift to the laft drop of blood, and fooner die than fuffer myfelf to be taken by boorifh, rafcally Dutchmen, who had arts to torment beyond death itfelf.

But now, thank kind Heaven, being afhore, our old pilot procured us a lodging and a warehoufe for our goods; it was a little hut with a large warehoufe joining to it, all built with canes, and pallifadoed round with large ones; to keep out pilfering thieves, which are very numerous in that country. The magiftrates allowed us a little guard during the night, and we employed a centinel with a kind of halbert for three pence a-day. The fair or mart, we found, had been over for fome time; however, there remained in the river four Junks and two Japan fhips, the merchants of the latter being on fhore. In the firft place, our old pilot brought us acquainted with the miffionary Roman priefts, who were converting the people to Chriftianity: two of them were referved, rigid,

C c 3

and

and auftere, applying themfelves to the work they came about with great earneftnefs; but the third, who was a Frenchman, called father Simon, was of a freer converfation, not feemingly fo ferious and grave, yet no worfe Chriftian than the other two, one of whom was a Portuguefe, and the other a Genoefe. Father Simon, it feems, was appointed to go to Pekin, the royal feat of the Emperor of the Chinefe: and he only waited for another prieft, who was ordered from Macao to accompany him. We never met together, but he was prompting me to keep him company in his journey: Sir, faid he, I will fhew you the glorious things of this mighty Empire, and a city, the city of Pekin, far exceeding London or Paris, put them both together. One day in particular, being at dinner with him, I fhewed fome inclination to go; which made him prefs the more upon me and my partner, to gain our perfect confent. *But, father* Simon, faid my partner, *what fatisfaction can you have in our company, whom you efteem as* heretics, *and confequently objects not worthy your regard?* Oh! faid he, you may be as good Catholics in time as thofe I hope to convert to our religion. *And fo*, faid I, *we fhall have you preaching to us all the way, inftead of pleafing us with a defcription of the country.* Sir, faid he, however our religion may be vilified by fome people, it is very certain it neither divefts us of good manners or Chriftian charity; and as we are gentlemen, as fuch we may converfe together, without making one another uneafy.

But we fhall leave him a while, to confider our fhip and the merchandife which we had to difpofe of. There was but very little trade in the place where we were; and I was once refolved to venture to fail to the river Kilam, and fo to the city of Nanquin: but Providence ordered it otherwife,

by

by our old pilot's bringing a Japan merchant to
us, to fee what goods we had. He immediately
bought our opium, for which he gave us a very
good price in gold by weight, fome wedges of
which were about ten or eleven ounces. It came
into my head, that perhaps he might buy the fhip
too; and I ordered his interpreter to propofe it
to him. He faid nothing then, but fhrunk up his
fhoulders; yet in a few days after he came accompanied by a miffionary prieft, who was his interpreter, with this propofal, *That as he had bought
a great quantity of our goods, he had not money
enough to purchafe our fhip; but if I pleafed, he
would hire her with all my men, to go to Japan,
and from thence with another loading to the Philippian iflands, the freight of both which he would
very willingly pay to us before; and at their return
to Japan, would buy the fhip.* Upon this we afked
the captain and his men, if they were willing to
go to Japan; to which they unanimoufly agreed.
While this was in agitation, the young man my
nephew left to attend me, told me, *That as I did
not care to accept this profpect of advantage, he
would manage it for me as I pleafed, and render
me a faithful account of his fuccefs, which fhould
be wholly mine.* Indeed I was very unwilling to
part with him; but confidering it might be for the
young man's good, I difcourfed my partner about
it, who, of his own generofity, gave him his fhare
of the veffel, fo that I could do no otherwife than
give him mine; but however, we let him have but
the property of half of it, and referved a power,
that when we met in England, if he had obtained
fuccefs, he fhould account to us for one half of
the profits of the fhip's freight, and the other
fhould be his own. Thus having taken a writing
under his hand, away he failed to Japan, where
the merchant dealt very honeftly by him, got him
a li-

a licence to come on fhore, fent him loaded to the Philippines with a Japanefe fupercargo, from whence he came back again loaded with European goods, cloves, and other fpiceries. By this voyage he cleared a confiderable fum of money, which determined him not to fell his fhip, but to trade on his own account: fo he returned to the Manillas, where getting acquaintance, he made his fhip free, was hired by the governor privately to go to Acapulco in America, on the Mexican coaft, with a licence to travel to the great city of Mexico. This traffic turned out greatly to account, and my friend finding means to get to Jamaica, returned nine years after exceeding rich into England.

In parting with the fhip, it comes in courfe to confider of thofe men who had faved our lives when in the river of Cambodia: and though, by the way, they were a couple of rogues, who thought to turn pirates themfelves, yet we paid them what they had before demanded, and gave each of them a fmall fum of money, making the Englifhman a gunner, and the Dutchman a boatfwain, with which they were very well contented.

We were now above 1000 leagues farther from home than when at Bengal: All the comfort we could expect was, that there being another fair to be kept in a month's time, we might not only purchafe all forts of that country's manufactures, but very poffibly find fome Chinefe junks, or veffels from Tonquin, to be fold, which would carry us and our goods wherefoever we pleafed. Upon thefe hopes, we refolved to continue; and to divert ourfelves, we took feveral little journeys in the country. About ten days after we parted with our fhip, we travelled to fee the city of Nanquin. This city lyes in latitude 30 deg. north of the line; it is regularly built, and the ftreets are ex-

                                    actly

actly ftraight, and crofs one another, in direct lines, which fets it out to the greateft advantage. At our return, we found the prieft was come from Macao that was to accompany father Simon to Pekin. That father earneftly folicited me to accompany him, and I referred him to my partner. In fhort, we both agreed, and prepared accordingly; and we were fo lucky as to have liberty to travel among the retinue of one of their Mandarines, who is a principle magiftrate, and much reverenced by the people.

We were five and twenty days travelling thro' this miferable country, infinitely populous, but as indifferently cultivated; and yet their pride is infinitely greater than their poverty, infomuch that the priefts themfelves derided them. As we paffed by the houfe of one of their country gentlemen, two leagues off Nanquin, we had the honour, forfooth, to ride with the Chinefe fquire about two miles. Never was Don Quixote fo exactly imitated, never fuch a compound of pomp and poverty feen before!

His habit, made of calico, was dirty, greafy, and very proper for a Merry Andrew or Scaramouch, with all its tawdry trappings, as hanging fleeves, taffels, &c. though torn and rent in almoft every part: his veft underneath it was no lefs dirty, but more greafy, refembling the moft exquifite floven, or greafy butcher. His horfe (worfe than Rofinante, or the famous fteed of doughty Hudibras) was a poor ftarved, decrepit thing, that would not fell for thirty fhillings in England: and yet this piece of worfhipful pomp was attended with ten or twelve flaves, who guarded their mafter to his country-feat. We ftopped at a little village for refrefhment: and when we came by the country-feat of this great man, we found him fitting under a tree before his door, eating a mefs
of

of boiled rice, with a great piece of garlic in the middle, and a bag filled with green pepper by him, and another plant like ginger, together with a piece of lean mutton in it; this was his Worſhip's repaſt: but pray obſerve the ſtate of the fool! two women ſlaves brought him his food; which being laid before him, two others appeared to perform their reſpective offices; one fed him with a ſpoon, while the other ſcrapped off what fell upon his beard and taffety veſt, and gave it to a particular favourite to eat. And thus we left the wretch pleaſed with the conceit of our admiring his magnificence, which rather merited our ſcorn and deteſtation.

At length we arrived at the great city of Pekin, accompanied by two ſervants, and the old Portugueſe pilot, whoſe charges we bore, and who ſerved us as an interpreter by the way. We had ſcarce been a week at Pekin, but he comes laughing to us, *Ah! Signior* Ingliſe, ſaid he, *me ſomething tell you make your heart glad, but make me ſorry; for you bring me here* 25 *days journey, and now you leave me go back alone: and which way ſhall I make my port after, without de ſhip, without de horſe, without* pecune? ſo he called money in his broken Latin. He then informed me, that there was a great caravan of Muſcovite and Poliſh merchants in the city, who were preparing to ſet out for Muſcovy by land within ſix weeks; and that he was certain we would take this opportunity, and conſequently that he muſt go home by himſelf. Indeed this news infinitely ſurpriſed and pleaſed me. Are you certain of this? ſaid I, *Yes, Sir*, ſaid he, *me ſure it's true.* And ſo he told me, *that having met an old acquaintance of his, an* Armenian, *in the ſtreet, who was among them, and who had come from* Aſtracan, *with a deſign to go to* Tonquin, *but for certain reaſons having altered*
his.

his refolution, he was now refolved to go with the caravan, and to return by the river Wolga *to* Aftracan. Well, Signior, faid I, don't be difcontented about your returning alone ; and if by this means I can find a paffage to England, it will be your own fault if you return to Macao at all. And fo confulting with my partner what was beft to be done, he referred it to me as I pleafed, having our affairs fo well fettled at Bengal, that if we could convert the good voyage we had made in China filks, wrought raw, he would be fatisfied to go to England, and fo return to Bengal in the company's fhips. Thus refolved, we agreed, that if our pilot would go with us, we would bear his charges either to Mufcow or England ; and to give him in a prefent the fum of 170 pounds Sterling. Hereupon, we called him in, and told him the caufe of his complaint fhould be removed, if he would accompany us with the caravan ; and therefore we defired to know his mind. At this he fhook his head, *Great long journey*, faid he, *me no pecune, carry me to* Mufcow, *or keep me there.* But we foon put him out of that concern, by making him fenfible of what we would give him here to lay out to the beft advantage : and as for his charges, we would fet him fafe on fhore, God willing, either in Mufcovy, or England, as he pleafed, at our own charge, except the carriage of his goods. At this propofal he was like a man tranfported, telling us, he would go with us all the world over ; and we made preparations for our journey ; but it was near four months before all the merchants were ready.

In the mean time, my partner and the pilot went exprefs to the port where we firft put in, to difpofe of what goods had been left there, while I accompanied a Chinefe merchant, who was going to Nanquin, and there bought 29 pieces of damafk,

with

with about 300 more of other fine filks; and by the time my partner returned to Pekin, I had them all carried thither: our cargo in filks amounted to 4500l. Sterling, which, together with tea, fine calicoes, nutmegs, and cloves loaded 18 camels for our fhare, befides what we rode upon, with two or three fpare horfes, and two more loaden with provifions: the company now was very great, making about 400 horfe, and above 120 men, well armed and provided. We were of feveral nations, among whom were five Scots merchants inhabiting in Mufcow, and well experienced in trade.

We fet out from Pekin the beginning of February our ftyle; and in two days more, we paffed through the gate of the great China wall, which was erected as a fortification againft the Tartars, being 108 Englifh miles long. We then entered a country not near fo populous, chiefly under the power of plundering Tartars, feveral companies of whom we perceived riding on poor ftarved horfes, contemptible as themfelves, without order or difcipline. One time our leader for the day gave us leave to go a hunting. But what do you think we hunted, only a parcel of fheep, which indeed exceeded any in the world for wildnefs and fwiftnefs; but while we were purfuing this game, it was our chance to meet with about forty Tartars, who no fooner perceived us, but one of them blew a horn, at the found of which there foon appeared a troop of forty or fifty more, at about a mile's diftance. Hereupon one of the Scots merchants (who knew their way) ordered us to advance towards them, and attack them immediately. As we advanced, they let fly a volley of arrows, which happily fell a little fhort of us: this made us halt a little, to return the compliment with bullets; and then being led up by the bold Scot, we fired our piftols in their faces, and drew out our

fwords;

fwords; but there was no occasion; for they flew like timorous sheep, and only three of them remained, beckoning to the rest to come back. But our brave commander gallops up to them by himself, shot one dead, knocks another off his horse, while the third ran away: and thus ended our battle with the Tartars.

We travelled a month more through the emperor of China's dominions; and at length coming to one of their towns about a day and a half's journey from the city of Naum, I wanted to buy a camel. The person I spoke to would have brought me one, but, like a fool, I must go along with him, about two miles from the village. My old pilot and I walked on foot, forsooth, for some. variety, when coming to the place where the camels were kept as in a park guarded by Chinese soldiers, we there agreed and bought one, which the Chinese man that came with me led along the road. But we had not gone far, before we were attacked by five Tartars, mounted on horseback, two of whom seized the man, took the camel from him, and rode away, while the other three approached us, the first of whom suddenly seized me as I was drawing my sword, the second knocked me down; but my old trusty Portuguese, taking a pistol out of his pocket, which I knew nothing of, and coming up to the fellow that struck me, he, with one hand, pulled him off his horse, and then shot him dead upon the spot; then taking his scymitar, he struck at the man that stopt us, but missing him, cut off one of his horse's ears, the pain of which made him throw his rider to the ground. The poor Chinese, who had led the camel, seeing the Tartar down, runs to him, and seizing upon his pole-axe, wrenched it from his hands, and knocked his brains out. But there was another Tartar to deal with, who seeming

                    neither

neither inclined to fight, nor to fly, and my old man having begun to charge his piftol, the very fight of it ftruck fuch a terror into the wretch, that away he fcoured, leaving my old pilot, rather my champion and defender, an abfolute victory.

By this time being awakened from my trance, I began to open my eyes, wondering where I was, having quite forgot all that paffed; but my fenfes returning, and feeling a great pain in my head, and feeing the blood was running over my cloaths, I inftantly jumped upon my feet, and grafped my fword in my hand, with a refolution to take revenge; but no enemies now remained, except the dead Tartar, with his horfe ftanding by him. The old man feeing me recovered, whom he thought flain, ran towards me, and embraced me with the greateft tendernefs, at the fame time examining into my wound, which was far from being mortal; when we returned to the village, the man demanded payment for his camel, which I refuling, we brought the caufe before a Chinefe judge, who acted with great impartiality: having heard both fides, he afked the Chinefe man that went with me, whofe fervant he was? Sir, faid he, I am nobody's, but went with the ftranger, at his requeft: why then, faid the judge, you were the ftranger's fervant for the time, and the camel being delivered to his fervant, it is the fame as tho' delivered to himfelf, and accordingly he muft pay for it. Indeed the cafe was fo fairly ftated, that I had nothing to objeft to it: fo having paid for that I was robbed of, I fent for another, but did not go myfelf to fetch it, as I had enough of that fport before.

The city of Naum is a frontier of the Chinefe empire, fo fortified, as fome will tell you, that millions of Tartars cannot batter down their walls;

by

by which certainly one might think one of our cannons would do more execution than all their legions.

When we were within a day's march of that city, we had information that the governor had sent messengers to every part of the road, to inform the travellers and caravans to halt, till a guard was sent to protect them from the numerous bodies of Tartars that lately appeared about the city. This news put us into great consternation; but, obeying the orders, we stopt, and two days after, there came two hundred soldiers from a garrison of the Chinese, and three hundred more from Naum: thus guarded both in the front and rear, with our men on the flanks, we boldly advanced, thinking we were able to combat with ten thousand Mogul Tartars, if they appeared.

Early next morning, in our march from a little well situated town called Changu, after having passed a river, and entered upon a defart of about 15 or 16 miles over, we soon beheld, by a cloud of dust that was raised, that the enemy was approaching. This much difpirited the Chinese. My old pilot took notice of it, and called out, Signior Inglefe, thofe fellows muft be encouraged, or they will ruin us all: and I am afraid, if the Tartars attack us, they will all run away. Why Signior, faid I, what fhall be done in this cafe? Done, fays he, why, let fifty of our men advance, and flank them on each wing. I know the fellows will fight well enough in company. We accordingly took his advice, and marched fifty to the right wing, and the fame number to the left, and with the reft made a line of referve, leaving the laft two hundred men to guard the camels, or to affift us as occafion required.

Thus prepared, a party of the enemy came forward, viewing our pofture, and traverfing the

ground

ground on the front of our line. Hereupon we ordered the two wings to move on, and give them a falute with their fhot; which accordingly was done. This put a ftop to their proceedings; for immediately wheeling off to their left, they all marched away, and we faw not more of them. They had undoubtedly given an account to their companions of what reception they might expect, which made them fo eafily give over their enterprife.

When we came to the city of Naum, we returned the governor hearty thanks, and difperfed a hundred crowns among the foldiers that guarded us. We refted there one day, and then proceeded on our travels, paffing feveral great rivers and defarts; and on the 13th of April, we came to the frontiers of Mufcovy, the firft town of which was called Argun.

This happy occafion, as I thought, of coming into a Chriftian country, made me congratulate the Scots merchant upon it: he fmiled at that, telling me not to rejoice too foon; for, faid he, except the Ruffian foldiers in garrifon, and a few inhabitants of the cities upon the road, all the reft of this country, for above a thoufand miles, is inhabited by the moft ignorant and barbarous Pagans.

We advanced from the river Arguna by moderate journeys, and found convenient garrifons on the road, filled with Chriftian foldiers, for the fecurity of commerce, and for the convenient lodgings of travellers; but the inhabitants of the country were mere Pagans, worfhipping the moon, fun, and ftars. We particularly obferved this idolatry near the river Arguna, at a city inhabited by Tartars and Ruffians, called Nerifinkey. Being curious to fee their way of living, while the caravan continued to reft themfeives in this city, I went to one of their villages, where there was to

be

be one of their folemn facrifices.   There I beheld,
upon the ftump of an old tree, an idol of wood,
more ugly than the reprefentation of the devil
himfelf: its head refembled no living creature::
its ears were as big and as high as a goat's horns,
a crooked nofe, four cornered mouth, and horrible teeth : it was clothed in fheeps fkins, had a
great Tartar bonnet, with two horns growing
through it, and was eight foot high, without feet,
legs, or proportion.   Before this idol there lay
16 or 17 people, who brought their offerings, and
were making their prayers, while at a diftance
ftood three men, and one bullock, as victims to
this ugly monfter.

   Such ftupendous facrileges as this, in robbing
the true God of his honour, filled me with the
greateft aftonifhment and reflection; which foon
turning to rage and fury, I rode up to the image,
and cut in pieces the bonnet that was upon his
head with my fword, fo that it hung down by one
of the horns, while one of my men that was with
me, pulled at it by his fheep-fkin garment.   Immediately an hideous howling and outcry ran through
the village, and two or three hundred people
coming about our ears, we were obliged to fly
for it.

   But I had not done with the monfter ; for the
caravan being to reft three nights in the town, I
told the Scots merchant what I had feen, and that
I was refolved to take four or five men well armed with me, in order to deftroy the idol, and fhew
the people how little reafon they had to truft in
a god who could not fave himfelf.   At firft he
laughed at me, reprefenting the danger of it; and
when it was deftroyed, what time had we to preach
to them better things, whofe zeal and ignorance
was in the higheft degree, and both unparalleled ?
that if I fhould be taken by them, I fhould be fer-
D d 3   ved

ved as a poor Ruffian, who contemned their worfhip; that is, to be ftripped naked, and tied to
the top of the idol, there fhot at with arrows till
my body was full of them, and then burnt a facrifice to the monfter: but, Sir, faid he, fince
your zeal carries you fo far, rather than you
fhould be alone, I will accompany you, and bring
a ftout fellow equal to yourfelf, if you will, to
affift you in this defign: and accordingly he brought
one captain Richardfon, who hearing the ftory,
readily confented; but my partner declined it,
being altogether out of his way: and fo we three,
and my man-fervant, refolved to execute this exploit about midnight; but upon fecond thoughts
we deferred it to the next night, by reafon that
the caravan being to go from thence next morning, we fhould be out of the governor's power.
The better to effectuate my defign, I procured a
Tartar's fheep-fkin robe, a bonnet, with a bow
and arrows, and every one of us got the like habits.   The firft night we fpent in mixing combuf-
tible matter with aqua-vitæ, gun-powder, &c. having a good quantity of tar in a little pot; next
night we came up to the idol about eleven o'clock,
the moon being up.   We found none guarding it;
but we perceived a light in the houfe, where we
had feen the priefts before.   One of our men was
for firing the hut, another for killing the people,
and a third for making them prifoners, while the
idol was deftroyed.   We agreed to the latter; fo
knocking at the door, we feized the firft that opened it, and ftopping his mouth, and tying his feet,
we left him.   We ferved the other two in the like
manner; and then the Scots merchant fet fire to
the compofition, which frightened them fo much,
that we brought them all away prifoners to their
wooden god.   There we fell to work with him,
daubing him all over with tar mixed with tallow
and

and brimſtone, ſtopped his eyes, ears, and mouth full of gun-powder, with a great piece of wild fire in his bonnet, and environed it with dry forage. All this being done, we unlooſed and ungagged the priſoners, and ſet the idol on fire, which the gun-powder blowing up, the ſhape of it was deformed, rent, and ſplit, which the forage utterly conſumed; for we ſtaid to ſee its deſtruction, leſt the ignorant idolatrous people ſhould have thrown themſelves into the flames. And thus we came away undiſcovered, the morning appearing as buſy among our fellow-travellers, as no body could have ſuſpected any other, but that we had been in our beds all night.

Next morning we ſet out, and had gone but a ſmall diſtance from the city, when there came a multitude of the people of the country to the gates of the city, demanding ſatisfaction of the Ruſſian governor for inſulting their prieſts, and burning their great *Cham Chi-Thaungu*, who dwelt in the ſun, and no mortal would violate his image, but ſome Chriſtian miſcreants; and being already no leſs than thirty thouſand ſtrong, they announced war againſt him and all his Chriſtians.

The governor aſſured them he was ignorant of the matter, and that none of his garriſon had been abroad; that indeed there was a caravan that went away that morning, and that he would ſend after them to inquire into it; and whoever were the offenders, ſhould be delivered into their hands. This ſatisfied them for the preſent, but the governor ſent to inform us, that if any of us had done it, we ſhould make all the haſte away poſſible, while he kept them in play as long as he could. Upon this we marched two days and two nights, ſtopping but very little, till at laſt we arrived at a village called Plothus, and haſted to Jarawena, another of the Czar's colonies. On the third day, having

having entered the defart, and paffed the lake called ohaks Ofer, we beheld a numerous body of
horfe on the other fide of it to the north, who
fuppofed we had paffed on that fide of the lake;
but having either found their miftake, or being
certainly informed of the way we took, they came
upon us towards the dufk of the evening, juft as
we had pitched our camp between two little but
very thick woods, with a little river running before our front, and fome felled trees, with which
we covered our rear; a precaution we always
took, and which we had juft finifhed, when the
enemy came up. They did not fall on us immediately, but fent three meffengers, demanding the
men who had infulted their priefts, and burnt
their god *Cham Chi Thaungu*, that they might be
burnt with fire, that if this was complied with,
they would peaceably depart; but if not, they
would deftroy one and all of us. Our men fta-
red at one another on receipt of this meffage, but
Nobody was the word, as indeed nobody knew it,
but he who did it. Upon which the leader of the
caravan returned for anfwer, That they were
peaceable merchants, who meddled with none of
their priefts and gods; and therefore defired them
not to difturb us, and put us to the neceffity of
defending ourfelves. But fo far was this from
fatisfying them, that the next morning, coming
to our right, they let fly a volley of arrows a-
mong us, which happily did not hurt any, becaufe
we fheltered ourfelves behind our baggage. We
expected however to come to a clofer engagement;
but were happily faved by a cunning fellow, a
Coffack, who obtaining leave of the leader to go
out, mounts his horfe, rides directly from our
rear, and taking a circuit, comes up to the Tartars, as though he had been fent exprefs, and tells
them a formal ftory, that the wretches who had
burnt

burnt the *Cham Chi Thaungu*, were gone to Siheil-ka, with a refolution to burn the god *Shal Ifar*, belonging to the Tonguefes. Upon which, believing this cunning Tartar, who was fervant to our Mufcovites, away they drove to Siheilka, and in lefs than three minutes were out of our fight, nor did we ever hear of them more.

When we came to the city of Jarawena, we refted five days, and then entered into a frightful defart, which held us twenty-three days march, infefted with feveral fmall companies of robbers, or Mogul Tartars, who never had the courage to attack us. After we had paffed over this de-fart, we found feveral garrifons to defend the ca-ravans from the violence of the Tartars. In par-ticular the governor of Adinfkoy offered us a guard of fifty men to the next ftation, if we ap-prehended any danger. The people here retained the fame paganifm and barbarity, only they were not fo dangerous, being conquered by the Mufco-vites. The clothing, both of men and women, is of the fkins of beafts, living under the ground in vaults and caves, which have a communication with one another. They have idols almoft in e-very family ; befides, they adore the fun and ftars, water and fnow ; and the leaft uncommon thing that happens in the elements, alarms them as much as thunder and lightning does the unbe-lieving Jews.

Nothing remarkable occurred in our march through this country. When we had got through the defart, after two days further travel, we came to Jenezo, a Mufcovite city, on the great river fo called, which, we were told, parted Europe from Afia. The inhabitants here were very little better, though intermixed with the Mufcovites ; but the wonder will ceafe, when I inform my rea-der of what was obferved to me, that the Czar

rather

rather converts the Tartars with foldiers than clergymen, and is more proud to make them faithful fubjects, than good Chriftians.

From this city to the river Oby, we travelled over a pleafant, fruitful, but very uncultivated country, for want of good management and people, and thofe few are moftly pagans. This is the place where the Mufcovite criminals are banifhed to, if they are not put to death. The next city we came to, was the capital city of Siberia, called Tobolfki, when, having been almoft feven months on our journey, and winter drawing on apace, my partner and I confulted about our particular affairs, in what manner we fhould difpofe of ourfelves. We had been told of fledges and rein-deer to carry us over the fnow in the winter feafon, the fnow being frozen fo hard, that the fledges can run upon the furface without any danger of going down. As I was bound to England, I now behoved either to go with the caravan to Jeroflaw, from thence weft to Narva, and the gulf of Finland, and fo by land or fea to Denmark; or elfe I muft leave the caravan at a little town on the Dwina, and fo to Archangel, where I was certain of fhipping either to England, Holland, or Hamburgh. One night I happened to get into the company of an illuftrious but banifhed prince, whofe company and virtues were fuch as made me propofe to him a method how he might obtain his liberty. *My dear friend*, faid he, *as I am here happily free from my miferable greatnefs, with all its attendants of pride, ambition, avarice, and luxury; if I fhould efcape from this place, thefe pernicious feeds may again revive, to my lafting difquietude; therefore let me remain in a bleffed confinement, for I am but flefh, a mere man, with paffions and affections as fuch; O be not my friend and tempter too!* Struck dumb with furprife,

prise, I stood silent a while, nor was he in less disorder ; by which perceiving he wanted to give vent
to his mind, I desired him to consider of it, and so
withdraw. But about two hours after he came to
my apartment : *Dear friend*, said he, *though I cannot consent to accompany you, I shall have this satisfaction in parting, that you leave me an honest
man, still ; but as a testimony of my affection to
you, be pleased to accept this present of sables.*

In return for this compliment, I sent my servant next morning to his Lordship, with a small
present of tea, two pieces of China damask, and
four little wedges of gold : but he only accepted
the tea, one piece of damask, and a piece of gold,
for the curiosity of the Japan stamp that was upon
it. Not long after, he sent for me, and told me,
That what he had refused himself, he hoped upon
his account I would grant to another, whom he
should name ; In short, it was his only son, who
was about 200 miles distance from him, on the
other side of the Oby, whom he said he would
send for, if I gave my consent. This I soon complied with : upon which he sent his servants next
day for his son, who returned in twenty days time,
bringing seven horses loaded with valuable furs.
At night the young lord was conducted *incognito*
into our apartment, where his father presented
him to me. We then concerted the best ways for
travelling, and after having bought a considerable
quantity of sables, black fox skins, fine erminies,
&c. (which I sold at Archangel at a good piece,)
we set out from this city the beginning of June,
making a small caravan, being about thirty-two
horses and camels, of which I represented the head.
My young lord had with him a very faithful Siberian servant, well acquainted with the roads : we
shunned the principal towns and cities, as Tumen,
Soli Kamoskoi, and several others, by reason of
their ·

their ftrictnefs in examining travellers, left any of
the banifhed perfons of diftinction fhould efcape.
Having paffed the river Kama, we came to a city
on the European fide, called Soloy Komofkoi,
where we found the people moftly Pagans as before. We then paffed a defart of about two hun-
red miles over; but in other places, it is near
feven hundred. In paffing this wild place, we were
befet by a troop of men on horfeback, and about
five and forty men armed with bows and arrows.
At firft they looked earneftly on us, and then placed themfelves in our way. We were above fixteen men, and drew up a little line before our
camels. My young lord fent out his Siberian fervant to know who they were; but when he approached them, he neither knew a word they faid,
nor would they admit him to come near them at
his peril, but prepared to fhoot him. At his return he told us he believed them to be Calmuck
Tartars, and that he thought there were more of
them upon the defart. This was but a fmall comfort to us; yet feeing a little grove about a quarter of a mile's diftance, we moved to it, by the
old Portuguefe pilot's advice, without meeting
with any oppofition. Here we found a marfhy
piece of ground, and a fpring of water running
into a little brook on one fide, which joined another like it a little farther off, and thefe two formed the head of the river called Writfka. As foon*
as we arrived, we went to work, cutting down
great arms off the trees, and laying them hanging
(not quite off) from one tree to another. In this
fituation we waited the motions of the enemy,
without perceiving any advancement they made
towards us. About two hours before night, being joined by fome others, in all about fourfcore
horfe, among whom we fancied were fome women, they came upon us with great fury. We

fired

fired without ball, calling to them in the Ruſſian tongue to know their buſineſs; but they, either not knowing, or ſeeming not to underſtand us, came directly to the wood-ſide, not conſidering that we were ſo fortified, as that they could not break in. Our old pilot the Portugueſe proved both our captain and engineer, and deſired us not to fire, till they came within piſtol-ſhot; and when he gave the word of command, then to take the ſureſt-aim: but he did not bid us give fire, till they were within two pikes length of us, and then we killed fourteen of them, wounded ſeveral, as alſo their horſes, having every one of us loaded our pieces with two or three bullets at leaſt. So much were they ſurpriſed at our undauntedneſs, that they retired about a hundred roods of us. In the mean while, we loaded our pieces again, and ſallying out, ſecured four or five of their horſes, whoſe riders we found were killed, and perceived them to be Tartars. About an hour after, they made another attempt, to ſee where they might break in; but finding us ready to receive them, they retired.

All that night we wrought hard, in ſtrengthening our ſituation, and barricading the entrances into the woods; but when day-light came, we had a very unwelcome diſcovery; for the enemy being encouraged by their aſſiſtance, had ſet up eleven or twelve tents in form of a camp, about three quarters of a mile from us. I muſt confeſs, I was never more concerned in my life, giving myſelf and all that I had over for loſt. And my partner declared, that as the loſs of his goods would be his ruin, before they ſhould be taken from him, he would fight to the laſt drop of his blood. As we could not pretend to force our way, we had recourſe to a ſtratagem; we kindled a large fire, which burnt all night; and no ſooner was it dark,

E e .   but

but we purfued our journey towards the pole, or north ftar, and travelling all night, by fix o'clock in the morning we came to a Ruffian village, called Kertza, and from thence came to a large town named Ozonoys, where we heard that feveral troops of Calmuck Tartars had been abroad upon the defart, but that we were paft all danger. In five days after we came to Veuflima, upon the river Witzedga; from thence we came to Lawrenfkoy, on the third of July, where, providing ourfelves with two luggage boats and a convenient bark, we embarked the feventh, and arrived at Archangel the eighteenth, after a year, five months, and three days journey, including the eighth months and odd days at Tobolfki. We came from Archangel the twentieth of Auguft in the fame year, and arrived at Hamburgh the thirtieth of September. Here my partner and I made a very good fale of our goods, both thofe of China and Siberia; when, dividing our effects, my fhare came to 3475 l. 17 s. 3 d. after all the loffes we had fuftained, and charges we had been at. Here the young Lord took his leave of me, in order to go to the court of Vienna, not only to feek protection, but to correfpond with his father's friends. After we had ftaid four months in Hamburgh, I went from thence over land to the Hague, where, embarking in the packet, I arrived in London the tenth of January 1705, after ten years and nine months abfent from England.

Robinſon Cruſoe's *Viſion of the* Angelic World.

Chap. I. *OF SOLITUDE.*

HOWEVER ſolitude is looked upon as a reſtraint to the pleaſures of the world, in company and converſation, yet it is a happy ſtate of exemption from a ſea of trouble, an inundation of vanity and vexation, of confuſion and diſappointment. While we enjoy ourſelves, neither the joy nor ſorrow of other men affect us: we are then at liberty, with the voice of our ſoul, to ſpeak to God. By this we ſhun ſuch frequent trivial diſcourſe, as even becomes an obſtruction to virtue; and how often do we find, that we had reaſon to wiſh we had not been in company, or ſaid nothing when we were there? for either we offend God by the impiety of our diſcourſe, or lay ourſelves open to the violence of deſigning people by our unguarded expreſſions; and frequently feel the coldneſs and treachery of pretended friends, when once involved in trouble and affliction; of ſuch unfaithful intimates (I ſhould ſay enemies) who rather by falſe innuendoes would accumulate miſeries upon us, than honeſtly aſſiſt us when ſuffering under the hard hand of Adverſity. But in a ſtate of ſolitude, when our tongues cannot be heard, except by the great Majeſty of heaven, how happy are we, in the bleſſed enjoyment of converſing with our Maker! It is then we make him our friend, which ſets us above the envy and contempt of wicked men. When a man converſes with himſelf, he is ſure that he does not converſe with an enemy. Our retreat ſhould be to good company, and good books. I mean not by ſolitude, that a man should retire into a cell, a defart, or a monastery: which would be altogether an useless and unprofitable restraint: for as men are formed for society, and have an absolute necessity and dependence upon one another; so there is a retirement of the soul, with which it converses in heaven, even in the midst of men; and indeed no man is more fit to speak freely, than he who can, without any violence to himself, refrain his tongue, or keep silence altogether. As to religion, it is by this the soul gets acquainted with the hidden mysteries of the holy writings; here she finds those flood of tears, in which good men wash themselves day and night, and only makes a visit to God, and his holy angels. In this conversation the truest peace and most solid joy are to be found; it is a continual feast of contentment on earth, and the means of attaining everlasting happiness in heaven.

Chap. II. *Of HONESTY.*

HONESTY is a virtue beloved by good men, and pretended to by all persons. In this there are several degrees: to pay every man his own, is the common law of honesty; but to do good to all mankind, is the chancery law of honesty: and this chancery-court is in every man's breast, where his conscience is a lord chancellor. Hence it is, that a miser, though he pays every body their own, cannot be an honest man, when he does not discharge the good offices that are incumbent on a friendly, kind, and generous person: for, saith the prophet Isaiah, chap. xxxii. ver. 7, 8. *The instruments of a churl are evil: he deviseth wicked devices to destroy the poor with lying words, even when the needy speaketh right. But the liberal soul deviseth liberal things, and by liberal things*
shall

shall he stand. It is certainly honesty to do every thing the law requires ; but should we throw every poor debtor in prison till he has paid the utmost farthing, hang every malefactor without mercy, exact the penalty of every bond, and the forfeiture of every indenture, this would be downright cruelty, and not honesty : and it is contrary to that general rule, *To do to another that which you would have done unto you.* Sometimes necessity makes an honest man a knave : and a rich man an honest man, because he has no occasion to be a knave. The trial of honesty is this : Did you ever want bread, and had your neighbour's loaf in keeping ; and would starve, rather than eat it ? Were you ever arrested, having in your custody another man's cash, and would rather go to goal, than break it ? if so, this indeed may be reckoned honesty. For King *Solomon* tells us, *that a good name is better than life, and is a precious ointment, and which when a man has once lost, he has nothing left worth keeping.*

Chap. III. *Of suffering* AFFLICTIONS.

AFFLICTIONS are common to all mankind ; and whether they proceed from losses, disappointments, or the malice of men, they often bring their advantages along with them : for this shews man the vanity and deceitfulness of this life, and is an occasion of rectifying our measures, and bringing us to a more modest opinion of ourselves : it tells us, how necessary the assistance of divine grace is unto us, when life itself becomes a burden, and death even desirable : but when the greatest oppression comes upon us, we must have recourse to patience, begging of God to give us that virtue ; and the more composed we are under any trouble, the more commendable is our wisdom, and the

E e 3

larger

larger will be our recompenfe. Let the provocation be what it will, whether from a good-natured and confcientious, or a wicked, perverfe, and vexatious man; all this we fhould take as from the over-ruling hand of God, as a punifhment for our fins. Many times injured innocence may be abufed by falfe oaths, or the power of wicked, jealous, or malicious men; but we often find it, like the palm, rife the higher, the more it is depreffed; while the juftice of God is eminently remarkable in punifhing thofe, one way or other, who defire to endeavour to procure the downfal of an innocent man: nor does God fail, comforting an afflicted perfon, who with tears and prayers folicits the throne of Heaven for deliverance and protection. *David* fays, *that his foul was full of trouble, and his life drew near unto the grave.* But certainly David's afflictions made him eminently remarkable, as particularly when purfued by King Saul, and hunted as a partridge over the mountains. But one thing which ftands by innocence, is the love of God; for were we to fuffer difgrace, nay, an ignominious death itfelf, what confolation does our innocence procure at our lateft conflict, our laft moments!

Chap. IV. *Of the immorality of converfation, and the vulgar errors of behaviour.*

As converfation is a great part of human happinefs, fo it is a pleafant fight to behold a fweet-tempered man, who is always fit for it; to fee an air of humour and pleafantnefs fit ever upon his brow, and even fomething angelic in his very countenance: whereas, if we obferve a defigning man, we fhall find a mark of involuntary fadnefs break in upon his joy, and a certain infurrection

in

in the foul, the natural concomitant of profligate principles.

They err very much, who think religion, or a strict morality, difcompofes the mind, and renders it unfit for converfation; for it rather infpires us to innocent mirth, without fuch a counterfeit joy as vitious men appear with; and indeed wit is as confiftent with religion, as religion is with good manners; nor is there any thing in the limitation of virtue and religion that fhould abate the pleafures of this world, but on the contrary rather ferves to increafe them.

On the other hand, many men, by their own vice and intemperance, difqualify themfelves for converfation. Converfation is immoral, where the difcourfe is indecent, immodeft, fcandalous, flanderous, and abufive. How great is their folly, and how much do they expofe themfelves, when they affront their beft friend, even God himfelf, who laughs at the fool *when his fear cometh?*

The great fcandal atheiftical and immoral difcourfe gives to virtue, ought methinks, to be punifhed by all good magiftrates: make a man once ceafe to believe a God, and he has nothing left to limit his foul. How incongruous is it to good government, that a man fhall be punifhed for drunkennefs, and yet have liberty to affront, and even deny the Majefty of heaven? when if, even among men, one gives the lie to a gentleman in company, or perhaps fpeaks an affronting word, a quarrel will enfue, and a combat, and perhaps murder be the confequence: at the leaft, he will profecute him at law with the utmoft virulence and oppreffion.

The next thing to be refrained, is obfcene difcourfe, which is the language only of proficients in debauchery, who never repent but in a goal or hofpital; and whofe carcafes relifh no better than
their

their difcourfe, till the body becomes too nafty. for the foul to ftay any longer in it.

Nor is falfe talking to be lefs avoided; for lying is the fheep's cloathing hung upon the wolf's back: it is the Pharifee's prayer, the whore's bufs, the hypocrite's paint, the murderer's fmile, the thief's cloak, it is Joab's embrace, and Judah's kifs; in a word, it is mankind's darling fin, and the devil's diftinguifhing character. Some add lies to lies, till it not only comes to be improbable, but even impoffible too: others lie for gain, to deceive, delude, and betray: and a third lies for fport, or for fun. There are other liars, wro are perfonal and malicious; who foment differences, and carry tales from one boufe to another, in order to gratify their own envious tempers, without any regard to reverence or truth.

Chap. V. *Of the prefent ftate of religion in the world.*

I doubt, indeed, there is much more devotion than religion in the world, more adoration than fupplication, and more hypocrify than fincerity: and it is very melancholy to confider, what numbers of people there are furnifhed with the powers of reafon and gifts of nature, and yet abandoned to the groffeft ignorance and depravity. But it would be uncharitable for us to imagine (as fome Papifts abounding with too much ill-nature, the only fcandal to religion, do) that they will certainly be in the ftate of damnation after this life; for how can we think it confiftent with the mercy and goodnefs of an infinite Being, to damn thofe creatures, when he has not furnifhed them with the light of his gofpel; or how can fuch proud, conceited, and cruel bigots, prefcribe rules to the juftice and mercy of God?

We

We are told by some people, that the great image which King Nebuchadnezzar set up to be adored by his people, held the reprefentation of the fun in its right hand, as the principal object of adoration. But to wave this difcourfe of heathens, how many felf-contradicting principles are there held among Chriftians? and how do we doom one another to the devil, while all profefs to worfhip the fame Deity, and do expect the fame falvation.

When I was at Portugal, there was held at that time, the court of juftice of the inquifition. All the criminals were carried in proceffion to the great church, where eight of them were habited in gowns and caps of canvafs, whereon the torments of hell were difplayed, and they were condemned and burnt for crimes againft the catholic faith and bleffed virgin.

I am forry to make any reflection upon Chriftians; but indeed in Italy the Roman religion feems the moft cruel and mercenary upon earth: and a very judicious perfon, who travelled thro' Italy from Turkey, tells us, " That there is only the
" face and outward pomp of religion there; that
" the church protects murderers and affaffins, and
" then delivers the civil magiftrates over to Satan for doing juftice; interdicts whole kingdoms, and fhuts up the churches for want of
" paying a few ecclefiaftical dues, and fo puts a
" ftop to religion for want of their money; that
" the court of Inquifition burnt two men for
" fpeaking difhonourably of the bleffed virgin:
" and the miffionaries of China tolerated the worfhipping the devil by their new converts: that
" Italy was the theatre, where religion was the
" grand opera; and that the Popifh clergy were
" no other than the ftage-players."

As to religion in Poland, they deny Chrift to
be

be the Meſſiah, or that the Meſſiah has come in the fleſh. And as to their Proteſtants, they are the followers of Lælious Socinus, who denied our Saviour's divinity; and have no concern about the divine inſpiration of the Holy Ghoſt.

In Muſcovy their churches are built of wood, and indeed they have but wooded prieſts, though of the Greek church: they pray as much to St. Nicholas, as Papiſts do to the Virgin Mary, for protection in all their difficulties and afflictions.

As to Lutherans, they only differ from the Romans in believing conſubſtantiation, inſtead of tranſubſtantiation; but, like them, they are much pleaſed with the external gallantry and pomp, more than the true and real practice of it.

In France I found a world of prieſts, the ſtreets every where crouded with them, and the churches full of women; but ſurely never was a nation ſo full of blind guides, ſo ignorant of religion, and even as void of morals, as thoſe people who con-feſs their ſins to them.

Does it not ſeem ſtrange, that while all men own the Divine Being, there ſhould be ſo many different opinions as to the manner of paying him obedience in the Chriſtian church? I know not what reaſon to aſſign for this, except it be their different capacities and faculties.

And indeed, upon this account, we have per-ceived in all Chriſtian countries what mortal feuds have been about religion: what wars and blood-ſhed have moleſted Europe, till the general pacifi-cation of the German troubles at the treaty of Weſtphalia; and ſince thoſe times, what perſecu-tion in the ſame country among the churches of the Lutherans: and ſhould I take a proſpect at home, what unhappy diviſions are between Chriſti-ans in this kingdom, about Epiſcopacy and Pref-bytery, the church of England men and the dif-

ſenters;

senters; oppoſing one another like St. Paul and St. Peter, even to the face; that is, they carry on the diſpute to the utmoſt extremity.

It might be a queſtion, why there are ſuch differences in religious points, and why theſe breaches ſhould be more hot and irreconcilable? All the anſwer I can give to this, is, that we inquire more concerning the truth of religion, than any other nation in the world; and the anxious concern we have about it, makes us jealous of every opſnion, and tenacious of our own: and this is not becauſe we are more furious and raſh than other people; but the truth is, we are more concerned about them, and being ſenſible that the ſcripture is the great rule of faith, the ſtandard for life and doctrine, we have recourſe to it ourſelves, without ſubmitting to any pretended infallible judge upon earth.

There is another queſtion, pertinent to the former, and that is, what remedy can we apply to this malady? And to this I muſt negatively anſwer, Not to be leſs religious, that we may differ the leſs. This is ſtriking at the very root of all religious differences; for certainly, were they to be carried on with a peaceable ſpirit, willing to be informed, our variety of opinions would not have the name of differences; nor ſhould we ſeparate in communion of charity, though we did not agree in ſeveral articles of religion.

Nor is there a leſs uſeful queſtion to ſtart, namely, where will our unhappy religious differences end? To which, I hope, I may anſwer, in Heaven; there all unchriſtian and unbrotherly differences will find a period; there we ſhall embrace many a ſinner, that here we think it a diſhonour to converſe with; and perceive many a heart we have broken here with cenſures, reproaching, and revilings, made whole again by

the

the balm of the fame Redeemer's blood. Here
we fhall perceive there have been other flocks
than thofe of our fold; that thofe we have excom-
municated, have been taken into that fuperior
communion: and, in a word, that thofe contra-
dicting notions and principles, which we thought
inconfiftent with true religion, we fhall then find
reconcilable to themfelves, to one another, and
to the fountain of truth. If any man afk me, why
our differences cannot be ended upon earth; I
anfwer, were we all thoroughly convinced, that
then they would be reconciled, we would put an
end to them before; but this is impoffible to be
done: for as mens certain convictions of truth
are not equal to one another, or to the weight or
fignificancy of fuch veracity; fo neither can a general effect of this affair be expected on this fide
of the grave.

Before I conclude this chapter, I fhall beg leave
to difcourfe a little of the wonderful excellency
of negative religion and negative virtue. The
latter fets out like the Pharifee, with, God, I thank
thee; it is a piece of religious pageantry, the hypocrite's hope: and, in a word, it is pofitive vice:
for it is either a mafk to deceive others, or a mift
to deceive ourfelves. A man that is clothed with
negatives, thus argues: I am not fuch a drunkard
as my landlord, fuch a thief as my tenent, fuch a
fwearer as his neighbour: neither am I a cheat,
an atheift, a rakifh fellow, or a highwayman: no!
I·live a fober regular retired life: I am a good
man, I·go to church, God I thank thee. Now,
though a man boafts of his virtue in contradiction
to the vices mentioned, yet a perfon had better
have them altogether, than the man himfelf; for
he is fo full of himfelf, fo perfuaded that he is
good and religious enough already, that he has no
thoughts of any thing, except it be to pull off his

hat

hat to God Almighty now and then, and thank him, that he has no occasion for him; and has the vanity to think that his neighbours must imagine well of him too.

The negative man, though he is no drunkard, is yet intoxicated with the pride of his own worth: a good neighbour and peace-maker in other families, but a tyrant in his own: appears in church for a show, but never falls upon his knees in his closet; does all his alms before men, to be seen of them; eager in the duties of the second table, but regardless of the first; appears religious, to be taken notice of by men, but without inter-course or communication between God and his own soul: Pray, what is the man? or what comfort is there of the life he lives? he is insensible of faith, repentance, and a Christian mortified life; in a word, he is perfectly a stranger to the essential part of religion.

Let us for a while enter into the private and retired part of his conversation: What notions has he of his misspent hours, and of the progress of time to the great centre and gulf of life, eternity? does he know how to put a right value on time, or esteem the life-blood of his soul, as it really is, and act in all the moments of it, as one that must account for them? If then you can form an equality between what he can do; and what he shall receive; less can it be founded upon his negative virtue, or what he has forborn to do, and if neither his negative nor positive piety can be equal to the reward, and to the eternity that reward is to last for, what then is to become of the Pharisee, when he is to be judged by the sincerity of his repentance, and rewarded according to the infinite grace of God, with a state of blessedness to an endless eternity?

When the negative man converses with the in-
F f

visible

vifible world, he is filled with as much dread and horror as Felix, when St. Paul reafoned to him of temperance, righteoufnefs, and of judgment to come: For Felix, though a great philofopher, of great power and reverence, was a negative man, and he was made fenfible by the apoftle, that as a life of virtue and temperance was its own reward, by giving a healthy body, a clear head, and a compofed life; fo eternal happinefs muft proceed from another fpring; namely, the infinite unbounded grace of a provoked God, who having erected a righteous tribunal, Jefus Chrift would feparate fuch as by faith and repentance he had brought home and united to himfelf by the grace of adoption, and on the foot of his having laid down his life as a ranfom for them, had appointed them to falvation, when all the philofophy, temperance and righteoufnefs in the world befides had been ineffectual. And this, I fay, it was that made Felix, this negative man, tremble.

Chap. VI. *Of liftning to the voice of Providence.*

THE magnificent and wife King Solomon bids us cry after knowledge, and lift up our voice for underftanding; by which is meant, religious knowledge; for it follows: *Then fhalt thou underftand the fear of the Lord, and find the knowledge of God.* By which undoubtedly he meant, to inquire after every thing that he has permitted us to know, and not to fearch into thofe ways that are unfearchable, and are effectually locked up from our knowledge. Now, *as liftning to the voice of providence* is my prefent fubject, I intend, in the firft place, to write to thofe who own, 1. That there is a God, a firft great moving caufe of all things, and eternal power, prior, and confequently fuperior to all created power or being. 2. That
this

this eternal power, which is God, Is the sovereign creator and governor of heaven and earth.

To avoid all needless diftinctions, what perfons in the Godhead exercife the creating, and what the governing power, I offer that glorious text, Pfal. xxxiii. 6. where the whole Trinity is intit-led to the whole creating work; and therefore, in the next place, I fhall lay down thefe two pro-pofitions.

I. *That the eternal God guides by his providence the whole univerfe, which was created by his power.*

II. *That this providence manifefts a particular care over, and concern in the governing and directing man, the moft noble creature upon earth.*

It is plain, that natural religion proves the firft, by intimating the neceffity of a providence guiding and governing the world, from the con-fequence of the wifdom, juftice, prefcience, and goodnefs of the Almighty Creator: for otherwife, it would be abfurd to think, that God fhould cre-ate a world, without any care or providence over it, in guiding the operations of nature, fo as to preferve the order of his creation.

Revealed religion gives us a light into the care and concern of his providence, by the climafe's being made habitable, the creatures fubjected and made nourifhing, and all vegetative life made me-dicinal; and all this for the fake of man, who is made viceroy to the King of the earth. The fhort defcription I fhall give of providence is this: That it is that operation of the power, of the wifdom, juftice, and goodnefs of God, by which he influen-ces, governs, and directs, not only the means, but the events of all things, which concern us in

this

this fublunary world; the fovereignty of which we ought always to reverence, obey its motions, obferve its dictates, and liften to its voice. The prudent man forefeeth the evil, and hideth himfelf; that is, as I take it, there is a fecret providence intimates to us, that fome danger threatens, if we ftrive not to fhun it.

The fame day that Sir John Hotham kept out Hull againft the royal martyr King Charles I. the fame day Sir John Hotham was put to death by the parliament for that very action; the fame day that the king himfelf figned the warrant for the execution of the Earl of Stafford, the fame day of the month was he barbaroufly murdered by the blood thirfty Oliverian crew: and the fame day that King James the Second came to the crown againft the bill of exclufion, the fame day he was voted abdicated by the parliament, and the throne filled with King William and Queen Mary.

The voice of fignal deliverance from fudden dangers, is not only a juft call to repentance, but a caution againft falling into the like danger; but fuch who are utterly carelefs of themfelves after, fhew a lethargy of the worft nature, which feems to me to be a kind of practical atheifm, or at leaft a living in a contempt of Heaven, when he receives good at the hand of his Maker, but is unconcerned from whence it comes, or to thank the bountiful hand that gave it; neither when he receives evil, does it alter his manner of life, or bring him to any ftate of humiliation.

We have a remarkable ftory of two foldiers being condemned to death in Flanders. The general being prevailed upon to fpare one of them, ordered them to caft dice upon the drum-head for their lives; the firft having thrown two fixes, the fecond fell a wringing his hands, having fo poor a chance to efcape; however, having thrown, he

was

was furprifed when he alfo threw other two fixes.—
The officer appointed to fee the execution, ordered them to throw again ; they did fo, and each of
them threw three fives ; at which the foldiers that
ftood round, fhouted, and faid neither of them was
to die. Upon this the officer acquainted the council
of war, who ordered them to throw a third time,
when they threw two fours ; the general being
made acquaint with it, fent for the men, and pardoned them : I love, fays he, in fuch extraordinary cafes, to liften to the voice of providence.

We read in the holy writings, how God fpeaks
to men, by appearance of angels, or by dreams
and vifions of the night. As God appeared to A-
braham, Lot, and Jacob ; fo angels have appeared to many in other cafes, as to Manoah and his
wife, Zachariah, the virgin Mary, and to the a-
poftles ; others have been warned in a dream, as
king Abimelech, the falfe prophet Balaam, and
many others.

It is certainly a very great and noble inquiry,
what we fhall be after this life ? for there is fcarce
a doubt, that there is a place referved for the reception of our fouls after death : for if we are to
be, we muft have a where, which the fcriptures
affert by the examples of Dives and Lazarus. The
doctrine of fpirits was long believed before our
Saviour's time ; for when the difciples of the bleffed Jefus perceived our Saviour walking on the
fea, they were much furprifed, as though they
had feen a fpirit. Nay, in thofe ages of the world,
it was believed that fpirits intermeddled in the affairs of mankind ; and throughout the Old Tef-
tament I do not find any thing that in the leaft
contradicts it. All the pains and labour that fome
learned men have taken, to confute the ftory of
the witch of Endor, and the appearance of an old
man perfonating Samuel, cannot make fuch ap-

F f 2

paritions

paritions inconfiftent with nature or religion: and it is plain, that it was either a good or a bad fpirit, that prophetically told the unfortunate king what fhould happen the next day; for faid the fpirit, *The Lord will deliver thee into the hand of the Philiftines: and to-morrow fhalt thou and thy fons be with me.*

Abundance of ftrange notions poffeffed me, when I was in the defolate ifland; efpecially on a moonfhine night, when every bufh feemed a man, and every tree a man on horfeback. When I crept into the difmal cave, where the old goat lay expiring, whofe articulate groans even refembled thofe of a man, how was I furprifed! my blood chilled in my veins, a cold fweaty dew fet on my forehead, my hair ftood upright, and my joints, like Belfhazzar's knees, ftruck againft one another. And indeed, though I afterwards found what it was, the remains of this furprife did not wear off for a great while; and I had frequently returns of thofe vapours on different occafions, and fometimes without any occafion at all.

One night, after having feen fome appearance in the air, as I had juft lain down in my bed, one of my feet pained me; after that came a numbnefs, fucceeded with a tinkling in my blood; when on a fudden I thought fomething alive lay upon me, from my knee to above half my leg. Upon this I flung myfelf out of bed where I thought the creature lay: but finding nothing, *Lord deliver me from an evil fpirit,* faid I, *what can this be?* When I lighted a candle, I could perceive no living creature in the place with me but the poor parrot, who being frighted, cried out, *Hold your tongue,* and, *What's the matter with you?* which words I taught him, by faying fo to him, when he made fuch fcreaming noifes as I did not like, *Lord,* faid I aloud, *furely the devil has been here: Hold your tongue,*

tongue, says Poll. I was then mad at the bird, and putting on my cloaths, cried, I am terrible frighted, *What's the matter with you?* says Poll. You toad, said I, I'll knock your brains out. *Hold your tongue*, cried he again, and so fell a chattering, and calling Robinson Crusoe as he did before. But after I had composed myself, and went to bed again, I began plainly to see it was a distemper that affected my nerves, and so my terrors vanished at once.

How intelligences are given or received, we do not know; nor are we sensible how they are conveyed from spirits unembodied, to ours that are in life; or on the contrary from us to them: the latter certainly is done without the help of the organs, and the former is conveyed by the understanding, and the retired faculties of the soul.

The spirits, without the help of voices, converse, and the more particular discoveries of the converse of spirits, seem to me as follow; to wit, dreams, voices, noises, impulses, hints, apprehensions, involuntary sadness, *&c.*

Dreams of old were the ways by which God himself was pleased to warn men what services to perform, and what to shun. Joseph was directed of God in a dream to go to Egypt; and so were the wise men warned in a dream to depart into their own country another way, to avoid the fury of Herod. I am not like those who think dreams are the mere dosings of a delirious head, or the relics of a day's perplexities or pleasures; but, on the contrary, I must beg leave to say, I never met with any capital mischief in my life, but I had some notice of it by a dream; and had I not been a thoughtless unbelieving creature, I might have taken many a warning, and avoided many of the evils I afterwards fell into, merely by total neglect of those dreams.

I was

I was once prefent at a difpute between a layman and a clergyman, upon the fubject of dreams. The firft thought no regard fhould be given unto them : that their communication from the invifible to the vifible world was a mere chimera ; without any folid foundation. For, 1. faid he, if dreams were from the agency of any prefcient being, the motives would be more direct, and the difcoveries more plain ; and not by allegories and emblematic fancies, expreffing things imperfect and obfcure, 2. Since, with the notice of evil, there was not a power given to avoid it, it is not likely to proceed from a fpirit, but merely fortuitous. 3. That the inconftancy of fuch notices, in cafes equally important, proves they did not proceed from any fuch agent. 4. That as our moft diftinct dreams had nothing in them of any fignificancy, it would be irrational and vain to think that they came from heaven. And, 5 that as men were not always thus warned or fupplied with notice of good or evil, fo all men are not alike fupplied with them; and what reafon could we give, why one man or one woman fhould not have the fame hints as another.

To all this the clergyman gave anfwer ; 1. That as to the fignification of dreams, and the objections againft them as being dark and doubtful, they are expreffed generally by hieroglyphical reprefentations, fimilies, allufions, and figurative emblematic ways, by which means, for want of interpretation, the thing was not underftood, and confequently the evil not fhunned. 2. That we charge God foolifhly, to fay, that he has given the notice of evil without the power to avoid it ; for if any one had not power to avoid the evil, it was no notice to him ; and it was want of giving due heed to that notice, that firft men neglected themfelves, and then charged the Judge of all the earth.

earth with injuſtice, 3. That we ought not to find fault with the inconſtancy of theſe notices, but rather with our weak underſtandings, by pretending dreams were not to be regarded, and negligent when the voice really ſpoke to us for our good. It is a miſtake to ſay, dreams have no import at all: we might with more reaſon have ſaid, none that we could perceive the reaſon of, owing to our blindneſs and ſupine negligence, too ſecure at one time, and too much alarmed at another; ſo that the ſpirit, which we might be ſaid to be converſing with in a dream, was conſtantly and equally kind and careful; but our powers are not always in the ſame ſtate of action, not equally attentive to, or retentive to the hints that were given. And, 5. to anſwer the laſt queſtion, why people are not equally ſupplied? This ſeemed to be no queſtion; for Providence itſelf might have ſome ſhare in the direction of it, and then that Providence might be limited by a ſuperior direction: That as to the converſe of ſpirits, he could not call it a ſtated converſe; ſuch a thing there was, by why there was ſo much of it, and no more,, was none of his buſineſs, and that no ſuch diſcovery had ever yet been made to mankind. Nor were we to imagine leſs of waking dreams, trances, viſions, noiſes, hints, impulſes, and all the waking teſtimonies of an inviſible world, and of the communication that there is, between us and them, which commonly entertain us with our eyes open.

One time my fancy ſoared on high, to ſee what diſcoveries I could make in thoſe clearer regions. I found that ſuch immenſe bodies as the ſun, ſtars, planets, and moon, in the great circle of the lower heaven, are far from being found in the ſtudy of nature on the ſurface of the earth. Here I ſaw many things that we can entertain little or no

notion

notion of in a ftate of common life, and the emp-
tinefs of our notion, that the planets are habitable worlds, that is, created like ours for the fubfiftence and exiftence of man and beaft, and the
prefervation of the vegetative and fenfitive life:
no, no; this is, I affure you, a world of fpirits;
for here I faw a clear demonftration of Satan being
the *prince of the power of the air*, keeping his
court or camp, with innumerable angels to attend
him; but his power is not fo great as we imagine,
he can tempt us to the crime, but cannot force us
to commit it: *Humanum eft peccare.* Neither has
the devil power to force the world into a rebellion
againft Heaven, though his legions are employed
among favage nations to fet up their mafter for a
god, who make the Heathens either worfhip him
in perfon, or by his reprefentatives, idols, and
monfters, with the cruel facrifices of human blood.
Now, as to the limitations of the devil's power,
you muft underftand, that as there are numbers
of evil fpirits employed in mifchief, fo there are
numbers of good angels fent from the higher and
bleffed abodes to difconcert and oppofe their meafures; and this every Chriftian, I hope, believes,
when he prays to God, the Father of fpirits, to
give his angels charge over him while he flumber-
eth and fleepeth. For if thefe preventing powers,
the devil was not reftrained, the earth would be
fubjected to dearth, droughts, and famine; the
air infected with noxious fumes; and in a word,
mankind would be utterly deftroyed, which might
oblige our Maker (if I may be allowed the expref-
fion) to the neceffity of a new Fiat, or elfe have
no more creatures to honour and worfhip him.

As the devil never wanted infinuatois, I fhall
obferve, that I learned a way how to make man
dream of what I pleafed. For inftance let us fuppofe one to be found afleep; let another lay his
mouth

mouth clofe to his ear, and whifper any thing fo
foftly as not to awake him, the fleeping man fhall
dream of what has been fo whifpered in his ear;
nay, I can affure you, thofe infinuating devils can
do this even when we are awake, which I call impulfes of the mind: for from whence, but from
thefe infinuators, come our caufelefs paffions, involuntary wickednefs, or finful defires? Who elfe
form ideas in the mind of man when he is afleep,
or prefents terrible or beautiful figures to his fancy? Mr. Milton reprefents the devil tempting Eve
in the fhape of a toad, lying juft at her ear, when
in her bower fhe lay faft afleep; and brings in
Eve telling Adam what an uneafy night's reft fhe
had, and relating her dream to him. And likewife
I believe that good fpirits have the fame inter-
courfe with us, in warning us againft thofe things
that are evil, and prompting us to that which is
good.

Were we to have the eyes of our fouls opened,
through the eyes of our bodies, we fhould fee this
very immediate region of air which we breath in,
thronged with fpirits now invifible, and which
otherwife would be the moft terrible: we fhould
view the fecret tranfactions of thofe meffengers
who are employed when the parting foul takes its
leave of the reluctant body, and perhaps fee things
nature would fhrink back from with the utmoft
terror and amazement. In a word, the curtain
of providence for the difpofition of things here,
and the curtain of judgment for the determination
of the ftate of fouls hereafter would be alike drawn
back; and what heart could fupport here its future
ftate of life, much lefs that of its future ftate after
life, even good or bad.

A gentleman of my acquaintance, being about
feven miles diftant from London, a friend that
came to dine with him, folicited him to go to the
city.

city. What, faid the gentleman, is there any occafion for me? No, Sir, faid the other, nothing at all, except the enjoyment of your good company; and fo gave over importuning him. Juft then a ftrong impulfe of mind urged the gentleman, and purfued him like a voice, with *Go to London, Go to* London. Hark ye, fays he to his friend, is all well at London? Am I wanted there? Or did you afk me to go with you on any particular account? Are all my family well? Yes, indeed Sir, faid he, I perceived them all very hearty; and I did not afk you to go to London upon any particular account whatfoever, except it was for the fake of your good company. Again he put off his refolution: but ftill the impulfe fuggefted to him, *Go to* London, and at length he did fo. When he came there, he found a letter and meffenger had been there to feek him, and to tell him of a particular bufinefs, which was firft and laft above a thoufand pounds to him, and which might inevitably been loft, had he not gone to London that night.

The obeying of feveral hints, or fecret impulfes argues great wifdom. I know a man that was under misfortunes, being guilty of mifdemeanors againft the government; when, abfconding for fear of his ruin, all his friends advifing him not to put himfelf in the hands of the law, one morning as he awaked, he felt a ftrong impulfe darting into his mind thus, *Write a letter to them:* and this was repeated feveral times to his mind, and at laft he anfwered to it, as if it had been a voice, *Whom fhall I write to?* Immediately it replied, *Write to the judge*; and this impulfe purfued him for feveral days, till at length he took pen, and ink, and paper, and fat down to write to him; when immediately words flowed from his pen, like

ftreams

ftreams from a fair fountain, that charmed even
himfelf with hopes of fuccefs. In fhort, the letter
was fo ftrenuous in argument, fo pathetic in its
eloquence, and fo perfuafively moving, that when
the judge had read it, he fent him an anfwer he
might be eafy, he would endeavour to make that
matter light to him; and indeed never left exhort-
ing himfelf, till he had ftopt the profecution, and
reftored him to his liberty and family.

I know a perfon who had fo ftrong an impreffion
upon her mind, that the houfe fhe was in would
be burnt that very night, that fhe could not fleep;
the impulfe fhe had upon her mind preffed her not
to go to bed, which, however, fhe got over, and
went to bed; but was fo terrified with the thought,
which run in her mind, that the houfe would be
burnt, that fhe could not go to fleep; but com-
municating her apprehenfions to another in the
family, they were both in fuch a fright, that they
applied themfelves to fearch from the top of the
houfe to the bottom, and to fee every fire and
candle fafe out, fo that, as they all faid, it was
impoffible that any thing could happen then, and
they fent to the neighbours on both fides to do
the-like. Thus far they did well; but had fhe
obeyed the hint which preffed upon her ftrangely,
not to go to bed, fhe had done much better; for
the fire was actually kindled at that very time,
though not broken out. About an hour after the
whole family was in bed, the houfe juft over the
way, directly oppofite, was all in flames, and the
wind which was very high, blowing the flame
upon the houfe this gentlewoman lived in, fo filled it with fmoak and fire, in a few minutes, the
ftreet being narrow, that they had not air to
breathe, or time to do any thing, but jump out
of their beds, and fave their lives. Had fhe obeyed the hint given, and not gone to bed, fhe might
have faved feveral things; but the few moments

G g

fhe

she had spared to her, were but just sufficient to leap out of bed, put some cloaths on, and get down stairs, for the house was on fire in half a quarter of an hour.

While I am mentioning these things, methinks it is very hard that we should obey the whispers of evil spirits, and not much rather receive the notices which good ones are pleased to give. We never perceive the misfortune of this, but when in real danger: and then we cry, *My mind misgave me when I was going about it;* but if so, why do you slight the caution? Why not listen to it *as to a voice?* and then there had been no reason to make this complaint.

I remember about 14 or 15 years ago (as to time I cannot be very positive) there was a young clergyman in the city of Dublin in Ireland, who dreamed a very uncommon dream, That a gentleman had killed his wife, a relation of his, by stabbing her in several places; the fright of this awaked me, but finding it a dream, he composed himself again to sleep, when he dreamed a second time the same dream. This made him a little uneasy; but thinking it proceeded from the impression made on his mind by the former, he went to sleep again, and dreamed the same dream a third time also. So troubled was he at this, that he arose, and knocked at his mother's chamber, told his concern, and his apprehensions that all were not right at his relation's house. Dear son, says the good old gentlewoman, do not mind these foolish dreams: and I very much wonder, that you, being a person in holy orders, should have regard to such illusions. Upon this he went to bed again, fell asleep, and dreamed a fourth time as before. And then indeed he put on his night-gown, and went to Smithfield, the place where his relation dwelt. Here it was, alas! he perceived his dream too sadly fulfilled, by seeing his relation, the young lady,

.big

big with child, who was a Proteſtant, ſtabbed in
ſeven places, by her barbarous huſband Mr. Euſ-
tace, a violent Papiſt, only for ſome diſcourſes of
religion that happened the day before. After the
wretch had ſtabbed her in three places, he went
to make his eſcape out at a window; but ſhe cried
out *My dear! don't leave me, come back, and I
ſhall be well again.* At which he returned in a
helliſh rage, and gave her four wounds more,
when, even in this condition, riſing from her bed,
ſhe wrapped herſelf in her night-gown, and went
to the Lord Biſhop of Rapho's chamber-door (the
biſhop lodging at that time in the houſe,) My
Lord, ſaid ſhe, *O my Lord make haſte unto me;* but
as ſoon as his Lordſhip came ſhe expired in his
arms, reſigning her precious ſoul into the hands
of Almighty God. The cruel wretch her huſband
was ſhot by the purſuers, too good a death for
one who deſerved the gibbet; and the lady was
univerſally lamented by all tender and religious
people. And this tragical relation I have mentioned upon the account of that impulſe or dream
that the clergyman had at the fatal time of the
bloody action.

It might be expected I ſhould enter upon the
ſubject of apparitions, and diſcourſe concerning
the reality of them; and whether they can reviſit
the place of their former exiſtence, and reſume
thoſe faculties of ſpeech and ſhape as they had
when living; but, as theſe are very doubtful matters, I ſhall only make a few obſervations upon them.

I once heard of a man that would allow the reality of apparitions, but laid it all upon the devil,
thinking that the ſouls of men departed, or good
men, did never appear. To this very man ſomething did appear: he ſaid, he ſaw the ſhape of an
ancient man paſs by him in the duſk, who, holding up his hand in a threatening poſture, cried
out, *O wicked man, repent, repent.* Terrified with

this

this apparition, he confulted feveral friends, who advifed him to take the advice. But after all, it was not an apparition, but a grave and pious gentleman, who met him by mere accident, and had been fenfible of his wickednefs; and who never undeceived him, left it fhould hinder his reformation. Were we always willing to make good ufe of Satan's real appearances, I know not but it would go a great way to banifh him from the vifible world; for I am very pofitive, he would feldom vifit us, if he thought his coming would do us any good: but fo abfolutely is he at the command of Heaven, that he muft go, even to do the work he abhors.

Some people make a very ill ufe of the general notion, that there are no apparitions nor fpirits at all; which is worfe than thofe who fancy they -fee them upon every occafion: for thofe carry their notions farther, even to annihilate the devil, and believe nothing about him, neither of one kind or other: the next ftep they come to is to conclude, *There is no God*, and fo atheifm takes its rife in the fame fink, with a carelefsnefs about futurity. But there is no occafion to enter upon an argument to prove the being of the Almighty, or to illuftrate his power by words, who has fo many undeniable teftimonies in the breafts of every rational being, to prove his exiftence; and we have fufficient proofs, enough to convince us of the great fuperintendency of divine Providence in the minuteft affairs of this world; the manifeft exiftence of the invifible world; the reality of fpirits, and intelligence between us and them. What I have faid, I hope will not miflead any perfon, or be a means whereby they may delude themfelves: for having fpoken of thefe things with the utmoft ferioufnefs of mind, and with a fincere and ardent defire for the general good and benefit of the world.

THE END.